ABDUCTION

ABDUCTION

Dwayne Morrow Mystery #6

DARIN MILLER

ISBN: 979-8-9867566-8-4 (Paperback)

Library of Congress Control Number: 2024900147

Any references to historical events, real people, or real places are used fictitiously. Names, characters, and places are products of the author's imagination. No portion of this book was created through use of artificial intelligence (AI), nor may any portion be used to train AI.

Cover image licensed for commercial use from Adobe Stock Images (stock.image.com)

Printed by Kindle Direct Publishing, in Columbus, OH, USA.

First printing edition 2024. Current printing edition 2025.

www.darin-miller.com

DARIN MILLER
Dwayne Morrow Mysteries

For Debbie Stephens:

In my mind, I see you
in Heaven's library, feet up,
with a stack of books at the ready.

These books will never steal your sleep again,
for now, you have all the time in the world.

Say hello to my Mom when you see her.
I guarantee she's got some great recommendations
for you.

TABLE OF CONTENTS

PROLOGUE

"*Stop the car! Stop the car!*"

My eyes flickered sideways toward the passenger seat where I found Melanie doubled over in the eerie luminescence of my Hyundai's dashboard lights. She looked awful.

I cut to my right with little regard for the traffic around me. I was greeted by a chorus of angry horns as I awkwardly bumped my front passenger tire up onto the curb and slammed on my brakes. Rain fell in sheets across the pavement, illuminated by headlights as cars swept by on this dark, dismal evening I desperately wished belonged to anybody else.

"I'm going to be sick," she mumbled, covering her mouth with one hand while fighting the seatbelt with the other.

I unlatched my own and threw my door open into oncoming traffic. More angry honking, and as I stepped down to the glistening pavement, I alternated between flipping a pair of angry birds and apologetic, palms-forward hand waving. I scurried around the back of the car to where Melanie knelt by the curb, retching herself into dry heaves. I helped to steady her against the car as she gulped for air between expulsions.

I've never felt so helpless in all my life.

Cars continued to whiz by in both directions along the two-lane city street, and I hated everyone inside of them. They were bound for destinations made by choice, and absolutely no one would choose to go where Melanie and I were heading.

Woefully inept at saying the right things at times like these, I stuck with the simple and inane, soothingly repeating things like, "I'm right here, sweetheart," and "Just breathe…breathe…"

Eventually, her hiccupping breath slowed and settled into a pattern approximating normal. I held her steady with my right hand as I rubbed her back with the palm of my left. "Do you think you can stand?" I asked.

She nodded, wiping the corners of her mouth with the back of her hand. I helped her to her feet, and once she was upright, she leaned against the SUV, a fresh wave of anguish sweeping over her. "Oh, God—I don't think I can *do* this," she cried.

"*Shhh, shhh,*" I soothed, folding her into my arms and tucking her head beneath my chin. I could feel rather than hear the sobs that caused her body to quake against mine. I was afraid to say anything more as we clung to each other in the pouring rain.

For everything I *had* been through, I'd never attempted to identify the body of a loved one, much less someone so young.

CHAPTER ONE

One week earlier...

A black, furry arm slowly extended through a checkerboard of circular cutouts in the bright green laundry basket sitting on the far end of the dinette table. The basket was empty, save for one ornery cat who had grown weary of being ignored. Oblivious, Jasmine sat nearby, drumming a well-worn pencil against her chin as she puzzled through a math problem that was part of her evening homework, her ever-present earbuds firmly in place. Flattened to the bottom of the laundry basket, Dexter's goal was the thin white plastic-coated cable trailing from Jasmine's earbud to her phone. From the far end of the table, I looked up from my laptop where I had been catching up on email to observe as Dexter's plan slowly unfolded.

His arm stretched closer...and closer...

He flexed his little hand and one razor sharp claw emerged from what I'd think of as his 'middle finger.' He watched her intently, looking for any sort of reaction whatsoever. In my head, I could almost hear a countdown.

Three...two...one...

"*Hey!*" Jasmine cried, startled as the earbud was plucked from where it rested in her ear, whipped away on its own cord by a cat who was busily reeling in his prey. "Oh no, you don't, you little monster."

Jasmine jabbed the eraser end of her pencil through a neighboring hole in the clothes basket, attracting Dexter's attention while freeing her earbud. He attacked the pencil, wrapping it tightly in his claws and chewing on its end while Jasmine squealed with delight.

"Let—go—of—my—pencil, you awful, *awful* cat," she giggled, pulling the pencil free only to attack him with it again through any number of the holes along the lower portion of the basket. Never one to be short on common sense, Dexter called her bluff and launched himself like a black, fuzzy missile over the edge of the basket, flipping it to the floor and prompting another squeak from Jasmine as she dropped out of her seat and onto the floor to avoid him. He landed in her chair where he crouched, tail flicking wildly while his backside twitched, waiting for her next move. With a sly grin, she eased to her hands and knees before springing towards the stairs, screeching in a range that's only accessible to girls her age. Dexter was after her in a flash, and they thundered up the stairs and down the long hallway.

I propped my chin on a fist and smiled, shaking my head as the hysterics above continued unabated. Things had certainly changed around here.

My name is Richard Dwayne Morrow and absolutely no one calls me Richard, or any variation thereof, anymore. Well, except for my mother, and when she does, I know I'm in big trouble. I've swung around this sun thirty-four times and am rapidly approaching thirty-five. Until very recently, I lived by myself in an old two-story farmhouse along Orin Way in Grove City, Ohio. A largely unused barn sits across the gravel drive, and both weatherworn, whitewashed facades are long overdue for a touchup. My nearest neighbors are entirely beyond detection, and I have always found the solitude most agreeable. Well—*almost* always. I reinforced some doors after my home had been vandalized the previous year and added a Ring doorbell to both the front and rear entrances after a psychotic lunatic had deposited a severed human foot on my porch by the light of the moon, but what are the odds of something like *that* happening again?

On second thought, in my current line of work, all bets were off…

Until recently, I had been working solely as a freelance information technology consultant, growing a small but loyal customer base whose individual needs couldn't support even a part-time IT position on staff. My skills might be self-taught, but I have loads of experience and plenty of glowing references available upon request. I'm also more affordable than my competition, and it should come as no great surprise this is often the deciding factor in corporate finance. But after nearly a decade of upgrading operating systems, configuring and securing database connections, and diagnosing any multitude of networking issues, I was bored. My incentive for getting up in the early morning—okay, as late in the morning as I could possibly negotiate—was becoming strictly a matter of survival. Like everyone else, I have bills to pay and require income.

Just a little over a year ago, I inadvertently stepped into the next act of my life when I fumbled my way through the murder investigation of my best friend from high school, Ryan McGregor. Helping to bring the responsible party to justice had awakened something inside of me I never knew existed. I had spent the past year worming my way into a former classmate's good graces so I might be able to function as a sort of apprentice in his private investigation business. Logging hours in the field under the guidance of a licensed private investigator was a way to satisfy one of the many requirements of obtaining my own private investigator's license, and for whatever reason, that seemed to be something I was determined to do, despite the fact that working for Doug Boggs was at best demeaning and at other times completely infuriating. He had opened a satellite office on West Broad in Columbus, and both he and his mother, Loretta, were underfoot far more often than I liked, although admittedly, the last month or so had been better. We had recently survived an exercise in teamwork, and although it had gone completely off the rails, we seemed to have actually learned a little something from the experience. I didn't know how long it would last, but I would take what I could get.

My association with Boggs Investigations wasn't the only big change that happened to me in this past year. I had gone from confirmed bachelorhood with nary a prospect in sight to a fella completely smitten with the widow of my deceased best friend. Neither Melanie nor I was looking for it, but from nearly the first moment we met, something just clicked, and despite my occasional idiocy, we were still going strong. In fact, the young lady who just bounded away from my dinette table and up the stairs with my cat in hot pursuit was Ryan and Melanie's daughter, Jasmine. She and her mother had been living with me for all of about ten minutes—okay, maybe just a bit longer than that.

A scant few months prior, Melanie had made the decision to pick up stakes and move from our hometown of Lymont in southern Ohio to a small, two-bedroom apartment on Wilson Road in west Columbus. Like myself, she attended online classes, although she also worked full-time for a company that manufactured fertilizer. She wanted better opportunities for her daughter and for herself, and it made me giggle to think she considered me one of them. Long distance relationships are a bitch, and neither of us had wanted to rush into anything, so it all seemed like a good idea at the time.

So much had happened since then, all of it documented elsewhere, but every single event had brought us both to the realization we were simply wasting time. I invited Melanie and Jasmine to move in with me—they were here all the time anyway. Melanie left the invitation contingent upon Jasmine's approval, and I was utterly relieved when she couldn't pack quickly enough. You see, I have next to no experience with children. I am the youngest of three and have never had the need to communicate with one. The past year had been a minefield of missteps and make-rights, but I think I was beginning to get the hang of it. The fact that I found the squalling, thumping, and thudding above my head amusing, despite the fact it was currently quaking the globes protecting the bulbs in the chandelier over the table, was most definitely progress. Such a thing would have previously shredded my nerves.

I returned my attention to my laptop just in time for the storm door to swing outward as Melanie breezed in, a messenger bag over one shoulder and a tiny little purse over the other. "Hey, you," she said, slinging both onto one of two matching leather sofas in the living room. She turned back to the door, shielding her eyes against the setting sun while waving toward the driveway.

"Is someone here?" I asked, pushing away from the table, and crossing to where she stood.

"Matt," she answered, referencing my older brother. "Weren't you expecting him?"

"Uh-unh," I said, shaking my head and shielding my own eyes. "Did he bring the whole crew?"

"Doesn't look like it."

"Damn," I said. My brother and his wife, Sheila, had recently welcomed the newest generation of Morrow into the world by way of my first niece, Abigail Regina. I mean, Matt and Sheila were fine, but I would rather spend time with little Abbie any day of the week. "I wonder what's up. This is a little out of the way for him."

We stepped out onto the porch just as Matt killed his engine. "Dwayne Morrow," he said in a monotone as he opened his door and alit from the driver's seat of his champagne Honda CR-V.

"Matt Morrow," I replied in a matching drone.

We cycled through this exchange two more times before Melanie laughed and interjected, "Why do you two *always* do that?"

I shrugged. It had been our usual greeting for one another ever since Matt had left home for his freshman year at the University of Kentucky. After nearly two decades, I was strictly on autopilot.

"Because we always were weird little kids," my brother answered with a grin. He joined us on the porch and wrapped an arm around Melanie. "How are you, pretty lady?"

She squeezed him back. "Just fine. Where's Sheila and the baby?"

"This is Sheila's folks last night in town before they head back to Florida."

"I didn't realize they were here again," I said. "Weren't they just up a month or so ago?"

Matt laughed. "I'm pretty sure this was a stealth maneuver. The last time they came up, Mom found reason after reason to extend her and Dad's stay. Penny and Burt barely got any alone time with their new granddaughter. I'm gonna have to have a long talk with that mother of ours."

"Good luck with that," I said.

"Thanks, I'm sure I'll need it. They wanted to take Abbie around and introduce her to some of their own relatives who live in Dublin and Muirfield before they headed for their condo in the morning. After a week of having her parents underfoot, Sheila cut me a break this evening and let me beg off. I thought I might take the opportunity to give my own family a visit."

I eyed him suspiciously. "You usually call before you do that."

"Dwayne," Melanie elbowed me gently. "Matt doesn't need an appointment to stop by. He's welcome whenever."

Matt gave her another sideways squeeze. "I always did like you better than Dwayne."

"Uh-huh," I nodded, still unconvinced. *"Something's* going on. Spill it."

Matt finally released his grasp on my lady's shoulders and aimed for a look that conveyed nonchalance. "It's nothing, really. I just wanted to touch base with you guys about Thanksgiving and see what your plans are."

I blinked. Thanksgiving was only a week away, and I hadn't given it a single thought. "I don't know. Melanie and I really hadn't discussed it. I guess we'll be going down to Mom and Dad's like usual—"

Melanie held up a finger. "Yeah, I wanted to talk to you about that. Jasmine and I usually celebrate Thanksgiving twice. Once with Cheryl and later out at Sarah's." She was referring to one of her sisters who lived in Ironton and Jasmine's paternal grandmother. "But of course, we want to spend Thanksgiving with your family, too. We'll need to figure out the timing."

In my thirty-four years on this planet, I had never once spent my Thanksgiving holiday anywhere other than under the roof of Todd and Jo Morrow. I might sneak out to Ryan's house for a little bit after dinner, but everything about the day's agenda revolved entirely around Jo Morrow's set-in-stone schedule. I could already see the look on her face when I told her our attendance would be somewhat abbreviated. Melanie already thought my mom didn't like her; it wasn't true, but I sure as hell didn't want to give Mom a reason to feel that way. One look at Melanie told me how important it was to her.

I nodded slowly. "I'm sure we can work out some sort of schedule."

Compromise would be key in folding our families together, and the smile on Melanie's face told me I had answered correctly.

Matt plodded forward. "We've worked it out with Sheila's folks that we'll do Thanksgiving at Mom and Dad's and do Christmas with them, switching it around next year. With all of Abbie's stuff, I figure we'll need to take the old bedroom you and I shared."

We stared at each other for a long moment, and I suddenly realized why Matt had chosen to discuss this in person. His plan only left one other bedroom for us, and that was the one belonging to our sister, Gina, who we had lost several months ago. There were a multitude of reasons I couldn't stay in that bedroom, but nothing I was willing to share.

I struggled to hold his gaze, afraid he might read my thoughts, and ended up both shaking and nodding my head, looking like an indecisive Bobblehead. "We'll figure it out."

"Thanks, brother," he said, clapping my arm. "I knew you'd understand."

Truth was, I knew he *wouldn't* understand. No one would. I hadn't yet discussed my near certainty that our sister was still alive with anyone, not even Melanie, although I had come close more times than I could count. I had promised Gina I wouldn't, and I had promised her I would investigate no further, two of the most difficult promises I had ever made. It was everything I could do to remain patient and hope things worked themselves out. Unless, of course, I was completely crazy and clinging to nothing more than fervent hope. But as time passed, I was growing more confident that my beliefs were correct.

This was the first big family holiday since her funeral, and her absence would undoubtedly hang like an albatross over the entire weekend. I'm sure we would spend the day dancing around the subject and hiding from one another when it got to be a little too much to bear. Especially Dad. He would rather die himself than allow anyone to see him in what he considered a weak and vulnerable state.

I realized the silence was lengthening as I sorted through my thoughts, and it suddenly seemed like a complete blessing that Melanie and I would otherwise be obligated to spend portions of our visit with other folks. Now, if I could only figure out where we might sleep *other* than my sister's old room...

Thunderous footsteps approached the storm door before it was flung open and Jasmine burst through, throwing herself at my brother. "Uncle

Matty!" she cried, as he boosted her up into his arms and swung her around, nearly clobbering me and Melanie with her outstretched feet. I had urged her to start calling him Uncle Matty, certain it would vex him as it was barely a variation of the Fatty Matty I so often utilized when we were kids, but my scheme had backfired spectacularly as my brother genuinely seemed to embrace the moniker when it came from Melanie's daughter—well, and minus the 'Fatty' part.

I looked down just as Dexter took a tentative step out onto the porch, keeping a steady eye on me to see if I would notice. I scowled and blocked his path with one stockinged foot. When we were growing up, far too many of our outdoor pets had become inadvertent roadkill. Dexter had the entire run of my farmhouse, and he was just going to have to be satisfied with that. Feigning surprise, he peeped and backed up, allowing me to latch the door and keep him safe and sound.

"Good Lord, child!" exclaimed Matt. "You've grown two feet since the last time I saw you. What's it been, five years?"

She giggled as he put her down. "A week ago, Sunday," she said. "Remember? We came over to your place to visit Abbie, and you burned everything on the grill."

Matt adopted a look of shocked indignation, his hand fluttering to his chest. "I most certainly did *not* burn our meal! In the South, that's what is called *blackened*, my child, and it's utterly delicious."

Jasmine's grin widened. "Especially if you use half a bottle of barbeque sauce to rehydrate it."

"Why, you little—"

Matt grabbed for her as she ducked around him squealing, and as they engaged in a bit of horseplay, I had to marvel at how quickly my brother had learned to engage with children. I had been around Jasmine for over a year now, and I still felt like I was making it up as I went along. Matt had no more experience than me, yet he was a complete natural. I was more than a little jealous. They settled after Matt let Jasmine get the better of him for a few moments more.

"So, what did you bring me?" Jasmine asked, her eyes twinkling.

"Jasmine Marie!" Melanie was appalled. "You don't ask someone a question like that!"

Jasmine barely paid her mother any attention. She knew better. She kept her eyes on the prize as Matt exaggeratedly avoided her probing eyes.

"Why would you think I'd bring you something?" Matt teased. "I mean, didn't you just have a birthday?"

"That was almost a whole month ago!" Jasmine reminded him, her smile never faltering. "So, what did you bring?"

"Jasmine!" Melanie looked at Matt apologetically. "I'm so sorry, Matt. I promise you, I've made every attempt to teach her manners, but—"

He cut her off with a wink, returning his attention to Jasmine. "I don't know, little lady. I'm starting to think you're nothing more than a pint-sized gold digger. Maybe you ought to see if there's anything in my passenger seat."

Matt had barely gotten the words out, and Jasmine was off like a shot, vaulting over the short set of steps leading to the drive.

"Matt," chided Melanie. "You don't have to bring her something every time you stop by."

Matt was watching her progress with a big smile, waiting for the moment of surprise. "I'm her uncle. Spoiling her is my prerogative."

"I think what Melanie's trying to say is you're making us look bad," I elaborated.

"That, dear brother, is my pleasure."

Birds took flight at the shrill outburst of delight that erupted from the driveway. Jasmine practically flew back to the porch, clutching a sealed plastic package to her chest in a bear hug, releasing it only to throw her arms around Matt and hug him fiercely. "How did you know? This only came out today!"

Matt beamed. "I pay attention to these things. I couldn't have your friends getting their hands on one before you now, could I?"

Jasmine looked at the package in awe, then back to Matt, hugging him again and kissing him on the cheek. *"Thank you*, Uncle Matty."

"Well, for heaven's sake, what is it?" I asked. I had only been able to catch a blurry glimpse as it passed me by.

Jasmine turned around and proudly displayed her new acquisition. "It's from the latest Demon Academy line—Expectra Autopsa. Isn't she *beautiful?*"

I didn't think I could go *that* far. It was an emaciated corpse with fully articulated limbs and multi-colored neon hair piled on top of its cadaverous skull. A graphic 'Y' incision etched across a surprisingly ample breastplate trailed down to a waist so small I couldn't even imagine it passing gas. My first thought was, *Yikes!* but Jasmine had been into these creatures for some time now, and I had learned to modulate my reaction to a mere *Eek!*

"Why don't you go inside and open her up," suggested Melanie, dropping her forehead into an open palm, and groaning when she realized what she'd just said.

Jasmine thanked Matt again before racing inside and leaving a bewildered cat in her wake to wonder what had stolen her attention away. I hurried across the porch to close the door, tossing Dexter a shrug, and keeping him inside where he belonged.

"I probably oughta go," said Matt. "I'm sure Sheila and her folks will be getting back soon. Thanks for being so accommodating, bro." He gave me a quick hug and moved on to Melanie, kissing her lightly on the cheek, which she reciprocated.

"Sure," I said. "We'll be down sometime on Wednesday. See you then."

He jogged down the stairs to his car and waved one last time before driving off.

"You're going to have to talk to him about that," said Melanie as we went back inside. "He's spoiling her rotten." She went to the bottom of the stairs and called up, *"Jasmine?* Did you get your homework done?"

After a lengthy pause, Jasmine called, "Almost."

"All right, then. You know the rules. Homework first, and then the doll."

"Mo-o-om!"

"I mean it," Melanie warned, and Jasmine came stomping down the stairs, clutching the partially opened package in one hand and wearing an expression best not put into words. She slumped back into her chair at the dinette table and positioned the package so Expectra could observe while she toiled in servitude, subjected to our cruel and unreasonable demands.

"Do it right, not fast," I added, earning a white-hot glare of my own. I really *was* going to have to talk to Matt. By comparison, we were practicing child abuse.

I dropped onto the leather sofa closest to me while Melanie fished her cell phone out of her purse, unlocked it and tapped its screen a few times before placing the phone against her ear. She paced in front of me as she waited for her call to be answered.

"Hey, Sarah, it's me," she finally said, cluing me in that she was talking to her former mother-in-law. "Did I catch you at a bad time?"

I followed the one-sided conversation as best as I could.

"It just occurred to me that we really hadn't discussed Thanksgiving. We're trying to coordinate with Dwayne's folks and Cheryl, and I just wondered—oh." She listened. "Okay, then. Sure. That makes sense." Another pause. "Of course. Yeah, that would be pretty far out of the way, but we want to see you, too." Another pause. "I'm sure we can figure out something. Is everything all right? You sound funny. Do you have company? I could've sworn I heard a child." I could hear Sarah's laughter through the phone, and even from a distance, it sounded odd. "I'll let you get back to it, then. Sure. We can do that. Love you. Bye."

Melanie disconnected and plopped down beside me, tucking her phone back into her purse. "Hmmm."

"Something wrong?" I asked, hooking an arm around her, and pulling her closer to me.

"I guess not," she said, snuggling in. "She's not making dinner this year. She's going to her parents' over in South Shore."

"Yeah?" I frowned.

Sarah had been hosting Thanksgiving dinner at her house on Brenner Hollow as far back as I could remember. I think I attended my first at age 14 as a guest of Ryan's. Essentially, it was a Savitch family reunion—Savitch being Sarah's maiden name. Usually in attendance were her parents, Joe and Ann, as well as her four younger brothers, their wives, and any number of extended family members who had blossomed from (or attached like a fungus to) the family tree throughout the years. It was quite the event, and Sarah had taken charge of it to relieve her aging parents of the burden. It seemed odd for her to toss it back to them all these years later.

"Did she say why?" I asked.

"Not really," said Melanie. "But it will actually make our day a little easier. Since Joe and Ann live all the way out on Route 7, she told me not to try and work it in and to focus on our own folks on Thanksgiving Day. She wants to see Jasmine, of course, so she suggested we figure something out before we head back home."

"Okay," I said. "Sounds reasonable."

Melanie nodded, but she didn't look completely convinced.

"What is it?"

She shrugged. "I'm sure it's nothing. She just sounded—odd. She told me to call before we came to make sure she was home, and she said it more than once. When have you ever known Sarah to request a phone call before we stop by?"

"I'm sure she's just being considerate. With all the driving we're going to be doing between Ironton and Lymont, I imagine she doesn't want us to waste our time trying to meet her when she's not available."

"I guess," said Melanie, still not convinced.

Absently, I turned on the television and fired up Netflix, looking for something inane to fill the next half hour or so. For the life of me, I'll never understand why we consistently choose to ignore those niggling little voices whispering in our ears, doing their very best to forewarn us of trouble in the road ahead.

This business with Sarah would only be the tip of the iceberg.

CHAPTER TWO

Is there really any point to a three-day work week that culminates in a four-day holiday weekend? I guarantee you the majority of nine-to-five workers are simply phoning it in, counting the minutes until the whistle blows on Wednesday. It's all about shuffling things and rescheduling as much as possible to keep from having to commit to any real work before you're finally set free. I had managed to do exactly that with a couple of clients in my consultant business, scheduling their non-emergent cries for help for the following week, but I had been saddled with a routine surveillance assignment by my stubby little overlord at Boggs Investigations very first thing Monday morning, and there would be no early release until I had completed the job.

We were hired by the counsel for Allswell Insurance. Surely, you've heard their slogan: *All's Well that Ends Well with Allswell Insurance!* No? Okay. Doesn't really matter. We were tasked to get evidence disproving Willard J. Tansky's disability claim against his employer to put a halt to the sizable payments he had been collecting for almost half a year now. There had been just enough eyewitness accounts of Tansky's unimpaired behavior to warrant the investigation, but to date, no smoking gun to allege fraud. Leave it to Doug Boggs to pollute my otherwise open schedule with such tedium.

Things were looking mighty grim on Monday and Tuesday, as I followed Mr. Tansky from doctor's appointment to doctor's appointment, watching him hobble about with a cane and a back brace the first half of each day before surrendering to the use of a wheelchair once we were into the afternoon hours. He was accompanied by his nephew, Jason, and if either of them had any idea they were being followed, they certainly gave no indication. I mostly observed from my driver's seat, boredom perverting the flow of time and making those twelve-hour days feel endless.

By the time Wednesday morning arrived, I was already mentally rehearsing what I would say when Doug tried to derail my holiday plans and insist that I continue to monitor Mr. Tansky into the weekend. While I'm actively working at being a better team player, I knew full well Doug would be hitting U.S. 23 South just as early as he possibly could, heading to Lymont where his mother, who is also our office manager, Loretta, was already waiting. She had taken the entire week off to prepare for the holiday, and I'm pretty sure Doug wasn't foolish enough to task her with anything before getting the all-clear to depart. Melanie's employer, A-1 Fertilizers, was closing shop at noon and even South-Western City Schools had given their charges an extra day off to enjoy time with their families. Everyone would be stuck waiting for me to finish another lengthy and ultimately pointless excursion, wasting my time and fouling my mood. I was *not* open to working through the holiday, regardless of whatever justification Doug was likely to attempt. Five o'clock would be the end of my day, period.

For once, I was actually lucky.

As I pulled up to the curb across the street from Tansky's tiny little house in Groveport, I couldn't believe my eyes. It was unseasonably warm, and Tansky was pushing a lawn mower across his front yard in what was probably his final cut for the season, creating a neat checkerboard pattern within the chain link fence that kept neighbor pets from doodling in his lush green grass. He wore sunglasses and earbuds and appeared to be singing along with whatever was playing via Bluetooth. He even managed a little fancy footwork as he changed direction, twirling on his heel like a middle-aged Michael Jackson with only the teensiest fraction of the skill. He paid me no attention whatsoever as I recorded a high-definition video of his antics on my smartphone, and it took incredible restraint to keep from contributing my own giddy giggles to the soundtrack of the evidence.

It was barely eleven o'clock when I tucked my SUV beside Doug Boggs' ugly, partially white but mostly rust-colored Pontiac Aztek in the gravel lot near the rear of the building that housed Boggs Investigations' Columbus office. It occupied the top half of what had formerly been a two-story residence on West Broad Street. Our entrance was once the back door, its foyer modified to provide access to our space via a narrow staircase leading up, and a secondary entrance to the first-floor occupant, a taxidermist named Charley Morse. I noted his perfectly preserved periwinkle blue mid-80s Cadillac on the opposite side of the lot and didn't even wonder what sort of pressing taxidermy-related emergency might keep him in his office when the rest of the working world was busy checking out for the Thanksgiving holiday. Charley was a man who loved his work. I didn't even know if he *had* family, although admittedly, I sometimes wondered if he had already stuffed them all, and they were mounted here and there amongst his first-floor furnishings. The whole thing gave me the willies, and frankly, I blame Alfred Hitchcock.

A bell jangled as I opened the outer door, and Charley looked up from his worktable, a lighted magnifying visor wrapped around his balding head. He normally kept the foyer door to his suite open while he was working, making it impossible to sneak upstairs without catching a glance of whatever Charley's latest project was. Today's work was a huge, angry-looking turkey, its beady eyes staring directly at me while its beak was partially open, wings stuck in mid-flap, legs frozen in mid-strut.

Charley plucked the visor from his head and ran fingers through what wiry gray hair ringed his liver-spotted head. "How do, Mr. Morrow?" he called, waving before indicating the monstrosity before him. "So whaddaya think?"

"Hey, Charley. She's a real beaut, although I don't think this is what they mean by stuffing a turkey," I said with a wink.

He chuckled good-humoredly. "Never heard *that* one before," he replied facetiously, reseating the visor onto his head before returning his attention to his project. He was getting ready to manipulate the eyes, something I really didn't want to witness.

"Enjoy your holiday, Charley," I said before trotting up the stairs, the laptop bag I had slung over my shoulder bouncing with each step. His reply was congenial if unintelligible, and I opened the door at the top of the stairs, practically catching Doug in the face as he was preparing to leave.

"Tell me you've got something good to report," said Doug, clearly expecting nothing. In response, I pulled my cell phone out and queued up the video, relishing the joy that blossomed on his stubbly face as he watched.

There was a time in the not-so-distant past when I collected my evidence on a 35mm long-lens Minolta, operating under the premise that bigger was better, but after the camera had gotten destroyed during my escapades in West Virginia, I realized quickly how much smartphone cameras had improved since I'd last paid attention. I could get higher resolution pictures and high-definition video on demand, all from a device that fit neatly in the palm of my hand. Best of all, it was so much more unobtrusive during a stakeout.

"I think Allswell should be thrilled with this," I said, heading over to my WWII-era metal desk and pulling my laptop out of its case. "Are you headed out?"

"Yep. Ma's sister, Verna, is coming in from Pittsburgh with her twin little yapping poodles. Ma asked if I could help her get the guest room set up, and I'd like to get it done and get out of there before they rope me into their evening."

"You don't get along with your aunt?" I asked, logging in to my MacBook and pulling up Outlook to check my email. On my phone, I set the video as well as a few stills I had snapped to upload to a OneDrive folder I had created so we could transfer such electronic media more efficiently. It had only taken me several months to convince my obstinate employer and his equally obtuse office manager/mother that the internet was more than just the devil's plaything.

"Oh, sure, although I'm sure Ma will spend a decent amount of time grinding her teeth. For two sisters raised by the same parents, they ain't got much in common. But for me, it's those damned dogs! Nasty little ankle biters, and I just know if I accidentally step on one, she'll think I did it on purpose."

I laughed. "All right. Safe travels, then. I'm going to write up a quick report and email it along with the video to Cassidy at Allswell. Then, Mel, Jasmine, and I are headed to Lymont ourselves. Maybe we'll run into you while we're down there."

"Maybe," said Doug. "If not, I'll see you next week. Enjoy your time off."

"You too, buddy," I said as he closed the door behind himself.

My mood was good. I had spent the entire morning preparing for a confrontation that didn't occur. In fact, this latest exchange may have been our most civilized to date, and for that, I was truly thankful.

"Cheryl has agreed to move her meal up to one o'clock, so we don't conflict with your mom's dinner," said Melanie as we traveled south in heavier-than-usual traffic on U.S. 23. It seemed as though everybody had gotten an early start on their holiday travel plans. After bottlenecking near the Eldorado Gaming Scioto Downs and creeping our way through multiple speed traps in South Bloomfield, we were finally moving at a pace that approximated the speed limit.

"That was nice of her," I said. "I hope she's not going to a bunch of trouble on my account, though."

"Nah," said Melanie, adjusting the volume down on the radio. "The family starts arriving in the morning anyway, and folks will come and go all day. She's just moving the main feast up, and she said she was fine with that as long as I could give her a hand in the kitchen."

I glanced in the rearview mirror and spotted Jasmine rearranging the fashions on her latest Demon Academy acquisition as well as two of her necrotic sisters. They were all easily transported in a black, coffin-shaped backpack emblazoned with the Demon Academy insignia. Jasmine had started carrying it everywhere. I hoped there wouldn't be a pop quiz on their names. Try as I might, I couldn't retain them for shit. Jasmine's omnipresent earbuds were in place and tethered to her phone, cycling through a playlist far cooler than anything we might stumble across on the radio. I looked back at Melanie who was reading a novel on her iPad.

"Maybe I should ask Mom to move our dinner up instead," I suggested. "I mean, there'll be more people at your place than at mine, and—"

"It's already settled. Why are you futzing?"

I sighed and studied the road ahead. "I just don't want your family to think I'm difficult, that's all."

"We-e-ll—"

"I'm *serious*, Mel! This is a big deal to me. You only get one chance to make a first impression, and I don't want to blow it."

She shifted in her seat to study me. "What are you talking about? You've met both Cheryl and Molly before. They like you just fine."

My laugh was doubtful. "We've said 'hey' through a car window or over the phone as I've passed you over to them. It's not like I *know* them. I mean, really—I don't know anything about them."

"You know that Cheryl is a cosmetologist and Molly is an ICU nurse at Lymont Memorial."

"I don't know their husbands' names or what they do for a living. I don't know how many kids they have. I don't know—"

"Good *gravy*, Dwayne!" she interrupted with a laugh. "Are you really this stressed out? There's no reason for you to know all of those things. It'll give you something to talk about. They don't know much about you either, so what I'm seeing is a golden opportunity for conversation. You worry too much."

I grinned. "That's rich, coming from you."

"What do you mean?"

I looked pointedly at the cherry cobbler she had in a covered container between her feet. "I don't recall Mom asking us to bring anything, but what's that I see?"

"Knock it off."

"Cherry cobbler, my mother's favorite dessert! *Oh!* And my grandmother's cranberry relish! What are the odds?"

Melanie sighed. "I'm telling you, I will win that woman over one dessert at a time, if that's what it takes."

"She doesn't dislike you."

"Interesting word choice," she noted. "And you will ask your mother to move her mealtime over my dead body. Are we clear?"

I grinned. "Crystal."

We settled into companionable silence for several miles before another worry landed. I glanced in the rearview mirror again to make sure Jasmine's earbuds were still in place and she wasn't paying us any attention.

"You don't expect your father—"

"*No,*" said Melanie, firmly. "Cheryl would never invite him. Kristi might come, but that's fine."

"Kristi? Who's that?"

"She's my half-sister. I don't get to see her often."

I nodded slowly. I didn't want to press the issue. Melanie and her siblings had grown up in an abusive household with a sexual predator for a father. He had never been forced to answer for his crimes and likely never would be. Like with so many families in similar circumstances, it was considered a shameful bit of family history that shouldn't be discussed outside the walls of the family home. While I had no intention of bringing it up over Thanksgiving dinner, I thought it wise to find out if I might be seated across from a man I would seriously like to throttle. My poker face was shit, and I wasn't convinced I'd be entirely successful at exhibiting restraint.

• • • • • • ◦ ◯ • • • • • •

It was almost three-thirty when we turned onto Topenga Avenue in Lymont. The Morrow homestead was the next to last on the right, down a road that gently sloped to a dead-end on Marjorie Lane. The entire neighborhood had been erected in the 1940s, and while many of the houses started with the same basic blueprint, customizations and improvements over the years had morphed the block into its current state of middle-class tranquility. Two-story dwellings anchored by mature oaks and evergreens were equidistant from one another, each with its own postage-stamp front yard, some fenced, others not. By this time the following day, the street would be lined on both sides with vehicles of relatives celebrating the holiday with friends and family, but only a few of those spots were occupied now. Naturally, the one in front of my parents' house was occupied by a cherry red Mustang, and their driveway was at capacity with Dad's minivan pulled underneath the carport and Matt's SUV tucked in behind it. I settled for a spot straddling a storm drain across the street, turning my wheels to the left and setting the parking brake.

"I see Matt and Sheila have already arrived," said Melanie, unbuckling her seat belt. "Who belongs to the Mustang?"

"If I'm not mistaken, I think it belongs to—"

I was startled by a sharp rap on my driver's side window. I turned to find Matt pulling a ridiculous face less than an inch from the glass. Jasmine giggled as I opened the door and gently whacked him with it.

"Are you trying to give me a heart attack?" I asked. "I didn't even see you approach."

"With my superior stealthy capabilities, maybe *I* should be the big-shot private detective," he said, stepping aside to let me out of the car.

"It also requires persistence, cunning and intellect, and I think you're a few ingredients short, dear brother. Why so eager to see me?"

"Just wanted to give you a heads up," he said, nodding toward the Mustang. "Aunt Jane is here. Got here this morning before we did."

Jane Freeman was Mom's older sister. She lived in Cincinnati and pretty much thought the world revolved around her.

"Wasn't Mom expecting her?" I asked. Mom had appeared behind the storm door on their porch and was waving. I smiled and returned the wave, and Melanie nearly dropped her cobbler doing the same. Jasmine was still busy in the backseat, packing her Demon Academy dolls and all their assorted accoutrement into her coffin-shaped backpack.

Matt wavered his hand. "Depends on who you believe. Mom says no, Aunt Jane insists she had announced her attendance months ago."

I grimaced. "And Dad?"

The grin on Matt's face was all the warning I needed. Todd Morrow gets along with every single person on this planet with the exception of one heavyset woman with a blonde beehive and thin-lipped mouth without filter. She just happened to be my mother's only sibling, and these impromptu get-togethers had a way of turning ugly on a dime.

"Shit," I said.

"And that's not all!" said Matt, sounding like a game show pitchman while continuing to smile with all his teeth in an effort to keep Mom from realizing he was running interference.

"Oh, God," I groaned. "What?"

"She's already staked a claim to Gina's old room," he said. "It's starting to look like there's no more room at the inn."

I nearly grinned but caught myself. I had no intention of staying in that room anyway, and now I had a perfect excuse. But with one problem solved, another one loomed. Where were we going to stay?

"Are you going to spend the whole weekend standing in the street?" Mom had grown impatient and stepped out onto the porch, urging us toward her. "Get over here, people! We were just getting ready to sit down to a game of Yahtzee!"

I smiled apologetically at Melanie and shrugged. We crossed the street, feigning enthusiasm the whole way.

· · · ·•••••●◯◯●•••••· · · ·

We spent the next couple of hours tumbling dice around the oblong dining room table in the folks' dinette, which occupied a third of the enormous addition Dad had tacked onto the rear of the house. The idea was to give the family a little more space, but by the time Dad had finally taken on the project, Gina and Matt had already moved out and I was well on my way. It was much appreciated at times like these, however, when the tight spacing of the original blueprint would have caused tempers to flare a little more quickly. Doing his part to keep the peace, Dad had spent the entire afternoon mowing the grass, but we all knew the lawn wasn't that big.

Jasmine was a real trouper, enduring Aunt Jane's eyerolls and general impatience as she attempted to learn the rules of Yahtzee, which was essentially poker set to dice. After the third time she had been corrected for carelessly allowing a die to skid over the edge of the table and onto the floor, Melanie suggested she go get her Demon Academy dolls from the car, effectively ending Jasmine's punishment for her earlier bad behavior, and Jasmine couldn't have bailed on the game more quickly. She was currently occupying herself with Spongebob on television and Demon Academy scattered around her on the couch. I suspected one of the little corpses was currently being referred to as Enflamed Jane. Melanie was leaving marks on my leg with her fingernails as she struggled to hold her tongue, worried about offending my mother by laying into my aunt at our first mutual family event. In all fairness, Mom wasn't exactly shy in her attempts to shame her sister for bullying a child. Words had a way of bouncing off Aunt Jane's thick skull, and Matt and Sheila were first to push away from the table when my aunt crowed in victory after tallying her score card.

Dad chose that particular moment to enter through the back door, bare-chested with a sweat-soaked t-shirt wrapped around his balding head, a sheen of perspiration on every square inch of exposed flesh.

"Perfect timing, Todd!" said Mom, already bracing for whatever might come next. "I was thinking maybe we could just pick up some carry-out from Frisch's. How does that sound to everyone?"

"*Ooo*, that sounds divine!" enthused Aunt Jane. "I just love their pumpkin pie. Let me get a piece of paper, and I'll jot down everyone's order. And I really *do* appreciate you picking it up, Todd."

Dad was busily mopping his forehead and shoulders with his saturated t-shirt but froze. "Excuse me? I'm not going anywhere. I need to get through the shower."

Aunt Jane sighed dramatically. "Well, I'm simply exhausted from the trip from Cincinnati. *I'm* not picking it up."

Melanie and I were already heading for the living room, silently instructing Jasmine to collect her things as the tension in the room began to ratchet up. Mom was helpless to interject because she had never learned how to drive. *She* certainly couldn't pick up the food.

Dad chortled, a sound Matt and I had learned to recognize as a warning sign. Shit was about to get *real.* "You've been sitting on your considerable backside for the past couple hours playing a dice game while I've been working up a sweat out in the yard. If *you* can skip a meal, I assure you, *I* can."

Matt interjected, literally stepping between the two and breaking their steely-eyed standoff. "I can pick up the food. Just tell me what you want, Dad, then go hop in the shower. Geez."

I was already guiding Melanie and Jasmine toward the front of the house. "And we need to head out," I said.

"But Dwayne," protested Mom. "I thought you were spending the night. I'm sure we could rig up something on the sofas, or—"

"It's all right, Mom," I said. "We'll just crash at Sarah's tonight. She's got plenty of room. We have to be up early in the morning so Melanie can help her sister, anyway. It'll be more comfortable for everyone, and Jasmine will get the chance to visit with her grandmother. We'll be back in plenty of time for dinner tomorrow. I promise."

I gave her a quick hug, waved to the room, and we were out of there just as fast as we could go.

"Are they always like that?" Melanie asked as we wound our way down the narrow, unkempt and leaf-covered trail that was Brenner Hollow. It was barely a lane-and-a-half wide with more than its share of hairpin curves and driving any faster than twenty miles per hour was taking your life into your own hands. At nearly six, the sun had completely set, so we could at least depend on the headlights of oncoming traffic to provide some sort of warning. Probably.

"Oh, that was nothing," I said. "You should see it when they *really* get going."

"Yeah? No thanks," she said, watching as an endless parade of evergreens crept by through the passenger window. "I swear, I don't know how she lives out here all by herself. It reminds me of *The Evil Dead.*"

I laughed. "That's half of its charm. And I'm pretty sure Sarah could hold her own against an army of the undead."

The woods abruptly dropped away on our right, revealing a clearing with a large gravel drive skirting the lawn of Sarah McGregor's mud-brown single-story bungalow. Her SUV was parked at the end of a sidewalk that ran parallel to the front of the house, vaguely illuminated by the single porch light by the entrance and a flickering sodium vapor lamp mounted high on a utility pole near the mouth of the driveway. A low fog had begun to roll in, underscoring Melanie's earlier observation.

I turned in, and my headlights had barely skirted across the glass of the living room's bay window when the front door opened, and Sarah hustled out into the front yard. She wore a red checkered button-down shirt and jeans but hadn't bothered to slip on shoes. I turned the engine off and exchanged a puzzled glance with Melanie as we unfastened our seatbelts and got out of the car.

"Hey, you guys!" Sarah said, and her voice was unusually cheerful. She shifted on her bare feet as Melanie rounded the back of my Hyundai and helped Jasmine down from the backseat. "I wasn't expecting you tonight. I, uh, thought you were going to call first."

"My bad," I said, as she quickly leaned down to give her granddaughter a hug and a kiss on the top of her head. "Mom's sister showed up unexpectedly and stole our room out from under from us. Naturally, we thought of you."

Sarah's expression was unreadable, and that was a first. She was desperately aiming for normal, but her eyes were tight, and she looked unusually worried. It also felt like she was blocking our path towards the house, and I had never known this woman to be anything other than welcoming.

"Is everything all right?" I asked, my smile beginning to falter. I leaned to my right to look around her, and she only shifted to block my view.

Her laugh was the phoniest thing I had ever heard. "Of course, everything is all right. What could possibly be wrong?"

"Who is that, Gramma?" Jasmine pointed to the door, and Sarah's expression completely fell.

She might have been able to distract me and Melanie, but it was physically impossible to cover all three of us, and she didn't even attempt to block me as I peered around her again.

Standing behind the glass of the storm door with a forefinger lodged firmly in his mouth was a pencil-thin little boy in Teenage Mutant Ninja Turtle pajamas. Even from this distance, there was no mistaking his striking resemblance to Melanie's late husband, Ryan.

CHAPTER THREE

"Jasmine, get in the car," Melanie said through clenched teeth, attempting to turn her daughter away.

"But, Mom, I—"

"Just do what I say." She practically lifted Jasmine into the back seat and shut the door. "What's going on, Sarah?"

Sarah sighed. "I was hoping I'd have a little more time to get my thoughts in order before we discussed this, but—"

"Just tell me," Melanie said flatly.

I was still transfixed by the child standing behind the storm door. I hadn't met Ryan until we were both thirteen and in the seventh grade, and even though this boy was not even three years old, it didn't take any imagination at all to see the uncanny resemblance. The last time I had seen him, he was being cradled in the arms of his mother, Rita Wiggins, as she smugly refused to apologize for the dalliance with Melanie's husband that had eventually produced this child.

"You knew I was trying to get visitation," said Sarah. "I'm sorry if this is hurtful, but Jordan is my grandson. Surely, you understand."

"I do," said Melanie, hugging herself tightly and staring at the ground while furrows sprung out across her forehead. "I just would have appreciated a little more warning. I thought Rita wouldn't allow you to see him. What's changed?"

Sarah's laughter was full of everything but mirth as she ran a hand through her short-cropped strawberry blonde hair. "What *hasn't?*" She forced Melanie to meet her eyes. "Rita's dead."

That caught my attention. "Rita's *what?!?*"

"They found her in her apartment. She'd been dead for days, and that poor child—" Sarah choked up, something I had rarely seen before. She cleared her throat and dabbed clumsily at her eyes. "Jordan hadn't eaten in all that time. I still can't *believe* it took those idiots who run the dry cleaners on the first floor of her building so long to request a wellness check. They said he cried all the time, anyway, so how would they know the difference?" She shuddered in disgust.

I looked at Melanie, but she was still rooted in place, processing.

"What happened to her?" I asked.

"Fentanyl," said Sarah. "It's all the rage down here—haven't you been paying attention to the news? When I think of how easily Jordan could have accidentally—"

She couldn't continue, nor was there any need. We were both fully aware of the escalating fentanyl problem in Scioto County and the surrounding areas. I looked back toward the door, and my heart nearly broke as I realized the poor little guy had burst into tears at some point during our exchange. He began to thump his tiny hands on the glass, drawing Sarah's attention.

"Look, you all are welcome to stay," she said. "You're *always* welcome. But I have to get back inside. He's having a hard time adjusting." She paused and looked at Melanie. "And you should know, I plan to file for custody. At my age, I can't imagine raising another child so young, but I will not allow Rita's family to get their hands on him—not that anyone has even tried. And I'm not putting him into the care of the State. He's already been through enough. He's going to know he's got at least one person in his corner."

Melanie nodded awkwardly. "I get that. I just think I—I just need a little time—"

"Take all the time you need, sweetheart," said Sarah. "I'll be right here when you're ready to talk, but at some point, we're going to have to talk about it. Jasmine's got a little half-brother. I don't think it's fair for us to keep them apart."

She strode back to the house, opening the storm door and scooping Jordan into her arms before disappearing inside. His wails were wrenching as they carried out to us.

Melanie was staring at her feet, and I crossed to her, attempting to fold her into my arms, but she stood ramrod straight and unyielding.

"I can't talk about this right now," she said into my chest, and I just nodded.

After a moment, I guided her around to the passenger side of my car and helped her inside. Jasmine's mouth was dangerously close to running as soon as I opened the door, but I managed to gain her reluctant silence with a purposeful glare.

Once I was settled behind the steering wheel, I said, "All right, ladies. Let's see if we can find ourselves a place to stay."

We took a detour to Rosemount where we decided to grab a dinner no one wanted at McDonald's. I made good use of their free wi-fi to learn the only hotel vacancies in the area were at places we would never take a child, not that the child in question wanted anything to do with either of us at the moment. She picked at her French fries listlessly as she stared out the plate glass storefront, watching the traffic whip by on U.S. 23.

"I guess I could call Cheryl," said Melanie finally, pushing her own cheeseburger aside. "She had a guest room last time I was there, but she was talking about turning it into a crafts room. I don't know if that ever happened."

"I know who he is, you know," muttered Jasmine, refusing to look at either of us. She slurped the last of her Coke through her straw, loudly expressing her displeasure via obnoxious behavior.

Melanie clamped a hand over her daughter's as other patrons began to stare. "I know you do," she said tightly. "I don't want to discuss this right now, all right?"

Jasmine pulled her hand away and slumped back in her plastic molded seat. If it hadn't been bolted to the floor, it would have likely toppled over. *"When?"* she demanded, determined to draw the attention of other patrons one way or another. Her face was pure fury, and I could see Melanie counting to ten in her head—possibly twenty.

"Soon," she said evenly. She pulled out her phone and unlocked it, preparing to call her sister.

"It's been over a year," muttered Jasmine, refusing to let it go. "It's too late for soon."

"Jasmine," I warned, and she turned her full fury on me.

"Could you just stay out of it, please?" she said sharply. "Not really interested in your opinion—"

"Jasmine Marie!" Melanie's eyes radiated heat as the rest of the customers tuned in to our unfolding drama. "Don't you *dare* speak to Dwayne that way. I will not have it."

"Why should *he* have more say in this than I do, hunh? Jordan is my *brother*—"

Melanie slammed her hands down on the table, and it felt like time stopped. Even the workers at the counter had abandoned their duties and were tuned in. "You need to shut your mouth this very instant, young lady, or—"

"Or *what*, Mom?" she challenged, and I felt my own patience evaporating. I was completely unqualified to weigh in on the ongoing debate over corporal punishment as my experience with children was largely limited to the one melting down in front of me, but it was nearly impossible to suppress the undeniable urge to slap her smart mouth.

"I want your Demon Academy dolls," Melanie finally said, after an excruciating standoff.

"They're in the car," Jasmine sassed.

"Fine. I'll collect them when we go. You can have them back once you've learned how to control yourself."

Jasmine sputtered, her eyes bulging. She pushed her uneaten McNuggets across the table and leapt to her feet.

"And just where do you think you're going?" Melanie asked.

"I have to pee," she announced to the room, and as she stormed off toward the public facilities added, "This is such *bullshit!*"

Melanie dropped her face into her palms, and I faced the room full of blatant voyeurs. "Show's over, folks," I said, waving them away and returning their stares until one by one, they grew uncomfortable and turned away. "Time to get back to your own happy little lives."

Melanie groaned. "This isn't the way I pictured this weekend. Maybe we should just go home."

I took her hands into mine. "Here's a thought. How about you step outside and call your sister? See if she's got room for us. Give me a crack at your demon spawn, and let's salvage what we can of the holiday, okay? It's not fair to your family or mine if we just turn tail and run."

She looked pensively toward the bathroom. "Are you sure you wanna take that on? I don't even have any holy water to leave with you."

I grinned, leaning in to kiss her forehead before handing her my keys. "I'll survive. Just go make your call and wait for us in the car."

She collected her things and stepped outside while I tried to project a confidence I didn't exactly feel. Jasmine emerged from the restroom and was halfway to our table before she realized her mother was no longer seated.

"Where'd she go?" she asked, looking around.

"Sit." I pointed to the chair across from me. "We need to talk."

Her eyeroll was instantaneous. "I already *told* you—"

"So, you did," I cut her off. "But I'm asking for the courtesy of just a couple minutes of your time before you shut me out. You owe me that."

I could see the wheels turning behind her eyes, deliberating whether she should remain insufferable or acquiesce to my request. This time around, good prevailed over evil. She dropped into the bright red plastic seat and gave me her reluctant attention.

"First of all, I don't think you're wrong for feeling the way you do," I said. "If I had a brother or sister out there, I would want to know them, too. I get it."

"Then why can't *she?*"

"I think she does," I said. "But you need to cut her a little slack here. She's had less than an hour to get her mind around this."

"It's been over a year—"

"Not really," I interjected. "Yes, we've known about Jordan for that long, but Jordan's mother wouldn't allow us to see him. She absolutely forbid it." I paused, weighing my words. "How much of the conversation did you hear back at your grandma's?"

"Enough."

"So, you know that Jordan's mother is—"

"Dead. Yeah, I caught that."

I sighed. "This changes everything—for everyone. And it only just happened. Your mom is going to need a minute, and is it really that much to ask? You and I both know when the dust settles, you're going to get the chance to meet that little guy. You just need to be patient."

We lapsed into silence as I gave Jasmine a little space. After a few moments, her hand snaked across the table to grab a stone-cold McNugget and pop into her mouth. Much of the aggression had left her posture.

"So, can we call a truce here?" I ventured.

She nodded as I nudged my Coke towards her so she could steal a drink. "I'm sorry I snapped at you," she said. "That woman just makes me crazy."

I had to laugh. "That 'woman' is your mother."

"I just wish she'd *talk* to me. That's what makes me so mad. I'm not a baby anymore. She can't protect me from *everything*."

I shrugged. "She's your mother," I echoed. "It's her first instinct. She can't help it. My mom still doesn't think *I'm* old enough to hear some things."

She laughed. "You're kidding me."

I shook my head and crossed my heart. "Just cut her a little slack, okay?"

"Fine," she agreed, snatching up another McNugget. "So, can I have my Demon Academy dolls back?"

"That's not up to me," I said to her obvious disappointment. "Let's just focus on getting this weekend back on track, and the rest will work itself out, okay?"

"Fine," she repeated with exaggerated resignation.

I gathered our waste onto the plastic tray that came with our food, and we made our way towards the exit. As I emptied the contents into the trash, I nudged her.

"I might be able to put in a good word for you, though," I said with a wink, earning a hint of a smile before we went out to face her mother.

Yeah, I was making this shit up as I went along, but for me, it felt like a win.

·•••••●⊖⊙●•••••·

I was kinda buzzin' as I escorted Jasmine back to the car. There is a certain appeal to saving the day, and I felt like I had really accomplished something big. There was a little extra spring in my step as I crossed that McDonald's parking lot, causing not one, but two vehicles to lurch to a stop. Once Jasmine was in the backseat, I headed for the driver's side, opening the door, and shooting Melanie a quick, *'I've got this!'* look, complete with a confident wink and a shot from a hand pistol.

I was a little surprised when she flinched. She couldn't have possibly missed the befuddlement on my face except she had quickly looked away.

We spent the next forty-five minutes in a deep freeze, with no one talking and the radio off. I attempted to turn it on near Sciotoville but got my hand smacked. True to her word, Melanie had seized all the Demon Academy paraphernalia from the backseat and hidden it somewhere in the confines of my Hyundai. Somehow, I felt responsible because it was my car. I was deflating like a balloon with a slow leak.

I couldn't imagine what I'd done to piss her off, but clearly, I had.

Although I knew my way to Ironton, as we neared our final destination, she was forced to bark short, sharp directions since I'd never been to her sister's house before. After taking the exit for State Route 93 North, we continued for several miles before she indicated a poorly marked offshoot I would've never found. Often, these directions came with little to no warning, and I gained an entirely different perspective on terror as I essentially drove those back roads as Melanie by proxy. I'll be the first to admit I'm a control freak with driving, but this woman scares the living shit out of me.

It was with the greatest relief when we finally pulled into a gravel clearing separating two structures on a hilly parcel of land. A two-story home-on-the-range was situated on the lower end of the property while a brightly lit aluminum mobile home was nestled against the woods to the north. At the far end of the clearing was an enormous five-bay garage that looked newer and more valuable than either of the other structures, and I noticed a professionally rendered sign mounted to the front, proclaiming 'Craig's Automotive' bookended by graphics of a wrench. A handful of cars were visible behind the windows in the closed garage doors, and a motion-activated security light sprang to life as I eased to a stop amongst four other vehicles that were parked haphazardly in the clearing.

The security light attracted as much attention as if I had laid on my horn. No less than six people and an overweight hound dog swarmed the car from both directions, veering toward the passenger side as soon as they realized they had no idea who the strange guy piloting this barge was. I recognized Cheryl from the time or two I had dropped Melanie off at her beauty shop, and I was pretty sure the square-jawed fellow standing at her side was her husband, the aforementioned Craig. He helped Melanie down from the passenger seat before giving her a quick hug and passing her over to her sister, who squeezed her tightly and began whispering a steady stream of inaudible assurances into her ear. It was pretty obvious Melanie had already shared our evening's shocking news. Craig nodded to me amicably, and I returned the gesture. He wore a Cincinnati Bengals jersey and ballcap to cover his thinning hair, and I was already dreading the inevitable sports banter he would use in an attempt to break the ice. My mother's rabid fandom had spoiled those pastimes for me since childhood, stripping away one of the most common conversation pieces men lean on once introduced. I always felt an extra obligation to justify my manhood after admitting my complete disinterest in these all-American activities, because for many, it was an automatic strike against me.

A band of giggly young ladies surrounded Jasmine as she got out of the back seat, their conversation high-pitched, rapid-fire, and completely unintelligible. The dog, a basset hound I would later learn was called Betsy, insisted on putting her two cents into the fray as well. All but one of the girls looked older than Jasmine, but when I spotted one with chestnut, shoulder length curls and an easy smile that could have been Melanie's own, I figured she must be Maggie, the youngest of Melanie's siblings. As I recalled, she was living in the mobile home rent-free while attending Ashland Community and Technical College part-time and working as a server at Applebee's. It was a perk of being the youngest sister-in-law of Craig Mullins, who had inherited the business, land, and family homestead when his folks decided to spend their retirement exploring this great land of ours via Winnebago. The trailer had once been home to Craig's grandmother until it was no longer deemed safe to leave her on her own. I was unaware of her current status.

I watched as the two groups moved toward the rear of my car, Jasmine activating the power hatch. She and her mother retrieved all of our bags save for my duffle and laptop bag which were carelessly pushed aside. Like the parting of the Red Sea, Maggie led Jasmine and her gaggle of friends back to the trailer while Cheryl guided Melanie toward their wide covered porch, her arm still wrapped protectively around her sister as she continued to offer words of encouragement close to her ear. I stepped down from the driver's seat and retrieved my own bags, closing the hatch and sighing. Craig and I were the only two remaining outside, and once we had confirmed we knew each other's names and awkwardly shook hands, we struggled to make eye contact amid our discomfort.

"So, how about them Bengals?" he finally offered.

Shit.

............●◎◉◉●●●●●............

"Care for a brewski?" he asked, settling into one of two mismatched rockers that sat on either side of a battered dorm fridge on the back porch.

Betsy snored alongside his chair, her tail dangerously close to the chair's rockers. We only had ambient light spilling through the windows behind us for illumination as the motion-sensor spotlight had darkened once the activity in the driveway had diminished. The porch light remained off as a conscious choice, typical of any property surrounded by woods on three sides. Even at this time of year, it would attract unwanted airborne creatures of the night.

"Sure," I said, easing myself into the other. I wasn't sure it would support my weight, but after an initial groan, it felt fairly solid. "I'd take something stronger, if you have it."

He grinned. "Let me see what I can rustle up."

He ducked into the house, giving me the opportunity to openly gawk at the clutter on the porch. At the far right was a washing machine, its hoses and electrical cords tucked into its basin and secured with the lid. Firewood was stacked waist high along the other end of the porch, and a wooden cable reel had been turned on its end and positioned in front of the mini fridge, acting as an end table. I found it a little surprising there wasn't an ashtray. I thought everybody smoked down here.

"Let's see what you make of this," he said, bringing out a mason jar nearly full of a dark liquid.

"What is it?" I asked, aiming for curious rather than suspicious.

"Old family secret," he nodded, handing me the frosty jar. He retrieved a longneck bottle of Heineken from the dorm fridge and twisted off its cap. He lifted it in my direction. "Cheers."

We clinked glasses, and I took a sip, not wanting to appear too wary. Liquid fire spilled down my throat and my sinuses opened wide as I gasped for air. Chuckling, Craig leaned sideways to pull a can of Pepsi from the fridge, offering it to me.

"Never said it was a smooth secret," he said with a wink. "So, Cheryl says you're some kind of hotshot detective or something." I couldn't tell if he was challenging me or simply asking.

"I wouldn't go that far," I answered, taking a more cautious sip of his home brew, which I immediately chased with Pepsi. I still couldn't keep from grimacing at the aftertaste. "More like I've been in the right place at the right time."

"You caught those fellows who killed Melanie's husband," he noted. "She seems to think an awful lot of you."

I laughed. "I wouldn't ask her right now," I said. "She's barely talking to me."

"Something happen on the way over?"

"Damned if I know," I said, unwilling to go into the long version with a man I had only just met and who was likely predisposed to taking Melanie's side once his wife brought him up to speed.

"Sounds about par for the course," he said. "Even after twelve years of marriage, I can't figure out what's going through Cheryl's mind half the time. She also said you do something with computers, is that right?"

I nodded. "I freelance as an IT consultant as my bread and butter. The whole private eye thing is something I'm just trying on for size."

"Man, I hate those fucking things," he said. "But I can't run the business without one. Everything from billing to ordering parts and keeping all my tax shit straight—it's all stored on that damned device."

I nodded, indulging him. It was a complaint I'd heard a million times before, although rarely from someone of his age, which I guessed was approximately close to my own at thirty-four. "Don't know what to tell you, man," I said. "I don't see 'em going anywhere anytime soon."

"Oh, I know, it's just that mine's been running like shit lately," he said. "It's not that old, either. Say, I don't suppose you'd—" He stopped himself, looking sheepish. "I'm sorry. That was rude of me. You're not here to work."

I'd seen *this* a million times, too. You'd be surprised at how quickly your circle of friends expands once they realize what you do for a living. Still, having been completely abandoned by Melanie and Jasmine, it beat the hell out of awkwardly manufacturing small talk, a skill I doubted I would ever master.

"Let's take a look," I offered, getting to my feet. "Is it cool if we take our drinks?"

CHAPTER FOUR

Craig let us in through the "people" door along the left side of the building, flipping up a set of four light switches which flooded the space with bright, fluorescent light. The second, fourth and fifth bays were occupied by vehicles in various stages of repair, but the space was almost clinical in its cleanliness and order. The unmistakable scent of rubber permeated the air. The open office was tucked into the corner immediately to our left, and Craig led the way, sliding into the single task chair at the hand-crafted counter he had undoubtedly built himself.

"Let me get you logged in, and I'll get out of your way," he said, his fingers clumsily hunting and pecking the correct combination of keys. I winced inwardly when he entered '1234' as the password. It was a perennial favorite amongst those who hated remembering passwords, and therefore one of the easiest to crack. "I can't tell you how much I appreciate this."

As the familiar Windows start-up jingle played, he traded me spots, offering me the seat. The computer was a late model HP desktop with decent specs and a 23" widescreen monitor. It appeared to be in pretty good shape, save for its mouse and keyboard, both of which showed ample evidence of the greasy fingerprints you would expect in an environment like this. Its fan was so quiet I reached behind the unit to make sure it was running—it was.

"So, what's going on with it?" I asked.

"Every time I go on the internet, I get all of these little pop-up windows. They open quicker than I can close 'em, and they're—well, they're—embarrassing."

I nodded, aware of where this was heading but playing it cool. In my particular line of work, I was much like a priest in a confessional, and seeing as how I had only just met the man, I didn't expect him to be any more forthcoming than absolutely necessary. This plague of runaway pop-ups is most frequently caused by dipping a curious but entirely inexperienced toe into the internet's murkier waters, where pornography proliferates with no predilection left hard up. Craig had more than likely infected his system with adware, the technological equivalent of a sexually transmitted disease. The goal was to eradicate the problem, educate on safe surfing and save face for a guy at whose dinner table I would be seated the following day. Delicacy and tact would be required.

"So, what do you primarily use the computer for?" I asked.

"Customer invoicing, locating and ordering parts, bill pay." He ticked the items off on his calloused fingers. "That's about it, really."

"Maybe some sports scores?" I suggested.

"Oh, sure, I guess so."

"How about email?"

"Oh—yeah, that too," he nodded.

"You don't ever click on links in emails or open attachments, especially from people you don't know, do you?"

He looked a little less sure on that one. "I don't think so."

"Do you have an anti-virus program?"

He shrugged. "Only if it came with the damned thing."

A little investigation uncovered an expired subscription to McAfee, but for some time, Windows had been bundling its own Microsoft Defender program with its operating systems, and it had taken over monitoring once the subscription had lapsed. While it was decent, it was no match for someone determined to see a free peep show, and as in life, such things are rarely free. I suspected Defender alone wouldn't be able to clean this mess up.

"I need to grab a flash drive out of my laptop bag," I said. "I think you've picked up some adware along the way, but I've got a great tool for clearing it out."

"I hope this isn't putting you out," he said, stepping aside so I could get past him.

"Not at all," I said. "The program does all the work. It just takes a little time to scan the system and quarantine anything it finds."

"How about I get us some refills on our drinks and maybe grab a deck of cards? We can hang out here until it's done scanning."

"Works for me," I said, holding the door open for him. The motion-activated lamp sprang to life as soon as we stepped outside. We crossed the wide gravel patch towards the house, and ascended the wood plank stairs to the porch, where I collected my laptop bag from beside the rocker, and he continued into the house. I could hear a television playing somewhere inside, but there was no sign of Melanie or Cheryl anywhere.

As the guardian spotlight winked out again, I caught the unmistakable smell of weed drifting down from the general vicinity of the trailer, and I looked up to see one of Maggie's friends watching me from its cinderblock stoop, the end of her blunt flaring brightly as she took a long, slow drag. She was barelegged under an oversized t-shirt featuring Minnie Mouse, but there was nothing adolescent about this girl whatsoever. Her platinum blonde hair was a disheveled shag with dark roots and her very stance was an invitation to come join the party. She waved two fingers in my direction and offered up the joint from afar. I nodded my acknowledgement but waved her offer away, wishing like hell Craig would get back and relieved when I heard the screen door slam against its frame behind me.

"Hey, Katie," he called, dragging an Igloo cooler on wheels off the porch. "Smoke enough of that shit?"

"Hiya, Mr. M.," she returned, utterly unfazed by his question. In fact, she took another slow, deliberate drag. "Just about."

"Jasmine still up there?" he asked, and I was embarrassed the thought hadn't even occurred to me. It hadn't been so many years since I had partied with my friends as Maggie was apparently doing with hers, but at twelve, Jasmine had no business being up there.

Katie nodded. "They're inside watching *Mean Girls*. And that's why I'm out here. Separation of church and state, so to speak."

"See that you keep it that way," he said, waggling a forefinger in her direction.

"Aye-aye, Mi Capitan," she returned with a salute, stubbing her blunt. She looked me over once more with a crooked grin before going back into the trailer.

"Do I need to let Melanie know what's going on up there?" I asked.

"If it'll give you peace of mind, but I'm sure Mel has an idea of what's going on up there. Oh, and those other two girls are my daughters, Amanda and Mackenzie, so maybe you're second-guessing *my* parental judgment?"

He looked at me pointedly, and I sputtered before he finally grinned and let me off the hook.

"Maggie adores Jasmine, as do my girls, and they wouldn't let anything happen to her, I promise you that. I'm not saying I condone every little thing they do, but I remember being that age not so long ago, and personally, I'd rather them be a little ornery right here on my own property than doing who-knows-what with who-knows-who and who-knows-where, you know?"

I followed his reasoning, and my only real choice was to nod. Anything else was a challenge to his years of cumulative parenting, and I couldn't think of a way to be more offensive. I hated this. I was the odd man out

47

here. It appeared that every single person on these premises had a lengthier history than me with both Melanie and her daughter, even the sultry little nymphet who had just flirted with me while getting her buzz on. Did I really want my first impression to be that of a snitch who didn't trust Melanie's own family's judgment with the care of their niece? I reluctantly followed Craig back to the garage, our approach heralded once more by the sudden burst of man-made security lighting.

• • • • ● ● ⊖ ⊙ ● ● ● • • • •

I started a deep scan with Malwarebytes to seek out any malware or rootkits that might be resident on the hard drive of what I had begun to think of as Craig's X-box, and all we could do was wait for it to finish. Craig had topped off my mystery concoction and was on his second Heiny. I could feel the faintest trace of warmth in my cheeks and my discomfort was starting to ebb. He let me retain use of the task chair as he pulled up a backless stool on wheels that had been positioned next to the open hood of a crimson Pontiac Sunfire. We sat across from each other at the open end of the handmade counter, as far away from the computer and assorted stacks of paperwork as possible in case we got clumsy with our beverages. He pulled a blue pack of Diamondback playing cards from his pocket and casually employed an overhand shuffle, shifting the cards from his left hand to his right.

"So, what's your poison?" he asked, shifting to a riffle shuffle and bridge with ease. In my hands, the cards would undoubtedly be raining down from the rafters in no time. "How about rummy?"

"Can't say I've ever played that," I said.

"It's easy. I can teach you."

My laughter was a little more robust than intended. "When it comes to cards, I'm pretty unteachable."

48

"Pinochle?"

I shrugged.

"Texas Hold 'Em?"

I took another drink from my mason jar and chased it quickly with a swig of Pepsi. "Stop when you get to Uno."

He grinned and shook his head. Typically, when I found myself in a conversation such as this, I was accustomed to condescension, but all I saw was a twinkle of amusement in his eyes. I was beginning to think Craig was an okay guy.

"Let's go with Crazy Eights," he said. "It's pretty much Uno but with regular cards. Sound good?"

"I don't know about good, but it sounds possible," I countered. "No promises, though."

He gave me a quick rundown of the game rules as he dealt the cards, then leaned to his right, reaching into his workspace and snagging a pipe. "Do you mind? I quit smoking last year, but still sneak a pipe here and there." My first thought must have been written across my face, because he laughed. "It's just tobacco. I promise."

"Of course," I said awkwardly, wondering anew if I should be extricating Jasmine from the trailer of questionable judgment. I now understood how my parents must have felt every single weekend of my high school senior year. "I gave it up, too, but still slip up sometimes when I drink."

"Well, hold on just one minute, my friend," he said, easing off of the stool and heading toward a bank of worktables at the rear of the garage. After rummaging around for a bit, he grunted in satisfaction, a pack of Camels clutched high in his right hand.

I could have kissed the man.

He tossed me the pack as he settled back onto the stool. "Chip usually leaves a pack out here. He doesn't want Cheryl to know he smokes."

"Chip?" I asked.

Craig nodded, lighting his pipe before passing his Bic to me. "Guess you haven't met him, either. Chip is Cheryl and Mel's brother. He's next to the youngest and the only boy. You'll get the chance tomorrow. He's out with his lady tonight, but he never misses a free meal. He's enlisted in the Army but managed to get leave for the holiday. Boy's real good with his hands. He helps me out around the garage when he's home."

"I guess that only leaves Molly," I said, arranging my cards in my hand. "Will she be here tomorrow, too?"

"Oh, yeah," he groaned, taking another pull from his beer.

I chuckled. "You sound thrilled."

"Oh, she's all right, I guess," he said, setting aside his ballcap and running his hand through his thinning sandy hair. "Very opinionated, that's all. She works at Lymont Memorial and her husband, Gordon, is a CPA in Huntington. I'm telling you all this because you probably won't even realize he's here. She does all the talking, and he just sort of fades into the background. They've got a pair of twin boys, Jacob and Jedediah, and I'd be hard pressed to tell you which of the two is the weirdest—not that I said that out loud." He shot me a quick wink.

I grinned, laying a card of matching suit onto his discard. "Nice alliteration there," I noted. "Very—biblical."

He snorted. "Very perceptive, and just you wait and see! Molly will undoubtedly attempt to rescue you from the clutches of Satan before the weekend is over."

I took another gulp from the mason jar and finished off my Pepsi, motioning for another as my eyes began to water uncontrollably. "Kill me now," I implored.

"You've seriously never met *any* of the family?"

"Not really," I said. "Other than a quick hello to your wife when dropping Mel off at her shop, I've never met any of them. Molly *was* very helpful when I first met Melanie in giving me updates on a friend who was in the ICU."

He laid a card over mine and shook his head in disbelief. "Well, that's a first. Molly breaking a rule? I can't imagine what Melanie promised in exchange for that. It'll be *years* before that score is settled."

I extracted a semi-crushed Camel from Chip's crumpled pack and lit it, launching myself into a horrific coughing fit. Craig watched intently as I got myself back under control. "I'm fine," I finally managed to wheeze, taking a much smaller hit as if to prove my point.

He laughed and began drawing cards from the deck. "Are you sure? I mean, I've heard smoking kills, but I didn't expect it to happen quite so quickly."

"Not my brand," I said, grimacing.

"Sorry, it's all I've got," he said, nudging an ashtray in my direction, but I waved it away.

"It's like smoking a turd, but beggars can't be choosers."

"If you say so," he said, finally drawing a card he could use.

The card I was in the process of playing froze in midair as a chorus of frightened shrieks upended our quiet evening.

The girls were huddled just outside the trailer running nearly the full gamut of the emotional spectrum. One of Craig's girls was crying while the other kept a protective arm around her. Jasmine stuck close to her Aunt Maggie, aiming for consciously aloof, but I could tell she was just a smidge from tears herself. Katie smoked a cigarette on the other side of Maggie, making sure to blow her exhaust away from the other girls but looking positively bored. Craig and I arrived in tandem, and I was reminded yet again that I needed to resume my former habit of jogging three miles in the morning. I was notably more winded than Craig.

"What's going on? Is everyone all right?" he asked while I caught my breath.

Their uncoordinated response was an assault on the auditory canal, urgent yet entirely unintelligible.

Craig urged the girls to bring it down a notch and grabbed his daughter who was the most distraught by both shoulders, pivoting her towards him. "Kenzie, honey, *shhh*," he said, inches from her face. "What's wrong, baby?"

"He-he-he was *watching* us!" she sobbed, tears streaming down her face. "Th-th-through the window!"

Craig looked questioningly to Maggie. "What's she talking about?"

Maggie looked sheepish as she fiddled with her nest of chestnut curls. "I'm honestly not sure, Craig. I didn't see anything."

Craig looked at the other girls, who had calmed considerably since we had joined their ranks. "How about you girls? Did anyone else see this face Kenzie saw? Katie? Amanda? Jaz?"

Their heads slowly began to shake, which only served to upset Mackenzie more. "I didn't just *imagine* it, you assholes!"

"*Whoa!* Hey, let's watch with the a-bombs, darlin'," Craig interjected while pulling his daughter in for a quick hug. "Just because they didn't see it, doesn't mean it didn't happen. So, let's go have a look-see, whaddaya say?"

She nodded, clearly less than convinced it was a good idea, but with her father at her side, she finally got her tears in check.

"Now, which window was it?" Craig asked, looking back toward the trailer. There was a wide picture window to the right of the cinderblock stoop, but with no porch to front the house, a Peeping Tom would have been over ten feet tall to make use of that one.

"The little one behind the dinette that looks out into the woods," she said meekly, dabbing at her eyes underneath a pair of glasses. She couldn't have been much older than Jasmine and looked very vulnerable in her thin cotton pajama top and matching shorts, her feet encased in oversized Bugs Bunny slippers.

Craig fished his cellphone from his pocket and activated its flashlight, keeping hold of his daughter's hand while signaling for the other girls to follow along. "Let's check it out."

I was slightly startled to feel a cold set of fingers inch its way into my palm, and I looked down to see Jasmine had hung back, staying by my side. I squeezed her hand. "You okay, kiddo?" I asked.

She nodded, waiting for the others to gain a little distance. "Love her to death, but Kenzie is like the Queen of Drama," she said with a bit of exasperation. "I doubt she saw anything. She probably just got spooked."

"Spooked? By what?" I asked. "Surely not *Mean Girls*—"

Jasmine giggled and shook her head. "No. We finished that a half hour ago. Katie was setting up her Ouija board and—"

"Her *Ouija* board?" I interrupted. "Why in the world would she be setting up a Ouija board—or is this just a 'normal' Katie thing?"

Jasmine shrugged. "I don't know. She's got all sorts of cool stuff in the trunk of her car. She thought of the Ouija when Kenzie kept going on and on about some girl at her school who disappeared a couple of weeks ago. Apparently, she left a really weird note for her mother saying she was running off, and that's the official story, but that hasn't stopped the rumor mill from coming up with one of its own."

"Yeah? And what's the story there?"

"There's actually two. There's one that says she's been sold into a human trafficking ring as a sex slave. The other thinks she got in over her head with a bunch of people who deal drugs. They think she's probably dead."

53

"Ah," I said, connecting the dots. "And thus, the Ouija board. You don't really believe in those things, do you?"

"I don't know," said Jasmine, avoiding my gaze as she minimized her own level of engagement. "Probably not. But Katie was really leaning into the whole thing, and Kenzie was getting all worked up. It might have been a little bit contagious."

Craig and the other girls came back from around the rear of the mobile home, looking visibly more relaxed. Mackenzie was no longer clinging to her father, and Maggie and Katie stayed back, laughing conspiratorially. Amanda, the youngest of the bunch, was simply along for the ride, shuffling along on the other side of her father, lips moving soundlessly to whatever music was playing inside her head. Restrained dance moves occasionally threatened to erupt but her self-consciousness kept them mostly at bay. She looked like she was maybe nine yet entirely more grounded than any of the others, save for Jasmine.

"No boog-uns to report," Craig announced. "We did spot an owl, and I'm guessing their imaginations did the rest, considering what they were up to in there."

"Geez, Mr. M.," said Katie. "It's only a Ouija board. It's vintage *Parker Brothers*, for heaven's sake. It's just a little fun, that's all."

"Not when you've got *this* one around," he said, pulling Mackenzie in for a quick squeeze. He turned to Maggie. "You *know* she's prone to nightmares, Mags."

Mackenzie pulled away, thoroughly embarrassed. *"Dad!"*

"I'm sorry, Craig, honest," Maggie said. "I wasn't thinking."

"Well, you're not the one who gets yanked out of sleep when she wakes up screaming in the middle of the night," said Craig, much to Mackenzie's mortification. She pushed past her father and marched toward the house, every step an expression of fury. Craig seemed content to let it ride, but Jasmine chased after her, working to calm her down.

"Oh, *c'mon*, Craig," implored Maggie. "Don't let this ruin our girls' night. We don't get the chance to do this very often since Melanie and Jasmine moved up north. Katie will put the Ouija away, and I'll do my best to get the subject changed, although it won't be easy. Kenzie's really fixated on that McAlister girl who ran away from home. There's a bunch of rumors about what really happened to her running rampant at school, and Kenzie can't seem to let it go."

Craig frowned. "I heard something about it at church, but we were never really close to the family. I didn't realize Kenzie even knew Tina McAlister."

Maggie shook her head. "She doesn't. Tina's a senior, and they don't even go to the same school. But you know how Kenzie is—these kids all know each other from the sporting events, and this is what all her friends are talking about."

"Well, *you* know how Kenzie is, too, so I'm counting on you to keep her from coming up out of her hair," said Craig, and Maggie crossed her heart. I couldn't help but notice the slight eyeroll from Katie over Maggie's shoulder.

Jasmine had apparently been successful in talking Mackenzie down from the ledge, and they were slowly returning to the group. We escorted them as far as the cinderblock stoop at the front of the mobile home.

Craig kneeled down to bring his face level with his oldest daughter's, forcing her to reluctantly look at him. "No more of this nonsense tonight, Kenzie. Do you hear me? There's nothing to be afraid of here. This is your home. Maggie isn't going to let anything happen to you, you got me?"

Mackenzie nodded, but still looked completely unconvinced. Katie sighed and headed for the door. "I'll go put the offensively evil board game away." She muttered something else as she went inside, and while most of it was unintelligible, I was pretty sure I detected the word, 'bullshit' somewhere in the mix.

As Craig continued to make peace with his daughter, I stepped up to hold the storm door open for the others, but before anyone else had a chance to ascend the block steps, another blood-curdling scream sounded from inside the trailer. I was operating on adrenaline and autopilot as I cut in front of Maggie and stepped up into the small living room.

A lanky man in navy coveralls had Katie pinned to the far wall, his face buried in her neck and his hands working their way underneath her Minnie Mouse tee.

CHAPTER FIVE

The element of surprise was all mine as I crossed the room in four long strides and clamped a hand over the punk's shoulder. I pivoted him around and put everything I had into the punch I threw, connecting solidly with his startled face and knocking him to the ground. I felt something give in his nose as blood spurted down onto his chin.

Chaos erupted all around me. Katie looked at me like I was from Mars as she called me a few choice names and pushed me away before kneeling down to her attacker. The other girls burst through the door, bypassing me, and making a beeline for the guy who was bleeding onto the carpet. The combination of five female voices competing to be heard made it impossible to understand any of them, and I looked back to find Craig standing just inside the door, clearly amused, and struggling to keep a straight face.

"*Sumbitch!* I think that asshole broke my nose!" said the intruder, dabbing at his bloodied snout and wincing. The girls began to help him off the floor.

I was completely perplexed with my mouth hanging open and fists still drawn.

Craig clamped a hand on my shoulder, and I nearly jumped out of my skin. "Dwayne? Meet Melanie's little brother, Chip. Chip? This is the fella your sister's been hooking up with." From there, he doubled over, howling with laughter he could no longer contain.

"Oh, my God—" I hurried forward to assist, thoroughly mortified. Now that I had a second to think, I *did* sort of recognize the guy from some of the family pics Melanie has scattered around my living room. "I am *so* sorry—"

"Shit *fire!*" he said, clamping onto my hand as I helped him the rest of the way to his feet. "When I was little, I got hit by a car once, and it ain't got *nothin'* on you, mister!" Maggie handed us each a wet washrag to clean ourselves up as Chip's blood was still free-flowing and getting all over everything. All of the other girls seemed as amused as Craig, with the exception of Katie, who still looked like she wanted to drive a knee into my crotch.

"Thought you were out for the evening, Bub," noted Craig.

"Naw, just to the dog tracks for a bit with Bobby," he said, tilting his head back and using the dampened rag to tenderly stanch the flow of blood dribbling from his nostrils.

"And you got back just in time to play a prank on the little ladies, I'm guessing."

Chip grinned sheepishly. "Just a little fun is all," he said. "I wasn't standing outside that window five minutes before Kenzie lost her freakin' *mind.*" He started to laugh, but his face wasn't quite up for that yet.

Mackenzie was thoroughly offended and desperate to save face. "I didn't lose my *mind.* I was just—startled, that's all."

None of the other girls were buying what she was selling, and it was fairly obvious, so Craig opted to put the subject to bed. "Well, seein' as how the only one who got hurt was you, wiseass, I think you should wish your nieces a goodnight and head on over to the house to get some sleep. We've got a lot to do before everyone shows up for lunch, capiche?"

"Got it, got it," he said. He gingerly tested the area below his nose and discovered the blood had stopped flowing.

"Is Jenny coming tomorrow?" asked Craig, and I could only assume this was the lady with whom Craig had earlier indicated Chip was spending the evening.

Chip shrugged. "Maybe. We're a little on the outs right now."

I stole a glance at Katie, and she couldn't have looked happier.

"All right, then. We're heading back over to the garage then," said Craig, moving toward the door. "Dwayne's trying to get my work computer straightened around for me. No more screaming and no more nonsense."

"I really am sorry," I added. "I thought you were—well, I didn't know what was going on." It didn't feel appropriate to share what I thought I'd seen between Chip and Katie when Craig and the others seemed entirely oblivious. "It didn't occur to me that you might be Melanie's brother."

"No worries, man," he said, offering a hand. As soon as I took it, he squeezed hard and pulled me toward him, grinning beneath a blood-crusted upper lip. "Just remember—payback's a bitch."

He held on for just a second longer than was comfortable, and I wasn't sure at all whether he was toying with me or completely serious. Once he finally let go, I awkwardly followed Craig through the door and back to the garage.

"Scan's finished," I announced, clicking a few buttons onscreen to quarantine and eradicate the malware it had found.

Craig indicated the pile of cards spread out at the far end of the counter. "Any interest in picking this back up?"

"Not really," I said. "If you don't mind, I think I'm about ready to call it a night." Frankly, I wanted to go inside and hide behind Melanie. After the incident with Chip, I was done with being left unsupervised.

59

"Not a problem," he replied, scooping the cards together to put them back in their pack. "Did you find anything?" He pointed to the computer.

I nodded. "A little over 50,000 pieces of malware and a rootkit."

"What?!?"

"I've flushed it all out. It should run like a top now."

"But—how did that happen? I mean, if that anti-viral thingy was doing its job—"

I was past the point of diplomacy. I didn't relish the next few minutes, but sometimes, you've just got to call it for what it is. "Can I be direct? No judgment, I promise."

His cautious expression belied his words. "Sure, I mean—I guess so."

"If you enjoy looking at folks doing things best done naked, do yourself a big favor and pick up a magazine or maybe a DVD porno or two."

I wouldn't have thought his ruddy complexion could flush the color of crimson he was currently sporting. He sputtered, looking for some sort of rebuttal, but I just shook my head and held up a finger.

"No judgment, remember? The internet is full of ads promising free this, that, and the other. But just like in life, is anything ever *truly* free?" I paused, shaking my head. "Sadly, no. And when it comes to computer malware, you could inadvertently be exposing your customers' personal or financial information to who knows who, and Lord only knows in what country. It's just not worth it."

His face drained of color just as quickly as it had reddened when he realized the full impact of my words.

"Am I gonna need to disclose all this to my customers?" he asked, and I suspected his customers weren't the only ones he was worried about. This was a locally owned business operating on the cusp of the Bible Belt. It wasn't the sort of thing you wanted getting around.

"Do you store customers' credit card or checking account numbers on there?" I asked.

He shook his head vehemently. "I don't take checks, and I have a POS terminal for credit card payments." He thought about it for a moment longer. "I *have* used my own company credit card to purchase parts."

I nodded. "That's good. Monitor your own credit card statements for any fraudulent activity. You might want to cancel your card and request one with a new number, just to be safe. If customer name and address and order history is all that you've kept on there, you're probably in pretty good shape."

He sighed with relief as his color began to return to normal. "Thank God."

"So, what's the deal with that Katie girl?" I asked, pocketing my thumb drive, and stepping out from behind his computer.

"She and Mags go way back—all the way to junior high, I think. Why do you ask?" He shot me a sly grin. "You *dog*—"

I laughed. "No, nothing like that, although she was kinda flirty before you came out. It's just that—" I hesitated, not sure I wanted to engage in what amounted to little more than gossip.

Craig stared at me. "It's just what?"

I regretted bringing it up, but I really didn't see a way out now. "I think she and Chip may have a little thing going, that's all. That's why I was so aggressive. His hands were underneath her shirt, and I—I'm pretty sure I completely misjudged her reaction. It wasn't the assault I thought it was. She seemed pretty pissed at me."

Craig shrugged, scooping his empty bottles into a trash can near the end of the counter. "She'll get over it. That little lady's always runnin' a little warm, and Chip? Well, boys will be boys, I guess."

I opened my mouth to say more but thought better of it. These people had only just met me, and I had already busted Chip's nose. Did I also want to come across as pious and morally superior? For all I knew, Chip and Jenny could have a completely open relationship, and just because I was barely able to navigate a relationship with a single monogamous partner didn't mean I should pass judgment on anyone else.

I collected my mason jar from the countertop and lapsed into silence, following Craig toward the exit, where he paused and turned around. "One more thing," he said. "Can we keep all this—" He gestured toward the computer then back to himself. "—to ourselves? I would really be embarrassed if Cheryl found out."

I grinned and nodded, clapping him on the shoulder. "Say no more. You're secret's safe with me, Mr. M."

* * *

Craig and I entered from the porch, leading us into a fairly narrow kitchen that already bore ample signs of the upcoming feast. The space was dimly lit by a hood light over the stove and a single covered bulb over the kitchen sink, above which was a window looking out onto the back porch. Cookies and other assorted desserts covered a fair amount of counter space as well as the top of a small dinette table to our left, and it smelled like a little bit of heaven inside.

Everything about the house seemed dated but clean. The kitchen linoleum was of a pattern like what had been in my own kitchen when I was a child. The ceiling was unusually low, and none of the angles seemed entirely flush, as if whoever had built the house did so without proper measurement and was just sort of winging it. Straight ahead through a wide, arched opening was the living room, where Cheryl and Melanie had taken up residence on the rust-colored shag carpeting, using the base of the L-shaped sofa and loveseat arrangement to lean against. They sat directly in front of an entirely unnecessary fire, blazing away in the fireplace, and elevating the indoor temperature well beyond my comfort zone.

"Well, *there's* our fellas!" called Cheryl, lifting a mostly empty wine glass in salute. She wore a knee-length red flannel shirt, and her feet were bare. She finished what was left in her glass and stood, crossing the room to greet her husband with a hug and a kiss. He patted her backside, and she giggled.

Melanie remained seated, nursing her own wine glass, but it seemed like some of the fire had left her eyes and settled warmly into her cheeks. She had changed into sleep pants and a thin cotton tee, and it was impossible not to notice she had retired her bra for the evening. She offered me a slight smile, giving me hope our cold front might have thawed.

Cheryl abruptly pivoted toward me and smacked my arm. "What's this I hear about you beating up my little brother?"

I froze, my mouth working soundlessly. I couldn't tell if she was serious or not from the expression on her face, and Melanie looked away, offering no clues.

Thankfully, Cheryl couldn't hold her mock outrage for long and slipped back into giggles. "What I wouldn't give to have seen that! Little asshole! What was he doing up there scaring the girls anyway?" She turned to Craig. "I thought he was out with Jenny tonight."

"Guess not, babe," he said, sliding an arm around her waist but offering nothing more. Apparently, the Boys' Club took care of its own here.

"Well, come on in and have a seat," said Cheryl, plopping back down on the floor catercorner from her sister and patting the carpeting. "It's only right that we should take a moment to prepare Dwayne for all he's signed up for. Besides, we've got just a *smidge* of chardonnay left, and we don't want that to go to waste, now, do we, Mel?"

Craig shook his head and grinned, then turned to me. "You up for another drink, brother?"

"Just half," I said handing him the empty mason jar I still held. He took it and disappeared into the kitchen. Sweat was beginning to spring out across my forehead, and I started plucking at my shirt to keep it from sticking to my chest. "Does anyone else think it's a little warm in here?"

Cheryl eyed the fire blazing away in the mantel. "I guess I did build it up a little more than I meant to. We'll have to let it die down, but in the meanwhile, you could open those two windows at the front of the house."

As I followed her direction, she stretched to her limits to reach a handheld remote from the nearest end table and aimed it at the lighted ceiling fan hanging directly above us. She activated its stationary blades, and what began as a slow rotation was soon a drunkenly wobbling guillotine of terror, threatening to break free from the ceiling and behead us all in one fell swoop. Neither she nor Melanie seemed particularly concerned. I tried to pull my head down into my shoulders as I lowered myself to the carpet beside Melanie, keeping a cautious eye on the fixture. I was a little surprised when I felt her fingers slip through mine.

Craig returned, handing me a mason jar that was a little more than half filled along with a fresh can of Pepsi. He popped the top of a bottle of Heineken and dropped down beside his wife. I wasn't sure why we weren't using the actual furniture. I was getting a little too old to find the floor particularly comfortable, but I wasn't hosting this shindig.

Cheryl topped off hers and Melanie's wine glasses, setting the empty bottle aside. She raised her glass and waited expectantly for us all to do the same. "To new family," she said with a smile.

We repeated her toast surprisingly in sync and stretched forward to click our various refreshments. I was the only one to clumsily chase my drink as my throat once again burst into flames, and Cheryl and Craig exchanged a bemused look that might have made me uncomfortable if Melanie hadn't given my hand a tiny squeeze. I looked at her, and she tossed me a quick wink.

Cheryl cleared her throat. "There is one little piece of—oh, I don't know—*awkwardness* that I'd like to get out of the way, if you don't mind," she said, looking directly at me as I froze like a deer in headlights.

"Um, sure," I said. "What's that?"

"As you can probably tell, me and my big sister have had just a little bit to drink here," she said, and out of the corner of my eye, I spotted a second empty bottle of Chardonnay tucked halfway beneath the loveseat. "I'm not good with stuff like this to begin with, so I'm going to apologize before I even open my big mouth—"

"Oh, for heaven's sake, Cheryl, spit it out," urged Melanie.

Cheryl tossed her a dark glare before returning her attention to me. "I am just so sorry about your sister." She grabbed Melanie's free hand. "I can't even imagine."

I nodded, frankly relieved it wasn't something else. "Thank you. I appreciate it."

"Mel's just the best friend I've ever had," she said, and my relief was short-lived when she started to mist over. She lifted Melanie's hand to her cheek and leaned into it.

"C'mon, honey," urged Craig, trying to ease her into his direction. "You're bringing everybody down—"

"He's right," said Melanie, gently extricating her hand from Cheryl's, while giving mine another gentle squeeze with the other. "You just got me up out of my funk. Let's keep it upbeat, upbeat!"

Cheryl nodded, snuffling, and dabbing at her eyes and fanning herself. "I'm sorry. It's the wine. You all *know* how I am with the wine."

"You started to warn Dwayne about what he'd signed up for," reminded Craig, wrapping an arm around his wife.

I looked at them warily. "I'm not sure I like the sound of that, either."

"She's talking about Molly and her family," said Melanie, attempting to urge her sister back on topic as she gently slid her fingers back and forth through mine.

Cheryl gasped as if remembering the cure for cancer. "That's right, I *was!* Oh, it's not too late to run. C'mon—let's do it! Let's all just run!" Melanie joined her in a chorus of wicked laughter. "Can you imagine her face when she and Mr. CPA pull into the driveway with the two J's and no one's here to answer the door?" The laughter quickly got guttural as the sisters leaned into one another conspiratorially, but Melanie held fast to my hand, and I was beginning to feel heat that wasn't from the fireplace.

Craig looked at me apologetically. "I think they may be a little more lit than we realized. They do this every time."

"Oh, hush," said Cheryl, gently elbowing him in the ribs as she came up for air. "It's not nice to mix our drinking with Molly." That sent them both back over the edge as they realized Cheryl's statement could also apply to the street name for the drug, Ecstasy.

"Oh, Lord," said Craig, cupping his forehead into his palm.

"Oh, Cheezits, that's *right!* The Lord!" Cheryl's eyes widened as she was pulled back on topic. Her focus shifted back to me, and she cleared her throat, digging deep for a little composure. "Molly and her family will be here at 9AM sharp. Not one minute early, not one minute late. She will bring every vegetable side dish that you ever avoided as a kid, and they will be every bit as tasteless and gross as you remember. She will spend most of the day making snippy little pronouncements while looking down her pointy nose about the way we keep house or conduct our lives and how we really need to spend a little more time with her in church. By the time dinner is served, she will have invited you to Sunday service at New Life Apostolic in Flatwoods and the upcoming jamboree, revival, and community baptism next week at Spit Lick Creek. She will also undoubtedly try to secure a sizable donation to support Apostolic missionaries and the orphans of the

South American rainforests, so guard your wallet. She's aggressive and judgmental, and a perfect example of the typical parishioner at New Life, and that's exactly why I stopped going there."

Melanie snorted. "You stopped going there because they cast you out as a Jezebel just as soon as word got out that you were pregnant with Kenzie. Same as they did to me when they found out I was pregnant with Jaz." She shook her head. "I never could understand how a church, of all places, could spew so much hatred and prejudice. It's obscene. You would have thought we were killing someone instead of bringing new life into the world, and all because we were unwed."

"And Daddy was right there leading the charge," added Cheryl, finishing off her wine and setting her glass aside.

We slipped into a few moments of awkward silence. I certainly didn't have anything to add, and I was finished tempting blindness with Craig's home brew. Craig reclined against the base of the loveseat with his eyes closed, his head tilted up toward the wobbly ceiling fan, and both Cheryl and Melanie were busily being consumed by memories from a much darker time.

I was contemplating the best way of extracting myself and calling it an evening when Melanie's hand tightened in mine. She downed the remainder of her drink and stood, pulling me to my feet with a little effort. "Enough of this nonsense," she said. "We're going to scare the shit right out of Dwayne, and you're making Molly out to be a lot worse than she actually is."

"If you say so, dear sister," said Cheryl, looking leery. "But then again, you always did get along with Molly better than me. I feel like everybody deserves a little heads-up before being exposed to her, that's all."

"And your work here is done," said Melanie, stifling a yawn. "But it's been a very long day, and if it's all the same to you two, I'd like to call it a night. We can let Dwayne draw his own conclusions after 9AM sharp." She slipped her arms around my midsection, and I had zero idea of how I had gotten out of the doghouse, but I clearly understood that I somehow owed it to Cheryl. "Where are you putting us?"

Cheryl pointed to the hallway that branched left just before the kitchen. "You can take Mags' old room. Chip laid claim to the attic." She groaned as she struggled to her feet, pulling Craig up after her. "You ready to hit the hay, mister?"

He nodded, playfully swatting her backside. "Good night, kids. Thanks for all your help, Dwayne. I really do appreciate it. It's really nice to finally put a face to the name."

I nodded. "Same here. Good night."

We watched as Craig guided Cheryl toward the stairs and spotted her as she began her wobbly ascent. Melanie took my hand and led me back through the darkened hallway to the last door on the left. The predominantly pink room was bathed only by soft light from a lava lamp on an end table beside a bed covered in frilly pillows. We had barely closed the door when Melanie pulled me to her and kissed me deeply.

"I'm sorry about earlier," she said, and her fingertips were raising gooseflesh along my back. "I didn't handle Sarah's news very well. I'm *still* not handling her news very well, but that's not your fault."

I kissed the tip of her nose. "It's some pretty big news. We've got time to work through it."

She nodded, still pressed firmly against me. "That wasn't all, though."

"No?"

"Huh-unh," she said, and she kissed me again, longer, and more slowly than before. I was afraid of saying something stupid and shattering the moment, seeing as how all of the blood had rushed completely away from my brain, so I just stood there, drinking in her beauty and trying not to actually drool. "I was jealous because of how easy you make it seem to rein Jasmine in when she's pushing every single one of my buttons. I hate it that

I'm always the bad guy, but again, that's not your fault. I need to stop pushing you away and recognize that we're much, much better as a team."

Her mouth found mine again, and I literally felt dizzy as she backed me toward the bed. I felt her fingers fumbling with my belt, and out of the corner of my eye, I saw something that gave me pause.

"Um—Mel?" I managed.

"Mmm?" She had moved to my neck and was nibbling at my jawline.

"It's only a twin bed."

Her hand abruptly slipped below the equator, and I gasped.

"Do you really mind?" she purred in my ear.

Not in the least.

CHAPTER SIX

I awoke with my face pressed against the pretty pink wallpaper, a steady stream of drool escaping the corner of my mouth and running down the wall. I was tangled up in bedsheets, and half of me had slipped into the space between wall and mattress, my left foot trapped between the rails of the footboard. It and its attached leg were completely useless as I had deprived them of blood flow for God only knows how long. The enticing aromas of bacon and coffee wafted down the hallway, as did smatterings of conversation, and I recognized the sound of Melanie's laughter. It took a moment longer to get my bearings, and despite my straining bladder, I still wasn't quite willing to move just yet, delaying the inevitable pins-and-needles agony awaiting me for just as long as humanly possible.

I must have drifted off again for a second, because the next thing I heard was two sharp raps on the door behind me as it swung inward. I smiled into the wall, anticipating Melanie with a cup of coffee, but the smile quickly fell away as the screaming began. I was suddenly made aware by an unexpectedly cool breeze that my bare backside was on full display to whoever stood screaming in the doorway. I nearly broke my foot wrenching it free from the footboard and adjusting the covers while keeping my face completely hidden, only to howl like a wounded animal as the pins-and-needles arrived with a vengeance.

I tucked myself into a fetal position as the scream faded down the corridor, pulling the sheet over my head and praying for a swift and painless death. I practically jumped out of my skin when I felt a finger poke my side through the sheet.

"You can come out now," Melanie managed, but there was no hiding the amusement in her voice.

I flopped over and peeked at her over the edge of the sheet. "Please tell me that wasn't one of the girls."

Melanie grinned, her eyes twinkling. "Nope, not one of the girls."

I let the sheet fall below my chin as I considered the other options. "Surely, it wasn't—"

She nodded, grin still firmly in place. "Oh, yes. That was Molly, and let me say, you made one *hell* of a first impression."

·····•••••◉⊖⊙◉•••••·····

I slunk toward the kitchen, hugging the wall to remain as unobtrusive as possible as I neared the arched entryway. Melanie and Cheryl bantered back and forth, laughing frequently, and my face was completely flushed. While I couldn't determine actual words over the steady clatter of knife against cutting board, I was certain they were talking about me. I had forgotten to bring my overnight bag in from the porch and had no choice but to slip back into my clothes from the previous evening—well, sans my underwear. I couldn't find it, and going commando didn't feel as liberating as it was made out to be. I hadn't showered and looked like I'd rolled out of a hamper. My hair was a little on the long side with a towering cowlick that resisted every attempt to tame it. I briefly considered crawling out a window in the bedroom and making my escape, but sadly, it was painted shut.

I took a deep breath and closed my eyes, counting to three and steeling myself for whatever abuse was coming my way. As I rounded the corner

71

into the kitchen, I almost ran straight into the butcher knife Molly held before her, and she let out a shorter version of the shriek that had started my day, nearly dropping an enormous bowl of peeled potatoes she had tucked into her elbow. She didn't even begin to resemble her sisters and was built like a pencil, a helmet of shoulder-length mousy brown hair sprayed to withstand hurricane force winds.

"Oh, shi-i-i—um, *shoot*, I'm so sorry, I—uh," I stammered, steadying the bowl but unable to meet her eyes as we did an awkward dance around each other. A card table had been set up in the living room, and she scurried over to it with her bowl and placed it beside a cutting board, unable to face me either.

When I looked up, Melanie and Cheryl were all smiles, their eyes fixed on me and having far too much fun at my expense.

"Good morning, *loverboy*," Cheryl said throatily, winking and blowing me a kiss.

"Oh, *God*," I groaned, looking to the ceiling as she and Melanie fell into hysterics, propping each other up and cackling as only a coven of sisters could.

"Now, I'm just teasin' you, Dwayne," said Cheryl, but the twinkle in her eye warned me she wasn't quite done yet—maybe she never would be. Melanie handed me a cup of black coffee and winked, providing absolutely no assurances whatsoever. "I'm just so pleased that Mel's finally found someone who can put a smile on her face like the one she's been wearing this morning. I've always heard doing it someplace different—you know, sorta like sneaking, makes it all so much more *exciting*, and we barely heard you at *all*—"

Melanie swatted her sister with a dishtowel while I continued to plumb the depths of mortification. "Would you *stop* it? You're going to scare him away." She turned to me. "They didn't hear a thing, I'm nearly sure of it."

It was cold consolation for me. I stood there slack jawed, trying to keep my coffee cup level as words completely failed me.

Cheryl had returned her attention to the counter where she was in the process of chopping fresh fruit into fruit salad. I had almost gathered the courage to sip at my steaming coffee when she casually added, "Even Molly said you've got a nice ass."

"I DID NOT!!!" shrieked Molly from the living room, and while Mel and Cheryl resumed cackling, I simply wanted to die. So much blood rushed to my face, I was dizzy, my heartbeat thudding in my ears.

In my life, I was never so grateful as when the back door opened, and Jasmine, Maggie, and Mackenzie came inside in search of sustenance for themselves and to carry back to the other two girls who weren't quite ready to face the world. They were immersed in their own giggle-filled conversation, and it immediately drew attention away from me. As they filed into the kitchen, I slipped out onto the porch, just as my cell phone began to ring.

Noting it was barely nine-thirty, I checked the Caller ID, and saw it was Brady Garrett, a newspaper reporter who had attached himself to me during a few of my earlier exploits. I was slowly beginning to think of him as a friend rather than a complete pain in the ass, but I vacillated easily. Today, he was my savior. "Hey, Brady. Little early for a social call, isn't it?"

"Sorry to bug you, buddy. I know you don't do mornings, but I thought I better check in to make sure we don't have a problem here."

That certainly got my attention. He had offered to check in on Dexter while we were away to keep him hydrated, fed, and his litterbox strained. I was surprised when he volunteered, but I didn't hesitate to take him up on it. Travel isn't one of Dexter's favorite things, and much of this holiday would be spent in the car. "What's going on? Is Dexter okay?"

"Well, that's why I'm calling," he said. "He *appears* to be. He met us at the door and seemed very pleased to see us. But if I didn't know better, I would swear he's spelling out a curse word in cat sick on the floor—in cursive. Is this a normal thing?"

I breathed a sigh of relief and chuckled. "He shows his displeasure by virtue of expulsion. I'm sure it was intended for me, and you can feel free to leave it. It won't hurt the floor. I'll clean it up when we get home. Jasmine probably overdid it when she was setting out dry food, and he's also known to gorge himself. But otherwise, he's okay?"

"I think so," he said. "How's your trip been so far?"

I laughed. "Starting to wish we never came. It's kinda been one thing after another." I could hear someone in the background cooing to Dexter. "Is that Billy you've got with you? Make sure you tell him Happy Thanksgiving from all of us. Nora and Wendell, too."

Billy was Brady's ten-year-old wheelchair-bound son, and Nora and Wendell Caudill were an elderly couple who cared for them both, acting as parents and grandparents without all of the messy legalese that adoption would entail. Brady had already told us they would be giving thanks with their found family, and it seemed especially appropriate.

However, the growing silence on the other end of the phone did not.

"You still there, Brady?" I asked.

"Um, yeah," he said. "It's not Billy who's with me."

I closed my eyes, pinching the bridge of my nose while my imagination ran wild. "Who have you brought into my house, Garrett?" I managed tightly, frankly appalled at the total lack of consideration that was the norm for this guy.

"It's not like she's some *stranger*," he said, keeping his volume subdued. "It's just Anyssa. She agreed to spend the holiday with us."

"Hi, Dwayne!" I heard Anyssa call from the background, and although I genuinely liked Anyssa, I was still galled by Brady's presumptuousness with my residence. Anyssa had hosted a mystery weekend we had all attended a little while back, and she and Brady had been flirty ever since. I still would have preferred her introduction to my home to have been at my own invitation. I was currently racing through my recollection of the state of the house before we left, and I knew at the very minimum, I had left the kitchen less than pristine. Lord only knew what else they might stumble across.

"Hey, look, I didn't really think you'd mind," said Brady, sensing my frustration. "It didn't feel right to leave Anyssa behind with the Caudills while I tended to your cat. She's only just met them, and—"

"No, no, it's fine," I said. "Tell her I said hello."

Another thought landed with a thud, so vivid I could practically hear Cheryl's voice in my head, *I've always heard doing it someplace different—you know, sorta like sneaking, makes it all so much more* exciting...'

"Just no funny stuff," I mumbled, as Craig and Chip walked through the yard in front of the porch carrying what appeared to be a decent size turkey fryer between them.

"Well, now *shoot*," said Brady, instantly picking up my meaning and seizing the opportunity to lampoon me. He pulled his mouth away from the receiver and called, "Anyssa? Baby? Can you toss me my undies? You might as well put your clothes back on, too. I'll help pack the whips and chains just as soon as—"

The phone was yanked from his hand, and at least Anyssa had the good grace to sound as flustered as I felt. "Dwayne, hi—it's me, Anyssa. Please ignore this guy. I don't know what's wrong with him."

"Nobody does," I said. "Hey, Anyssa. I'm sorry about the mess. I wasn't exactly—"

"Do not give it a thought," she interjected. "I wanted to wait in the car, but Brady insisted I come in. I think he's a little intimidated by your sweet cat. I have been no farther than your living room, I promise."

I felt some of my tension ebb. "Thank you for that. And you *know* it's not you I don't trust, right?"

"You're sweet," she said. "We'll all have to get together sometime after you're back in town. I'd love to see you all again."

"Likewise," I said. "Happy Thanksgiving to you and the asshole. And please send our best to Billy and the Caudills."

"Will do," she said, and we disconnected.

At this point, I had two, maybe three choices.

I could follow Craig and Chip out into the yard and offer to help with the turkey preparation, but Chip was still shooting me some serious side eye as fallout from the previous evening. His prominent, angular nose was even more so now, swollen and shiny in a palette of hues that pretty well covered the entire spectrum of purple.

I could go back inside and endure more of Cheryl's humiliating banter, but some of her taunts would undoubtedly include Molly, and I was already pretty sure I'd never be able to look directly at her without my head exploding.

I looked longingly at my SUV. I could slip behind the wheel and make my escape while no one was paying attention. Melanie would forgive me. Eventually. My last, best option evaporated as I patted my pockets and realized my key fob must have fallen out of my pocket somewhere in Maggie's room.

Shit.

Craig made my decision for me. "Hey, Dwayne! Can you bring me that big box of peanut oil on the porch?"

"Sure," I said, locating the box and carrying it out to where he and Chip had positioned the large metal pot on its stand near the edge of the back corner of the house. I scowled, eyeballing the fryer's positioning as I set the box of oil at Craig's feet. I had no trouble whatsoever picturing the entire house engulfed in flames. "Don't you think you're a little close to the house, there?"

Chip looked at me like I was stupid while Craig inspected the setup more closely. "You think? Guess it's better to be safe than sorry. Let's move it out about halfway to the garage, eh, Chip?"

Chip grunted something unintelligible but moved into position, helping Craig boost the apparatus to a safer distance from all flammable structures. Once in place, Craig went back for the propane tank he had left behind.

"You ever done this before?" I asked, shielding my eyes from the morning sun.

"Nope," said Craig, breaking the seal on the peanut oil.

"Is there any sort of safety documentation?"

Craig and Chip exchanged a quick glance that reminded me I was *never* the coolest kid in my class. I assumed it meant no.

"It's not really rocket science, man," said Chip. "There's a max fill line inside the pot and a dial to set the temperature."

Across the yard, the trailer door flew open, and Craig's youngest daughter sprinted across the gravel drive towards the main house. "Morning, Daddy!" she called out with a quick wave.

"Morning, booger!" he returned.

Chip waited all of about five seconds before digging his hands into his pockets and taking a few steps away. "If that's all you need me for, Craig—"

His eyes flitted to the trailer and, to borrow his own phrase, it didn't take rocket science to know what was on his mind. Katie was still in the trailer. Alone.

Craig gave him a warning glare. "Don't be lettin' my girls walk in on something they aren't old enough to see."

Chip gave him a lopsided grin before turning and jogging towards the trailer.

···•••••●◎◉●•••••···

The next few hours passed quickly as I assisted Craig with the chores assigned to the menfolk, namely us, as Chip was otherwise occupied in the trailer. Molly's husband, Gordon, remained inside, glued to the Macy's Thanksgiving Day Parade on TV while one of their sons assisted the ladies with deviled eggs and desserts and the other was combing the front yard for insects of interest for a science fair project. At this point, I couldn't tell you which was which. They both had jet-black hair shorn close to their oversized heads with eerily translucent skin that looked like it would burst into flame if it ever encountered sunlight. Melanie and Cheryl took turns checking in with us and keeping us hydrated, first with coffee before switching to the most amazing sweet tea I had ever tasted. Apparently, it was 'sun brewed,' and I didn't even know that was a thing.

A twenty-five-pound turkey had been immersed in a bath of Cajun spices and left to brine overnight in the refrigerator Craig kept in his garage. A little alarmed by Craig's laissez-faire attitude towards safety protocol, I snuck away to consult Google on my laptop for recommended temperature and cooking time for the deep fryer. Once we had the turkey submerged in the preheated peanut oil, we set about preparing the area for the day's festivities. We dragged four eight-foot folding tables out into the gravel expanse beyond the cars, setting three of them in a 'U' formation for dining with the other offset at the open end to serve the food buffet style. Once they were in place, Maggie, Jasmine, and Craig's girls came out with disposable Thanksgiving-themed tablecloths, securing them to the tables with tape. We carried two sets of cornhole boards out and positioned them in the front yard near a sandy patch in the lawn with a stake driven into its center for horseshoes. The sun continued to rise in a nearly cloudless sky, and while the temperature was unseasonably warm, it was never uncomfortable.

With less than a half hour for the bird to cook and our obligations otherwise satisfied, we settled into the rockers we had occupied the previous evening on the back porch. Craig reached into the dorm fridge between us, extracting a Heineken for himself before offering me one. I only hesitated a second before taking it. Soon enough, every single person I had only just met would be sitting across from each other, breaking bread. Cheryl would continue to needle me to see exactly how bright my cheeks could glow while Molly—good God. The woman had seen my ass. I felt an obligation to apologize for even *having* one. I needed reinforcement but wasn't quite ready to face whatever liquor bomb Craig had laid on me the previous evening. The Heineken was chilled to almost freezing, and for the first time, I thought I might understand the appeal of beer.

"You guys do this every year?"

"Pretty much," he said, producing his pipe from nowhere as well as Chip's crumpled pack of cigarettes. He tossed them to me, followed by a lighter. I was really beginning to like this guy. "We have the best space to do it, and Maggie already lives here. We usually pick up one or two of the girls' friends along the way. They're at that age, you know?"

I nodded but had no idea what he was talking about. Jasmine had only just turned twelve. We were still sizing each other up, figuring out boundaries while building a grudging respect for one another. She didn't share information about girl friends with me. We hadn't reached that level yet.

"Do you know their dad?" I asked, tipping my beer back and nodding towards Melanie and her sisters. The question had been on my mind since the previous evening.

"*Hoo*, yes, I know that son of a bitch," he said with a pained grin.

"Melanie's told me some things about the family," I hedged, choosing my words carefully. "She told me what kind of father he was. How he

79

treated her, the things he did—Mackenzie's almost three years older than Jasmine. It had to have been so much worse for the two of you."

He looked at me, surprised. "I wouldn't know. I didn't meet Cheryl until the next year. I adopted Kenzie after we got married. What sort of things did Melanie tell you he did?"

Well, shit. Melanie may have casually mentioned that both she and Cheryl had been cast out of their father's church over unwed pregnancies, but I had mistakenly assumed Craig and Cheryl simply weren't married yet. I didn't realize he also wasn't Mackenzie's birth father. Melanie had once told me her father's abuse had also been sexual, sparing none of her siblings. Did that also include Chip? And how much of *any* of this had Cheryl shared with Craig? It was suddenly crystal clear how very little I actually knew about Melanie's family—and that my own most special skill was planting both feet firmly inside my mouth. I shifted into damage control mode.

"Oh, you know. Like Cheryl was saying last night. How the church turned their backs on them and all that. Pretty hard to get away from all that judgement when their father completely agreed," I said. "You were the one to call him a son of a bitch. Where'd that come from?"

He chuckled. "It's pretty clear *you* haven't met him yet or you wouldn't have to ask. You'd never believe it now, but he was a very menacing man back in the day."

"Yeah?"

He nodded. "Had a stroke about ten years ago, and that took most of the fire out of him. Hasn't been welcome here since he pushed me off my own damn roof."

I gaped at what I had surely misheard, but the screen door suddenly swung outward, clacking into the arm of Craig's chair. Cheryl, Melanie, and Molly emerged, followed by their children, each of them carrying various side dishes and desserts to the designated table. Their playful banter immediately overwhelmed any conversation we had been having. Jedediah or Jacob—I wasn't sure which—followed with paper plates and cups, and a large container of plastic flatware.

"Guess we'll save that story for another time," said Craig, getting out of his chair. "Better check on that bird."

Surviving an awkward moment during which I was certain Craig would either send the bird tumbling across the drive or splash me with remnants of scalding hot peanut oil, he managed to safely convey the golden-brown beast onto the serving platter I held for him. I carried it to the head of the table reserved for food and set it beside an electric carving knife Cheryl had brought, along with a 50-foot orange industrial extension cord for power. Poor old Betsy trailed along, tail wagging, hoping against hope that bird would hit the ground so she could get to it.

I stepped back to let Craig tend to business, and Melanie slipped an arm around my waist. "Hey," she said. "Are you surviving?"

I kissed the top of her head. "No thanks to your sister. Craig seems like a decent guy."

"He is," she confirmed. "He's been there for me more than once, no questions asked. And I promise you, Cheryl *will* settle down. She wouldn't tease you if she didn't like you. Now, *Molly*—"

"Oh, hush," I said, nibbling at her neck and making her squeal. I was vaguely aware of Molly's unamused glare casting judgment from across the way, but I had decided to ignore her as much as I could and just enjoy the day. Melanie's spirits were noticeably brighter, and Jasmine was having a ball with her cousins. I was about to nibble my way from Melanie's neck to her shoulder when I felt her stiffen at my touch.

I looked up as a late model, pearl-white Chevy Malibu nosed into the drive, pulling off into the grass on the right. All three of the younger girls raced toward the car as its rear driver-side door opened, and a pencil-thin girl with shoulder-length ringlets of auburn hair emerged. She wore a pale-yellow sundress that fell well below her knees. She had a bright smile full of orthodontic hardware and freckles scattered liberally across her nose and cheeks. I was able to pick *'Kristi!'* out of the cacophony of excited voices and realized the half-sister must have arrived. I was a little surprised when the engine cut, and the driver's door opened. A taller, fuller version of the girl emerged, stooping to fawn over Jasmine, Mackenzie, and Amanda. Her own auburn hair was pulled into a tidy chignon, and her pale-blue church suit fit her like a glove. I guessed she was the stepmother.

Melanie wasn't looking at either of them.

I followed her gaze across the Chevy's hood to the stooped old man using it to prop himself up. Wispy strands of white hair trailed out from underneath his black Fedora, framing a face that was both gaunt and lined. His mouth was predisposed to sneer and that's exactly what he did as he surveyed the scene in front of him.

It looked like I would be meeting Melanie's father today, after all.

CHAPTER SEVEN

Melanie stepped up beside Cheryl and took her arm. "You didn't—"

"*No!*" Cheryl's answer was immediate as she shielded her eyes and watched their father slowly make his way around the front of the car. "Never. I would *never.*"

Molly's husband, Gordon, had shuffled around the front of the car to assist the old man, and they were currently shaking hands, exchanging pleasantries. He didn't seem particularly surprised to see his father-in-law, and I suddenly realized I didn't even know the old man's name—first or last. After all this time, how could I not know Melanie's maiden name?

I shifted my attention back to Melanie and Cheryl just as Molly approached, and she was already on the defense. "I invited them," she said, holding her hands out to ward off their anticipated angry response.

"Why would you *do* such a thing?" implored Melanie, visibly upset.

"You had no right, Molly," added Cheryl, hugging herself tightly and rocking on her heels. "This is *my* house, not yours."

"Don't you think that after all this time, Daddy deserves a little more?" asked Molly, sending both her sisters' eyes soaring into the heavens. Before they had a chance to protest, she plodded forward. "Now *listen* to me. I know there's been lots of hurt feelings and a bunch of he-said, she said, and whatever all else you want to drag back up, but today is important. Daddy's making an effort, so why can't the two of you?"

"You know damn well why," Melanie said hotly, her cheeks flushing. "And I won't have him anywhere *near* my daughter."

It was Molly's turn to roll her eyes. "So, it's *that* again, huh?"

Melanie staggered backward as if she'd been slapped, her mouth dropping open in disbelief. "Yes, it's fucking *that* again!" she hissed, struggling to control her volume. The girls were still gathered around Kristi and hadn't taken much notice of their grandfather. Craig was busily carving the turkey, oblivious to the entire thing. "What in the hell is *wrong* with you, Molly?"

Molly's cheeks brightened at each curse word, and her jaw set as she straightened, brushing imaginary lint from her skirt. "I'm not interested in rehashing it all over again. There's always gonna be two sides to this story—"

Melanie barked an incredulous laugh, drawing unwanted attention from the girls. "Is that *really* how you want to play this, Molly?"

Molly bridged what little distance remained between herself and her sisters in an effort to keep their conversation private. "At this point, does it really matter? I mean, look at him. He couldn't even make it to the table without Gordon's help." She sighed. "He's dying, Mel."

······•••••◉◎•••••·····

Tense doesn't even *begin* to describe the mood that descended on the holiday meal. I would have much rather been at my own parents' house watching Dad and Aunt Jane fistfight in the front yard than participate in this family showdown. It was reality TV minus the cameras, and I couldn't change the station.

Melanie and Cheryl had ensured their daughters would be seated together at the folding table nearest the house along with Maggie and Kristi, placing them as far away from their father as possible. They seated us to

84

the kids' right, at the table running perpendicular to the other two and serving as the bottom of the 'U' in the configuration. Still far from ideal, the kids were directly across from the old bastard, and while they mostly kept their conversations contained amongst themselves, it was impossible not to notice the furtive glances stolen by Jasmine and Cheryl's daughters at a man they knew only from a distance but never quite *this* close. Chip and Katie had slunk over from the trailer at some point, fingers linked and guilt flushing their faces as they joined the table with the girls, presenting their backs to our unanticipated guests.

Melanie and I took the end of the table closest to the kids with Cheryl and Craig separating us from Gordon and Molly, who sat closest to her father, Charles, and stepmother, Tangie. I had finally managed to discreetly glean their names from Craig as I not-so-discreetly relieved him of the carving knife he was wielding. I didn't know him well enough to have any real sense of his temperament, and my imagination went wild at what he might do with the knife once he realized what was happening in his own yard. Molly's own children, Jedediah and Jacob, looked like Addam's Family bookends seated on either side of Charles and Tangie, and if this was unusual for them, they gave no indication.

Molly stood, clapping her hands sharply before putting her thumb and pinkie finger to the corners of her mouth and renting the air with a sharp blast that echoed down the hollow. "If I could have everyone's attention, please?"

It was a saccharine-sweet command, not a request, and we fell into awkward silence.

"Daddy? Would you care to give the blessing?" asked Molly brightly, her eyes shining with nothing short of adoration for her father. I felt Melanie stiffen beside me.

Charles cleared his throat and licked his purplish lips in a decidedly serpentine fashion before removing his Fedora and placing it on the table, pushing himself unsteadily to his feet. Tangie rose with him, steadying him at the elbow, but he brushed her aside, mildly annoyed. He clasped his hands together and closed his eyes. When he spoke, his voice was a rusty nail. "Dear Lord in Heaven above, thank you for the bounty of the feast before us. God bless the hands that prepared it and every single person who is seated at these tables to partake in its sustenance."

He paused to scan for each of his children, nodding as he located each one. I hadn't noticed the visible tremors in his hands until then.

"Today is indeed a day to give thanks," he continued. "And to be in the presence of my dear Lord and Savior with all of my children and grandchildren by my side is truly a blessing. Amen."

Cheryl stood, struggling for words, and carefully avoiding eye contact with her father. "All right, everyone! There's plenty to eat, so don't be shy. Line forms behind your extraordinary grill master and man of *this* house, Craig!" She pulled her husband to his feet and gave him a quick kiss before aiming him toward the offset table holding all of the food. She hooked a hand over the back of his belt and followed him along, and the children followed suit.

I looked at Melanie and cupped my hand under her chin, nudging her gaze to mine. "Are you okay?" I asked. "We don't have to stay, you know."

She shook her head and sighed. "It's fine."

I raised an eyebrow and she allowed herself a small laugh before groaning.

"Okay, *fine* isn't the right word," she admitted. "But for now, I can cope. I'd be lying if I said I wasn't curious about that bomb Molly dropped. There have been plenty of times I prayed that sorry excuse for a father would—"

"Melanie?"

We both turned to find Tangie standing across the table from us, nervously rotating a paper plate between her fingers.

86

"Tangie," Melanie acknowledged tonelessly. I had no idea how she felt about her stepmother, so I opted for a curt nod.

"Listen, honey, I'm so sorry this seems to have taken you and Cheryl by surprise," she said, and she seemed sincere. "When Molly invited us to come, I just *knew* something was up. I wish I had picked up the phone."

Melanie shook her head, smiling tightly. "It's fine, Tangie, really. Molly loves nothing more than a good show, so I guess we all walked right into this one. How have you been? You look nice. Haven't had much of a chance to talk to Kristi yet, but she looks well."

"Aw, sweetheart, thank you," she said, beaming. "She was so excited to come over and see everyone today. She loves you all so much! This whole thing with your father has been terribly stressful for both of us."

"Molly says he's dying," said Melanie bluntly. "Is it true?"

Tears welled in Tangie's eyes as she struggled for composure. "Afraid so. He was just diagnosed with Parkinson's last spring, but his balance kept getting worse and worse. In July, he took a tumble and broke his arm. It was when they ran the additional tests that they discovered the tumor."

"Tumor?" Melanie echoed vacantly.

She nodded. "Glioblastoma, grade four. It's inoperable, and he won't put himself through chemo or radiation. I'll be surprised if he sees the new year." She pulled a tissue from her pocket to catch tears that had finally spilled over onto her cheeks while Melanie averted her eyes, unwilling to risk hurting her stepmother any more with her true feelings.

"I don't know what to say, Tangie," Melanie stumbled. "I—"

"You don't have to say a thing, sweetheart," interrupted Tangie, reaching out to take Melanie's hand into her own. "Whatever happened between you and your father happened long before I ever knew him. I wasn't about to get tangled up in a bunch of 'he said, she said' back then, and I'm not about to now. I just wanted you to know that none of this was our idea. Molly made it sound like—well, I guess it doesn't matter. But I can tell you that all of this has been weighing on your father's mind for some time. He's been looking so forward to seeing you all again—at least one last time. If we could just make it through this day, I'd consider it a personal favor."

It was everything I could do to keep my mouth from falling open. This woman was *good.* The only other woman I had witnessed apply guilt so masterfully was my own sweet mother.

Melanie nodded. "I'll try not to throw any gasoline on the fire."

"Awww, now *that's* my girl," Tangie said, pulling Melanie in for a quick hug. "Now, I'm going to put a plate together for Charles. We'll talk more later." Her eyes finally landed on me, as if she'd only just noticed I was standing there. She extended a dainty hand. "Hello. I'm Tangie Vogt, Melanie's stepmother. And you are?"

"Dwayne Morrow," I said, gently taking her hand. "Melanie's—friend." That earned a sharp glance from Melanie, but it felt moronic to say 'boyfriend,' and I wasn't about to test Tangie's ethical waters by announcing we were currently living in sin.

"It's nice to see you're dating again, honey. Jasmine really needs a father figure in her life. But you really might want to tell your beau his barn door's open, and it looks like he's riding bareback," Tangie said with a wink before turning away.

I looked down just as I felt the first gentle stirrings of a breeze.
Shit.

Plates were loaded and everyone had returned to their seats. Conversation was minimal as we sampled from the variety of deliciousness before us. No one would have ever guessed this was Craig's maiden voyage frying a turkey. It had emerged from its peanut oil bath a golden, crispy brown, and the expertly sliced portions were juicy and flavorful. I'm not a big turkey fan, but even I could get on board with this. Hand-whipped potatoes were pale yellow with real butter and frankly needed no gravy, but the gravy served was savory and plentiful, pairing well with the turkey, potatoes, and stuffing. In fact, all of the food was amazing.

This wasn't the way my mother cooked.

Mom relied on recipes and exacting portions, and without them, she had no idea whatsoever how to season her dishes or how much food to make. She expected a minimum of leftovers. Here, things were thrown together in excess and on a whim. Ingredients and spices were selected by intuition. The only thing that *wasn't* homemade was the stuffing, and quite frankly, I balk at eating anything that's been prepared in the anal cavity of—well, *anything*. Conversation had largely been replaced by the sounds of mastication, as you would expect. Even amongst the girls, only an occasional ripple of giggles managed to escape the vicinity of their table.

Molly deliberately avoided her sisters' telegraphed glares which alternated from anger to fury and back again. Craig ate with purpose, his expression largely blank, but his cheeks were dangerously crimson, and I wouldn't have been surprised if he were to suddenly stand and flip the table in front of him over, lunging for the old man he clearly loathed. I tried to focus on my own plate and will myself invisible, but it wasn't working.

I couldn't shake the feeling of eyes persistently invading my personal space, and despite my determination to avoid engaging with Melanie's father, my own eyes kept involuntarily stealing a glance. Every single time, he was staring directly at me, sloppily chewing with his moist purple lips smacking audibly.

We had nearly made it through our first course when he suddenly boomed, "You, over there!" His voice was deceptively robust, and everyone snapped to attention.

A forkful of mashed potatoes froze midway to my mouth as I realized he was pointing at me. For confirmation, I indicated myself. "Me?"

He nodded, his bony, crooked finger still waggling in my direction. "You're new. I don't recall ever seeing your face before."

Melanie sighed, dropping her head. "This is Dwayne Morrow, Daddy. He's here with me."

He nodded, dropping his finger but not his invasive gaze.

"Does he speak?" he finally asked.

I was a stammering fool. My parents had raised us to always be polite and courteous to everyone, especially our elders, but this particular scenario hadn't been documented in any of the playbooks. I felt Melanie stiffen as I blurted out, "It's a pleasure to finally meet you, Mr. Vogt." I awkwardly moved to stand, but Melanie grabbed my arm, urging me back into my seat.

"You don't need to talk to him," she whispered darkly. Her eyes were fixed on her father, shooting a steady stream of daggers in his direction. He merely looked amused by our fluster and began to slowly lick the tips of his fingers, refusing to look away. Whatever remained of my appetite completely evaporated.

"So, what does *this* one do for a living?" Charles asked, once he had finished his cat bath. "Does he *actually* work, or does he only talk about it, like your last one?"

Melanie's knuckles turned white, and I glanced sideways towards Jasmine at the other table. Mercifully, she was still lost in conversation with Kristi and Mackenzie and had missed the jab at her father. All of the adults were attuned, wondering exactly how ugly this was going to get.

"Now, Charles," said Tangie, patting the old man's arm. "I've told you about Dwayne. He's the one who was on the news earlier this year for helping to catch that maniac who was killing all those women up near Columbus."

Recognition dawned, and he nodded slightly. "That's right. You're also the one who figured out who killed that son of a bitch who ruined my little girl's life," he said, the hint of a smile playing at the corners of his mouth. I

90

could only gape at the man's bold impertinence. This wasn't about making amends; it was about twisting the knife one last time. "I guess you really had your work cut out for you, son. The list of suspects had to have been at least ten miles long. I mighta done it myself if I had half a chance."

Hot tears had collected in the corners of Melanie's eyes, and I felt a dangerous fury building within. He wasn't just talking about Melanie's former husband and the father of her child, but he was also badmouthing my best friend. Sure, he had his issues—which of us doesn't? But this was wildly inappropriate, especially coming from a man whose ideals were supposedly rooted in his religious beliefs. I couldn't imagine a congregation that would condone speaking ill of the dead, especially in front of the deceased's young daughter. Jasmine and the others at her table had begun to pick up on the electricity in the air and were starting to tune in to our unfolding drama. I took a deep, steadying breath and placed my hands flat on the table in front of me. My eyes locked on his.

"With all due respect, Mr. Vogt," I began, keeping my tone even. "This is neither the time nor the place to discuss this."

The old man was only amused. "Fancy that. Does this *stranger* really think he can control my content?"

His laugh was a sputter that devolved into a wet cough before finally subsiding. He wiped sputum from his chin and returned his attention to me, looking even more determined than before. I couldn't even begin to anticipate his next move, but in my peripheral vision, I could see Jasmine pivot in her seat, tuning in completely now. I couldn't allow him to continue along his current trajectory.

"Sir," I said, my voice exceedingly tight. "I'm going to kindly ask you to change the subject one more time, and then—"

My still-evolving threat was interrupted by the roar of an engine rounding the bend on the road to our north. An orange Dodge Challenger with black racing stripes nosed into the drive, just far enough to be off the road. The passenger window powered down, and a gangly teen stuck his head through the passenger window, his dark frizzy hair held to his head by a knit cap.

"Yo, Chip!" he called across the yard above the throaty idle of the engine.

Chip wiped his hands on a napkin and pushed away from the table. "S'up, Scootch?"

"Get over here and hop yer bony ass in!" he returned, slapping the side of the car urgently.

"Where's the fire, boss?" Chip asked, but he was already halfway across the yard while the rest of us gawked, thankful for the distraction.

"Body washed up near the bridge, man," the young man said, his eyes practically glowing with excitement. "We're headin' down to check it out. They think it's that McAlister girl!"

He opened the door and leaned forward to allow Chip to slide into the backseat while a wave of murmuring washed over our gathering. With a bark of tires, the Challenger lurched back out onto the road just as Mackenzie started to scream.

Lunch was effectively derailed by this latest development.

Cheryl and Melanie took Mackenzie inside to try and calm her down while Maggie and the other girls were locked in animated conversation at their table. Molly had fluttered over to her father and Tangie, tending to their every need while Gordon helped himself to the largest portion of pecan pie I had ever seen a grown man take. Craig wandered back to the mini fridge on the back porch and returned with a Heineken, a Pepsi, and a partial bottle of Jim Beam. He placed the last two in front of me and dropped into the seat formerly occupied by Melanie. I contemplated the bourbon only slightly before pushing it away and snagging the Pepsi. I still had to drive to my parents' in a bit, and while tempting, it was still a bit early for serious consideration. Craig, however, twisted the top of his green bottle and downed almost half its contents with the first swig.

"I'm really sorry about all this," he said. "That motherfucker knows he's not welcome here, dying or not. I'm about to tell Cheryl the same thing goes for Molly. I would never hit a woman, but that scrawny beanpole can't seem to keep her long bony nose where it belongs."

I stole a glance at Molly, tittering away at something clever her father had said. Craig was right. Her nose *was* long and bony.

"What do you make of Tangie?" I asked.

He shrugged. "She's alright. She's just not willing to believe things she hasn't seen herself, and with Cheryl, Melanie, and Molly on different sides of the fence, all she wants to do is keep the peace. She and Charles hadn't been married long before he had his stroke. While he's still just as mean as a snake with his words, he's not the physical threat he used to be."

I studied the old buzzard as I took a sip from my Pepsi. He was chatting with one of Molly's sons—was it Ichabod and Igor?—but I couldn't tell which. At a glance, he looked frail and congenial, but it had only taken a brief conversation to shatter the illusion. Was Tangie *really* that blind?

"Pushed you off the roof, huh?" I asked, leaning back in my chair.

Craig took another long pull from his beer and stifled a belch. "Yep. Broke my shoulder and shattered two vertebrae when I fell. We were fixing a leak in my roof, although I never asked for his help, and he was really only here to try and start some shit between me and Cheryl. Claims he lost his balance, but when I reached over to steady him, he pitched me over the side. He says it was an accident, but we both know better." He finished his beer and set it aside. "What say we put those cornhole boards away? I don't see 'em getting any use today, do you?"

I couldn't see it, either.

....•••••●◎◎●•••....

After loading Charles back into their car, Tangie made the rounds once more, checking in with each of us to apologize for Chuck's earlier bad behavior. She really did seem sincere, and I merely nodded when it was my turn, considering myself lucky he hadn't had the opportunity to really sink his teeth in. Cheryl and Melanie were still seething at Molly, and they kept their distance as she instructed her husband and sons to collect the leftovers from her own contributions and load them into their car. Tension dissipated considerably once both parties cleared the drive.

Kristi had brought along a carryover bag and was planning to spend the night with Maggie and the other girls so they could get an early start on Black Friday, hitting the Ashland Town Center in the morning before heading over to the Huntington Mall in the afternoon. They worked as a team to coax Mackenzie out of hysterics, and it was everything they could do to get her to stop crying. Despite the fact we had yet to receive confirmation that whatever was going on was related to the McAlister girl, I didn't have a good feeling about things. Melanie, Jasmine, and I opted to take our leave before any such news could break.

Melanie looked like she hadn't slept in days. She laid her head against the headrest and shielded her eyes from the westering sun as we drove along US 52 toward Lymont. My eyes flicked to Jasmine through the rearview mirror to find her in much the same position, although wires from her ever-present earbuds trailed down to the phone in her lap. Her eyes were closed, but I couldn't tell if she was sleeping.

"Are you okay?" I asked Melanie quietly.

Her smile was tired, but she reached out for my hand, and I took hers. "It wasn't my first rodeo."

94

"How about Jasmine? How much did she hear?" I scanned the rearview mirror again for any sign she was paying attention but saw none.

"Not much—at least, I don't think so. She was more upset about Kenzie. All those girls are so protective of one another, and poor sweet Kenzie has always been a little high strung."

"Didn't Cheryl say Kenzie didn't even know this McAlister girl?"

"Doesn't matter. It just hits a little too close for comfort," said Melanie, giving my hand a little squeeze. "Would you mind if I try to catch a little snooze before we get to your parents' house? I'm beat."

I squeezed her hand right back. "Not at all. You just relax, and I'll wake you when we're there."

Traffic was fairly light at this particular hour, and the study thrum of tires against pavement threatened to lull me to sleep as well. I added a tiny bit of volume to the radio and rubbed my bleary eyes with a little more force than necessary. The four-lane highway stretched on monotonously with what appeared to be largely the same scenery playing out mile after mile. Through my driver's window, the murky water of the Ohio River reflected sunlight while the passenger side bordered on magnificent striations of rock exposed by the blasting necessary to lay a navigable path for the highway.

I spotted the first billboard shortly after passing Hanging Rock. The second, handmade and less noticeable was just a few miles beyond. Both were pleas for information regarding the whereabouts of missing women, complete with sun-bleached pictures taken in happier times. As I neared New Boston, I had counted a total of seven signs, and I was fairly certain there were no repeats among them.

CHAPTER EIGHT

"*D*^{uh}*-WAYNE!*"

I had barely stepped foot from my SUV after parking it across the street from the old homestead when I heard my name echo throughout the neighborhood. I looked up to find a 6½ foot man barreling across our front yard toward me, and I barely had time to brace myself before he grabbed me in a bear hug and lifted me off the ground, swinging me side to side like I was absolutely nothing.

"Myron! Good to see you, buddy!" I managed to squeeze out, returning his hug before gently patting his shoulders in the hopes that he would take the hint and put me down. He was beaming like a child on Christmas morning, and it was impossible to do anything other than smile right back at him. Luckily for me, he took the hint and returned me to the earth before shifting to Melanie and Jasmine to greet them with decidedly more restraint.

"Yeah, yeah, Mr. Morrow told me to come, so I did," he said, still grinning from ear-to-ear. "Your dad is such a nice fella."

I nodded, pleased to see that Dad was keeping tabs on the gentle giant. I had met Myron Peters while investigating Ryan McGregor's murder the previous fall. In retrospect, it seemed ridiculous he'd ever been one of the suspects, but he could be very intimidating when agitated. I soon discovered his erratic behavior was a byproduct of a learning disability, and the elderly mother who had always been his caretaker had recently passed. Myron was largely capable of taking care of himself and was able to remain in the small townhouse he had shared with his mother. However, he required a little assistance with managing his finances and making smarter choices in the grocery store. Left to his own devices, Myron would subsist entirely on nothing but brightly colored breakfast cereal and soda pop, and that's where Dad stepped in.

"It's been a while," I continued, looking him over. "Looks like you got a haircut."

"Yeah, yeah," he said, running his gigantic fingers through the closely shorn brown fuzz that ringed his bald head like an open-ended hemorrhoid pillow. Previously, it stretched nearly to his shoulders, reminiscent of the late comic Gallagher. "Mr. Morrow takes me along when he goes to Eddie's."

A wistful smile played across my face as the recollection of many an unwanted childhood haircut washed over me—the kind that can only be achieved with a guide, electric clippers, and a steady hand. Poor old Eddie only had those first two bases covered back when I was a child. Eyeing the poorly framed work on Myron's head, it explained what I had initially attributed to self-mutilation. Yet Dad continued to feed his friend business, because that's the kind of loyalty you could expect with Todd Morrow. It was oddly comforting.

"For the life of me, I don't know why I always find you all out in the street!" It was my mother, hands on hips and looking at us expectantly. "Come on, in! Dinner's served!"

Compared to the lunchtime fiasco at Craig and Cheryl's, dinner with my folks was an absolute walk in the park. Sure, Aunt Jane gave Myron the occasional reproachful glare for his less than stellar table manners, but thankfully, she managed to keep her judgment non-verbal, and I suspected my mother had everything to do with that.

As much as Dad liked to spar with his sister-in-law and as protective as he was about Myron, things could have gotten ugly real fast. It was a little unusual to see Myron occupying the spot at the dinner table normally occupied by my sister, Gina, but somehow, it bothered me less than had it been anyone else.

The table only seated six, so Dad set up a card table in the space between the dining and family room areas for me, Melanie, and Jasmine. I think Matt would have much preferred it if he and his family had been seated at the temporary accommodations. From my vantage point, I had a clear view of a football game that was quietly playing on the flatscreen TV in the family room, a thing I could care less about. There was simply no way Mom was going to have little Abbie any further away than necessary, and she was currently out like a light in a baby swing near the head of the table.

"You did a marvelous job with Mama's cranberry relish, Melanie," Mom called to Melanie. The salad was a Thanksgiving tradition and my grandmother's annual contribution to the holiday meal up until she passed away nearly ten years ago. Mom's version never quite seemed to gel, and she didn't even hesitate to pass the recipe along when Melanie had asked what she could bring.

"You think?" asked Melanie after swallowing a forkful of yams. "The recipe called for red Jell-O, and I wasn't sure which red Jell-O it meant, so I went with cherry. I hope that was okay." For whatever reason, Melanie believed Mom was on a never-ending quest to find fault with her, but I'm pretty sure it was only paranoia.

"Delicious, dear," added Aunt Jane. "Much better than Jo's version."

Mom laughed. "Well, thanks for that, dear sister. And what, may I ask, was your contribution to this meal?"

"I brought two pumpkin pies," Aunt Jane said, feigning indignation. "I did my part."

"*Frisch's* pumpkin pies," laughed Mom. "Not the same."

"I *love* punkin pie," enthused Myron, and everyone laughed.

It was a real Hallmark moment that passed as quickly as it came. From the corner of my eye, I realized coverage of the football game had been interrupted by a news bulletin from WSAZ News, reporting live from Ironton where the body of a young woman had washed up on the bank of the Ohio River. According to the ticker at the bottom of the screen, the body had been positively identified as that of Tina McAlister, 18, of Ironton, Ohio. I subtly nudged Melanie and nodded toward the screen. She tilted her head toward the remote control on the table at Mom's end of the couch, and I excused myself, snagging it and changing the channel to Nickelodeon, where Spongebob and Patrick were up to their usual shenanigans.

"Hey, I was following that game," Matt complained almost immediately.

"And it will still be going when Spongebob is over," I said, sitting back down and shooting him a non-verbal warning I hoped he would catch. "All day long, it's football, football, football. It's not gonna hurt anyone if Jasmine gets a turn."

Jasmine looked startled. "I'm okay with the football. You don't have to change it on my account."

My chuckle was off-key. "All right, then, it's not gonna hurt anyone if *Dwayne* gets a turn."

Mom gave me a questioning glance, but she picked up on the warning shot I fired at my brother and just rolled with it.

Never one to hold back her opinion, Aunt Jane whined, "But *Spongebob?*" She shuddered. "I can't get past the sound of that laugh. Ugh. You could at least pick something entertaining, Dwayne."

Seeing an opportunity to play devil's advocate and seizing it, Dad winked at me. "Oh, I don't know, Jane. I think ole Spongebob is pretty clever if you're not too uptight to give him a chance. Let the boy watch his cartoon."

I smiled at her and shrugged apologetically, hoping she would drop the matter. In my peripheral vision, I could tell Mom was very much hoping for the same. Dad and Aunt Jane were so volatile that practically anything could serve as a flashpoint, and while I wanted to protect Jasmine from the unfolding news, I didn't want to spark a battle during what had so far been a very pleasant meal.

"So, Sheila," Mom slyly interjected, an expert in diversionary tactics. "Is Abbie sleeping through the night yet?"

That received a wistful snort as my sister-in-law dabbed at the corners of her mouth. "If only. Most nights, she's up at least twice, but occasionally she cuts us a break and keeps it to once."

Whew.

Danger averted as conversation shifted to the sleeping, eating, and pooping habits of my tiny, adorable niece, and the rest of the meal passed without incident.

Once sufficiently stuffed, Dad and I wandered out to the covered deck that spanned the width of the back of the house. He had added it almost as an afterthought when he had practically doubled the size of the home's original blueprint by adding an open concept extension that currently housed both the dining and family rooms. If I haven't mentioned it lately, Dad is very good with his hands, and there's practically nothing he can't do—well, except adhere to Ohio's Building Codes, but I'm not turning him in. His work is sound, if his occasional design choices are not, such as placement of the doorknob on the door leading to the deck. It's practically level with my shoulders, which is aesthetically—odd. Functional, but odd.

We stood side-by-side, leaning against the wooden rail as we stared vacantly at the trio of towering pines that marked the end of his property. He had donned a sweater as the night air was getting chilly, but I tend to run warm and hadn't thought to bring one. We had both eaten ourselves into misery, but the dinner had been delicious and the desserts divine. Myron was on his second piece of pumpkin pie while Matt had returned the television to football and was currently seated in Dad's recliner, screaming like a lunatic as the team he supported fumbled and bumbled, time and again. Aunt Jane was catnapping in the chair to Matt's left while Jasmine was sprawled on the couch, focused on her phone with earbuds in place. Abigail had woken during dessert, and Sheila was discreetly breastfeeding her while Melanie assisted Mom with clearing the tables and loading the dishwasher. I thought it was good for them to spend a little time together. Maybe Melanie would begin to believe me when I told her my mother actually *likes* her.

"So, what was all that business with the television?" Dad asked, breaking the silence.

"Hmm?"

"You're not going to try and sell me on that whole Spongebob baloney, are you? I mean, sure, it's got its moments, but..." His sentence trailed away.

"No," I admitted. "There was a breaking news bulletin I was trying to keep Jasmine from seeing. Some girl that Jasmine's cousins knew was found floating in the Ohio River. She'd been missing for a couple of weeks."

"That's awful."

I nodded. "It is."

Dad turned my way as he lowered his voice. "Was it some sort of—you know, foul play?"

"I have no idea. I turned the channel before much of anything was said. Jasmine's cousin Mackenzie spent a whole lot of last night in hysterics over the situation. I guess there's all sorts of speculation with the kids at school."

"Yeah, well, teenagers really excel at spreading rumors and gossip," he said, finishing my thought. "It's a damn shame, no matter what."

"Yes," I agreed. "It sure is."

Crickets chirped as we stared into the starry, cloudless sky for a long moment, lost in our own thoughts as the silence grew. As badly as I felt about the situation, I imagine my father was empathizing with the girl's parents, only too well aware of exactly how it felt to face such a loss. His own grief was still fresh and raw, and I looked away as tears collected at the corners of his eyes.

"Dad?" I asked after giving him a moment to collect himself.

"Hmm?" He kept his focus on the night sky.

"Ever notice all those billboards along 52?" I asked. "The ones with all the missing women? I mean, I must've counted seven or so."

He cleared his throat and nodded. I was beginning to think that was the end of his response when he cleared his throat again. "The old hometown isn't at all like it was when you were kids. We didn't have to worry so much back then. You were safe pretty much anywhere you went in our neighborhood. Well, you remember how it was."

It was my turn to nod. When we were kids, if school schedules didn't dictate the day's agenda, we were turned loose in the great outdoors to occupy ourselves with our neighborhood friends and enemies, our activities limited only by our own imaginations. The only caveat was we must remain within earshot at all times and return home before the sun had fully set. *Everyone* knew bad things only happened after dark. It was a once-in-a-lifetime freedom we wouldn't fully appreciate until we were already saddled with the never-ending burdens and responsibilities of adulting.

Dad sighed. "Now, you barely go a day without reading about another bad batch of fentanyl making the rounds, and people dying in their own front yards with needles sticking out of their arms. With unemployment so high in these parts, people tend to get a little creative about how they make ends meet. Most folks believe those girls got on the wrong side of a drug deal, or maybe they even dabbled in prostitution but got in over their heads. Those billboards have been slowly going up over the past five years or so, but none of those girls have ever turned up. I don't expect they ever will— at least not alive. And the parents—wondering where they went wrong, what they might have done differently to keep their keep their babies safe..."

His voice was getting thicker, and he refused to look in my direction. Of course, I knew where his mind was, and I wanted to reach out, put an arm around his shoulders and provide a little comfort, but that wasn't what we did, and so I didn't. I just stood there like a big schmo, waiting uncomfortably for the moment to pass.

I jumped when he cleared his throat again.

"Will you do me a favor, son?"

"Sure, Dad. Anything."

"Would you mind giving Myron a ride back to his place? I'm not feeling—"

"Of course, Dad," I interrupted. The least I could do was save him from inventing an excuse that was painfully transparent to us both.

He finally looked my way, relief evident on his face. "Thank you. I'm going to lie down for a bit. The tryptophan in that bird is really doing a number on me."

He turned and shuffled to the door, and I was a little startled to watch him go.

For the first time in my life, he seemed—older.

．．．．●●◉◎●●．．．．

I waited long enough for Dad to clear the scene before going back in. Matt was still raging like a loon as his team's scores worsened, and Aunt Jane had awakened to add her own two cents to the fracas, as well. If Mom weren't otherwise occupied cooing over her granddaughter, she would have been right in there with them, shrieking her disapproval at the referees, the coaching, and who knows what else. For the life of me, I'll never understand what it is about sports that causes people to lose all sense of themselves. I have exactly zero desire to follow a thing that does nothing but make me angry. Myron was perched on the edge of the couch beside Jasmine, looking more than a little uncomfortable at the escalating volume of the critical commentary. I held a finger up to let him know I'd be back to rescue him shortly.

Melanie was handwashing the last of the dishes that wouldn't fit in the dishwasher while Mom and Sheila had pulled chairs into the kitchen and were taking turns bouncing Abigail on their knees. They were sharing a laugh as I entered the room, and I was happy to see that Melanie actually looked comfortable. I bent down to 'gitchy-gitchy' my niece, and she promptly spewed a steady stream of off-white regurgitant down her pudgy little chin. I recoiled like she had peeled her face off.

"Can you hand me a damp rag, please?" Mom asked Melanie, who wordlessly complied.

I leaned in and kissed Melanie's forehead. "Dad asked me if I would mind giving Myron a ride home. Frankly, he looks scared to death stuck with Statler and Waldorf in there. Will you be much longer?"

"Well, surely you're not leaving yet, babe," said Mom, catching my words and passing Abbie back to Sheila. "We were just about to break out the cards and play a little 'I Buy.' It isn't often I have both the ladies in my boys' lives here with me. We've barely had a chance to chat."

Melanie smiled and gave the subtlest of nods.

"No problem," I said. "I'll just run the big guy home and then I'll be back."

Myron was already on his feet when I returned to the living room, eager to escape the lunacy. I looked to Jasmine, who was busily skating her thumbs across the surface of her cell phone with just a hint of a smile on her face. I waved my hand between her face and the screen to get her attention.

"Whatcha doin'?" I asked.

"Group chat with Billy and Scott," she said, and I should have guessed. No mere physical distance could separate the Three Musketeers, at least not since the advent of 5G and wi-fi.

"You wanna get out of here for a few? I'm getting ready to take Myron home." I snagged my dark brown barn coat from where it hung on a hook by the back door.

"Is Mom going?" she asked.

"Nope, she's gonna hang out with my mom for a while," I said, sliding into the coat.

"If it's all right with you, I'd really rather stay," she said. She indicated her phone. "We're kinda in the middle of something here."

"Sure," I said, turning to Myron. "You ready?"

He couldn't have been readier.

He grabbed his own fluorescent orange coat and made the rounds, telling everyone good night and what a nice evening he had, and only Aunt Jane balked at his attempt at a hug, offering to politely shake hands instead. He didn't appear to be offended in the least, especially once we entered the kitchen, and he caught sight of the Tupperware containers chock full of leftovers that Mom had packed to send with him.

"Oh, Ms. Jo, are you *sure?*" Myron asked, already loading the containers into a pair of plastic grocery bags.

"Of course, Myron," she said, rising to her tiptoes to riffle his hair. "I insist."

As I've already mentioned, Mom isn't big on leftovers, and Myron is a human garbage disposal, so this wasn't exactly the sacrifice it may have seemed.

"Please tell Mr. Todd thanks from me," said Myron as we continued to the front door. "I think he ate too much. He looked like his belly hurt."

A bellyache was only a couple of inches away from a heartache. Close enough.

"I will," said Mom, seeing us out onto the porch. "And you're welcome to join us for Christmas dinner, too."

Myron was so excited at the prospect that he nearly dropped his leftovers. I helped him load his bounty into the back seat and got him situated on the passenger side, buckling him in. Soon enough, we were on our way.

······●●●◎◎●●●●·····

I never fully realized what a chatty monkey Myron could be.

We were barely underway when, once freed from the intimidating atmosphere fostered by my brother and aunt's aggressively unpleasant sportscasting, his dam of pent-up observations finally burst. He flowed from one topic to another with little regard for logical segues, and his penchant for using ill-defined pronouns made his stories a bit hard to follow. However, his enthusiasm was contagious, and I was happy just to slip my mind into neutral and go along for the ride.

Although the sun had set long ago, it was still barely seven, and the streets were practically empty. Dayton Avenue transitioned into Main Street as we passed over the viaduct and continued through the handful of blocks that comprised downtown Lymont. As we neared the waterfront, I was suddenly aware Myron had stopped talking and was looking at me expectantly.

"I'm sorry, buddy," I said, patting his arm. "I must have been daydreaming. What was that?"

He grinned, his eyes twinkling with excitement. "I was just sayin' that was four. *Four!*"

I didn't even begin to follow. "Four what?"

"Four lights!"

My face remained a total blank.

He sighed. "You got through four green lights and didn't have to stop! My mama said that if you make it through seven, you're in for a run of good luck! Oh! Look! Here comes the next one."

As we approached the intersection, the light turned yellow.

"Go! Go! Go!" he urged, slapping on the dashboard. "Yellow don't count!"

I goosed the gas pedal and slid through without ever detecting red. Myron rocked in his seat, laughing and clapping like we'd won the lottery, and soon, I was laughing, too.

"Don't get too excited," I said. "We still have two more to go. Do you really believe this?"

"My mama wouldn't lie," he reasoned.

"No, I guess not," I said. "Okay, here we go. Next up, Second Street. Are there even two lights left before we reach your place?"

He nodded enthusiastically. *"Exactly* two. Get ready, here's the first, and so far, so good."

I had surrendered to the frivolity and was fully invested now. "It's green and holding—holding—holding—"

I turned right at the intersection just as it was turning yellow.

"Woo hoo!" bellowed Myron, doing another drumroll on the dash with his hands. It occurred to me this wasn't so very different from what my

107

brother and aunt had been doing, only these were the sounds of victory, not the agony of defeat.

Myron's residence was one of several identical timeworn townhomes that sat shoulder to shoulder on the left side of the next block. With only one final opportunity before victory would be ours, I found myself surprisingly dismayed when the light shifted to yellow before I had traveled even half the block.

"Go! Go! Go!" Myron repeated, and even though I knew I'd never make it, I have to admit I considered it for just a moment. That is, of course, until a Lymont Police cruiser approached the intersection from my right and slowed to a stop as the lights continued to cycle.

Sanitizing an expletive mid-flight, I slapped my hands against the steering wheel and eased to stop.

"Well, *shoot,*" was all Myron could say as the cruiser cut in front of us and turned left, traveling back in the direction from which we came. "Oh, well. Easy come, easy go."

It seemed that I was more distraught by the turn of events than he would ever be. I pulled to the curb and shifted the engine to park.

"Thank you so much for the ride," said Myron, unfastening his seat belt and stepping out onto the uneven sidewalk. He moved to the rear seat where he retrieved the bags Mom had loaded for him. "Tell Mr. Todd and Ms. Jo how much I appreciate them, and it's always great to see you!"

"You too, buddy," I said.

"Don't forget to count the lights on the way home," he reminded me. "It's never too late for good luck."

I nodded. "Will do, and hey? If I don't catch you again before we leave town, I'll see you at Christmas, okay?"

His smile was wide, and his head bobbed up and down before he stepped around the front of my SUV and carefully crossed the street. I watched him fumble with his house key and let himself in. With a sigh, I slipped my vehicle back into drive and eased away from the curb.

I passed through a green light at the first intersection.

"One," I said aloud and laughed, marveling at how I had allowed myself to become so focused on Myron's silly little game. If I hadn't, I might have noticed the headlights pulling away from the curb just behind me.

I might have realized I was being followed.

CHAPTER NINE

Hindsight is 20/20.

I just wanna punch whoever came up with that little nugget right in the throat. I mean, *of course*, it is! But it doesn't change the fact that I was too lost in my own thoughts to notice my surroundings, although in retrospect, I certainly should have.

Determining the car behind me had no police lights, I executed a sloppy five-point turn to reverse direction and therefore avoid dipping down onto Front Street, where the brick-lined roadway was riddled with potholes big enough to challenge my Hyundai's suspension. It didn't strike me as particularly odd when the car eased right into the parking lot of a defunct "Buy Here-Pay Here" lot and eventually turned around, looping back in behind me. It kept a safe distance, and I had other things on my mind.

This was the first time I had been home since Gina's funeral. It was the first extended period of time I had spent with the folks where the unspoken topic wasn't offset by something wondrous, such as the birth of my niece. It was the first real look I had taken at my father, and what I saw frightened me. Todd Morrow was this family's rock, its calm in a storm, its invincible guardian. His armor was supposed to be impenetrable, and yet, I had gotten a glimpse through the titanium, and I wasn't in any hurry to go back to the house.

Besides, I had only been gone for about a half hour, and that was barely enough time for Mom and Aunt Jane to explain the rules of this mysterious 'I Buy' game, much less play it. Matt had undoubtedly moved on to the next football game and was likely screeching himself hoarse at the television screen, and Jasmine certainly didn't need me to entertain her. She had online access to her friends and the means to keep her devices charged. I couldn't top that. I decided to kill a little time on my own and hooked onto US 52, heading east toward Portsmouth. While the car behind me matched my moves, it fell further behind once we hit the highway, and I didn't give it a second thought.

Traffic was light, and I set SiriusXM to *70s on 7*, but it only stayed there for a second, as the smooth harmonies from the Eagles only brought Dad back to the forefront of my mind. He was a huge Eagles fan, and my siblings and I spent many a summer's evening in the back of his company car, listening to any number of their greatest hits while accompanying Dad on whatever task was at hand. Sometimes it was bowling, and others it was slow-pitch softball. My thoughts darkened as I realized I couldn't remember the last time Dad had even mentioned softball. I wondered if he still played. I advanced to *80s on 8* where Cyndi Lauper assured me that girls just wanna have fun, and thoughts of Dad trickled away. He had never been able to listen to her again after learning the innuendo behind "She Bop."

I caught the sign indicating the Portsmouth flood wall murals were off the next exit, and I decided I would venture down and take a look. It had been years since I had last seen them, and they had become a point of pride for the community. I nudged the turn signal up and veered right onto S.R. 852, following the signs for State Route 73 and the Scioto River Bridge.

Coming off the bridge, I practically had Second Street all to myself. Straight ahead and on my left was the Second Street Dari-Creme. It was strange to see its rainbow-hued fluorescent lighting shining down on a darkened and empty concrete and glass building. Even more so than for its frozen dairy concoctions, it is a local legend for its foot-long hot dogs with family secret sauce, onions and mustard—footers, to us natives. It is open year-round, and there is almost always a line stretching from its twin windows to the sidewalks. Naturally, they were closed for the holiday, but that didn't stop my stomach from objecting, despite how completely stuffed I already was. I may have whimpered slightly as I turned right on Madison Street.

"Shit," I muttered to myself, slowing as I neared Front Street. My headlights illuminated a one-way sign pointing to my right. I had forgotten all about that. The street used to be a two-way thoroughfare, but as murals depicting the chronological history of the Ohio Valley were added from east to west, City Council had decided it made the most sense to restrict traffic flow to that same direction to provide an unobstructed view for tourists. I tucked my car along the curb and sat idling for a moment before switching off my engine. I hadn't really intended to do a drive-by of the murals anyway. I still wasn't ready to head back to my parents' house, and quite frankly, I could use the exercise. I had missed so many of my three-mile morning jogs that I was beginning to feel a bit like pudding. It wouldn't kill me to walk the length of the floodwall and back. In fact, it might aid with digesting the ridiculous amount of food I had consumed over the course of the day.

As I stepped out onto the street, another car approached the intersection of Second and Madison and slowed, but only briefly before continuing east along Second Street. I locked my car and buttoned my barn coat up to my chin with a slight shiver. The evening had cooled considerably since the sun tucked beneath the western hemisphere.

I began my leisurely stroll, casually observing the area's progress dismantled mural by mural as I followed the timeline in reverse. The paintings are quite remarkable, rendered in a style that feels as though you might just step right into the scene, but let's face it. I wasn't really there to see the artwork. I was killing time, leaving Melanie and Jasmine behind to represent us while I avoided the ongoing effects my sister's passing had left behind. Mom seemed to be sublimating far better than Dad, and that was a real surprise. I desperately wanted to give Dad some modicum of hope, but I still couldn't be one hundred percent sure of myself, and even if I were, to say anything would be a violation of a promise I had made to Gina. And if I was wrong? I honestly thought it might kill him.

An elderly couple approached from the opposite direction, bundled in heavier coats than I would have thought necessary. The man pointed at the wall with a crooked finger and provided narration he had clearly committed to memory while the woman steadied herself on his arm and followed along intently. Her shoulders were stooped, and her gait unsteady, but her focus was on the man, not the murals, and the look in her eyes was unmistakable. I wondered how long they had been married. I wondered how many children they had raised. Grandchildren, great-grandchildren—

I wondered how much time they had left together.

Stop it, Dwayne, I told myself sharply, but I was having a lot of trouble finding the fucking serenity to accept the things I could not change. Hearing about the young woman pulled from the Ohio River and seeing all those billboards along US 52 weighed on me more than I realized.

I smiled and nodded as I passed the couple and noted the man's gallantry as he instinctively kept himself between me and his wife, just in case I was more of a threat than I seemed. I lowered my head, stuffed my hands into my pockets and continued forward.

I was approaching Market Street when I first got the feeling someone was behind me. Whether it was an audible footfall or the suggestion of conversation, I couldn't be sure. I paused to look at the mural so I might casually take a peek. More than block away and yet closer to me than the elderly couple were a couple of men traveling in the same direction as me. Their coats were hooded, and they clung to the shadows, pausing to converse with one another as I feigned interest in the mural. I saw a glowing ember pass between the two and suspected they were sharing a joint, which helped calm my nerves. It was probably their intention to keep a bit of distance between us to hide the tell-tale aroma. For all they knew, I could be a cop.

I continued walking and slid back into my darkening thoughts.

Maybe it would be best if we just went back home. I knew the holiday would be difficult, but I sort of thought there would be safety in numbers. We could pretend everything was alright as a team. Sure, there might be occasional awkward moments, but I certainly hadn't anticipated these startling glimpses at my father's vulnerabilities, and I wasn't prepared to handle this. Avoidance was probably the safest course from here.

Shit.

We couldn't go home yet. Melanie had plans with Cheryl, Maggie, and the others that would fill the entirety of the following day. Apparently, one of their holiday traditions included piling into Cheryl's minivan and attacking Black Friday sales with a vengeance. The plan was to start early and end late, taking advantage of the best deals in the tri-state area by combing the Ashland Town Center before heading to the Huntington Mall. Originally, I had planned to spend the day with Dad and Matt, but that wasn't happening. I might be able to insert myself into Melanie's day, but that could be problematic on several levels. First, there wasn't room for me in the minivan, so we'd have to take two cars. Second, they may not *want* me to tag along on what had always been an annual family event. Perhaps most importantly, I'd rather kill myself than spend an entire day having my personal space repeatedly violated by crowds in the throes of a Black Friday mob mentality.

I was between Court Street and Washington when I heard what sounded like some sort of odd bird call coming from behind me. It echoed across the empty street, and I caught a hint of laughter. I cast a quick glance over my shoulder and was startled to see the two men had somewhat closed the distance between us. Less than a full block separated us, and I subtly picked up my pace. I didn't want to project fear, but I was a little unsettled. Maybe strolling along a dimly lit avenue all by my lonesome hadn't been the wisest of choices. I ran my hands over my pockets, hoping to find something I might use as a weapon should I need one, but all I found were my keys, cell phone, and a rumpled tissue from the previous year's cold and flu season.

I passed Washington Street, barely looking at the last of the murals as the floodwall abruptly dropped away. My original plan, which included turning around and backtracking toward my car, seemed dangerously reckless at this point, so I started plotting an alternate course that might dissuade whatever was going on behind me. If I could just reach Second Street, the odds of running into somebody—*anybody*—would dramatically improve.

Another strange throat noise sailed past my ears, again followed by laughter. There was little doubt they were taunting me now, and when I looked back, I discovered they had gained even more ground. My heart knocked in my chest as adrenaline coursed through me, and I found myself half-walking and half-jogging to try and regain a bit of my lead. I knew the Portsmouth Police Department was in the next block, and I could already see a line of darkened police cruisers in the lot behind the building. What I *didn't* see was any actual police presence.

The next catcall was startlingly close, and I broke into a run without bothering to look behind me. I could already hear their shoes slapping against the pavement as they gave chase, and their laughter sounded anything but playful. I might get lucky and stumble across an officer on his way to his patrol car but, worst-case scenario, I needed to keep my lead long enough to make it to the front entrance of police headquarters. Once inside, I should be safe.

I skidded to a stop as I rounded the corner.

Another darkened figure stood in the middle of the sidewalk halfway to Second Street, arms splayed like a gunfighter as frosty breath plumed around his head. He was effectively blocking my flight to freedom. The two behind me had also paused, more visible than before under the ghostly luminescence of the corner streetlight. My heart did another hard lurch when I realized they all wore knit masks to cover their faces, and I had no delusion that it was to protect their fragile skin from the cold. This was about anonymity. They were the predators, and I was their prey.

I took a hard right and bolted diagonally toward the block that had been designated as the Spock Memorial Dog Park. They wasted no time converging into a pack and tearing after me as if they already had a taste of my blood. I ducked around the south side of the park, keeping its wrought iron fence between me and them, which bought me a little more time.

My breath was ragged in my own ears as I reached the corner of the park where Second Street met Chillicothe Street. To my left was a straight line of city blocks, darkened buildings staring each other down across an empty street. There wasn't a single car in sight, and I couldn't imagine the odds. Last time I checked, it was barely nine o'clock. At first, I didn't see any pedestrian traffic either, but then my eyes locked onto yet *another* masked figure waiting across the street, ready to intercept me should I attempt that route.

What the hell *was* this? Five against one. This was clearly an organized effort.

That only left one possible route, and I only hesitated for an instant.

To my right was the U.S. Grant Bridge leading to Kentucky, and the latest arrival sprinted across the crosswalk as I pivoted and pounded down the wide pedestrian corridor to my right. I tried to avoid looking over the edge as I raced up the incline toward the bridge's midpoint and the Ohio shore receded below my feet. A lone barge hauling who-knows-what crawled in slow motion through the water below, and I wasn't sure how much longer I could keep up this pace, but my incentive remained high. All five of my pursuers were on the bridge, too, whooping like wild animals. The cool night air stung my eyes and caused my vision to double as panic began to swallow me whole. I was about to give up hope when I spotted headlights shining from the Kentucky side of the bridge. I lurched across the lane diagonally, waving my hands above my head as I hopped up onto the median, frantically hoping against hope that I wouldn't scare away the first sign of life I had seen since being targeted in this pursuit.

I needn't have worried.

I struggled to catch my breath as I slowed to a stop, leaning forward with my hands on my knees. The car was idling in place, half on the roadway and half on the median, another darkened figure leaning against its hood, observing my progress with a curious tilt of his masked head. Even from a distance, I could tell he was a brute, taller and broader than me by more than just a little. He casually strolled in my direction as the others closed in from behind. I staggered back across the southbound lane, coming to a rest against the safety rail.

I couldn't even take my chances and throw myself over the side of the bridge. The odds for survival were slim enough under optimal conditions, but the barge passing directly below pretty much ensured my demise.

I was *beyond* fucked.

I was still breathing raggedly as the four from the Ohio side surrounded me. The larger fellow was in no hurry to join his mates, still approaching at a leisurely pace. I held my hands in front of me in surrender.

"Look, I'll give you anything I've got," I said, unfastening my watch and holding it out. I could feel my pulse throbbing in my temples. "I don't carry much cash, but you can have my wallet—"

"*Shut up!*" croaked the one closest to me, and it was obvious he was obscuring his voice. "Just keep your hands where we can see 'em."

I was catching a lot of nervous laughter, and it occurred to me that two of the masked figures were hanging back a bit, as if this whole thing was maybe a little more than they had signed up for.

"You know the police station is right over there," I said, nodding my head in the general direction. "One of those cops is bound to spot you any minute now."

There was nothing nervous about the laughter that trickled from the one near my face. "If I can't see the front of the building, they sure as fuck can't see me," he growled. He turned to the more courageous of his three buddies who stood to my left. "Hold the motherfucker for me."

In one quick move, his buddy slid behind me and snagged both of my arms through the elbows, pulling them behind me and exposing my midsection to the one I'd come to think of as their leader and therefore, Number One. I struggled to free myself as I watched the croaking miscreant form a fist and draw back, preparing to drive one into my gut. At that point, I completely stopped struggling. It surprised the goon holding me into relaxing just enough for me to plant my feet and lift him off the ground, pulling both of us to my right as Number One's fist sailed past and glanced off the guardrail behind me.

Spittle flew from my assailant's mouth as he tucked his hand against his side and spewed creative invectives against me and my mother. He turned to the two who seemed to be shrinking further and further away.

"Get your asses over here and help him!" he commanded, flexing and shaking his fist. He nodded toward the fellow behind me who had pulled me back and reestablished his grip through my elbows.

Only one responded, and warily at that. I was gaining confidence that not everyone was as committed to this endeavor as their fearless leader, but I was still outnumbered. The guy behind me surrendered my left arm to the new arrival, who was shorter than me by more than a head, and they each tightened their grip, positioning themselves in such a way that I couldn't shift in either direction. The behemoth—involuntarily tagged by my racing brain as Big Mo—was still lumbering towards us across the bridge from the Kentucky side, undeterred by our little kerfuffle.

There was no avoiding it this time. Number One drew his fist back and drove it into my abdomen with as much force as he could muster. It hurt like hell, and he knocked the wind completely out of me.

But that's not all.

As full as I was from back-to-back Thanksgiving feasts, the blow triggered a wave of nausea like nothing I'd felt since the time I had tangled with food poisoning. I felt a rollicking deep within my abdomen, and nothing was stopping the locomotion of regurgitant that came barreling up my esophagus. I spewed like a geyser, nailing my assailant on the lower half of his knit covered face and down the front of his hoodie. He recoiled and gagged as the horrific mess soaked into his mask and dripped from his chin. He turned away, averting his face as he peeled the mask off and tossed it aside, protesting, "It's in my fucking *mouth!*" And then he was making his own retching sounds as he sprinted toward the car that continued to idle on the median of the bridge.

The two who were holding me were understandably put off by this unexpected turn of events and offered little resistance as I pulled away from them, but not before Big Mo finally arrived on the scene, planting one meaty hand around the base of my neck, undeterred by any of the upchuck still dripping from my chin. In one fell swoop, he boosted me off my feet and pushed me back. I felt the safety rail slip below my equator, and suddenly my balance was in serious jeopardy. At this rate, I would be face-planting on the barge below us in about five seconds. My fingertips struggled for purchase as the safety rail slipped beyond my reach, and all I could think to do was grab hold of the thick forearm that was currently sending me over the edge.

A series of three gunshots sounded abruptly, followed by someone barking unintelligible orders not so very far away.

Suddenly, my makeshift safety tether released my throat and pulled free of my arms, and I was pinwheeling, my ultimate direction uncertain. A dozen footfalls slapped against pavement, most of which were fading toward Kentucky. One solitary pair approached from the Portsmouth side, amidst a fair amount of huffing, puffing, and grunting. I hate to seem ungrateful, but I wished whoever it was would hurry. I could feel myself losing the battle with gravity on the wrong side of the safety rail.

Two hands clamped down around my ankle and pulled me back to safety. I landed on my ass in a puddle of my own sick, nearly hyperventilating as my heart hammered away. I had never been so happy to be on—well, relatively dry land before. A series of stars swam across my vision as my panic began to ebb. My savior was shrouded in shadow mere inches from my face, his hands firmly holding my shoulders while he continued to blather words I couldn't decipher, but I could clearly smell the acrid stench of cheap cigar.

"Doug?" I finally managed to croak.

My former classmate and boss from Boggs Investigations rose to his full five-and-a-half feet, backlit by the moon. He stood with his hand on his hips, one of which was holding a snub-nosed revolver. "What the fuck, Morrow? Don't you understand the meaning of time off?"

I couldn't control the laughter that abruptly burbled up and out. Soon, I was on my side, tears streaming down my face, and it was contagious. Doug joined in, adding an occasional snort to the mix. In the distance, car doors slammed, and tires squealed, my attackers making their escape, cutting across the median and hightailing it back to Kentucky.

"Come on, man," said Doug, offering me his hand and helping me to my feet. "Let's get the hell out of here before they come back."

⋯•••••◉⊙◉•••••⋯

Doug had been on his way to fish when he spotted my Hyundai parked along Madison Street on his way to his favorite spot. Maybe it was because he knew I wasn't much for fishing, I don't know, but curiosity had gotten the best of him, and he decided to loop through the area to see if he could spot me. By the time he did, I was already being chased out onto the bridge by five should-be felons in masks. We returned to where he had parked his ugly old Pontiac Aztek at the entrance to the bridge, and after using some napkins he had stashed in his glovebox to rid myself of the last of my unanticipated expulsion, I slid into the passenger seat. I struggled to find a place for my feet amongst the collection of cans rolling around the floorboard, but I was too damn grateful to issue one of my customarily pithy observations.

"So, I'm guessing the police station is our next stop?" Doug asked, firing up the cranky engine and turning the car around.

"No," I said, barely even considering the notion. My personal experience with small-town law enforcement was less than positive, and while I shouldn't hold the Portsmouth P.D. to the same low standard as that of the Lymont police, it was difficult to be impartial when everything that had just transpired essentially happened right underneath their collective noses. "It would just be a waste of time. What could I tell them? Five masked silhouettes of varying height tried to pitch me over the bridge? No, thanks. Just take me back to my car. I need to pick up Melanie and Jasmine from my parents' house."

Doug glided past the police department without question. There was some fundamental distrust between private investigators and police that I didn't fully understand, but Doug wasn't going to make the offer twice.

"Any idea at all who those bozos were?" he asked. "I mean, is there a chance they'll be back?"

I hadn't had time to give it much thought. "I guess there's always a chance, but I can't imagine why. It's not like they were calling me out by name. Maybe it was one of those idiotic internet things where someone gets dared to knock some random guy out while his buddies film it. I think they may have followed me from Myron Peters' when I dropped him off, but I'm not even sure of that. It's been a weird evening."

"How so?"

I shifted in my seat to look at him. "Did you hear about that girl whose body was found near Ironton, down by the river?"

He shrugged. "Sure. It's been all over the news."

"She was around the same age as some of Melanie's nieces. We were there when they heard the news, and—I don't know. They're barely teenagers. They didn't take it very well. It just kind of cast an extra shadow over the whole day." I paused for a moment. "Have you ever noticed all those billboards along 52 on the way into town from the east?"

He looked mildly constipated. I didn't wait for a response.

"My dad says they've been going up over the last five years or so, girls from the area who've just vanished off the face of the earth. With everything that's happened with Gina—" I broke off and squeezed my eyes shut, pinching the bridge of my nose. "It's just got me in a little bit of a dark place. I had to get away for a little bit. I guess I let my guard down."

He made the left turn onto Madison and pulled in behind my car. "Don't you even carry your firearm?" he asked, somewhat incredulously. "I never leave home without mine securely strapped to my ankle."

I laughed. "And thank God for that. No, I never really got into the habit of carrying mine everywhere. I used to keep it in the trunk of my Optima before it got wrecked. I haven't figured out a good spot to store it in my SUV."

Doug tsk-tsked at that. "We'll need to make that a priority. Oh, and getting you enrolled in some of those self-defense classes Ma was tellin' you about. You looked damned ridiculous up there flailing around."

I unfastened my seatbelt to get out. "Yeah, well—we'll talk about that in the office on Monday. Sorry about ruining your fishing trip."

He waved my apology away. "It wasn't about the fishing. I needed my space, too. Ma invited a bunch of her church lady friends in for euchre. For a bunch of Christians, they're damned competitive. I'll stick around long enough to make sure you get underway alright."

I stepped out onto the curb but leaned back in before closing the door. "Hey, Doug?"

"Yeah?"

"Thanks. I owe you one."

He rolled the nauseating little tobacco turd around in his mouth. "By my count, I think you owe me two or three."

I shut the door and shook my head.

Asshole.

CHAPTER TEN

Friday morning was a whole lot less traumatic than the previous one.

Sure, I still woke up wedged into the crack between the twin mattress and the wall, but my backside was no longer on display. It was covered in its entirety by underwear, sleep pants, *and* a thin blanket. I rolled over and reached for my cell phone, which was charging on the small desk near the head of the bed. It was barely after eight, and I was used to waking up alone. Melanie was a freakishly early riser, even when she didn't have to be, although that wasn't the case this morning. Today was all about the shopping, and I could hear a variety of high-pitched voices floating down the hall from the kitchen. My stomach grumbled audibly as coffee and all sorts of delectable aromas wafted down the hall. I tossed the blanket aside and stood, stretching my back and groaning at the resplendent relief I felt as a ripple of cracks swept up my spine.

After double- and triple-checking myself for general decency, I wandered down the shag carpeting in the hallway on my bare feet, rubbing sleep from my eyes. I could still feel a twinge in my solar plexus from where a bony fist had been driven into it, but what I was most aware of was how entirely empty I felt after losing my dinner as a result. My body demanded sustenance, and I followed my nose to the kitchen.

"Well, there he is!" Cheryl said brightly as she passed glasses of orange juice around the small kitchen table to her girls and to Jasmine.

"Good morning," I said, looking around cautiously to see who else might be lurking about.

Melanie handed me a cup of coffee and kissed me on the cheek. "You're safe," she said. "Molly's not part of today's activities. Would you like some—"

I was already loading a plate with scrambled eggs, biscuits and gravy and a handful of bacon strips. When I saw the look on Melanie's face I hesitated. "Too much?"

I was ready to return some of the eggs and bacon when Cheryl laughed. "No worries, guy. We've got plenty. The girls already have theirs, and me and Mel are just snacking—just save some for Craig, okay? Good Lord, I'm still full from yesterday! I don't know where you put it all." I wasn't about to offer that I had left most of it in a steaming pile on the U.S. Grant Bridge. I had kept a lid on the previous evening's adventure, deciding there was no need to worry anyone unnecessarily. Cheryl stepped out onto the back porch and called for Craig, who was apparently already out in his garage. I found a clear space along the counter and slid my plate in, grabbing a fork and digging in.

"Isn't Maggie going with you?" I asked with my mouth full.

"She and Katie are meeting us in Ashland," said Melanie, spearing a wedge of cantaloupe from a bowl of fresh fruit she and her sister were sharing. "I guess Chip came back after we left yesterday, and they all spent the night at a friend's over in Flatwoods. What are you doing today? Still thinking about bowling with your dad and Matt?"

I shrugged noncommittally. It had been the original plan, but it currently had all the appeal of a root canal. "We'll see."

Craig entered through the back door and nodded, patting his wife on the bottom as he passed to get a plate. His OSU Buckeyes hat was drenched with perspiration, and his face was bright pink. "Morning, all," he said, sliding the rest of the eggs onto his plate. "Don't mind me. I'll be in and out in a jiffy. Toby Watkins is gonna be out here to pick up his car in about an hour, and I've still got to finish the brakes."

"Well, you're welcome to hang out here," Cheryl said to me. "As you can see, Craig's working today, so you wouldn't even have to fight for control of the television."

"Thanks, I might just do that," I said. I took a sip of my coffee and kept my eyes on Melanie. "I was thinking about visiting Sarah, unless you think that's something we might all want to do tomorrow. You know, as a family."

She stiffened only slightly, but from the corner of my eye, I could see I had Jasmine's attention. "I'm not really sure what our plans are for tomorrow," Melanie said coolly. "Maybe you should go ahead and do that just in case we don't have time."

"*Mom*," implored Jasmine, wisely leaving it at that one word.

"It's not a topic for today," Melanie said, a bit more sharply than intended. She shot me a dark look as Jasmine sighed and returned to her breakfast. So much for diplomacy. "Now, come on girls. Just as soon as you finish up, we can hit the road. We've got some serious shopping to do!"

She clapped her hands and brushed past me, clearly a little miffed at my timing, and admittedly, it could have been better. But we were going to have to face this situation with Sarah and Jasmine's half-brother sooner or later, and I was a big fan of sooner. It felt like we owed Sarah better than this.

I stood back, continuing to inhale my breakfast while the girls brought their plates into the kitchen and rinsed them, stacking them in the sink. As Jasmine passed, she nudged me and mouthed, *"Thanks for trying."*

I winked at her and kept chewing. I may be letting it go for the moment, but I wasn't done trying.

Everyone did a quick inventory for phones, pocketbooks, and perhaps most importantly, credit cards, before drifting outside towards Cheryl's minivan. Melanie paused in the doorway, shifting things around in her purse. "Don't look for us until late. We always take the girls for pizza at Gino's in Huntington before we come home. Do you want me to bring some back?"

"Yes, please," I nodded enthusiastically. I hadn't had Gino's in *years*. "Pep and sausage—maybe a little onion?"

She raised on her tiptoes to give me a quick kiss. "Fine. But you're sleeping in your car tonight."

"It felt like those odds were pretty good anyhow, I—" My thought tapered off as a small silver car nosed into the driveway. "Anyone you know?"

Melanie turned to follow my gaze as Cheryl crossed the driveway to greet the new arrival. "No, but Cheryl seems to know 'em. See ya later."

I watched from behind the screen door as Melanie joined the girls in the minivan and Cheryl continued to converse through the driver's open side window. Her usual buoyancy and easy smile had faltered, and she looked unusually solemn, nodding her head and listening intently. She cast a furtive glance in my direction, and I involuntarily stepped back, feeling like a voyeur, despite the fact it was unlikely she could see me hovering there. She briefly returned to her conversation before holding up a finger. She turned and headed directly toward me. I scrambled away from the door and dropped my plate with a clatter into the sink as she stepped inside.

"Hey, Dwayne?" She sounded uncharacteristically pensive which automatically drew my full attention.

"Something wrong?"

"No—*yes*—" She sighed, backing up to start again. "Look, I know you and Mel are here to relax and enjoy the holiday, but I promised I would at least *ask*."

I stared expectantly, but she was still flustered. "Ooo-kay. I'm guessing this has something to do with whoever you were talking to in the driveway?"

She nodded. "Yeah, um—yes. That's Anne Marie Brown. I barely know her, but she's the aunt of that girl they found in the river yesterday. Tina McAlister, you remember?"

I nodded, afraid I knew where this might be going.

"Anyhow, she'd really like a moment of your time, but if you don't have one to spare, I can just send her on her way. I just promised I would ask."

I shook my head slowly. "How did she even know I was here?"

Cheryl smiled apologetically. "Molly seems to be the gift that just keeps on giving. They all go to church together, and after the news broke yesterday, Molly made a beeline over to the McAlisters' for a big show of support. I'm afraid to think what all she promised them you could do for them. Listen, I really hate to even ask, but that poor girl out there is barely holding it together. I just couldn't tell her no without at least giving you the opportunity to speak for yourself."

She hovered at the doorway staring at her feet while I cursed the nonexistence of teleportation. I would rather be just about *anywhere* than here. In my current frame of mind, I wasn't sure how much more residual grief I could accommodate, and it wasn't like there was much of anything I could actually *do*.

Ah, but that was a lie I couldn't even sell to myself.

I could always listen.

"I can't tell you much I appreciate you talking to me," said the nervous young woman as she paced the living room. Her fine, frizzy hair was light brown streaked with gold, and fastened haphazardly at the nape of her neck. She wore blue jeans and a Marshall University hoodie, and I was startled to find she looked no older than the niece she mourned. "I feel so awful imposing on your family time, but Molly just insisted you wouldn't mind."

Yeah, me and Molly were *so* damned close.

She was making me crazy with all of the pacing, so I finally indicated the sofa. "Why don't you have a seat?" I suggested. "I'd offer you a drink, but I'm a little out of my element as it's only my first visit here."

She perched on the edge of one of the cushions and clasped her hands together between her knees. "That's quite all right. I won't stay long."

For lack of a better idea, I sat on the loveseat and faced her. "You've got my undivided attention."

I could almost see words forming behind her eyes, but instead, her shoulders hitched, and she bursts into sobs, covering her face and leaning forward. I scanned the room in vain for a box of Kleenex and found myself sprinting to the kitchen to snag a handful of paper towels. This time, I sat down beside her and handed her the paper towels as she leaned into me. I remained stiff as a board while she worked through her wave of grief, blotting her tears and seeping nostrils before regaining her composure and sitting upright.

"I'm so sorry," she said. "It just hits me in waves. I can't believe she's really gone."

I nodded, loathe to say anything, despite my absolute identification with the feeling. I don't shine in moments of anguish, and my propensity for poor word choice is a known commodity. I opted for the safest choice of all—silence—and waited for her to gather her thoughts.

"Tina and I were always close," Anne Marie finally said, almost apologetically. "I'm only a few years older."

"Cheryl said you were her aunt."

She nodded. "I was one of those 'change of life' babies, you know? Mama thought she was done with all that when I up and came along. Me and Tina were more like sisters than anything else."

"I'm sorry for your loss." *Shit*. It just slipped right out. She must have already been numbed to the inane, however, and she simply nodded, so I quickly moved on. "I'm not really sure how I can help you."

"I know it's too soon for an official cause of death, but deputies from the Lawrence County Sheriff's Office have already been out to the house, asking all sorts of questions, and it's just so obvious they're leaning towards suicide," she said, shaking her head in disbelief. "It *wasn't* suicide. I'd stake my own life on that."

I sighed and weighed my next words carefully. "What makes you so sure of that? My understanding is the people who succeed in committing suicide are the ones you least suspect might actually go through with it."

"*No*," she said firmly. "She wasn't like that. If anything, she was having the best year of her life! I think we both about fell out of our chairs when she won Homecoming Queen last month. She had everything going for her. She was excited about going to Marshall next fall and was applying for scholarships left and right—this was a girl who was planning for a future, not thinking about killing herself."

"So, why would the police think otherwise?"

"I don't—" she began, her hand flying up to her mouth as if to stop herself. Her mental gears were cranking so hard I could practically hear them, but she certainly wasn't one to wonder aloud. Finally, her eyes locked on mine. "Look, I was raised to never tell tales out of school—"

For some reason, she found that funny and broke off to chuckle and mutter under her breath to herself, and she seemed to be holding up both sides of the conversation, which I found a bit disturbing. I was beginning to think Anne Marie might not have both oars in the water. She cleared her throat, took a deep breath, and tried again.

"I don't have any kind of proof to back up what I'm telling you," she said. "It's just my gut feeling, and I've always been able to trust that. Do I sound crazy?"

Well, when you're conversing aloud with yourself, just a little, but I shook my head. "I've gotten out of more than one scrape by listening to my own. I can understand that. What is your gut telling you?"

She leaned forward, her intensity growing. "It's these kids she's been running with. I don't *like* them. And they never liked *her*. At least, not until this year."

"Is this a different crew than she normally hangs out with? Cheryl's sister, Maggie, said that Tina was very popular."

She laughed, again covering her mouth with steepled fingers as if staunching something blasphemous. "I'm sorry. I shouldn't laugh. But I would have never thought of Tina as popular until Chandler and his friends sort of adopted her. Don't get me wrong, she wasn't *un*-popular. She just wasn't—I don't know. She just wasn't anything *special*—"

She gasped, and there went those hands again, flying up and clamping over her mouth, but this time, they were accompanied by fresh tears.

"I didn't mean that," she repeated several times, rocking in place and whispering what sounded like a prayer in between iterations.

"I understand what you meant," I said, trying to soothe her. I considered putting an arm around her shoulders, but wasn't fully comfortable with that idea, and it didn't really matter in the long run. Her rocking momentum eventually brought her back to rest against my shoulder. "So, who is this Chandler guy and what about these friends of his?"

In my head, I was picturing a long-haired, tat-covered hoodlum with a penchant for body piercings and petty theft. Good girls and bad guys—a tale as old as time.

"He's the son of our preacher, Reverend Donald Keaton," said Anne Marie, dabbing at her eyes while continuing to use my shoulder for support.

A-ha! The son of a preacher man. Dusty Springfield has warned us well of the dangers there.

"I take it this Chandler is some sort of rebel—?"

She sat up straight and looked at me earnestly. "I don't know what he is. He just gives me the creeps. They *all* do."

"Was he Tina's boyfriend?"

She shook her head. "No, nothing like that, although they were closer than I liked. He has someone else. But I mean, when a guy pretty much ignores you your whole entire life and suddenly, he's everywhere you turn— well, there had to be a reason."

"Maybe they just never had the opportunity to get to know each other before this year," I suggested, but Anne Marie was already shaking her head vehemently.

"That wouldn't be the case with *all* of them," she said. "These aren't the sort of people who are looking to add people to their clique, if you get my drift."

I decided to cut to the chase. "Do you think they're in some way responsible for your niece's death?"

"I—I just don't know," she admitted. "But I think they *know* more than what's come out. In fact, I'm sure of it."

"And how are you sure of it?"

She looked at me like I pinched her. "I *told* you. My gut. I feel it in my gut."

"Have the police even talked to any of them?"

"I don't think so, but how would *I* know? It's not like *I'm* friends with any of them."

I sighed, closing my eyes, and pinching the bridge of my nose. "I'm not sure what you're asking me to do here."

She started rifling through a denim bag I hadn't even noticed was looped over her arm, pulling crumpled bill after bill out of it and smoothing them in her palm. "I don't have a lot of money on me, maybe sixty—one, two— um, oh, here's a couple more—and, oh, there's that too—" She laid it all out on the end table beside the sofa. "Sixty-four dollars and forty-two cents.

But I got more in my savings. I would like to hire you to look into this on behalf of my family."

I was already shaking my head. "I can't do that, Anne Marie. I'm not a licensed investigator yet."

She scooped up the money and thrust it toward me. "I don't understand. You've been on the news more than once. It was you that stopped that guy who was killing all those hookers—"

"That wasn't in any sort of official capacity, Anne Marie," I said as I watched her grow more agitated. "I was just trying to keep from getting killed myself with that one. I mean, *yes*, it is my goal to one day work as a private investigator, but right now, I'm only apprenticing under Doug Boggs with Boggs Investigations. I don't have the authority to accept new cases."

"Will you talk to him?" she begged as she refused to retract her fistful of crumpled money and her lips began to tremble. *"Please?"*

Fuck!

"I can't promise anything." My treasonous mouth was on autopilot, and the words were out before she had a chance to break down again. She practically threw the money into my lap, and I collected every rumpled bill and grimy coin and promptly returned them. "There's no need to put any money down at this time, Ms. Brown. If—and *only if* Mr. Boggs decides to take your case, he will negotiate a retainer and a fee schedule with you."

She grabbed my hand and pumped it up and down vigorously. "Thank you, Mr. Morrow, *thank you!* I can't *tell* you how much I—"

I pulled my hand free and held up a finger. "You really need to temper your expectations here, Ms. Brown. I'm not at all convinced this will be something Mr. Boggs will take on. He generally tries to keep out from underfoot of actual law enforcement." I was rather proud of the way I made it sound like more of a conscious choice than Doug's actual fear of failure with higher profile cases.

"But you *will* talk to him?"

"I will," I nodded. In fact, it gave me an actual excuse to bow out of bowling with my dad and Matt. "Hang on just a sec."

I stood and crossed the room, retrieving my laptop bag from where I had left it leaning against the wall. I sat beside her and pulled my laptop out, powering it up and opening a Word document.

"Give me your phone number."

She complied.

"How about Tina's parents? Names, phone numbers, address?"

"It's just my sister, Marlene," she said, reciting her address and phone number. "Harlan ain't been around for years. Hooked up with some skank from the Moose—I'm guessing every bit of ten years ago?"

Like *I'd* know.

"Did Tina have any brothers or sisters?"

Anne Marie gave another little jerky shake of her head. "Nope. Just our little Tina."

She groaned and doubled over, losing her composure all over again. I dug the soggy paper towels from where they had gotten wedged between the seat cushions and offered them to her again. I waited with my fingers on the keyboard for her to collect herself.

"How about boyfriends?" I asked.

"For who?"

I blinked, unaware of the ambiguity of my question. "Well—either of them, I guess," I said. "Mrs. McAlister or Tina?"

"Not that I know of," she replied, snuffling into the paper towels. "Well, for sure, not for Marlene. Pretty sure Harlan put her off men for good. Tina never mentioned anyone special to me, either, and I'd like to think she would have."

And she succumbed to her grief again. I set my laptop aside and went into the kitchen after more paper towels. By the time I returned, I had determined there wasn't much point in dragging our mutual discomfort out any longer. I snagged a business card and a pen from my laptop bag and flipped the card over, jotting my cell phone number down.

"I want you to text me the names of these friends of hers that give you the creeps. If you know phone numbers or addresses, that would be helpful, too."

She took my card and studied it, nodding.

"Also, if there's anything you think is important about them or anyone else, send that to me, too." I stood, indicating she should do the same, and began walking her toward the back door. "Does your sister know that you've reached out to me?"

Anne Marie shook her head as we stepped out onto the back porch. "No. I don't really think she understood what Molly was talking about when she came over and told us you were here. I'm not sure she understands too awfully much right at the moment, but I'd seen the news. I didn't want to get her hopes up, but I just knew you were the answer to our prayers."

I reached out and took her by the arms, aiming her gaze toward mine. "You need to keep your hopes in check, too, Anne Marie. If Doug Boggs says no, that's the end of the road. Do you understand what I'm telling you?"

Her eyes were wide as she slowly nodded. "But you *will* try, won't you? Try your very hardest?"

"I promise."

She threw her arms around me and squeezed with all her might, burying her face into my chest until I felt tears soaking through the fabric of my t-shirt. I carefully brought my arms around to pat her shoulders delicately until she finally turned me loose and raced off to her car. As she opened the driver's door, she turned, kissing her fingertips, and sending it my way with a quick wave. Despite all my careful warnings, there was no mistaking the hope that radiated from her expression, and I immediately realized I had once again stepped into what promised to be a messy pile of shit.

I just had no idea at the time *how* messy it would turn out to be.

CHAPTER ELEVEN

I decided to ease my car off the street across from the split-level, dark paneled abode that Doug Boggs had called home his entire life, as the driveway that sloped down to the garage on the lower level was already lined with a fair assortment of cars, minivans, and SUVs. For a fraction of a second, I wondered if Doug and Loretta were entertaining family, but then I remembered Doug's complaints about his mother's church friends, and my spirits sank. I sat with my engine idling, debating for a full five minutes whether I wanted to go through with this or not. I could have saved myself a lot of trouble and simply made a phone call, because I was certain Doug was going to take a pass, but it had made truth of the excuse I had finally texted my brother begging off from bowling with him and Dad.

And I had made a promise to Anne Marie.

I got out of my car and crossed the street, heading down the driveway. I hoped I might catch Doug outside, preferably alone, but God wasn't done amusing Himself at my expense for the day. It was warm for November, undoubtedly assisted by the bright sun hanging high overhead in a nearly cloudless sky. I was a little more than halfway down the drive when I was assailed by a matching set of twin furballs, one white and one champagne, both determined to chase me right back to my car with a barrage of angry yipping. I'm not exactly scared of dogs, but I'm not stupid, either. I froze as they took turns baring their teeth to dispel any doubts I had about their ferocity. They were nearly within ankle-biting range when a short, round woman in a leopard-spotted leotard rounded the corner. I frowned. I wanted to say it was Loretta, but only if she had lost a little height and gained a little girth since last week.

"Dooley! Pumpkin! Stop this very instant and come to Mother!" she commanded. They complied immediately—well, after one last round of warning snarls, and I realized this must be Doug's Aunt Verna whom he said would be visiting for the holiday. She waved me in. "Come on back. They won't hurt you, but I wouldn't make any sudden moves if I was you."

Not feeling particularly reassured, I rounded the corner into the backyard to find the lawn covered in almost its entirety by brightly colored yoga mats, all of which were held to the ground under ancient flesh of varying shapes and sizes, twisted into a variety of surprisingly flexible poses, and to what end I had no clue. They all wore leotards of differing propriety, but there was enough fleshy corpulence on display to stop me dead in my tracks.

"Dwayne Morrow!"

No mistaking *that* sonic cry. I looked up and spotted Loretta, clad in a lemon-yellow bodysuit with a beehive to match, weaving her way toward me through her group of elderly friends, all of whom were having a sudden attack of self-conscience.

"This is private yoga session for my ladies' league. What are you *doing* here?"

"Hi, Loretta," I called meekly, trying not to look at any one person for too long lest my eyes burst from my head. "Is Dougie home?"

"Doug-*ieeeeeee!*"

I jumped, along with half of the ladies, although we all should be accustomed to her shrieking by now. It was the Boggs' normal method of communication.

Doug appeared in the sliding glass door centered in the deck that ran the width of the upper level. "Jeez, Ma, do you have to blast it to the whole neighborhood?" He spotted me, and I offered a meager wave. "Oh. Dwayne. It's you. Come on up. I guess."

He turned and ducked back into the house, leaving the door open, which was more of an invitation than his words, so I ascended the wooden stairs before he had a chance to change his mind. *Anything* before his mother could lay into me. Well—that and for a change of view.

An unbidden and distant memory floated to mind as I reached the top step, and I was suddenly back in the fifth grade, attending a birthday party for a classmate I barely knew and was none too happy about it. I was missing a perfectly good *Six Million Dollar Man/Bionic Woman* reunion movie on MeTV. I remembered clutching a bag of green plastic army men I was ordered to give as a gift and feeling certain my present would be the very least of Doug's offerings. This wasn't about Doug's disappointment. Hell, it wasn't even about Doug at all. It was all about *me*—me and my embarrassment of having to give something that probably didn't even cost full price at the Dollar Tree because Dad had no interest in keeping up with the Joneses. I remembered all the brightly colored balloons anchored to the rails of the deck, and the festive paper tablecloth proclaiming the lucky little bastard's eleventh birthday. Oh, and Loretta…

She was much more threatening when I wasn't quite so tall. Fond of glow-in-the-dark, polyester couture even then, she was roving and raving, distraught at what she considered to be a low turnout for her Dougie's birthday, as if the nine or so of us who had been forced to attend didn't even count. I remembered Doug's father hiding in the living room, tucked behind his newspaper and reclining in a Barcalounger, only his pajama-bottomed legs and a wild tuft of hair visible around the top and bottom of *The Daily Times*. Doug had brought a bright red plastic cassette deck out and was blasting "We're Not Gonna Take It" by Twisted Sister through its shitty little speaker and dancing without the faintest sense of rhythm. He was just as happy as shit, oblivious to his mother's angst, his guests' reticence, and his own father's inattentiveness, and it struck me what a horrible, awful child I had been, worried about my own inconvenience and how quickly I could feasibly escape and return to my own world. Here was little Dougie, completely unaware he only had maybe two more years to spend time with his father before a massive coronary would take him, a fact I had gleaned only recently during what may have been our first *real* conversation in all the time I had known him. The recollection of my own father shuffling in from the deck the previous evening flashed before me, and my heart ached in a way I'd never experienced.

At this point, I was feeling like a pretty horrible, awful adult.

"Are you coming in or not?" Doug inquired from the darkness within, snapping me out of my reverie. "You're letting all the heat out of the house."

"Yeah, sure," I mumbled, stepping across the threshold, and sliding the glass door back into place. It took my eyes a moment to adjust to the walnut paneling and orange-flecked shag carpeting that was still in place, even after all these years. Doug sat in his father's Barcalounger, which had a few more pieces of duct tape holding it together than before, but otherwise, it looked largely the same. I expected to find football on the old-school tube TV but was surprised to find some sort of deep-sea fishing program in progress, its volume muted.

"What brings you here today?" asked Doug, taking a bite from an enormous Dagwood that was barely contained by the two slices of bread on either side. Having his mouth full did nothing to stop him from continuing his thought. "Let me guess: you've decided to report those goons to the police after all, and you need a witness?"

I shook my head. "No, nothing like that." I eyed the sofa to my right that was covered with newspapers, magazines, and knitting supplies.

"Just shove all that junk aside and have a seat," said Doug, making no more effort to move than a wave of his hand. I took him at his word and did exactly that, clearing off just enough cushion to perch my backside on the edge. "So, if that ain't it, what exactly *does* bring you out here?"

I sighed, remembering my promise to Anne Marie, and trying to formulate a persuasive argument for helping the poor girl out. Of course, I'd been working on that persuasive argument all the way from Ironton and hadn't really gotten very far. I didn't know how to play at Doug's sympathies. I wasn't even sure Doug *had* any sympathies.

"I've been thinking about that girl, you know? The one I told you about last night who got fished out of the river."

He nodded and slurped away an unsightly glob of mayo that was racing down his forefinger. "Yeah. It's been all over the news this morning. Real shame, that is." His focus went right back to his sandwich.

"Well, apparently, there's some overlap between the girl's family and Melanie's," I said.

"You don't say," he said, still concentrating on keeping his condiments under control. "You make sure and tell Melanie how sorry I am—*we* are, that is. I'm sure Ma would be sorry to know this, too."

A prolonged, disharmonious wail arose from beyond the sliding glass door, and Doug waved away my alarm.

"They're releasing their inner demons, or some such shit," he said, driving a forefinger into the corner of his mouth to pick at some buried treasure hiding between his teeth. "Ain't been the first, won't be the last. Anyway, you were saying?"

"I don't really think Melanie knows this girl or her family," I said. "But her sister, Molly, goes to the same church, and she kind of took it upon herself to recommend our services."

That brought a puzzled look to his face. "Our services? In what way? It sounds like things are pretty much wrapped up."

"Well, not according to the victim's aunt," I said. "She says the police have pretty much decided it was suicide, but she was close to the victim. She says it doesn't track."

"Well, of course she says that," said Doug, pausing to take a long slug of what appeared to be iced tea. "No one wants to believe someone in their family could do a thing like that. Does this woman have reason to think the police are missing something?"

"It's more like intuition," I said. "The victim had been running around with a different crowd at school, and the aunt thinks they know more than what they're saying. She'd like us to take a closer look at them, maybe ask a few questions."

He nodded slowly, savoring the latest bite of his sandwich. "And…?"

"What do you mean, *'and?'* There's no *'and.'*"

He shot me a disbelieving look. "There's *always* an *'and'* with you. What did you promise her?"

"Nothing!" I said, only to realize that wasn't exactly true. I decided to appeal to his despotic narcissism. "Well—*almost* nothing. Nothing *substantial.* I only promised her that I would talk to you about it. I made sure she understood that any case that comes in the door has to be approved by our commander-in-chief, and that would be you. So, here I am."

He basked in the glory of my acknowledgment of the pecking order while he finished his sandwich. Power-mad little fungus. "I planned to spend most of next week here in Lymont," he finally said. "I think I might have a little time on my schedule."

I narrowed my eyes. This was too easy. This was not a typical case for Boggs Investigations. It would involve actual questioning, not just observation. In my experience, Doug's comfort level involved keeping a safe distance and collecting photographic evidence of theft and more often, adultery, while attempting to blend in with one disgusting scenery or another. It was usually very passive.

My phone blipped, and I looked down at its screen. Anne Marie had just sent the first of her list of names.

"You need to get that?" he asked, his eyes shifting to my phone.

"No," I said. "It's fine. So, are you saying you'd be interested in taking the case?"

He leaned forward and snapped the recliner into its upright position, pushing himself to his feet. He carried his empty paper plate and napkin into the tiny, open kitchen that occupied one corner of the living space, its burnt sienna appliances the same as I remembered from the birthday party. He stepped on the pedal of a stainless-steel receptacle, flipping its lid up so he could toss his trash inside. "I don't know. What's your take?"

I was at a loss for words. He *never* asked for my take. My phone blipped again as another text landed. "Well, I have to admit, I feel really sorry for the aunt—her name's Anne Marie Brown, and she's just a few years older than the victim, Tina McAlister. She says they were very close, and Tina never showed any signs of being suicidal. She's very broken up about it, and she's worried about her sister, Marlene—Tina's mother. She says she's practically catatonic."

"What about the father?"

"Hasn't been in the picture for about ten years," I said. "I don't even know if he knows his daughter is dead."

"What do think is the likelihood there's anything to this?" He plopped back down into the recliner, but leaned forward, giving me his full attention, and I have to say, it was unusual bordering on unsettling.

"Well—I'm not sure." Another text landed on my phone. I peeked down to confirm it was also from Anne Marie. "I was very careful to keep her expectations low, but even if she's completely off-base, it might help the family process this tragedy without any lingering doubts. As it so happens, Melanie's out spending the day with her sisters and Jasmine, so I have a little free time myself this weekend. I thought it wouldn't *hurt* to ask around. I don't know. It just kinda feels like the right thing to do."

"Did you give her any idea of what our services would run?"

And here was where it would all fall apart.

Having seen Anne Marie scrape together what little she had in her purse, including loose change, I knew she couldn't afford even our meager fees, especially if the case took longer than a couple of days. I would be willing to donate some of my time, which could offset the overall cost, but would Doug be willing to do the same? It was the sort of thing anyone with a heart might do, but with Doug, I just wasn't sure.

"I didn't discuss fees with her," I hedged. "There didn't seem to be any point unless you were open to the case, and like I said, I was doing my best to keep her expectations low. Besides, your mom handles all of that shit, not me."

As if on cue, the sliding glass door glided along its track, and Loretta leaned inside, perspiration glistening from her brow and pit stains extending halfway to her waist. "We're almost finished, Dougie," she said, a bit winded. "The ladies are rinsing off in the shower downstairs and will be ready for you in about twenty minutes."

I looked from Doug to Loretta and back again, and it was impossible to keep my big mouth shut. "Ready for what? Exactly what kind of services are you offering here, Dougie?" I waggled my eyebrows lasciviously.

"Oh, hush up, you pervert," snapped Loretta. "Leave it to you to take it straight to Smut City—"

"Gee, Ma," Doug interrupted, rising from the recliner. "I don't think I'm going to be able to help out today, after all. Dwayne met with a new client of ours earlier this morning, and we were just on our way out to do a little legwork."

Her hands flew to her hips as her eyebrows skewed south. "Douglas Lee Boggs! You *know* I can't do this all by myself, and you promised you would help me!"

Another text landed as I sat back and watched, eager to see where this was going.

"I really don't know what to tell you, Ma—"

"*What* case? What could be so urgent?"

Doug scrambled, never really one for thinking on his feet. "You heard about that young girl that got pulled out of the river yesterday? Well, her family has hired us. The police think she killed herself, the family don't." I could nearly see the words forming behind his eyes as they flitted across me and, as an afterthought, he added, "And these folks are friends with Melanie's family—they all go to church together, in fact. It's the Christian thing to do."

As I watched Loretta process the case Doug was making, it suddenly occurred to me that Doug was never this selfless. I was close to finding out the *real* reason why he had been so receptive, and it might just be in my best interest to bolt for the front door and make my escape while that was still an option. Unfortunately, the thought was slow to fully realize.

"Fine," Loretta finally said. "I suppose we can get some of the other ladies' sons to help with the charcoal pit at the charity chicken booth this afternoon. But I'm still gonna need your help downstairs. I can't possibly handle twenty-three women by myself."

"But *Ma*—"

"No 'buts!'" she barked. "Lord, forgive me for saying this, but that girl is already dead, so what's another hour?" Her eyes flitted across me, and the suggestion of a smile played at her lips, instantly raising every fine hair up the back of my neck. "In fact, you could cut your time in half if you got Dwayne to help you."

I was on my feet in an instant, shaking my head adamantly. *"Me?!?* I don't even know what you're talking about, and I'm pretty sure I don't *want* to know. I'll just wait in the car while—"

"She's got a point, Dwayne," interrupted Doug. "With both of us, we could be finished in no time flat."

Finished? Finished with *what?!?* The things that raced through my head rendered me speechless.

"Thank you, son," said Loretta, her scowl softening by degrees. The look she sent me was pure satisfaction. She looked at the Fitbit that was sinking into the flesh of her wrist. "It'll only be about fifteen minutes now. I'll see you both shortly."

She stepped back out onto the deck and closed the door as another text landed on my phone and I gaped at Doug. "What in the hell—?" was all I could manage.

He sighed. "Look, I'm helping you with this loser case you seem to think is worthwhile, and you're getting me out of an afternoon of sheer hell. This is just the small price we both have to pay to get what we want. Don't worry—Ma's got a box of protective gloves down there, and it'll all be over soon."

•••••••●⊖⊖●••••••

The tiny Gain-scented vent clip in my Hyundai was no match for the overpowering stench of lidocaine and mentholated pain cream, both of which we had spent the past half hour massaging into flesh of indeterminant age but all of which was almost twice as old as my own. Shoulders, backs, arms, and legs—all to the soundtrack of moaning and groaning that would haunt my darkest nightmares for weeks to come. It was like *The Golden Girls* and all their friends reenacting the restaurant scene from *When Harry Met Sally*, and my ears were still burning bright red. The gloves that Doug had promised were a joke. They were sized for small little chubby hands like Doug's and Loretta's. My hands were anything but small. I laid waste to no less than seven of those suckers before we were finished and had touched enough old lady parts that I felt a confession to Melanie would be in order. Worst of all, the lidocaine and mentholated pain cream had collected underneath my fingernails, and no amount of handwashing had been able to clear it out. It was like traveling in a jar of Vicks VapoRub.

My phone continued to bleep notifications as more texts landed, and it seemed like Anne Marie must have sent a dozen by now. I hadn't stopped to review any of them, still in a state of shock from my entirely unexpected servitude. We were heading east toward Ashland on US 23 along the Kentucky side, figuring we would encounter fewer speed traps than the notorious ones found all along US 52 in Ohio. Doug had the good grace to guiltily stare through the passenger window and keep quiet. This had *never* been about doing a good deed for the McAlister family, and I could only imagine how quicky he was going to shatter Anne Marie's hopes. Sirius was set to 80s on 8, but when Twisted Sister started to play, I turned it off before Dee Snider even had a chance to rage against authority.

"Hey!" protested Doug. "That's a good song."

I just ignored him. I was feeling vindictive.

My phone rang through the car's Bluetooth connection, and Sarah McGregor's name appeared on the screen. I pressed the button in my steering wheel to answer the call.

"Hey, Sarah," I said. "What's up?"

"If I know Melanie, and I'm pretty sure I do, she's out scouring the Black Friday deals with Jasmine and her sisters today." It was an unsurprising statement of fact considering this was a tradition Sarah had been aware of for far longer than me. It was also unsurprising that Sarah wasn't among those making their annual pilgrimage to retail nirvana. She never was much of one for elbowing her way to the last of anything. She was just fine ordering from Amazon and patiently waiting for her merchandise to be delivered right to her front door.

"You are correct," I confirmed.

"Good," she said, sounding relieved. "I was hoping to catch you when she wasn't right beside you. I'm not used to being at odds with her, and I'm not sure how to make her see things differently. I *cannot* turn my back on my grandson. I just can't. Surely, you understand."

"I do. And I think Mel will come around. It was just very sudden. She needs a little time to process."

"*She* needs time to process? I thought I was long past my child-rearing days. I'm really struggling here. I could use the support of my family. Nothing about this is going to be easy."

"You know I'm here for you," I said. "And Jasmine wants to meet her half-brother. Just be patient. We're working on Melanie. She'll be more receptive once the shock has worn off."

"Well, I hope so," she said. "And I'd really like to see my granddaughter before you all head north. I'm sure I could get my folks to watch Jordan for a bit so he wouldn't have to be part of things this time around, but eventually, we're going to have to cross that bridge."

"Of course. I'm sure we can figure something out," I said, hoping I wasn't telling a lie. I had no real power to make anything happen here.

"The last thing I want is for that poor little boy to think he's the cause of any turmoil. It's bad enough I've got people like Loretta Boggs running her big, fat mouth with her group of cronies about Jordan's mother, and she's none too kind about Ryan, either. I mean, talk about a bunch of Sunday Christians, I'd like to—"

"Sarah, Sarah, *Sarah!*" I interjected, following with a laugh that started at the very highest end of my register before disintegrating into the fakest chortle ever known to man. We were way past the point of subtlety, and I could tell from the heightened color in Doug's cheeks he hadn't missed a word. "I should have probably mentioned that I'm in my car, and you're on speakerphone. Guess who's with me?"

Silence stretched out for an uncomfortable moment until Doug finally muttered, "Hello, Mrs. McGregor."

More uncomfortable silence.

"Is that—?" she began.

"It *is*," I confirmed. "Doug and I are on our way to visit a potential client. Have you heard about that young girl that was pulled out of the river near Ironton?"

"Of course," she said. "It's been all over the news. It's just awful."

"Not sure there's much we can do, but we're going out to talk to the family. They're not completely satisfied with what the police are telling them, and—well, you know how that can go. Why don't I give you a call later tonight or early tomorrow after I've had a chance to talk to Melanie?"

"That'd be fine," she said. "And Doug?"

"Yes, ma'am?" I wasn't sure if it was fear or genuine respect for his elders that Loretta had clearly drummed into him, but Doug remained polite.

"I wish I could say I was sorry about what I said earlier, but I really don't do well with gossip, especially when me and my own are at the heart of it. I hope you understand."

I hadn't really expected Sarah to take her words back. With her, what you see is what you get, and you never have to wonder what she's thinking.

"Yes, ma'am," he replied.

"But I do want to tell you how pleasantly surprised I am that you and Dwayne are looking into this girl's death. Take it from me, there's nothing worse than losing your child and feeling like nothing more than an inconvenience to the local authorities. I always got the impression you didn't care for cases like this, but if it hadn't been for you and Dwayne, I would have never found out what happened to my Ryan. This girl's family needs answers, and if you can help them in any way, you're doing a good thing here, and I admire that."

Doug was momentarily speechless. Whatever he was expecting, it wasn't praise.

"Thank you, ma'am," he finally said. "Hopefully we can make a difference."

I disconnected the call and tried my hardest to keep my smile to myself. Sarah had essentially eradicated any avenues of escape Doug may have been plotting to ditch this case once his services were no longer needed at the charity chicken barbeque.

I sobered up quickly when I realized that now came the hard part—interviewing the bereaved family.

CHAPTER TWELVE

We pulled into the lot at McDonald's in Flatwoods, and I had a momentary flash of déjà vu. It seemed like decades ago when Melanie and I had stopped at this very location investigating Ryan's murder. I remained behind the wheel as Doug shuffled inside to make a beeline for the bathroom. It only served to remind me how much I'd rather be doing this with Melanie. I think we've pretty firmly established by now I'm not at my best when dealing with bereavement. Melanie says things that are tactful and soothing. I'm prone to say things that are inappropriate at best and downright startling at worst. Based on his stubborn insistence on calling Tina McAlister, 'The Dead Girl,' I suspected Doug would sink us to a whole new low, and in very short order.

I took the opportunity to scroll through the text messages on my phone. Only a handful had actually been from Anne Marie, the others from someone desperate to locate a guy named Robert whose property on Lake Shore Drive was apparently a very desirable commodity. After reporting his string of texts as spam, I sifted through the ones from Anne Marie and was frustrated to find she had barely followed my instructions at all. While her first text included the street address for her sister, Marlene, conveniently linked to Google Maps for GPS guidance to her door, the next six were names only, save for the first, which signified he was the preacher's son.

She had supplied neither phone numbers nor addresses, and since most, if not all, would be minors, I couldn't even look them up on whitepages.com.

Chandler Keaton – Rev Keaton's son
Farrah Willey
Jesse Baker
Kaitlyn Hamilton
Tammy Tipton

I sighed, scrolling through the texts again. We hadn't even begun, and I was already stuck. Based off the various news coverage of my exploits over the past year, you might think I was born with a knack for deduction, but the sad truth is, I've just been winging it all along. Even after I had made the decision to shift careers, and enrolled in online courses, I was currently stuck with electives that would have been required whether I was going into private investigation, business management or taxidermy. Even once I started courses that were more focused on criminal justice, they would be courses like psychology and criminology, neither of which would serve as a 'how-to' guide to investigation. These were lessons to be learned as an apprentice with Boggs Investigations, but it had become readily apparent during the five months I had been under Doug's wing that he was no teacher. His idea of leadership was limited to shunting all the cases he felt were beneath his talents to me, so I could provide proof of transgressions that were already a foregone conclusion. There was never a question of what, and only occasionally a question of who. No creative sleuthing was required, just a lot of blending into frequently disgusting backgrounds.

Doug appeared in the McDonald's doorway and made a heavy-handed stab at charades, asking me if I wanted something to drink. I nodded as my phone rang again through the audio system. Melanie's name appeared on the screen, and I connected. "Hey, lady."

"Hey, guy," she replied, the background noise doing its best to drown her out. Any grudge she may have been holding from earlier appeared to have evaporated, and she sounded like herself again. I guess there's some truth to the healing power of retail therapy.

"I can barely hear you. Where are you?" I asked.

"Still at the Ashland Town Center. It's a freaking *madhouse*."

My idea of hell on earth. "Are you having any luck?"

"We are! You're gonna die when you see what Jasmine found for you." I could barely hear Jaz protesting in the background, and Melanie pulled the phone away from her mouth. "I'm *not* telling him, I promise. Fine. *Fine!*"

Doug returned with a drink carrier and slid into the passenger seat. He handed me a soda as he slurped whipped cream from the top of what appeared to be a strawberry shake.

"Listen," continued Melanie, her voice louder again. "I just wanted to apologize for my sisters. Molly had no business offering up your services, and Cheryl shouldn't have even bothered you with it. If I had any idea what that woman was there for, I would have put a stop to it myself. You had no clue what you were walking into when you agreed to meet my family, huh?"

"No apologies necessary," I said. "Especially as far as Cheryl is concerned. She was just trying to do the right thing. I'm not so sure about Molly's motivation. But either way, you can't control what they do or say."

"I know," she said. "But I would've kept Cheryl from encouraging the poor woman. I know this isn't the type of case Boggs Investigations takes, as much as you hate it."

I looked peevishly at Doug. "Um, Mel—"

"For the life of me, I don't understand it. Is Doug really so afraid to take on something that might actually be challenging? If I were you, I'd tell him to—"

"Mel!" I interrupted, speaking over her sharply. "Why don't you tell him yourself? He's sitting right here."

Cue uncomfortable silence, round two. Despite their great convenience, I was beginning to see how speakerphones might be more trouble than they're worth.

"You're with Doug?" she finally asked.

"I am," I confirmed, giving Doug an apologetic shrug as his face once again crept to crimson. It was hard to be sincere when his reputation had preceded him so effectively. I decided to plod forward before she said anything else that would make this day even less comfortable. "We're actually on our way to visit the girl's mother. You know, see if there's anything to the family's concerns."

"You're shitting me," was Melanie's blunt response. "I never thought I'd see the day—"

"Now, just hold on right there," Doug finally erupted. "You're talkin' about me like I'm some yellow chicken. You *do* remember I was the one who saved Dwayne and your daughter last year, don'tcha?"

"Well—yes, I do, but—"

Doug was testifying on his own behalf and wasn't about to stop now. "And if I hadn't been where I was last night—"

I launched into a coughing fit directed toward the mic embedded in the roof while frantically waving Doug to silence, but I was a tad late. Not much gets by Melanie.

"Last night? What happened last night?"

"It was nothing, really," I insisted while Doug looked outraged, his mouth hanging open, ready to continue defending his reputation. I snatched the shake out of his hand and powered down my window, holding it outside and well beyond his reach. It was my turn for charades, and I left absolutely no doubt his frozen treat was in jeopardy of hitting pavement if he didn't shut his mouth. "I'll tell you all about it tonight."

The silence that followed suggested she didn't exactly believe me, but ultimately, she decided to let it go. "Well, then. I guess I'll let you two get

154

back to it. I have to admit, I'm really surprised. I don't know what motivated you to step up, Doug, but it's a good look for you. You should try it more often."

"Thank you—?" was Doug's pensive reply, fairly certain he had just been insulted again, and I turned my face to hide my smile. My hat was off to both Melanie and Sarah. Neither one had backpedaled on their comments about Doug, choosing to remain within the confines of truth to soften the blow instead. They were so much alike it was scary. This conflict between them needed resolution, stat.

"Love you, lady," I said, handing the milkshake back to Doug which largely appeased him. "Have fun, and tell Jaz I love her, too."

"Right back at ya, mister. Will do," she said and disconnected.

I plunged a straw into the soda Doug had handed me and took a long pull. Fortunately, I hadn't rolled the window up, and I immediately leaned my head out to spit the foul beverage out onto the lot. "What the hell *is* this?!?"

"Diet Coke," he replied innocently. "You've been looking a little thick around the middle here lately."

Asshole.

•••••••●⊖⊖●••••••••

Doug and I sat uncomfortably close together on a floral upholstered loveseat that was completely sealed underneath clear plastic cover. Every movement we made registered in the crinkles like tiny bursts of flatulence. Lost in frumpy jeans and an oversized pink t-shirt that was littered in faded yellow daisies, Marlene McAlister sat catercorner to us in a wooden rocker, her hands folded in her lap. She stared blindly at a console television along the far wall that was switched on with the sound muted. Her focus was far beyond anything we could perceive. She barely blinked, and the only way I knew she was still with us was the slight pendulation of the chair.

The compact room was claustrophobic with too much seating, most of which was covered to overflowing by stacks of sewing patterns, skeins of yarn and piles of multicolored material. All of it was separated by a battle-scarred coffee table that left too little legroom for guests like me. Hanging crookedly on the wall in front of me was what appeared to be one of Tina's school pictures. It was the same one used by news outlets in reporting her death, and I studied it for a long moment. It seemed like the least I could do at this point was commit to memory her plain, expressionless features shrouded by long, stringy hair the color of sand. I immediately felt guilty for my frank assessment, but she was completely unreadable and wholly unremarkable.

Knick-knacks adorned every available square inch of surface, but the grand centerpiece was an enormous curio cabinet that sat along the eastern wall, filled to capacity with porcelain dolls from all around the world. They wore frills and bows and stared out into the room with creepy, soulless eyes. It was unnerving.

Anne Marie bustled in with a serving platter carrying a plate of cookies, a pitcher of lemonade and four ice-filled glasses. "I can't tell you how happy I am you decided to come," she directed this to Doug. "I apologize I ain't got nothing fancier, and the sugar cookies might be a little stale—"

"It's fine, Anne Marie," I said, taking one of the glasses of lemonade and trying to wash away the nasty aftertaste of Diet Coke that still lingered. "Why don't you make yourself comfortable?"

She nodded, choosing to perch on the arm of a chair that matched the loveseat we occupied. It, too, was covered in plastic, and I was surprised she didn't slide right off. Her left leg ticked away nervously as she gave us her full attention.

Doug cleared his throat. "So, Miss—Brown, is it?"

"Yes, sir."

"Dwayne tells me the police are leaning towards calling your niece's— incident—suicide."

"Yes, sir."

I jumped as Mrs. McAlister abruptly snorted, the first sound she'd made since we'd been seated, but when I turned my head to see if she had something to say, she only stared at the television as if she'd never made any sound at all.

Doug continued. "Why would the police think your niece killed herself?"

Anne Marie fidgeted with her fingers as she stole a glance at her sister. "She sort of left a note."

"How do you 'sort of' leave a note?" I asked, leaning forward.

"Marlene got a text from her last Friday," said Anne Marie. "Or at least, it *claimed* to be from her—but I just don't believe it. Neither does Marlene."

"Well, Ms. Brown, I can understand why you wouldn't want to believe your niece could do such a thing, but if the police seemed satisfied, they must have good reason," said Doug, and I could already sense him washing his hands of this whole affair.

Anne Marie sniffled, dabbing at her nose with a tissue. "They confirmed with Tri-State Cellular the text came from Tina's phone number."

"So, what makes you think there's more to the story?" I asked, trying to at least give Anne Marie a chance to expand on whatever facts she found troubling. Even if there was no real case to investigate, we might be able to give her and her sister a little peace of mind just by talking through it.

Anne Marie took a deep, fortifying breath and sat a little straighter on the arm of the chair. "Firstly, I don't believe Tina was the type for killin' herself, and as you don't know her, you're just gonna have to take me at my word on that." I started to interject, but she held up a finger. "But she never called Marlene, 'Mom.' *Never.*"

"I'm not sure I understand," said Doug, but at least he was paying attention once again.

"The text," she said, jumping to her feet and darting back into the kitchen. When she returned, she had a cellphone clutched in her hand, swiping its screen to unlock it with her thumb. "The so-called 'suicide' text. Here. You read it." She thrust the phone toward Doug.

He held the phone at arm's length to read the tiny text, which gave me the opportunity to read over his shoulder.

Can't be here anymore Mom. Goodbye.

"It doesn't say anything about killing herself," I muttered. I don't know why, but I expected something more dramatic and direct, like, *'You'll never forgive yourself once I'm dead.'*

"And that's why it didn't hit us at first. We thought she just took off in a huff. It wasn't the first time she ran off after her and Marlene had words, and it was always about those gosh darned kids. God help me, I wish she hadn't never *met* any of them!"

I re-read the message, my eyes coming to rest on the word, 'Mom.' "So, what did Tina call her?"

"Mo," said Anne Marie. "Mo or MoMo. That's what she always called her mama, even when she was just a wee thing. Don't ask me why. *Never* 'Mom.'"

I fiddled with the messaging app on my own phone and quickly learned that autocorrect would turn 'Mo' into 'More,' and 'MoMo' into 'Moment.' 'Mom' was one of the suggestions, but not the default.

"I have to say, I still don't see why the police would see that as a suicide message," said Doug. "Your sister got it last Friday? That's more than a week before her—" His eyes shifted to Marlene. "Before they found her."

Anne Marie lowered her voice and looked at her feet. "She'd been down there for a while. You know—underwater. I'm guessing the timing's close."

"There has to be something more than that," I said, and I was talking to Doug more than anyone else. "Unless, of course, the police in these parts are as inept as the ones in Lymont."

"Now, don't go generalizing," said Doug. "I'm sure there are plenty of good men on that force."

I could only stare in disbelief. I couldn't remember Doug ever having a kind word for local law enforcement. He was only marginally less critical of the Columbus PD. He only seemed respectful of officers who had some sort of specialized training, such as defusing bombs or hostage negotiations. He shot me a coded look that meant absolutely nothing to me. I made a mental note to ask him later and moved on.

"What was the argument about?" When Anne Marie looked confused, I elaborated. "Between Tina and her mother."

"That boy—"

It was a growl that slipped through Marlene's clenched teeth, but when I looked at her, it was as if she hadn't moved a muscle. She was beginning to freak me out more than just a little.

"She means Chandler," said Anne Marie. "She caught him in Tina's room. Again."

"You told me earlier that Chandler wasn't Tina's boyfriend," I said. "Are you sure about that?"

Anne Marie nodded. "He went with another girl. Farrah Willey or Whaley—something like that. She's on the list, too."

I wasn't naïve enough to question why else Chandler might have been there, and apparently on multiple occasions. Most teenage boys' mindsets had the rough moral equivalence of dogs in heat.

"So, she ran away with him?" I asked.

"I never said she ran away with him," Anne Marie corrected me. "I said she ran away over words she and my sister had over the boy."

"Didn't anyone talk to Chandler or his folks when she didn't come home?" asked Doug.

"They said they didn't know where she was."

"How about any of the other kids?" I asked.

She shrugged. "I got no idea who the police might have talked to, but I barely know most of their last names. I surely don't know their phone numbers or anything like that."

"So, these are school friends—?" I ventured.

"Some," said Anne Marie. "Most went to school with Tina here at Ironton High, but even though they're around the same age, they're not necessarily in the same grades or classes. A couple of 'em are from across the river and go to school over in Kentucky. Chandler's one. He goes to school at the New Life Academy. But they all were in teen fellowship together out to the church."

"Church friends?" It seemed like an odd choice for troublemakers to congregate, but then again, the old rugged cross casts a mighty long shadow, and darkness has a nasty propensity to breed darkness.

Anne Marie nodded. "New Life Apostolic. It's just outside Flatwoods on 207."

A tumbler fell into place. Molly's church. Of course.

"What was it about those kids that put you off?" I asked.

Anne Marie took a long moment to try and collect her thoughts but ended up just shaking her head. "I wish I could think straight. I know I'll think of something particular just the moment y'all walk out that door. But most of all, it was the way they looked at you. Lots of whisperin' and smirkin' like everything was some big secret, and they were above everybody else. Sure, Chandler's daddy is the preacher, and some of the others might have some money, but that don't give 'em the right to treat people the way they do. And if you found one, you usually found them all, like a pack of wolves. It didn't feel safe to be around 'em. I don't think I'm the only one who felt that way. You just knew they were up to no good but could never quite catch 'em in the act. The way they folded our quiet little Tina into their circle—it just didn't make no sense. It was out of nowhere. And suddenly, she started getting popular, both in church but especially at school. It just don't happen like that."

I thought back to my own high school days and couldn't argue. When life turns on a dime, it's almost always on a downward slope. I looked to Doug to see if he had any other questions, but all I saw was defeat in his eyes. If the conversation turned to fees, I figured it was all over but the shouting. I wasn't quite so willing to throw in the towel.

"Have the police searched Tina's room?" I asked.

Anne Marie blinked, surprised by the question. "What for?"

"To find some reason for her to do something so extreme."

She shook her head. "Other than the two officers who came out to tell us they found her, no. No one else has been here. Do you think they'll want to do that?"

"They might come around to it," said Doug, shifting on the loveseat. "If they were already convinced this was a suicide, they may not have thought it was worth the time nor trouble."

"Would you mind if we took a look around while we're here?" I asked. We had a limited-time opportunity to poke around before the police took anything of interest away. It seemed like a brilliant idea to me. Doug looked decidedly less sure.

Anne Marie looked to her sister to see if she registered any objection, and it was no surprise to find her attention firmly focused on another astral plane.

"I don't guess so," she said, shifting uncomfortably on the arm of the chair. She pointed to the arched open doorway to Doug's left. "Turn right.

It's down the hall, last room on the left. I'd show you myself, but I just can't bring myself to—"

"It's quite alright, Ms. Brown," I said, standing. "We'll be very careful to keep things just as they are."

Doug followed my lead, but once we were out of earshot, he muttered to me, "What in the hell are you doing? We ain't got no business going in that girl's room before the police. We're just causing ourselves a world of trouble. If they dust for prints, they'll know we were in there."

Well, shit. I hadn't thought of that, but a smile crept across my face as I patted my pockets and found a single disposable glove left over from our torturous administration of analgesics to the geriatric set. I dangled it in front of Doug's face.

"What are you giving it to *me* for?" He swatted at it like it was a bee.

"Unless you've got more gloves on you, this is the only one I've got, and you'll have to do the honors. My hands are too big for these damned things."

He scowled and reluctantly worked the glove over his thick, stubby fingers. We paused at the end of the darkened hallway, Tina's white bedroom door standing ajar. She had posters of boy bands and other teen idols tacked to its exterior, and I couldn't help but wonder if provocative pouting was the common denominator in the boys she found swoon-worthy. It opened with an assist from my knee, its hinges screaming for WD-40. I peered inside, but the room was surprisingly dark, considering the time of day. Doug fumbled along the wall with his gloved hand until he found a switch and flipped it up, triggering soft light from a pair of matching bedside table lamps. We stepped inside.

The entire room was faded cotton candy, pale pink and yellowing white with fragile-looking frills affixed anywhere you could place them—on pillows, on bedding, at the edges of the lacy window coverings.

"Hmm," I said, crossing the room to a small white desk positioned beside the bed and underneath the window.

"You find something?" asked Doug, whispering as though he was afraid we'd get caught. He quickly reminded me, "Don't *touch* nothing!"

"There's no glass in the window," I likewise whispered. It *did* feel wrong to be in the dead girl's room, looking at her things. Nevertheless, I leaned in for a closer look. "It's been covered over by a sheet of plywood. We should ask what that's all about."

"Agreed," said Doug, using his gloved forefinger to slide a closet door open and poke around.

I examined her sparse desktop, noting a couple of chargers that weren't plugged into anything as well as an ethernet cord for internet dangling off the edge of the desk. There was a cheap blotter in the center, and I could barely discern a rectangular shape in the hint of dust that covered the surface.

"Looks like she had a laptop, too, but it's not here now," I mumbled, thinking aloud. "We should ask—"

Another screech sounded like the one I had heard when I nudged open the bedroom door, but this time it came from right in front of me. I looked up just in time to see the working end of a crowbar slide up from the bottom right and reposition itself at the next point of resistance. A little torque was applied, and another yelp came from where the crowbar bit into the window frame. Unwilling to call out and scare away the intruder, I waved like mad to try and get Doug's attention, but he was busily fingering his way to the back of Tina's closet.

I scanned the desk for something I might use as a weapon, and grabbed a stapler, immediately kicking myself when I realized I had just left evidence of my presence. Oh, well. Maybe I could slide the stapler into my pocket and take it with me, no one the wiser.

Fingers appeared at the bottom and side of the plywood, poking in, and grabbing hold where the crowbar had loosened the nails. After a mighty pull and shriek of protest from the surrounding siding, the plywood dropped away, and sunlight flooded into my face, momentarily blinding me. All I could make out was the vague outline of a person, slight in stature, and judging from the gasp, as startled by my presence as I was of its. As it turned to flee, I lunged through the window to try and grab hold only to crack my forehead hard enough against the glassless frame of the bottom pane to blur my own vision. Dizzy, I pulled back, leaving a trail of handprints along the surface of the desk as I struggled to keep my balance.

I recovered quickly, but by the time I got my bearings, the intruder was long gone.

CHAPTER THIRTEEN

Doug and I sat side-by-side on the rickety front porch of the McAlister bungalow, our legs dangling over the edge and swinging freely in the overgrown weeds below. I couldn't shake the feeling we were back in high school, waiting for punishment to be administered by the principal.

When a couple of officers, one male and one female, arrived in a Ford SUV from the Lawrence County Sheriff's Office, it was impossible to miss Doug's heightened agitation, but I didn't see how it could be helped. I *had* to call the police. Someone attempted to break into the McAlister home in broad daylight, and we certainly weren't in any position to offer any sort of ongoing protective service.

Hmmm. I made a mental note to bring it up during our next office meeting. Maybe it's a service we *should* be offering. It would sure beat the hell out of chasing down horny adulterers in seedy hotels and other icky locales.

In this particular case, I thought it might help the police realize this whole thing might not be so open and shut. I didn't know exactly how much longer Doug was willing to hang in there, especially once he realized Anne Marie would be struggling to meet our retainer, much less pay for our actual services. If I could help reignite police interest, I wouldn't feel so bad about abandoning Mrs. McAlister and her sister once Doug declared it was time to go home.

The male half of our investigative team was middle-aged and soft, with a balding head and a chin that receded right down into the neckline of his white t-shirt. His crisp, black uniform shirt was adorned with patches identifying him as an officer of the Lawrence County Sheriff's Department, as well as a shiny gold badge pinned to the left side of his chest, and above that was a name badge reading, 'R. Palmer.' He stayed behind to take our statements in a monotone while his partner, a short, husky woman with strawberry blonde hair and an abundance of freckles covering her face and arms, went inside to speak to Anne Marie. Mrs. McAlister remained uncommunicative, and I wondered if she needed to be seen by a medical professional. In extreme cases, shock can be lethal.

Once Officer Palmer had exhausted his limited questions, he sauntered around back to see if he could find any evidence the intruder left behind. He was about a half-hour too late, but I wasn't going to point it out. Inside, Anne Marie continued to answer the other officer's questions animatedly and after a few moments, I began to wonder if she was even asking any questions. Anne Marie never seemed to pause long enough for the officer to speak.

When I had told Anne Marie about the attempted break-in, her agitation was immediate. She was practically bouncing off the walls with worry, a veritable fountain of imaginative suppositions that all culminated in her and her sister's murders. I was fairly certain if I hadn't called the police, she would have. Frankly, I don't know if I would have been comfortable staying there, either.

"Douglas Lee Boggs."

The voice came from behind us and startled us both. It was the short, stocky policewoman with an inflection suggesting both familiarity and reproach. She wore a name badge above her golden sheriff's badge that read, 'L. Graves.' She also kept her hand uncomfortably close to her holstered weapon, and I didn't think the smirk on her face bode well for us. She stepped off the porch and turned to face us.

"Lucy," Doug grumbled, offering nothing more and avoiding her gaze.

"What on God's green earth are you doing way out here?" she asked, putting one foot up on the stoop and leaning in to force him to look at her.

I was nervous, and when I'm nervous, I tend to blather. I offered her a hand. "Hey—hi. You all seem to know each other already. I'm Dwayne. Dwayne Morrow. I work out of Doug's Columbus office."

Her gaze flitted over my hand before landing on my face. "I know who you are. What I *don't* know is why the two of you are sticking your noses into an active investigation."

Doug cleared his throat. "Maybe 'cause the family of the victim don't think you're doing your job very well."

"Is that so?" she asked. He still wouldn't look at her, and she clearly found it amusing. All it did for me was heighten my discomfort, and I really wished she'd move her hand a little farther away from her holstered weapon. "So, is this some sort of publicity gimmick? Trying to squeeze a little business out of this poor family's misfortune?

"Not at all!" I protested. "Anne Marie—Ms. Brown came to see me this morning over at my girlfriend's sister's house, more or less asking if we might be able to do something since—"

She tilted her head, shifting her attention to me. "Since what?"

"Well," I hedged. "She was of the opinion you all had already decided it was a suicide."

Her response was half-snort, half-harrumph. "This is an ongoing investigation," she said, pacing a short line in front of us. "What would have given her an idea like that? Or maybe, I should be asking *who?*"

I was flustered at her implication. "I guess you'd have to ask Ms. Brown about that," I said, and her eyes locked back onto me at the sound of my voice. Whatever her tactic, it was certainly making a mess out of me. "I'm just down here visiting family for the holiday—ma'am."

"Officer Graves," she corrected.

"Yes, ma'am—um, Officer Graves. I certainly wasn't looking for her to come around asking for my help."

"Mmm-hmm." Her eyes continued to bore directly into my soul. "And how would she have even known you were here?"

I knew this one!

"Molly!" I practically shouted, and then I was off to the races. "My girlfriend's sister, Molly, convinced Anne Marie to come talk to me. I guess she goes to the same church as Anne Marie. She practically volunteered our services without even giving me a heads up, which is completely crazy considering I'm not the one who decides what cases we—and by we, I mean Boggs Investigations—takes. I'm learning really fast that Molly's super-opinionated and has a great big mouth—"

"Molly Ridenour?" she interrupted.

I blinked. "Well, yes. Do you know her?"

"Maid of honor at my wedding. Godmother to my little girl."

Shit.

I just sat there with my mouth working silently, trying to find anything else to say that wouldn't bury us any deeper.

She scowled at me. "I have to say, meeting you in person has been a bit of let-down after seeing all those heroic news stories where you seem to be the center of attention."

I was startled when Doug cleared his throat and decided he'd had enough.

"Would you just give it a rest, Lucy?" he said. "Dwayne was just tryin' to do the lady a favor is all. And the lady doesn't seem particularly satisfied with the work of you and your team, and I can hardly blame her. I mean, how long is that partner of yours gonna hide out in the backyard before admitting there's nothing out there to find? Whoever it was is long gone. You all seem to be taking your sweet time investigating *anything* around here. Ms. Brown's got a right to ask for outside help."

"From the likes of *you?* Don't make me laugh!" She laughed a big, ugly laugh anyway. "I just better not find a bunch of evidence you've trampled on or compromised."

Doug scooted off the front of the porch and landed on his feet. "I'd worry more about your partner finding his way back to the car," he quipped, nodding toward me. "C'mon, Dwayne. We've wasted enough time here."

Feeling a little less sure of myself, I got to my feet as well.

"Now, just wait a minute, there," she said, stepping into Doug's path. "I don't believe I said you could go just yet."

"*Lucy*—" Doug sighed, kneading his forehead and shaking his head. I've never seen him work so hard at choosing his words. "We've already told your partner what little we know including where we've been in the house and what we've touched. I will follow up with Ms. Brown on how else we may be able to assist her at a later time. But for now? I'm tired. This was supposed to be a day off for me, sittin' around the house in my Jockeys and watchin' TV. I didn't plan on any of this, much less runnin' into you. If you need anything, you certainly know how to get hold of me, but in the meanwhile, I'm goin' home. If that ain't okay by you, you'll just have to shoot me."

He headed toward my SUV while I cut a wide swath around Officer Graves, whose complexion was becoming more mottled by the second. Her hand was still scarily close to her holstered weapon, and I could only imagine the inner turmoil raging over the plausibility of her falsifying a report that could satisfactorily explain to Internal Affairs why she had shot us both in the back.

As I started the car, she was still scowling at us, unblinking and her elbow poised for the draw. I got us the hell out of there.

I remained on the Ohio side of the river for the journey back, and we traveled west on US 52 in silence for several long minutes. It was a little after five, and the sun was already on its way to bed. Traffic was relatively light, and I kept my cruise control engaged to thwart any of the speed traps for which this stretch of road had gained infamy.

Doug brooded in the passenger seat, and I fully expected him to demand I call Anne Marie at my earliest opportunity to extricate us from this matter. Still, I couldn't help but be curious. He obviously shared some history with Officer Lucy Graves, and inquiring minds wanted to know.

"So, who's Lucy?" I had held my tongue far longer than I thought possible.

He sighed. "Ancient history, that's all."

"Really?" Now I was intrigued. I muted the radio that had been playing softly in the background. "Did the two of you, like, *date* or something?"

"Shuddup!" he protested halfheartedly. He rubbed his face with one hand and stared out the window, and I could sense he was reminiscing, I just couldn't tell if that was a good thing or a bad thing.

"Oh, come *on*, man!" I needled him. "Don't just leave me hanging. You two were practically throwing sparks back there."

"We were not," he insisted, and he was beginning to get a little agitated, so I decided to cool it for a second to see if he might volunteer more on his own.

To the best of my recollection, Doug never had a steady girlfriend in high school, but I had no idea what might have happened in the years between then and now. They say everybody's got a soulmate somewhere, and I suppose that even applies to squirrelly little munitions nuts like Doug

Boggs. I was beginning to think he had closed the door on the matter when he cleared his throat.

"Back in the day, we went to the academy together," he said, adding, "She was Lucille Schultz back then. Musta gotten married at some point."

"You mean, like, the police academy?"

He glanced at me crossly. "Of course, I mean the police academy, and just one wiseass Steve Guttenberg crack will get you fired, you understand me?"

He stared at me until I nodded. "Sure, I mean—I guess I just didn't know that about you."

"How did you think I got *my* hours in to become a PI?"

I just shook my head and shrugged, never really having given it a thought.

"Actually coulda ended up in your neck of the woods," he said. "It was the Columbus Police Training Academy over there on Hague."

Try though I may, I couldn't keep a smile from creeping onto my face. "It's really hard to picture you as a policeman." At least my voice was steady.

"Yeah, well, I guess it wasn't meant to be," he said. "But that's where I met her, anyhow. We was both in the same class of cadets competin' for a handful of openings with the Columbus PD."

"And she made it, but you didn't?"

"No!" he barked. "That wasn't it at all!"

He lapsed back into pensive silence, watching the mile markers whip by through the passenger window, and I thought that was all I was getting.

"Neither one of us made it," he acknowledged, quickly adding, "But it wasn't like we were the bottom of the class or anything. There were seven openings and fourteen cadets. We *almost* made the cut. She was just closer to makin' the cut than me, is all."

Wow. I knew that had to be hard for him to admit, so I choked back every single snide comment that was fighting for control of my mouth. It wasn't easy.

"No matter what it was, she was always just one step ahead of me," he said before stealing a glance in my direction. "You know, there was a little bit of time there where I sorta took a fancy to her. She wasn't like all those foo-foo girls we went to school with, ya know? She could make you blush with that mouth of hers, and she gave as good as she got. She used to needle me when she'd outscore me in tests, whether they be written or tactical or whatever. It was never by much, and at the time, I thought it was her way of showin' me she liked me, too, but all she was doin' was gaging her competition and makin' fun of me the whole time."

"That's awful." And I meant it, too. There's not much worse than being put down by a person who is also failing, only less so than you.

He shrugged. "Whatcha gonna do? Her scores were high enough she was able to parlay herself into the sheriff's department over here in Lawrence County, and I went to work at the Walmart's in New Boston as undercover security until I logged enough hours to branch out onto my own. In the long run, I think it worked out best for both of us."

We fell back into silence for several more miles before I decided it was time to face the inevitable. "What do you want me to tell Anne Marie when she calls me? I'm kind of surprised she hasn't called already. I just want to let her down easy—"

"Let her down?" He raised a bushy eyebrow. "You throwin' in the towel already?"

"Well—*no*," I said, more than a little surprised. "I just figured after all that back there—"

"That I'd go runnin' off with my tail between my legs?"

Pretty much, I thought, but I kept it to myself.

172

"I'm not about to let that bigmouthed woman dictate my when and wheres," he said. "We've got a whole list of folks to talk to, and I ain't got nothin' set for tomorrow, how 'bout you?"

My surprise escalated into actual stammering. "Well, I-I-I've got a few things to do at some point in the day, but no real schedule, I guess. Sure, I'm up for it."

I guess the pissing contest between the two former cadets wasn't quite over yet.

......●●●●●⊖⊜●●●●●...

We drifted into our own thoughts for the rest of the trip back to Lymont until I started noticing the billboards again. The first that caught my eye was near Franklin Furnace. A pretty, if a tad overly made-up blonde woman caught mid-laugh, her eyes still twinkling at the camera, despite the sign's age and sun-bleached state. Cassie Martin, mother of two, was last seen with friends outside Nettie's Bar and Grill on 4th Street in Lymont. There was a desperate plea for tips, anonymous or otherwise, and a phone number. The date last seen was five years' past. In fact, I was pretty sure Nettie's has been closed for almost three years now.

The next was closer to Wheelersburg.

Kim Perkins, looking dazed, her unfocused eyes barely slits staring in the general direction of the camera. Her smile was a slash across the bottom of her face, suggesting few teeth remained and protruding collarbones that are prevalent among those with a taste for meth. Last seen near Tracy Park in Portsmouth over two years ago. Another desperate plea, another phone number.

"What do you make of these?" I asked Doug, startling him from near sleep.

"Make of what?"

I pointed but was a little too late as the homemade billboard sped past.

"All these missing women," I said. "Surely, you've noticed the signs along the roadside. You still live down here."

"Oh, sure," he said, yawning and wiping his eyes. "I guess after a while, I've gotten a little blind to 'em."

"It's sad," I said. "It's like everyone's forgotten about them except for their families. I mean, people don't just disappear."

He snorted, stifling another yawn. "That's where you're wrong, buddy. I mean, sometimes it's on purpose and sometimes not, but people disappear all the fucking time."

It was nearly six-thirty when my headlights swept over the entrance to the Boggs' driveway. It was practically empty now, with only Doug's ugly Pontiac SUV and some nondescript midsize sedan that I assumed belonged to his aunt parked at the bottom. I only pulled in far enough to get off the road, slipping my gearshift into park as the porchlight was tripped by an automatic sensor, and Loretta's silhouette appeared in the front window, her head swathed in the hardware necessary to construct her beehive in the morning. I could barely make out a chorus of angry poodle protests emanating from somewhere behind the walls.

"Why don't we meet at that McDonald's in Flatwoods around nine, nine-thirty?" Doug suggested as he unfastened his seat belt. "We could grab some breakfast and cobble together some sort of game plan for the day."

"Works for me," I said, turning on the inside light so I could waggle some fingers in Loretta's direction, and not just the one I wanted to. She pulled away from the window immediately, letting the curtain fall back into place. "I'll reach back out to Anne Marie on my way back to make sure they're doing okay and also to let her know we're still involved."

"Good idea," he said, stretching his back once he was out on the pavement. "I appreciate you bein' willing to put in a little extra time on your holiday."

"Not a problem," I said. If he wanted to act like this whole thing had been his idea all along, I wasn't about to stop him. I was still practically in shock that he was committing himself to the task at hand with exactly zero conversation about compensation. I mean, sure, Doug is probably more charitable than I'll ever admit in public, but this went against everything I knew about the man. Lucy Graves had scarred him in a way I didn't think was possible. With their paths intersecting on this case, his desire to cross the finish line before her was palpable. He was behaving in a manner most un-Doug-like. Loretta was going to have a cow when she found out her son had committed to a case without getting a contract signed or a retainer in hand. Oh, well. For once, it wasn't me in the doghouse with the woman.

I pulled up to a gas pump at the Speedeemart at Lymont Point and shifted the transmission into park. Not only was I low on gas, but I needed to fumble around to find Anne Marie's contact information so I could give her an update. I was still sifting through papers in my laptop bag when my phone rang, and her name appeared on the center console. I pressed the button on my steering wheel to answer the call.

"Hi, Anne Marie," I said. "I was just getting ready to call you."

"Please tell me it wasn't to tell me you're not takin' the case."

"No, not at all," I said. "In fact, Mr. Boggs seems uncharacteristically enthusiastic. We're putting our heads together tomorrow morning to come up with a plan of attack. I just wanted to make sure you and your sister are all right."

"They took Marlene to the hospital for observation," she said. "And I ain't gonna lie, I'm glad for that. I think that's where she's safest. She's worryin' me."

"How about you? Are you alright?"

She chuckled off-key. "Doin' my best."

"Are the police providing any sort of protection for your sister's property?"

"They said they'd send a car around every hour or so, and some fellas from the church were going over to secure the window, but I ain't stayin' there. I got my own little apartment, and I'll feel a whole lot safer there. Matter of fact, I'm gonna try to talk Marlene into staying with me over here once she gets out of the hospital, at least for a little while."

"Sounds like a good idea," I said. "Try and get some rest tonight, and we'll be in touch tomorrow, okay?"

"Okay, sure," she said. "And Mr. Morrow? Thanks for doing this. I can't tell you how much it means to us. I feel like you and Mr. Boggs are our only real hope."

She disconnected the call, and I killed the ignition, sliding out of the car to gas up. As soon as my feet hit the ground, I realized the wisdom of hitting the facilities before I started my journey back to Ironton. By the time I filled the tank, I was doing a less-than-subtle version of the pee-pee dance, and I hurried inside to take care of business. On the way back through, I snagged a 20-ounce Pepsi from the refrigerator case and a snack-size bag of Doritos. My stomach was reminding me I hadn't eaten since breakfast, and it wasn't happy with my lack of consideration. The bored teenaged girl entrusted with ringing sales and IDing minors was far more invested in the conversation she was having on her phone than tending to her line, which gave me a dangerous amount of time to eye the wall of cigarettes behind her. When it was finally my turn, I added a pack of Pall Mall Blue, king size, and a disposable lighter. Frankly, after the day I'd had, I was looking forward to a little decompressing once everyone got settled in for the night, even if it meant a little more of Craig's questionable alcoholic concoction. At least I'd have cigarettes of my own choosing.

Back at my car, I opened the driver's door and realized I had left my phone in the passenger seat where it was ringing. I slid behind the wheel and snagged it, hurrying to answer before the call went to voicemail. The screen read, "Mothra," and I smiled. Matt and I tagged Mom with the nickname ever since she indoctrinated us into the fandom of Godzilla back when we were teens.

"Hey, Mom," I said, putting the phone to my ear while I fumbled with my seatbelt. "Hang on just a sec." I started the car and waited for Bluetooth to grab the call. "There we go. What's up?"

"Hey, babe," she said. "I was just wondering if we were going to see you today. I know Melanie and Jasmine are doing the Black Friday thing, and I've been halfway expecting you all day. It's getting close to seven, and we were thinking about ordering pizza from Giovanni's. I wondered if we should order enough for you, too."

Giovanni's. My stomach gurgled, making sure I was paying attention, but I hesitated. I felt like a complete coward, but I just couldn't face everyone tonight, putting on a happy face and pretending everything was all right. Besides, Melanie would be bringing Gino's pizza home with her in a little while.

"Um, no, you go ahead," I said. "Doug and I actually picked up a case this afternoon, and it's kept me busy all day. It's likely to spill into tomorrow pretty heavily, too."

She was silent for a moment. "Are you okay? Is there anything you want to talk about? You know I'm—"

I forced a laugh and hoped it didn't sound too phony. "I'm fine, Mom."

"We *will* see you before you head back, won't we?"

"Yes, Mom. I promise."

She wasn't happy, but she let it go. "Well, all right, then. I'll talk to you soon."

I disconnected and took a quick moment to hang my head and feel like shit. I didn't like being less than honest with my mom. It didn't come naturally. When I opened my eyes, I noticed I had a missed text from my brother, sent earlier in the afternoon when Doug and I had been otherwise occupied. I opened it, and it read:

Of all the times to flake out, brother! You MISSED it! I took Dad down TWO out of THREE games today! I AM THE NEW BOWLING MASTER OF THE MORROW UNIVERSE!!! Mwa-ha-ha-ha!

Appended to his text were two pictures. The first was of the final scores projected from the monitor mounted above the lane. Matt had outpaced Dad by more than thirty pins in both games, and he had only lost the third by a handful. The second was a selfie of my brother looking smug and superior, smiling big with his arm slung around our father's drooping shoulders. Dad looked tolerant but defeated, his good sportsmanship presenting in more of a wince than a smile.

I dimmed the screen and put the phone face down in the passenger seat. The image had caught me by surprise, breaking a little more of my heart.

CHAPTER FOURTEEN

Craig nodded to me from his chair on the back porch as I climbed out of my SUV. "You came back!" he called out, tipping a Heineken to me and grinning. "I would have lost money."

I laughed, going to the backseat to retrieve some items I had picked up from Kroger in Portsmouth before heading back—namely Pepsi and Canadian Mist. I figured I might as well have what I wanted to drink, too. "You can't get rid of me that easily."

"Good," he said, tipping his beer back for a long swallow. "I like you better than most of Melanie's other fellas. Can I get you something to eat? I'm not much of a cook, but I could probably fry up a burger or slap together some cold cuts."

I shook my head as I settled into the chair beside him. "Thanks, but I'm good. Melanie's bringing some pizza back when they get here, which I'm guessing should be within the hour."

I omitted the part where I went back down to Second Street while I was in Portsmouth to treat myself to a couple of those famous Dari-Creme footers I had been denied the previous evening. My stomach wasn't about to let me wait until Melanie got back to the house with pizza. I had been so hungry I was starting to get a headache.

As I stood in line with a handful of others underneath the rainbow-hued fluorescent lights, I couldn't help but be hyperaware of my surroundings.

Despite the safety in numbers, I felt a little too exposed standing streetside within blocks of where I had essentially been assaulted just the previous evening. I kept expecting to see a masked face or two lurking amongst the smallish crowd, all of whom were simply there waiting for their hot dogs and frozen desserts. Frankly, it shook me up more than I wanted to admit, and I was more than a little relieved to take my dinner back to the safety of my vehicle and lock myself inside where I proceeded to wolf down those dogs like I hadn't eaten in days. *So* good…

Looking back toward Craig's garage, I noticed one of the previously occupied bays was now empty. "Looks like you had a productive day."

He laughed. "Depends on your definition of productive. I only had the one car to finish up this morning, so I've spent most of the day just lazing around. I might have even napped there for a few. Rare is the day I get the whole house to myself. How 'bout you? I heard Molly pretty much plotted your day for you."

"You heard right," I said as he opened his mini-fridge, and I slid a few of my Pepsis into some available space in the door. "Thanks. I came a little better prepared tonight." I slid the bottle of whiskey out of its paper bag along with some disposable shot glasses and set them on top of the fridge.

His laugh deepened. "Yeah, you're not even close to the first man Molly's driven to drink. I don't know how Gordon puts up with her."

"I had no *idea* she was like this," I said. "My only previous exposure to her came secondhand through Melanie when she was keeping us up to date on a patient's condition in the ICU back when I was trying to figure out what happened to Ryan."

He sucked in a breath through his teeth. "I keep forgetting Ryan was your buddy. I wasn't trying to say anything about him with what I said earlier, I was just—"

I waved his concerns away. "Think nothing of it. I couldn't blame you even if you did have some choice words about him. He wasn't exactly the best husband to Melanie. I'm not sure he was the type to ever settle down."

"I liked him well enough," said Craig. "He was a little too much of a people pleaser for me, but he had a damn good sense of humor. We used to occasionally go out and grab a couple of beers over in Ashland, maybe shoot a few games of pool. Always flirting with the waitresses and talking shit about his mad sharpshooter skills that frankly got a whole lot less mad the more he drank. I had to watch myself when I was hanging out with him. We had a way of landing ourselves in some hot water from time to time."

I smiled, pouring myself a shot before twisting the cap from one of my Pepsis. I knew exactly what Craig meant. I had plenty of my own adventures with Ryan to draw upon.

Thumping music and a muffler meant to be heard signified the approach of a car from the north, long before its headlights pierced the night sky, shining through the trees as it rounded the curve and slowed near the mouth of the driveway. It was the orange Challenger from the previous morning, and once again, it only pulled in far enough to be barely off the road. The music's volume cut off while the throaty exhaust continued to rumble. The passenger window slid down, and waves of smoke rolled out from the interior. Despite our distance, the sweet, cloying aroma of marijuana was practically a full-frontal assault. I watched Chip clumsily hook an arm through the opening and onto the roof, followed by his shoulders, head, and finally his bony little ass, which perched precariously on the edge of the window before he toppled backwards, loudly guffawing until his descent was cut short in a sea of gravel. His buddies were in hysterics, their laughter intensifying when Chip cried out from gravity's painful surprise. They pointed with fingers and phones, capturing what they could in videos and stills. For all I knew, they might be posting all this nonsense to social media to try and grab their fifteen minutes of fame in a world that was increasingly indiscriminate.

I started to get to my feet to give him an assist, but Craig laid a hand on my arm.

"Let him go," he advised. "He ain't hurt so bad he can't pick himself up."

I allowed myself another shot while I watched Chip awkwardly struggle to his feet, using the side of the car for support until his friends decided it would be funnier if they pulled forward—just enough to cost him his balance, and he fell hard against the passenger door, his face bouncing off the frame with a sickening *thunk*. Somehow, they kept from running him over as they pulled back onto the road and peeled away, barking tires laying a path on the asphalt while the tail end of the car struggled to hold the road. Chip was back on his knees already, flipping twin birds to his buddies who were long gone.

I raised an eyebrow, but Craig just shook his head, taking another sip from his beer. "This shitshow requires no audience participation."

Well, alright, then.

After several false starts, Chip found his way back to his feet, and when he turned, the motion-detected light by the garage activated, showing us the brand-new welt blossoming across his left cheek, the perfect accessory to the damage I'd inflicted on his nose Wednesday evening. He stumbled across the drive toward us, giggling about something and feeling not even a hint of pain. That would come later. He fanned his fingers out and waved at his brother-in-law.

"Hey, there, Craig," he slurred. "Sorry 'bout all that—"

He turned to indicate the driveway and nearly lost his balance. I couldn't help myself. I leapt to my feet and grabbed an arm, steadying him. His head bobbled loosely on his neck, and he turned toward me. "Hey, thanks, I 'preciate your—"

His eyes swam briefly into focus, and he stopped on a dime.

"You. What are *you* still doing here?" His goofy smile had morphed into a sneer, and it might have been intimidating if his eyes were anything more than the slits they were. He jerked his arm from my grasp and staggered again before grabbing one of the posts supporting the roof and hugging it like his life depended on it.

"He's being a far better houseguest than you, *Junior*," said Craig, setting his beer aside and standing.

"Pffft…don't call me that," he said. "I fucking *hate* that—"

"Yeah, yeah, come on," said Craig, taking hold of one of Chip's arms and guiding him toward the door. He paused just outside of it, turning to me. "Give me just a second here. I want to see that this idiot makes it safely to bed. I can't afford any more of his property damage."

I had been considering another shot of whiskey, but it suddenly lost all appeal. I pushed the shot glass away and nodded as Craig led Chip inside. After several moments and several less than graceful noises, Craig came back through the door still shaking his head.

"Boy can't hold his liquor for shit," he said, dropping back into his chair. "I'm really sorry about that."

"It's not your apology to make. He doesn't seem to like me very much, though," I said. "Of course, busting him in the nose probably wasn't the best way for me to introduce myself."

Craig laughed. "It certainly didn't help. But I think you were going to have a rough go of it anyway with that one." He hitched a thumb back towards the house. "He knows you and Ryan were good friends once upon a time, and that's an automatic strike against you. He never did like your buddy very well. They ran in close enough to the same circles that Chip had a pretty good idea of exactly how faithful Ryan was to Melanie. He even lit him up real good one night right here in front of where we sit. Thought I was going to have to call the police to bust 'em up, it was so bad. It was right around the time Mel and Ryan were separating. Ryan showed up here in not much better shape than Chip is tonight, demanding to see Melanie, begging her not to take their daughter away from him. With Chip being the only boy from that brood, he's always tried to be the big brother, you know? The protector."

Still unsure of the extent of Craig's knowledge about the abuse Melanie and her siblings had endured, I simply nodded. It made a certain sort of sense, though. If Chip couldn't protect his sisters from their father at home, he could do his best to run interference with anyone from the outside world.

"He doesn't seem to have it in for you," I noted.

"I never gave him any reason to. Me and Cheryl have always been steady, and we've given him a place to crash whenever he needs it. Honest to God, he's a good kid when he's not like this. He knows almost as much about fixing cars as I do, and he's always a big help in the garage whenever he's on leave."

Lights pierced the darkness from the south side of the road, and Cheryl's minivan nosed into the gravel. Craig and I were both on our feet in an instant, but not before Cheryl lowered the driver's side window.

"*Aaat, aaat, a-a-a-t!*" she called, ticking a warning forefinger at us like a metronome. Her call reminded me of my own when warning Dexter off the counter or against sharpening his claws where he shouldn't. "Much as I love you, darlin', I'm gonna need you to stay the hell away from me, and that goes for you too, Dwayne. In fact, we're gonna need you fellas to get yourselves indoors, please, and right now. We've got an entire van to unload over to Maggie's, and Santa's Little Helpers are *tired*. We have shopped until we dropped, then picked ourselves back up to shop a little more, and we've got a zero-tolerance policy for peepers."

Melanie leaned across her sister, smiling sweetly before blowing me a kiss. "Hey, fella! You glad to see me?"

184

"Depends," I said, with an ornery grin. "Did you remember the pizza?"

Her smile turned to a scowl as she turned to her sister. "Honestly, he's not an asshole *all* the time."

"Get inside!" barked Cheryl, pointing toward the house, and we threw our hands up in surrender, collecting our assorted beverages from the top of the mini fridge before heading inside.

........●⊝⊖●........

We sat in a circle on the floor in the living room, much as we had our first evening together. Cheryl popped the pizza onto a baking sheet and topped its temperature off before sliding it back into its box to bring it and some paper plates in. Betsy was sacked out on one of the couches but lifted her nose at the scent of food. The fireplace crackled softly in the background, and I appreciated it a bit more this time around, as temperatures had dropped since the sun had set. Episodes of *Ridiculousness* played soundlessly on the television as we ate pizza, sipped adult beverages, and caught up with each other's days.

"Are the girls crashing over at Maggie's again?" I asked. I kept expecting a small invasion through the back door and didn't want to get too comfortable until everyone was settled in for the evening.

Melanie slipped an arm though mine. "Nope. They're all staying at Katie's tonight," she said. "There's some new movie out that they're dying to see—I can't think of the name, but Cheryl and I don't really want to suffer through it."

"Not so appealing?" I asked, snagging another piece of pizza from the side with onion. I had nearly forgotten how good Gino's was.

"It's based on one of those video games Jaz is always playing with Billy and Scott, and I guess Brady took the guys to see it this afternoon. Jasmine's got to get up to speed before one of them accidentally spoils something.

It's of the utmost urgency." Melanie rolled her eyes and leaned forward to snag the glass of fruity concoction Cheryl offered her.

"Katie's got her own place?" I asked, more than a bit surprised. From what little I had seen, she came across as somewhat bohemian. I guess I had assumed she was crashing at Maggie's until she was forced to face some adult responsibility.

"Yeah, she's got a little apartment over in Flatwoods," said Melanie, sampling her drink. "And before you say anything, I *know*. Katie can get a little wild sometimes, but Maggie's there, so it's not much different than them being over in the trailer. They're also taking our girls to do a little bit of Christmas shopping for their mothers which they couldn't do while we were all together, and far be it from me to stop such a thoughtful gesture." She and Cheryl clinked their glasses together.

Cheryl shifted her attention to me. "Oh, and hey—let me apologize myself for siccing that woman on you this morning. I wish I had all that to do over. She just caught me off guard, and—"

"Stop it," I said, cutting her short with a smile. "I feel badly for her too. If we're gonna be upset with anyone, let's put our collective displeasure where it belongs and have a little sit-down with your sister, Molly. The surprises just keep coming with that one, don't they?"

"*O-o-o-h*, don't you worry," said Cheryl, pausing to take a drink. "There *will* be *words*."

Melanie shook her head. "I still can't believe she thought it was alright to have Daddy over. I mean, I know she doesn't believe us, and that's bad enough. But right in the middle of Thanksgiving? What did she really think was going to happen? I don't care if the old man *is*—"

Her lips clamped together and so did her eyes, refusing to finish the thought. Some things should just never be said aloud, no matter who was involved.

"Anyway," Melanie continued. "I told the girls to be back before dinner so we could do whatever you wanted to do tomorrow night. We could go back out to your folks, or—"

"Maybe visit Sarah?" I snuck in, and she stiffened, immediately trying to pull her arm from mine, but I held on. "Sorry. I thought I'd try when Jasmine wasn't here to give you her two cents. We'll talk about it whenever you're ready."

Slowly, she relaxed. "Thank you."

Cheryl reached out and snagged a piece of pizza en route to Craig's open mouth. "What did *you* do with yourself all day, you big goon?" she asked her startled husband, taking a sizable bite as he looked helplessly on.

"Fixed up Toby's brakes like I said I was going to, then spent the rest of the day looking for a new wife online," he said, pulling her closer so he could nibble at her neck before seizing what was left of his pizza while she squealed. Then they started doing that food sharing/kissing mashup that always signified true love back in high school, and I had to look away. It was gross then, it's still gross now.

"Tell me about your day," said Melanie, squeezing my hand. "Has Doug found a way to let poor Ms. Brown down yet?"

"Quite the opposite," I said. "In fact, we're meeting tomorrow morning to discuss strategy."

"*Really?*" Melanie sounded as surprised as I felt.

"Really. I hope I'm not messing up anything you had planned for tomorrow."

She shook her head. "Not at all. I was going to help Cheryl drag the Christmas stuff out and get it staged so we could decorate the tree as a family once everyone gets back here tomorrow night. So, what is it about this case that is different than every other interesting case he's turned away without a giving it a second thought?"

"Officer Lucy Graves," I said, smiling as the implication registered with Melanie. "She's a deputy with the Lawrence County Sheriff's Department, and apparently, she and Mr. Boggs have a little bit of shared history."

"Tell me more."

And so, I did.

I filled her in on Doug and Lucy's academy past, and moved on to what we knew about the case so far, which frankly wasn't a whole lot. I explained that Tina's mother was practically catatonic and had offered nothing substantive, while Anne Marie had provided us a list of the terrible teens with whom Tina had been associating. When I got to the part where we encountered someone trying to break into Tina McAlister's room, Melanie held up her hands to stop me.

"Wait a minute. You're telling me someone actually tried to break into the house while all of you were *inside?* That's nuts! Were they armed?"

"I can't really be sure, but I don't think so. I didn't get a really good look because the sun was in my eyes, but I got the impression they were as startled as I was when the plywood fell away. They took off like they were running for their life."

Her mind was working as she shook her head. "Why was their plywood on the window, anyway? Had someone already broken in?"

"I don't know," I said.

"Why not? Didn't you ask?"

"Didn't really get the chance. We were already taking a liberty we shouldn't have by poking around in Tina's bedroom. The police hadn't been through her room yet, and it seemed like a good opportunity to have a look before anything got bagged and taken away as evidence. We were careful not to leave fingerprints until the attempted break-in, and I—well, I guess I got a little careless with what I was touching. I really felt like we needed to involve the police at this point before we got accused of compromising any more evidence than we already had."

There was a creak from the top of the stairs as Chip cautiously began his descent to the first floor, clinging to the banister for balance. His eyes were barely open as he peered over the handrail, leaning into the living room with his nose working like a hound dog's. "Izzat pizza I smell?" he slurred.

"Sure is," said Melanie, plating up a piece and turning toward her brother. "Come on down and grab a piece, Bub."

He managed the rest of the stairs without incident and cut a wide path around me to retrieve the plate Melanie offered.

"Hey, hang on a minute there," she said, getting to her feet to have a closer look at Chip's newest bruises. "What happened to your face, Bub?"

He snorted. "Your *boy*-friend punched me in the nose."

"Not that, *this*," she said, carefully touching his cheek as he winced and pulled away. "Did you get into a fight?"

Craig laughed. "Only with the driveway, Mel. He faceplanted getting out of his buddy's car."

She leaned in for a closer look while Chip squirmed. *"Bub!* I certainly hope your friends weren't as drunk as you are. I'll be worried sick if I suspect y'all are out there driving in this condition."

He pulled away again, nearly losing his plate of pizza. "It's nothin'," he said, wobbling off toward the kitchen. He mumbled some other mishmash that might have included 'designated driver,' but who could say for certain?

Melanie took her seat beside me on the floor and leaned forward, lowering her voice. "Is it just me, or is Chip drinking more than usual?"

Cheryl shrugged. "Maybe a little. But he's on leave. He always cuts loose a little more when he's on leave."

The look on Craig's face more than suggested he didn't agree with his wife's analysis, but I wasn't about to weigh in. I still felt bad about the misunderstanding that led me to punch the boy in the nose. It was readily apparent that all was *not* forgiven, at least not yet.

"I'm really surprised that he and Jenny are having issues," said Melanie, still keeping her voice low so her brother wouldn't overhear. Based on the clatter from the kitchen, I doubted he was paying attention. He was currently rummaging through the cupboard, and I was braced for the sound of something breaking. "She's usually stuck to him like glue when he's home. What do you suppose happened?"

"They're young. Who knows?" Cheryl dismissed the question with a wave of her hand that also toppled her drink. "Well, shit! And now I've ruined our be-*yoot*-iful carpet!" She started to get to her feet, but I waved her back down as I stood.

"I've got it," I said. "I needed another Pepsi anyway."

I hustled back to the kitchen where Chip was filling a glass with water at the sink. It filled to overflowing before he turned the water off, and he hovered in place, taking long sips with his eyes closed. The paper plate he had carried in was face down on the floor, the pizza squashed underneath his bare right foot. I snagged a Pepsi out of the refrigerator and scanned the room for paper towels, spotting a countertop spindle on the other side of Chip.

"Excuse me," I muttered as I reached around him to snag the entire roll. He was muttering to himself under his breath, and he leaned in to refill his glass. As his right hand pushed the faucet handle up and to the right, I couldn't help but notice his knuckles were horribly swollen and bruised. He hadn't broken his fall from the car with his hands, so what in the hell had happened?

I was suddenly aware of his eyes locked on me, watching me watch him, and that's when I *knew*.

"You little piece of *shit*," I hissed, grabbing his arm, and roughly turned him to face me. White-hot anger swept over me.

And for the second time in as many days, I hauled off and clocked my girlfriend's brother square in the middle of his stupid face, snapping his

190

head backward as blood sprayed from his nose. He dropped his glass as he went down, and it shattered in the sink.

This time, I knocked him out cold.

CHAPTER FIFTEEN

I was on top of Chip, spewing a venomous stream of inventive pejoratives while nonsensically trying to revive him by lifting his shoulders and slamming his head back against the kitchen linoleum. I was only vaguely aware of protests gaining in volume as Melanie and Cheryl frantically attempted to pull me off of their brother only to be shaken away by the lunatic I had temporarily become. It wasn't until Craig clamped down on the back of my neck and hoisted me up by the seat of my pants that I could actually recognize the fear and panic I was causing for both Melanie and her sister. It was like a shot of cold water to the face, and I turned away, cheeks burning. I don't know if I've ever been so angry. It was frightening. The loudest thing in the room was my own heartbeat hammering away in my ear. I was surprised to discover my hot face was damp with angry tears, and I hurriedly wiped them away, embarrassed.

"What the *fuck*, Dwayne?" demanded Melanie, cradling her brother's head in her lap, her own tears flowing. She looked at me as if seeing me for the first time, and it wasn't a good thing.

Cheryl was busy trying to staunch the flow of blood from her little brother's nose with a damp kitchen towel that would never come clean. If I hadn't broken the bastard's nose on Wednesday night, I'm pretty sure I had succeeded this time. Craig remained on standby, keeping a careful eye on me, ready to leap back into action should the need arise, but my raw outrage had already peaked and was beginning to subside. I leaned my back against the wall and stared at the ceiling, taking deep breaths, exhaling slowly, forcing myself to calm down. As the sound of my heartbeat stopped pounding in my ears, I slowly became aware of the sisters' concerned, tearful voices, coaxing their brother back to consciousness. He was coming around, and they hurriedly propped him up when he started making noises like he might get sick.

"Are you okay, Bub?" Melanie asked soothingly while shooting me a dark look. "Can you say something to me? Anything at all?"

He looked around, and his confusion was evident.

"Over here, Bub," said Cheryl, snapping her fingers in front of his face. "How many fingers am I holding up?" She made a V of her forefinger and middle finger.

"Four," he slurred, and the sisters exchanged worried glances. "Two held up and two curled under. There's a thumb somewheres in there, too."

That brought some nervous laughter and another angry glare for me from Melanie.

Cheryl pointed her forefinger toward the ceiling directly in front of Chip's nose. "Now, don't turn your head, just follow my finger with your eyes."

"What are you doing?" asked Melanie.

"Seeing if he has a concussion." Cheryl slid her finger slowly to the left, and then to the right.

"How will you know if he's got one?"

Cheryl paused to scowl at her sister. "I don't know. It's what they do on *Grey's Anatomy*."

"Isn't this more of a Molly thing?"

Chip groaned at the mention of his sister's name. "Oh, God, not *Molly*. I'd rather die of internal bleeding."

There was more nervous laughter as they shifted Chip into a seated position with his back against the cabinets below the sink.

"What happened?" Melanie asked, and she was directing this at both of us.

"Tell them," I said gruffly, boring holes through Chip with narrowed and unblinking eyes. I was back under control, but I was still plenty hot. He couldn't hold my gaze and looked away, chewing on his bottom lip. He had tucked his hand with the bruised knuckles underneath his leg, as if I might forget what they signified.

"Tell us *what?*" asked Melanie, nearing the end of her patience. Her body language indicated the onus of responsibility was on me, and at this point, I thought it was probably wisest to get it out there before the little shit-heel made up some stupid lie and set me off again.

"Ask the ole *Chipper* what he was up to last night—oh, maybe a little after seven," I said, continuing to stare while he squirmed. "Does that sound about right to you, *Bub?*"

He continued to chew his lip, offering nothing.

"What is he talking about, Chip?" Melanie asked, cupping her hand under his chin, and easing his face toward hers. He started to shake his head, so I jumped back in.

"Is that the sort of fun you and your buddies have on a regular basis?" I asked. "What the fuck is *wrong* with you, man?"

Melanie put her hands to the sides of her head, shaking it. "Would you please speak *English?* None of this is making *any* sense—"

"Your brother and his buddies tried to pitch me over the edge the Grant Bridge last night."

She stared at me in disbelief, an uncertain laugh falling from her lips. "What?"

"They were dressed in black from head to toe. They even wore masks. *Tell her.*"

I took a threatening step toward him, and as he recoiled, Melanie and Cheryl closed ranks over top of him. Craig snagged my arm in a vice-like grip before I could get any closer.

"All right!" Chip cried, pulling his knees up to his chest. "We did."

Melanie's eyes went from me to her brother, stunned. "I don't understand. Why would you—"

"He ain't no good for you, Mel," Chip said. "Just *look* at him. And Ryan's *best friend*, I mean geez—how long before he's steppin' out on you, too?"

"You don't know what you're talking about, Chip," Melanie protested. "You don't even *know* Dwayne."

"It's kinda hard to do when the motherfucker keeps punchin' me in the face," he countered petulantly. "We were just puttin' a scare into that clown. It's not like we were *really* gonna go through with it."

"That's sure not how it felt from where I dangled," I said. "You know, I didn't file a police report, but it's not too late to change my mind about that—"

"Yeah, and I could file assault charges against you. Look at my face. Who you think they're gonna believe?"

"Fellas!" Melanie stood, massaging her temples. "Can we just stop this? *Please?"*

I was determined to win our current visual deadlock, and just as I thought my eyes would dehydrate and collapse, Chip finally looked away.

Cheryl helped him to his feet, reluctant to move the ruined kitchen towel too far out of reach. "Your nose really looks bad, Bub. I should probably run you into the ER and get you checked out."

He shook his head, gently nudging his sister away. "I just wanna go to bed," he said.

Melanie stepped around to his other side, placing herself between me and Chip. "We're not done talking about this," she said.

"Fine," he acknowledged.

"Can you make it upstairs alright?"

He scoffed. "Not a problem. My buzz is pretty much shot to hell at this point."

Cheryl handed him the kitchen towel, and he pressed it to his nose as he passed through, making his escape while the getting was good. Melanie continued to use her body as a shield to protect her little brother in a way that made me ashamed of myself, despite my utter sense of righteousness in the matter. I crossed to the sink and started picking the pieces of broken glass out of the basin.

"C'mon, babe," Craig said softly to his wife. "Let's give these two some space."

Cheryl nodded, struggling to contain what promised to be a scathing opinion before settling on one last withering glare in my direction. She allowed her husband to lead her back through the living room and upstairs to their bedroom. Somehow, I was getting the distinct feeling *I* was the one in trouble, and I wasn't exactly sure how that had happened.

I could feel Melanie's eyes on my back as I gathered the last of the broken glass into a paper towel and dropped it into the wastebasket beside the fridge. When I turned to look at her, she was regarding me coolly, hugging herself with crossed arms.

"Why is this the first I'm hearing about this?" she asked, her tone cool and controlled.

"I-I-I—" I was already stammering, trying to remember why it had seemed like a good idea at the time. I cleared my throat and collected myself a little better before making another attempt. "I wasn't really hurt. Doug was nearby and helped run them off before anything got too out of hand. At the time, I didn't know who it was. I thought it was over. I didn't see any point in getting anyone else upset."

She slowly began to nod, as my unease grew. "So, you're saying if you *hadn't* figured out that it was my brother and his pals, I would have *never* heard about it. Sound about right?"

I started toward her. *"Mel, I—"*

"God*damn* it, Dwayne!" Her eyes were ablaze as she shoved me away—hard. "If we're going to be together, you don't get to just pick and choose what you share with me. I got enough of that bullshit from Ryan, and you should know better than that."

"I *do*, Mel, I just thought—"

"No." She held up a hand, cutting me short. "You don't get to filter based on what you think I can handle. I know I've cut you some slack on whatever went down in West Virginia, but this is beginning to feel like a pattern here. This thing we've got—" She motioned back and forth between us. "—it's never gonna work if it's built on a foundation of secrets."

I tried again to reach out to her, but again she pulled away. I put my hands on my hips and sighed, ditching excuses, and going for the only tool I had left in my box. "I'm sorry, sweetheart. I really am. I didn't think this thing through. From now on, I promise—"

"Aaah!" she protested, shielding her ears. "The only thing worse than secrets is a pile of broken promises. I need a little time to myself to think. You'd be smart to do the same."

I was at a bit of a loss. "Are you saying—do you want me to go? I, uh, I'd need to call an Uber or something. I've had a little more to drink than I—"

"I didn't mean you should go," she said, crossing into the living room to snag an ancient, multi-colored throw from an overstuffed recliner tucked away in the corner. She tossed it onto one of the two couches. From the loveseat, she pried a thin pillow from underneath Cheryl's sleeping basset hound and tossed it to me. "Goodnight."

197

I watched helplessly as she breezed past me and continued down the hall, closing herself into the bedroom we had shared the previous two nights. I tossed the pillow onto the couch and took the remnants from our living room campout into the kitchen, putting the pizza box into the fridge and throwing away the paper plates we'd left behind. I soaked one end of a dishrag in warm water, wringing it out before using its dry end to absorb what I could of the wine that Cheryl had spilled, wishing I hadn't been so quick to volunteer the first time. After scrubbing the spot to the best of my ability and returning the dishrag to the sink, I turned off all the lights and the silent television, leaving only the dwindling firelight for illumination. Fully clothed, I set the alarm on my cell phone for 8:30AM before plugging it into its charger and crawling underneath the crocheted throw, doubling the distinctly canine-scented pillow before tucking it underneath my head.

"Goodnight, Betsy," I said quietly to the dog on the loveseat. She regarded me casually before yawning wide and settling back into sleep, blowing me a staggeringly fragrant kiss from her backside as a parting shot.

···••••◦◎◦•••••···

"What in the hell are you wearing?" asked Doug, giving me a serious once-over.

He approached my table inside the McDonalds in Flatwood where we had agreed to meet at nine-thirty. He carried a pile of breakfast burritos on a tray along with another strawberry shake.

I had been there since shortly before eight, and the evidence was piling up before me by way of two empty breakfast sandwich wrappers and three empty coffee cups, a fourth warming my hands. Sleeping on the couch in Cheryl's living room had proven to be nearly impossible, especially once Betsy decided she could use my backside as a replacement for the pillow I had stolen from her. I gave up around dawn. Other than the dog, no one else stirred as I prowled the first floor, wishing it were later than it was. Fearing I might disturb someone whose opinion of me had already clearly been lessened the previous evening, I bypassed the shower and wore the crumpled khakis and t-shirt I had slept in. The duffel with my clean clothes was in the room with Melanie, and I didn't want to wake her. I didn't want to wake anyone. In fact, I had snuck out of the house like a cowardly teenager.

"Never mind all that," I told Doug, waving him into the seat across from me. "Have you got any sort of game plan?" It was a ridiculous question. Doug rarely had a game plan that I thought was better than my own. But with as little sleep as I had gotten, I had done no planning whatsoever, so I was going to have to follow his lead.

"Well, actually, yeah, but you're kinda killin' it here with all this." As he once again indicated my sorry appearance, I focused on the too-tight number he had chosen. A mud brown sportscoat with tan patches at the elbows strained to cover a button-down white dress shirt with what appeared to be a boy's clip-on maroon-and-black striped tie digging into the flesh of his portly neck. The shirt strained at every buttonhole, and I expected those buttons to become airborne projectiles at any moment. His pants were dark brown corduroy, and he completed the ensemble with shiny plastic black dress shoes that couldn't have cost more than ten dollars at Walmart. For Doug Boggs, this was "black tie."

"What did you have in mind?" I asked, sipping on the tepid remains of my coffee.

Doug paused long enough to unwrap a breakfast burrito and drizzle it with hot picante. "Since our goal is to speak to as many of those kids as we can find whose names Ms. Brown provided to us, I got to thinkin' about the best way to go about doin' that. Do you remember what they all have in common?"

He shoved half a burrito into his mouth and ejected a stream of picante onto the table from its other end when he bit down. I just stared at him.

"The church!" he exclaimed, carefully mopping up his spillage before he managed to lean into it. "New Life Apostolic. I looked them up on the Google and saw they're having special Thanksgiving services this morning at ten. I thought we might be able to catch a bunch of 'em in one place if we swung by there and just sort of blended in, but—" For the third time in less than five minutes, he passed withering judgment on my appearance without so much as a word. His expression was loud and clear.

I sighed and pushed myself up from my seat. "Fine," I said. "I'll see if there's anything I can do to make myself more presentable."

He nodded, his mouth already full of the other half of his burrito. "At least see what you can do about this," he said, indicating a space near the top of my head. "Looks like a damn fright wig."

I used the camera in my phone to see what he meant and flinched, suddenly self-conscious. I had no idea how bad I looked and was instantly aware of all the lingering looks from passersby that had previously gone undetected.

"Oh, and one more thing," said Doug, fishing deep into his trouser pocket. His hand emerged with a lint-covered pack of Certs, and he thumbed two of them out onto the table. "Take these. You'll need them. I can smell your breath clear across the table, and it smells just like a dog's ass."

···•••●◎☉●•••···

We traveled together in my car, using GPS to find New Life Apostolic, although it would have been impossible to miss once we hit KY 207. It wasn't so much a church as a complex fronted by an enormous parking lot that seemed more appropriate for a hospital or a Walmart Supercenter, and all of the good parking spots were already taken. The centerpiece of the complex was its massive cathedral, at the back of the inclined lot and sitting high above the road below as if in judgment of those who dare pass before it. A ginormous crucifix depicting Jesus's final sacrifice in frightening detail was centered on a tall spire directly above the main entrance, soberingly stark in its imagery against pristine white siding.

As we entered the parking lot, it was impossible to see from our vantage point exactly how far back the main building ran, but it was surrounded by clusters of satellite buildings whose purposes were identified by directional signage in the lot. To the right were dormitories and Christian academy classrooms, and to the left was an event center and addiction recovery services. Families dressed in their Sunday finest drifted towards double doors that were held open by a pair of ushers whose smiles never faltered as they greeted parishioners, exchanging pleasantries and keeping the line moving.

I finally found an empty space in the extreme outer edges of the lot and parked, pausing to give my hair one last look in the rearview mirror. I had developed a stubborn cowlick in the night, and while I had dampened it in the Mickey D's restroom, it was attempting to rise like a phoenix from the ashes. I raked my fingers through it and sighed as that only seemed to awaken it more. This was as good as it was going to get. Doug and I ambled toward the entrance behind the last of the morning stragglers, ascending the stairs just as the church bells rang, signifying service would be beginning shortly.

Upon entering, we had our choice of stairs on either side, leading to some sort of balcony seating, and I wondered just how big this fellowship was. Straight ahead was where the bulk of the congregation appeared to be, so I guided us in that direction. While I'm sure it was only paranoia, it felt like all eyes were upon us as we entered the packed cathedral. Four sections of pews filled the room, countless rows deep, and they seemed filled to capacity. I nodded and smiled at those closest who regarded us with open curiosity and, in some cases, disdain at my apparent inability to dress appropriately for this morning's service. Scanning the room, I was relieved to find several other men who wore jeans and casual shirts, although no other ensemble quite as wrinkled as mine. The wall to our left featured four spectacular stained-glass windows, equidistant from one another and stretching nearly to the cathedral's high ceiling. They were impressively resplendent in the morning sunlight.

We found an empty spot at the end of the last pew on the right, and we squeezed into it as quickly as we could. The organist's music was drawing to a close, and the air was filled with the susurrating noise of a crowd that had not yet been called to attention. That ended abruptly with a rapid burst of chords announcing the arrival of Reverend Donald Keaton at the pulpit, adorned in a crimson robe with gold trim and smiling benevolently to his mighty flock below. He had a full head of steely gray hair, and its style brought Elvis Presley to mind, but not comically so. His pearly whites were an orthodontist's dream. We were so far away from what I can only call the stage, I would have needed opera glasses to actually see the man's face if it hadn't been for the dual high-definition monitors mounted high along each side of the stage. I could practically see his individual pores with their assistance. I scanned the elaborate racks of lighting and other equipment that occupied the area—was that a smoke machine off to the right of the stage? I'm not particularly good at math in my head, but even with conservative round numbers, the amount of money spent on technology alone was enormous. By comparison, when I was a child, the tiny little Methodist church to which I had occasionally been dragged by my Aunt Eunice had failed to raise enough money in a fundraiser to buy a small television and VCR for the Sunday School classes to share—I couldn't begin to imagine what was funding all this.

Reverend Keaton began to gently hush the crowd, the smile never completely leaving his face. "My goodness, what a crowd!" he enthused. "I'm so thankful that you've all decided to share your Saturday morning with me and with each other, and that seems appropriate, doesn't it? I'm thankful. *Thankful.*"

He paused, nodding and smiling, while the congregation sent audible sound bites of approval.

"Let us pray," he said, lowering his head and triggering the same with his abiding flock.

His words swam out of focus for me as I surveyed the room as best I could with my head slightly bowed and one eye open, scoping the human sea for a collection of teenagers that might fit the list provided by Anne Marie Brown. It was fairly easy to eliminate large swaths of possibilities based on teased silver hair and balding heads alone. Families tended to sit together, which also helped speed up my search. I spotted Anne Marie, herself, sitting near the front of the section to our left, her head bowed dutifully and nodding in agreement to whatever benediction the pastor was offering. Just over Anne Marie's left shoulder, Melanie's sister, Molly, sat ramrod straight with only her chestnut helmet of Aqua Net fixated hair tipped forward. Gordon sat beside her, somehow looking shrunken and completely kowtowed even from the rear. They were seated front and center where the good reverend couldn't help but see them. Their goth twins sat beside their father, and while the parents' heads were bowed, the twins were noncompliant, openly gawking at the crowd around them. I followed one of their roving gazes until it settled on a group of kids near the front at the far right.

Three boys and one girl, and they weren't particularly interested in the ongoing prayer either, whispering back and forth to one another conspiratorially just low enough to keep from drawing attention to themselves. I consulted the series of texts Anne Marie had sent me and while the count was off by one, it was close enough. If this wasn't the group of kids we were looking for, surely they would be able to point me in the right direction.

As if on cue, one of the boys rose from the pew, kneeling in to whisper something to one of the other boys. Tall, blond and wiry, he slipped out of the row and headed for the closest of three doors along the right wall, leading out into the vestibule.

I nudged Doug gently and leaned closer. "I think I might have a lead. Stay put."

A stern-faced octogenarian seated directly in front of me pivoted her head with the disconcerting speed of Linda Blair. *"Shhhh,"* she commanded, following up with a head-to-toe scan that suggested revulsion. I pressed my lips together and simulated a key in a lock before holding my hands up in surrender. She turned back to the prayer-in-progress and bowed her head.

I slid out of the pew and made for the door closest to where we sat. Once out in the vestibule, I spotted the young man rounding a corner to his left at the far end of the hall.

"May I help you?"

I jumped, startled to find one of the ever-smiling ushers standing directly behind me. "Looking for the restroom," I said, trying on a smile of my own.

"Yes, sir," he said, indicating the hallway that lay before us. "Just follow the corridor to the end. Turn left, and you'll see the restrooms straight ahead on the right."

I nodded my thanks and scurried off like it was of the utmost urgency, but by the time I reached the end of the long hall and turned left, the young man had disappeared. I slowed my pace, noting the series of closed doors lining each side of the corridor, identified with an engraved golden placard mounted at eye level to the right side of each door. They appeared to be offices for church staff, and I tentatively tested the first door on my left, finding it locked and accessible only by magnetic key card—pretty serious security for a neighborhood church, and again I found myself wondering what the operating budget must be for a place like this. All the offices and utility rooms had identical security, and all of the doors were closed. At the end of the hall was an emergency exit, complete with a crash bar that would trigger an alarm if anyone passed through, so that only left the bathrooms on the right. There was one for each gender and a family restroom, and I headed for the men's room, easing the door open and triggering the motion-detected lights.

Odd. I would have expected the lights to already be on if the young man had entered before me.

I eased the door closed behind me and took a few steps into the room. A bank of urinals was mounted to the left wall beside a handwashing station with four basins, none of which was in use. Six stalls were on the right, two of which were handicapped accessible. All of the doors swung inward, ready and waiting for an occupant.

The family restroom! Of course.

I backtracked, pulling the door open and nearly colliding with *another* young man from the group of teens in the cathedral, and the surprise elicited a sharp shriek from the dark-haired boy.

"Oh, hey, sorry about that," I said, trying on another smile that I hoped wasn't intimidating. "I was looking for Chandler Keaton, the preacher's son. I don't suppose that would happen to be you, would it?"

His eyes widened and the color drained from his face as he turned around and ran back toward the cathedral like his life depended on it.

CHAPTER SIXTEEN

Something about the kid's sudden movement triggered my predatory chase drive, and like a dog after the mailman, I was off, doing my own version of barking as I rounded the corner, determined not to lose sight of this one. Of course, that put us both on a collision course with the startled usher at the end of the hall whose persistent smile finally managed to falter. He clutched the collar of his shirt and whispered something into it while urging the fleeing teenager toward him. I was almost halfway down the hall when a brute of a man stepped into my path, seemingly out of nowhere but actually from a hallway that cut off to my left. His chiseled arms were folded over his muscular chest, and he wore an expression that just begged me to try him.

I skidded to a stop before colliding with the guy, and it unnerved me how much taller than me he was. I'm not accustomed to looking up at much of anyone. He scowled at me beneath bushy eyebrows the same salt and pepper as his military crew cut, and he placed a gigantic hand over my left shoulder, essentially pinning me in place. A small receiver was embedded in his right ear canal, and I mentally upped my estimate of the operating budget of New Life Apostolic to include the cost of robust security.

"I'm going to need you to stop right there, sir," he said, his deep voice calm and emotionless.

I was surprised at how winded I was from just that little burst of speed, but this wasn't the time to bemoan how lax my morning exercise routine had become. I nodded, offering half of what I hoped was a disarming smile while holding up a forefinger to buy time for a series of deep breaths to get my pulse regulated. I watched the young man exchange some quick words with the usher, glancing furtively back in my direction, before they both disappeared into the cathedral.

"I was just, uh—I just had a question for that—" I started and suddenly realized there were no words that could adequately explain what had just transpired. I was a stranger in this congregation, chasing one of its flock down a deserted hallway. These weren't good optics.

The usher reappeared and approached us. A version of his smile was back, but it was superficial and condescending. "I don't believe I've seen you at services before, Mr.—?"

"Morrow," I said, offering him my right hand to shake since my left was still pinned in place. It was all for naught, as the usher's smile shifted to a smirk, and he left it hanging in mid-air like I dripped contagion. I retracted it sheepishly. "Dwayne Morrow. And no, I haven't had the pleasure of—"

What the fuck was the word? Enduring? No—

"—joining in with, um, one of the good reverend's sermons, although I hear they're just out of this world." I was trying my very best to project sincere enthusiasm, but it sounded like horseshit to my own ears, so their unamused glares came as no real surprise.

The usher turned to the security goon. "Barton, why don't you escort Mr. Morrow to Consultation Room 1? I'm sure Reverend Keaton would like to have a word with our—*guest* once his sermon is complete."

"Oh, I don't think *that's* necessary," I said, shaking my head and trying to ease out from underneath Barton's vicelike grip. "Really, I can just—"

He squeezed my shoulder hard enough to make me wince and cry out. It would have taken a whole lot more noise than that to attract the attention of any of the parishioners who were visible through the open doors to my right. Reverend Keaton's amplified, mellifluous voice had the congregation under its spell, and all eyes were locked on either the stage or the screen—well, all except one. Just over Barton's shoulder and through the farthest door on the right, Doug openly watched us with his mouth agape. The reverend must have announced a hymn because the organ suddenly hit some warm-up chords while the audience shuffled to its feet and noisily retrieved hymnals from the backs of the pews in front of them. Doug awkwardly followed suit, flipping through the book while keeping an eye on us. It was too much to hope he'd rescue me when even *I* hadn't a clue how to explain myself.

Barton turned me around and began escorting me back down the hallway, with the usher following just long enough to say, "Make yourself comfortable, Mr. Morrow. Reverend Keaton's holiday sermons typically run a little longer than our usual Sunday worship. But don't worry! You won't miss a thing. Barton will activate the monitor in the room so you can follow along. Have a blessed day!"

I didn't need to look to know that shit-eating grin was back in place.

Consultation Room 1, my ass. This was a holding cell.

The room was near the end of the hallway and on the left, which meant no windows. Barton finally unclamped his fingers from my shoulder after guiding me inside.

"Turn your pockets out, please," he said, blocking the entire door with his frame.

"Excuse me?"

"Your pants pockets," he clarified while I stared at him as if I couldn't possibly comprehend his words. He sighed. "Look, we can do this the easy

208

way or the hard way—totally up to you. Either you show me the insides of your pockets, one at a time, followed by a peek at each of your gams, or I'm gonna search you. You decide."

When put like that, the answer was clear. I fished my cell phone, car keys and wallet out of my pockets and handed them to Barton so I could turn my pockets out to show they were otherwise empty. I then raised my khakis as close to my knees as I could get them, one leg at a time. When I was finished, I lifted my arms and turned slowly like a ballerina, making sure he could see there weren't any weapons hidden along my beltline. I reached for my personal items, and realized quickly I wasn't getting them back quite yet.

"Hey, those are mine," I said, embarrassed by the whine in my voice. "You can't *do* that."

With a smile, he tucked them into his own pockets. "I just did. And relax. You'll get 'em back after the Reverend has a word with you."

Thoroughly defeated, I slumped down onto a small loveseat just to the right of the door, ignoring the pair of matching beige chairs centered before a small oak desk that appeared to belong to no one. I wasn't here for a job interview, so I may as well be as comfortable as possible while I waited.

I watched while Barton fished a remote control out of one of the desk's drawers. He aimed it at a monitor mounted near the ceiling in the opposite corner of the room and activated it, filling the room with the closing bars of a hymn I wouldn't recognize no matter how much of it I heard. He tossed the remote to me and moved towards the door.

"I don't suppose I could get a bottle of water or a coffee?" I asked.

Barton rolled his eyes and made his retreat, stepping out into the hallway and pulling the door closed behind himself. The biometric lock buzzed and *thunked*, and I knew I was in for the duration. It didn't stop me from counting to thirty before hopping up to check the handle. Locked, just as I suspected. I looked around the room to see if there was anything else of note, and I spotted a pair of small black orbs mounted near the ceiling in the corner across from the video monitor. I took a moment to wave and flash a smarmy smile to whoever was on surveillance. It didn't stop me from rifling through the desk, only to find each drawer empty. The desktop itself was free of clutter and anything else, for that matter. No pens or pencils, notepads, computer monitor—nothing. Behind the desk was a black task chair that looked to be actual leather. Everything smelled new. My mental capacity for tabulating the church's operating budget was officially into numeric overflow.

I scooped up the television remote and flopped back down on the loveseat with an exaggerated sigh. This wasn't how I imagined this day would go, although I shouldn't have really been surprised. Once again, I had plunged headlong into a course of action with only the flimsiest framework of a plan. I was starting to wonder if I could be charged with breaking some sort of law, although I couldn't imagine what that might be. New Life Apostolic was in the middle of services that were open to the public, and while I might have spooked the young, dark-haired man in the hall, I hadn't harmed him or even threatened to harm him. It was all a misunderstanding.

So, what *was* I doing here?

I decided I should probably give some thought to that, but a quick glance at the monitor assured me I still had ample time for deliberation. The good reverend was only just beginning to turn up the intensity, his strong, baritone landing on certain words in that way common amongst clergymen and used car salesmen. I watched without listening, at first astonished by the multi-camera angles employed onscreen. This broadcast had some serious production values, and this surely wasn't a feed being piped in solely for my benefit. I made a mental note to see what sort of airtime the church commanded.

The organ was joined by a small string quartet as Reverend Keaton introduced a special guest singer, a petite, apple-cheeked young lady with twinkly eyes and a miles-wide grin bookended by dimples. She looked all of thirteen-years-old, but she took hold of the microphone and launched into her selection with the intensity of a seasoned professional. The cameras panned the enraptured crowd, and it was either all smiles or hands to heaven, raised in testament to a harmonious message, powerfully delivered. As she finished, several were openly weeping in the crowd, and for the briefest second, the camera panned across Doug, awkward and uncomfortable in his ill-fitting brown corduroy OshKosh B'gosh.

Reverend Keaton thanked the girl and summoned another round of applause for her before escorting her from the stage and picking up the thread of his sermon, smiling and gesticulating to his adoring audience. I had to admit, the man had charisma. His words were gentle and somewhat soothing, and soon, my eyelids were heavy. I really could have used that coffee. I slid down on the loveseat, making myself a little more comfortable, as I stopped focusing on the individual words coming through the monitor and more on their reassuring tone. Keaton had a certain cadence to his delivery that was pleasing and somewhat hypnotic. I blinked, resting my eyelids just a bit longer with each subsequent pass.

Before long, I was asleep.

••••••●◌◌●••••••

The sound of the maglock disengaging startled me from my unintended slumber, and I pushed myself into an upright position from where I had essentially faceplanted into the seat, my hand landing in a sizable puddle of drool that had escaped my mouth. I didn't need a mirror to know my cowlick had fully resurrected and was now pointing towards the ceiling. I noticed belatedly that the monitor had gone black, and the room was silent.

The door swung inward, and I stood, turning to find myself face-to-face with Reverend Keaton. He had changed clothes or at least abandoned one layer. Instead of the plum robe, he wore a simple blue-and-white checked button-down shirt, open at the collar and tucked into navy Dockers. What hadn't changed was his warm expression, which led me to believe it maybe wasn't just for show. I expected him to be followed by a security detail, but he traveled alone, closing the door behind him.

He smiled, extending his hand. "Good afternoon, Mr. Morrow. My name is Donald Keaton, but I suspect you already know that."

He winked at me as I took his hand and shook. "Um, yes, I guess I do."

"Why don't we have ourselves a little chat?"

Shit.

Instead of inventing a plausible cover story, I'd wasted all my time sawing logs and drooling onto the cushion. I sighed, resigned to an interrogation for which I was completely unprepared. I pulled out one of the twin chairs facing the desk and dropped down into it.

A few seconds passed, and I realized the reverend hadn't moved toward the leather chair behind the desk. I turned to find him staring at me with his hands on his hips, amusement evident on his face. "I thought we might go back to my office where it's a little more comfortable," he said. "I could get you something to drink, maybe a little something to eat. Or if you needed to make use of the facilities, I have my own private bathroom."

My bafflement was undoubtedly being captured in high definition by the security orbs in the corner.

His smile broadened. "This is just an empty consultation room. There really aren't any creature comforts here to speak of, but if it makes you happier, we can stay right here."

I was back on my feet in a flash. "Sure, yeah, that's fine. Whatever."

He waved a card over the maglock and held the door for me. "Right this way, please."

I fully expected Barton or maybe even the police to be waiting outside the door but was surprised to find the hallway completely empty and eerily quiet. I wondered exactly how long I had been asleep. I briefly considered bolting, but that would only make me look worse than I already did. Instead, I followed the reverend as he led me to the end of a hall that led to an emergency exit but turning left where a half-flight of stairs led to his suite of executive offices. Again, I was surprised at how bright and cheerful the space was, with skylights admitting ample natural light from above since there were no windows on either side of the room. There really couldn't be, based on the building's layout. The wall to my left abutted the cathedral, and the one to my right housed four doors leading to private offices. All were secured by maglocks.

A nearly circular desk occupied the central space in the room, looking more like a command center than anything else. It was elevated on a platform so whoever manned the station would have the height advantage over any visitors. I caught a hint of dual widescreen monitors as we circled it, but I wasn't tall enough to see much more. It was currently unoccupied. The walls were adorned with tasteful portraits of landscapes interspersed with the occasional obligatory cross or other tableau of dogma. Reverend Keaton continued to the last door on the right and swiped his badge over it, causing it to click, its indicator light glowing green. He ushered me into his spacious private quarters, and when I automatically turned right and headed toward one of the chairs positioned in front of his own massive desk, he caught my arm and redirected me to a comfortable seating area at the opposite end of the room. An off-white modular sofa, loveseat and armchair huddled around a low coffee table offering an arrangement of pamphlets covering a wide variety of topics, including but not limited to alcoholism and adultery—and that was just at a quick glance. Its centerpiece was an oversized Bible, spread open at its midpoint on a tabletop book stand. Reverend Keaton opted for one of the chairs, so I opted for the other, keeping the entire length of the coffee table between us. A breathtaking view of the campus was visible through the outer wall, which was comprised entirely of floor-to-ceiling glass. A handful of people were visible, engaged in amiable conversation or heading back to their cars in the parking lot, and what I would have given to trade places with any of them.

He steepled his fingers under his nose, watching me. "You seem awfully nervous, Mr. Morrow."

"Well, I've been stripped of my identification, cell phone, and car keys and locked in a holding cell for—" I glanced at my watch and was shocked to see it was nearly twelve-thirty. "—nearly three hours. Is this the sort of treatment everyone who visits your church should expect?"

"In all fairness, you were chasing a member of our youth group down the hall. Jonathan, one of our ushers, was only doing his job by notifying security. He had no way of knowing who you were or what you may be up to. Let's face it, Mr. Morrow, these are turbulent times. One report after another of yet another hate crime, and all too often, those crimes are committed against innocent people gathered together only to give praise in the house of the Lord. I have a duty to provide a place of reasonable sanctum. What, exactly, were you doing? You scared that poor young man half to death."

I mentally cringed. I really wish I could have a 'do-over' on that one. I couldn't imagine it would help to explain I was originally looking for one young man and only started chasing the other after the first one disappeared. All of it looked bad. I decided to stick to playing ignorant, since it shouldn't be much of a stretch.

"I can't really say what spooked him," I said, avoiding eye contact. "This is my first time visiting your church, and I only asked for directions to the restroom." I briefly considered the likelihood of lightning striking me down for lying so flagrantly in a house of worship.

He cocked his head, amused. "Oh, come now, Mr. Morrow. You asked for directions to the restroom from Jonathan before you ever headed down that hallway. He told me as much. You're not just *visiting* our church. You and your associate—it's Boggs, isn't it?"

I blinked, surprised into nodding.

"What is it that you're *really* here for? I suspect if you cut to the chase, we could both get back to our own days a whole lot sooner."

Hmmm. At this point, the truth was not only an interesting proposition, it was pretty much all that was left. Still, I wasn't quite ready to commit, so clearing my throat, I opted for a question of my own.

"I suppose you're holding Mr. Boggs in another room so you can question him separately and compare notes?"

His laughter was genuine, his eyes sparkling. "You really watch too much TV, Mr. Morrow. No, once I was made aware of what had transpired during the service, I made a point of looking Mr. Boggs up and personally extending an invitation for him to join our after-Thanksgiving luncheon in the dining hall downstairs. It's an annual Saturday tradition we do to provide a good meal for any and all who wish to come. It seems appropriate to the season, don't you think?"

At the mention of food, my stomach entered the conversation, gurgling mightily. "Well—yeah. Sure."

"So, how about it? I'd sure love to get a plate, and you're welcome to do the same, but I'd feel a whole lot better if we could just get this business out of the way first. I understand that you work for Mr. Boggs at his private detective agency, correct? I'll be right up front with you—I took a peek at your identification and had you Googled. It seemed only smart to have some idea who I was dealing with before coming to talk to you, but in your line of business, I would think you would understand that."

I nodded, kicking myself that I hadn't done the same on the good pastor. It seemed to fall into the category of basic good practice, but then again, so did having a plan. As it was, I was forced to take him at face value, and if he were harboring any dark secrets, they would remain as such, at least for the duration of this conversation. He settled back in his chair, crossing one leg over the other and folding his hands over his knee, patiently waiting for me to get to the point.

"We're looking into the death of Tina McAlister," I said, finally meeting the man's eyes. "I believe she was a member of your youth group?"

His face turned sympathetic. "Yes, oh my. Such a tragic turn of events. Her friends here are just devastated."

"I'm sure they are," I said. "We were hoping to talk to a few of them, maybe get some sense of how Tina was acting lately or if something had been bothering her."

"But I thought the police were calling this a suicide."

I shrugged. "Seems like that's the way they're leaning, but her family needs a little more reassurance. That's what Doug and I are trying to provide. We figured talking to her friends would be a good place to start."

"Well, I wish I'd known that from the beginning," he said, and it was impossible not to feel mildly chastised for our poor planning. "I could have gotten the group together and facilitated a meeting—provided, of course, that I could get their parents' consent, but I doubt that would be much of an issue. We are all grieving for that poor family. But by now, I doubt that any of them are still here. A community dinner doesn't have the same appeal for our teenagers as it does to our elderly members. We can certainly head down and see if we can catch anyone, but they tend to scatter as soon as services are over. If you'd like to leave a card, I can try and round some of them up and give you a call."

I smiled, feeling completely defeated. "My cards are in my wallet."

"And your wallet, phone and keys are in our security office," he said, grinning. He rose from the chair. "We can pick them up on the way downstairs."

Awesome! What a tremendous waste of a couple of hours. I pushed myself to my feet, and as I followed Reverend Keaton across the room, it occurred to me to ask, "Did you know her very well? Tina, I mean."

"I'd like to think I know all my parishioners," he said. "But with a congregation this size, that's not entirely possible. We exchanged pleasantries. I was better acquainted with her mother. She's been in counseling with me since her husband left. Some folks are better equipped to head a household than others."

"Did she have issues with her daughter?"

He stopped at the corner of his desk and turned, his smile turning rueful. "I've really already said more than I should. Let's see if we can catch some of Tina's friends. They might be able to satisfy some of your questions as they aren't bound by privilege."

He turned back toward the door when I noticed a family picture on the corner of his desk. Reverend Keaton smiling, his arm wrapped around the shoulders of a dark-haired beauty, her ebony hair pinned up above cascading ringlets. Between them in the foreground stood a pair of boys, the elder of the two staring straight ahead, stone faced, a full head taller than his brother. I recognized him as a younger version of the teen that had inspired this entire pursuit. Between them was an impish little girl with a cheese-eating grin, and only after a double-take did I realize she was the young lady who had sung so beautifully during the service.

"Your family?" I asked, indicating the picture.

The reverend beamed proudly. He picked up the picture and handed it to me. "It's a few years old, but it's the most recent I've got. That's my darling Maribel. I fell in love with her the moment I heard her sing. I was twelve, and she was eleven, and it was her first time attending New Life's Vacation Bible School. I know it sounds crazy, but we've been together ever since then. We'll be celebrating our twentieth anniversary this coming February."

"Wow," I said, handing the picture back to him. "Congratulations. Nice looking kids, too. So, this has been your church since—?"

"Since always," he said. "My father held the pulpit before me, and I imagine I'll eventually hand the reins over to Chandler when it's my time to retire." He indicated his younger son with his thumb.

"Isn't that a little unusual? I mean, doesn't the eldest son usually take those reins?"

For the first time, Reverend Keaton's face clouded over. "Yes, well, Dustin wants no part of it. No part of *us*, really. He's decided that he knows better than anyone else what's best for him, and he's not accepting advice from anyone, especially us. We just have to let him find his own way and pray he eventually does. In all my years of family counseling, I've certainly seen my fair share of this in families with multiple children. There's always one who seems more prone to cause trouble."

I understood his point. In my family, that would be me. "I'm sorry to hear that," I offered sincerely before attempting to get him off the hook. "If I'm not mistaken, that was your little girl I heard singing during the service."

His face lit back up. "Isn't she something? That's Tessa, and she just turned fifteen. She was truly blessed with her mother's gift. She used to have terrible stage fright, but this past year, she's gotten a lot more confident." He clapped his hands. "Enough about my family! We better get you downstairs if we have any hope at all of catching someone from the youth group. And I don't know about you, but I'm starving."

CHAPTER SEVENTEEN

By the time I arrived in the downstairs dining hall, almost all of the serving trays were either empty or home to something less-than-appetizing congealing in the bottom. Reverend Keaton apologized profusely, genuinely surprised at the robust turnout, and offered me the tray that had been reserved for him. I wasn't about to take the man's lunch, but decided in that moment the man's congeniality wasn't just for show. Besides, I felt like I'd already overstayed my welcome. What few parishioners remained were openly gawking, which only made me increasingly self-conscious about my rumpled clothes and flyaway hair. It didn't take long to determine there were no members of the youth group still on premises, so I gave the reverend a business card, and he promised to contact me as soon as he could arrange a sit-down with one or more from the group.

Doug was seated alone at the end of a long folding table, fuming and surrounded by a collection of spent dishes. It was easy to see how he had whiled away the time while I had been more or less held captive, and my stomach gurgled in protest, apparently equally upset with me. I quietly helped him collect his dishes and return them to one of the plastic tubs that were stationed around the room before we finally headed for the parking lot.

Doug alternated between angry silence and reading me the riot act once we got back to my car which, thanks to him, now smelled like gravy. He had managed to spill about a gallon down the front of his shirt while wolfing down a turkey dinner and waiting for me to be released. The short drive to McDonald's to retrieve his Pontiac seemed interminable.

"I can't imagine what you were thinking," he said for no less than the fifth time.

I sighed. "I don't know how many different ways I can explain it, Doug. I thought I had an opportunity to talk to one of those kids, and I took it."

"And there's your problem," he said. "You *'thought.'* Have you forgotten that you are the apprentice here? It's your job to follow my lead."

I was beginning to grind my teeth. "Well, then, it would have been really helpful if you had given me some direction. I didn't see *you* doing anything."

He was exasperated. "I was still formulating my plan! I would've found a way to get us an interview with at least a couple of those kids without scaring the pants off folks and causin' a full-fledged security situation!"

He lapsed back into angry silence, and I let him, despite my deep reservations about his ability to negotiate a peaceable gathering. There was no sense grinding my gears over an outcome that would never be realized. But like an angry little teapot on the verge of boiling over, he could only go short bursts before venting some more steam.

"And you *realize* who bore witness to this lunacy, right?"

His eyes bore holes through me as I cast a vacant glance in his direction and shook my head.

"Lucy freakin' Graves, that's who," he spat.

"The police lady?" I asked, surprised, although I guess I shouldn't have been. She *had* mentioned Molly being her maid of honor, so I guess it wasn't so farfetched they attended the same church.

"But *of course!* She had herself a field day ripping on our lack of professionalism and the sheer gall of us invading what should be a place of sanctuary for Tina McAlister's friends and family. And that's before she even got *started* on you chasing that boy down the hallway, and guess what? She managed to get a video of a little piece of that. You just might be the TikTok's next viral *sensation!* How about them apples?"

"Shit," I muttered, signaling left before easing into the McDonald's parking lot.

"Shit is right. But, *hey!* You might get lucky and instead, Lucy will convince the boy's parents to file charges against you for menacing their child, and guess what else? Since you were working for me, I could be found liable, too. Do you have any idea how happy that would make her? It could be the end of Boggs Investigations!"

"I'm *sorry*, Doug! I certainly didn't mean for this to go down like it did. Reverend Keaton seemed to recognize the misunderstanding. Maybe if I talk to Officer Graves, *explain* myself—maybe the parents—"

"Oh, good Lord, *no*," said Doug, unfastening his seat belt as I pulled into the spot beside his Pontiac Aztek. "Absolutely not. I don't want you talking to anybody else about this case, do you hear me? You're *done* here. I'm pulling you off it before you do any more damage."

"*What?!?* It was just a stupid mistake!" I pleaded as he got out of my car. "You can't *do* that!"

"The hell I can't. You're lucky I'm not firing your ass, and let me tell you, I'm not taking that option off the table just yet. You better just pray I can get this train wreck under control."

He slammed the door and got into his own ugly SUV, narrowly avoiding an elderly couple who were crossing the parking lot as he threw his car into reverse and lurched backward in his haste to put some distance between us, leaving me with only the scent of gravy and a very bad taste in my mouth.

Craig's truck and Cheryl's minivan were both gone when I pulled back into their drive, and I was surprised to find the back door standing open, the house protected only by its unlocked screen door. I knocked on its frame before pulling it open and poking my head into the empty kitchen. Straight ahead and through the archway into the living room, I could see a stack of plastic storage tubs as well as loose artificial tree limbs strewn about, but no sign of any human activity. Betsy was lying amongst the Christmas detritus, sprawled out and belly up, dead to the world. She didn't even flinch when I knocked. Despite his feline heritage, Dexter made an infinitely better guard dog.

"Knock, knock!" I called out tentatively, unsure if I was even still welcome.

Cheryl peeked in from the living room and only hesitated for a second before crossing the hallway into the kitchen and throwing her arms around me, giving me a big hug. I automatically stiffened. I wasn't much of a hugger, but I forced myself to relax and awkwardly return the gesture, unsure of what exactly prompted it.

"I am so sorry about how I acted last night," said Cheryl, stepping back but keeping hold of my upper arms. "I'm just used to running interference for my brother and sisters. It's what I do. Chip came clean about what happened when he dragged his sorry butt out of bed this morning. I knew he could be ornery, but this is more than I would've ever imagined. When I think about what could've gone wrong, I…" Her words trailed off, and she shuddered.

I smiled. "It's not your responsibility to answer for Chip. He's a grown man. Immature, but grown, and I should've handled myself better. I promise not to start any more fistfights in your home." I flashed her a three-finger Boy Scout salute before craning my neck to glance hopefully into the living room, but there was still no sign of Melanie. "Is she here?"

"Nope," she said, crossing the room and retrieving a couple of glasses from the dish drainer. "She had an errand to run, so I let her borrow my van. You want something to drink?"

"Thanks," I said absently, dropping into a chair at the dinette table and pulling out my phone. "Where'd she go?"

Cheryl gently pushed my phone to the table before I could connect to Melanie's number. "Slow your roll, fella. You and I may be good, but you're still in the doghouse as far as my sister's concerned."

"But I thought you said Chip explained—"

"Oh, he did, and she is plenty pissed at him, believe me," she said, carrying the glasses over to her fridge where she dispensed ice from the door. "But you're missing the point. Pepsi?"

I nodded, utterly perplexed. *What* point?

She poured herself a glass of sweet tea and returned the pitcher to the refrigerator before carrying the other glass and a can of Pepsi over to the table and putting them in front of me. She sat in the chair closest to me and studied me as she took a sip of her tea. "It's a good thing I like you. I get the feeling this won't be the *last* time you need me in your corner, at least as far as my sister is concerned."

I closed my eyes and sighed, leaning back in the chair, and mentally counting to ten. Why was it so hard to get a simple answer to a simple question? Despite my utter deficit of patience, I forced myself to hold my tongue until I had filled my glass with soda and felt I could express myself without being patently offensive. It wasn't Cheryl's fault my entire day had been a shitshow, and she was only trying to help me.

"Thank you, Cheryl. I like you, too, and I'm all ears if you're willing to clue me in. But right now, I'm just kinda hanging out here, swinging in the wind, so could you…?"

"You need to stop thinking of yourself as Melanie's Prince Charming."

I blinked. "I don't—"

"Ah, but you *do!*" she interrupted. "Maybe not that particular terminology, but the concept is the same. You want to protect her from everything, so you keep shielding her from things you don't think she can handle. This business with Chip is just the latest example."

"I don't do that," I protested.

"Ah, but you *do!*" she repeated. She stood and crossed to her sink, nabbing a plastic spray bottle out of her dish drainer, and filling it with water. "Look, I'm not gonna dig into specifics here, because if you won't talk about it with Melanie, you sure as hell won't talk about it with me, but Melanie's not just my sister. She's my best friend. We share everything, always have. Some of what you two have been through these last couple of months is giving her a serious case of déjà vu, and not in a good way."

She moved behind me and suddenly my hair was wet. *"Hey!* What are you—"

"I just can't look at this mess any longer," she said, and her fingers were working through the top of my hair. "Just relax. I do this for a living. This isn't hair, it's a cry for help."

I stiffened and sighed, submitting to her less-than-gentle manipulation, but ready to draw the line if a pair of scissors suddenly appeared. "Tell me about this déjà vu."

"Melanie's relationship experience is pretty much limited to what she had with Ryan McGregor, and let's face it, that was never really love. They bypassed all that 'getting to know you' stuff after a one-night stand resulted in a plus sign on a home pregnancy test. They went from nothing to family unit in no time. Can you imagine sharing your home with a virtual stranger? Someone who wants to mold you into his personal fantasy, and you're just insecure enough to go along with it all? You trust him to take care of things because you have no idea what to do. He finds housing, makes the financial decisions, and tells you what you can and can't do, and you don't question anything. You feel lucky that he comes home to you. Except when he doesn't. You want to believe he's working late when he says he is, but he's not nearly as good at hiding his shenanigans as he thinks he is."

"You make him sound like a monster," I said as she blasted my hair with the spray bottle again.

"He really kinda was, wasn't he? Look, I know he was your friend and all, but I just call 'em as I see 'em. Believe it or not, I actually liked Ryan. He was a real charmer. I don't think he ever set out to hurt anyone, but you can't be everything to everyone without eventually disappointing somebody. I knew he couldn't be trusted when he tried to get me into bed the second time I met him, and don't you dare say a word about that to Craig. He'd have an aneurysm. I only told Melanie about it after she laughed at the idea that Ryan might be unfaithful. I didn't know any other way to open her eyes."

"Sounds to me like you're no better than me about this selective honesty stuff," I said as she finished messing with my hair and stepped back to inspect her work. I checked myself in the selfie cam on my phone and had to admit, she knew what she was doing.

"Alright, fine, but it's a hard habit to break," she said. "I've been doing it my whole life, but to *protect* her. Ryan was only doing it to protect himself. At this point, Melanie doesn't give a shit about the *why*, she's just sick of people deciding what she's capable of handling. She's come a long way and is a lot stronger than she gets credit for. If she thinks you're holding something back, she automatically wonders what else you're hiding. She's pretty much done feeling like she's being made a fool of, and selective disclosure is currently working against you, my friend."

I took a sip of Pepsi, mulling her words over. "Thanks, Cheryl. I'll work on it. I promise, I'm not anything like Ryan—you know, in *that* way. I hope you'll believe that."

She smiled and patted my hand again. "I already do."

"Yeah?"

"Of course! We've been here alone this whole time, and you haven't so much as flirted with me. I'm starting to get offended. Hell, even Molly saw your naked backside, but me? I get nada," she said, her eyes twinkling.

Craig chose that exact moment to come banging in through the screen door. "Whose naked backside are we looking at?" he asked, putting a six-pack of Heineken on the counter and taking his wife into his arms.

"Why, yours, sweet darlin'! Most perfect bubble butt in all the land, or at least that's what Dwayne thinks." She crinkled her nose and pushed him away. *"Eww*…get away from me. You smell like fish."

"Awww," he said, hooking an arm around my neck and planting a big, wet kiss on my forehead. "Be still my heart."

I felt my face flush from my cheeks to the tips of my ears, and I knew I was never gonna live this down. "Yeah, yeah, yeah—knock it off," I said, squirming out of his grasp before he could transfer his fishy aromatics to me. He really *did* stink. "So, where did Melanie go?"

"She said she needed to clear the air with Ryan's mom," said Cheryl, sitting back down at the table.

"Sarah?" I was pleasantly surprised. "Did she take Jasmine with her?"

"Un-unh," she said. "We're not expecting the girls back until tonight. In fact, they're probably just now settling into that movie they wanted to catch. Why?"

I shrugged. "I know Sarah wants to see her granddaughter before we head back."

"And Jasmine wants to meet her half-brother."

"Oh. You know."

Cheryl smiled. "I told you, Melanie and I share everything. And for the record, I'm on your side on this one. I think Melanie's only delaying the inevitable by keeping them apart, and it's not helpful to anyone."

"Thanks," I said. "Maybe you can get her to listen to reason."

She laughed. "Fat chance of that. But in time, I'm sure it will all work itself out. So, where have you been all morning? You were up and at 'em bright and early."

I regaled them with mine and Doug's morning adventures, leaving nothing out—well, almost nothing. I may have downplayed my pursuit of the young man in the church hallway just a bit. By the end, they were both having trouble containing their laughter.

"So, this is a normal day in the life of a private eye?" asked Craig, loading his beer into the refrigerator.

"I have no idea what's normal," I admitted. "I seem to get benched more often than I actually get to work, and after what happened this morning, I'm off the case. It's frustrating."

"Well, at least you get your holiday weekend back," said Cheryl.

"Yeah, but poor Anne Marie Brown is now stuck with Doug, and I don't think she's gonna be happy about it. Of course, she was there for the service, too, so her whole opinion of me might be considerably less than it was yesterday."

"I don't know," said Cheryl. "She pretty much thought you walked on water when I spoke to her yesterday."

"I just couldn't get over the size of that church," I said. "Didn't you say it was your family church growing up?"

"Uh-huh," said Cheryl, sipping her tea. "But we haven't gone in—geez, how long has it been, babe? Ten years?"

Craig twisted the top of a beer and leaned against the counter. "More than that. Kenzie's fifteen, so at least that long."

"I guess so. Wow, time really flies, doesn't it? Of course, it was a lot different back then. It was at the old location out on Sweeney Hollow and services were led by the current pastor's father, Lawrence." She shuddered at the old ghosts stirred by the memory. "I'll never forget the way that man laid into me when I learned I was pregnant. I've heard that Donald is a lot

227

less fire and brimstone, but the church is still pretty unforgiving when it comes to the gays and other non-traditional lifestyles. It funds controversial practices like conversion therapy, and I don't know what all else. Donald took charge after his father retired, and he's grown the church into what it is today. *The New Life Hour of Power* is broadcast live every Sunday morning and Wednesday evening with a simulcast on YouTube, and every year, the congregation grows. He's drawing people from all around the tri-state area who want to see him do his thing live. Once they started televising services, they had to move out of the old location because they couldn't accommodate the crowds any longer. They rented the bingo hall out on 207 while the new campus was being built. He's recently added a private school and hopes to add team sports to the mix soon."

"He's like a next generation Jerry Falwell or Jimmy Swaggart," I said.

She rolled her eyes. "Or maybe Jim Jones."

"That's pretty harsh. He was surprisingly understanding about what happened this morning."

She rankled. "I have more experience with that particular group of people than you do. Tell a teenage girl she's ruined her life and is going to hell simply for bringing a child into this world—well, let's just say it left a bad taste in my mouth, but maybe you would have had to have been in my shoes to understand."

"No, of course not. I didn't mean to offend you."

She smiled apologetically and shook her head. "It's not you. Everything about that place offends me. The kind of money that's flowing through there is obscene, and I can only imagine the political clout and personal amenities the good reverend currently enjoys because of it. This isn't just passing around collection plates. You can tithe via every payment platform available—cash, credit, PayPal, you name it. Molly was telling me just the other day they started accepting Bitcoin, of all things. I just can't think about it for long. It's too scary."

Craig polished off his beer and tossed the bottle into the recycle bin. "And on that note, I'm going in to take a shower. Apparently, I smell like fish." He winked at his wife. "You wanna keep me company?"

"Such a sweet talker," said Cheryl, getting up from the table to carry her empty tea glass to the sink. "I've still got more Christmas boxes to unpack. I wanna be ready to decorate this tree once everyone gets back tonight."

"Do you need any help?" I volunteered to Cheryl as Craig crossed the living room to the stairs, on his way to the master bath in their bedroom.

"Not really," she said. "Why don't you just relax until Mel gets back? You've had a pretty full morning. The TV's all yours, if you don't mind me crossing back and forth in front of you constantly."

"I think I'll just sit out on the back porch with my laptop for a while if that's all right. I've got some busywork I've been putting off for my own consulting business."

"You're still keeping that up, too?"

I smiled. "That's what pays the bills. I can't seem to stay of out trouble long enough to earn any real money from Boggs Investigations. Maybe someday."

"There's a stack of TV tray tables beside the refrigerator. Feel free to use one for your laptop if you'd like."

"Thanks." I carried my glass to the sink and rinsed it and the empty can, crushing the latter before tossing it into the recycle bin.

I grabbed a tray table and carried it out to the back porch where I set it up in front of one of the chairs I had come to think of as my drinking spot. I had left my laptop bag in my car, and shivered slightly as I walked across the gravel to retrieve it. Clouds were beginning to multiply in the sky, obscuring the sun and dragging the temperature down to more customary November levels. It looked like it might rain. I snagged my lightweight hoodie from the backseat, too, pulling it over my rumpled shirt.

I activated the mobile hotspot on my phone and fired up my laptop, hoping its remaining charge would be sufficient for my needs. I hadn't thought to put it on its charger overnight, and I didn't care for the looks of the ungrounded pair of electric outlets that serviced the porch. Sure, the refrigerator was humming away just fine, but my power cord required a three-prong outlet, and these were one prong short, a fairly common occurrence in old houses like these. With just under fifty percent of my battery remaining, I changed the power plan to conserve power and set about my business, responding to a handful of emails including a request for a quote to upgrade a SQL database server for one of my longstanding clients. It was a little reassuring to have some things of my own on the books that Doug couldn't pull me away from. I sent a payment reminder to another customer who was reliably late with every single invoice, warning that a two percent late fee would be assessed if payment wasn't received within the next ten days. I knew it would get paid before then. It always did.

Once I had tidied up my own business, I killed the next nearly half hour attempting to solve the daily Wordle puzzle, which turned out to be a particularly archaic five-letter word I'd never even heard of. After that, I decided to take a gander at New Life Apostolic's web presence, unprepared for the auditory assault that was triggered from the laptop's speaker. It was a replay of this morning's sermon, and Reverend Donald Keaton was midway through announcing his daughter, Tessa's upcoming performance. Across the top of the web page was a horizontal menu bar with links labeled, *Past Recordings, Daily Scripture, Active Missionary Campaigns, Virtual Campus Tour, Applications for Student Enrollment, Staff Directory*, and a rather ambiguous *About*. Crawling above the whole thing was a banner reminding you, 'IT'S **NEVER TOO LATE** TO HELP YOUR FELLOW MAN! CLICK **HERE** TO **DONATE NOW!!!** IT'S **TAX DEDUCTIBLE!!!**' All of the underlined text were hyperlinks to a quick and dirty donation form that was already pre-populated with the suggested amount of one hundred dollars. Well, then.

I canceled out of the transaction and had to confirm my intentions no less than three times before being vaguely admonished and finally returned to the home page. From there, I clicked on the *About* link, which shrunk Tessa's performance to a small window in the lower right and opened a page featuring a yellowing photo of the original church building. A grim-faced couple stood just outside the main cathedral doors at the top of a steep set of stairs, one hand from each on the shoulder of the young, smiling boy between them. It was captioned, *New Life Apostolic Church, Sweeney Hollow, Reverend Lawrence Keaton, with his wife, Doralee and their son, Donald.* It was dated thirty-five years prior. Even if I hadn't known the backstory from Melanie and her sister, I could practically feel judgment and condemnation radiating from the former pastor's eyes.

I was just about to read the church's Mission Statement when a text landed on my phone. I used my fingerprint to unlock the screen and frowned when I saw the message was from 'CALLER UNKNOWN.' It read:

Tina McAlister not how people think. I help U U help me. 3:00 at rest area, Ohio side, Greenup Dam. Ten mins past, Im out. Come alone.

CHAPTER EIGHTEEN

I must have stared at the phone for a full minute before stupidly replying, *"Who is this?"*

No response.

Of course, there was no response. Why would someone go to all the trouble of blocking their Caller ID only to identify themselves now?

I toyed with my phone a moment longer. I should turn this over to Doug. I had been pulled from the case, and that's what he would expect me to do. Of course, the message had been directed to me with specific instructions to come alone. There was no guarantee whoever this was would even be willing to speak to Doug. In fact, he'd probably scare whoever it was away. I glanced at the clock on my phone and saw it read 2:36PM.

Shit.

Doug had almost certainly hightailed it back to Lymont after our disastrous morning at New Life Apostolic, and he couldn't possibly make it back to the Greenup Dam in time. My decision had been made for me. Knowing there would eventually be hell to pay, I tucked my laptop back into its bag and ducked into the kitchen to snag my keys.

"Going back out?" Cheryl called from where she stood untangling a knot of Christmas lights.

"Just for a bit," I said. "If Mel gets back, tell her I shouldn't be long."

........●—◯◯—●........

Apparently, déjà vu was the theme du jour.

I found myself squeezing the steering wheel in a death grip, traveling west on US 52 towards a destination that held less than pleasant memories for me, and the darkening clouds that continued to gather overhead seemed to be in on the joke. Had it already been a year since I was nearly killed atop the viewing platform at the Greenup Dam while rescuing Jasmine from a deranged psychopath? It seemed like only yesterday. I ran my tongue over the implant that now served as my right front tooth, a souvenir of lasting damage from that horrific night. I hadn't given much consideration to the psychological scars that lay dormant, but as I neared the infamous scene, I couldn't shake the sense of palpable dread that grew with each passing mile.

I thought long and hard about calling Doug to bring him up to speed before I had gone any farther. While I recognized it was the appropriate course of action in a normal employment relationship, ours was anything but normal. With Doug, it was always more productive to ask forgiveness later than permission in advance. Either one would be painful, and I would assuredly have to endure a booming lecture about protocol, but at least this way, I'd have my curiosity satiated. Hell, I might even have a workable lead.

I activated my right turn signal and slowed, easing onto the exit ramp before signaling left to cross the overpass. A cold and clammy sweat sprung across my shoulders, and the meager lunch I had picked up at McDonald's after getting my ass chewed by Doug felt like lead in my stomach. In the immediate aftermath of the events of the previous fall, I was plagued by vivid nightmares that put me right back here on that foggy night. These grotesque and nerve-shredding permutations of truth always ended the same way, with Jasmine running for her life while I was too slow to stop the gunshot that ended it. I would awaken with a jolt, tangled in

233

perspiration-soaked sheets with my heart galloping, momentarily unsure of exactly how that night had actually ended. By morning, I felt foolish for allowing a dream to affect me in such a way. To speak of it seemed an admission of weakness, so I never did, not even to Melanie.

Hmmm. Another example of my selective disclosure suddenly stared me in the face. For a guy who claims to be honest if nothing else, I had subconsciously been making a goddamn liar out of myself for months.

Mercifully, the frequency of the nightmares had diminished as the months passed, but as I turned right onto the sloping entrance to the rest area, it all came rushing back to me again. I was vaguely aware of pit stains spreading down my sides with a dogged ferocity I hadn't experienced since puberty.

Just breathe, I told myself, and since there was no one waiting behind me to enter the area, I lingered at the stop sign at the bottom of the entrance and did exactly that. I closed my eyes tight and drew in a deep breath before letting it out in a slow whistle. It somewhat helped that daylight eradicated many of the shadowy spaces from my recollection, and I also noticed the observation deck was currently blocked off, closed to the public. I wondered if it had been closed after two men lost their lives on its scaffolding. All that really mattered was that I wouldn't be lured back up there again this afternoon, and it acted like Alka-Seltzer on a roiling stomach for my frayed nerves.

I circled the lot slowly before pulling into a somewhat secluded spot on the far side where I could watch cars come and go. There were almost a dozen vehicles parked on both sides of the lot, and a handful of people milled about in the grassy central area, some on their way to the cinderblock restrooms while others trailed after canines with little plastic poop bags at the ready. Some were simply stretching their legs. None seemed to be waiting for me. I glanced at the clock on my dash and saw it was only 2:55PM. I sighed and settled in for the duration.

A late model dark blue Chevy Malibu eased into a spot on my driver's side, three down from where I was parked. I stole a glance from the corner of my eye, but could only determine the passenger seat was unoccupied, as was the back seat. The height differential between our vehicles put me at an angle that obscured any view of the driver. All I could see was the vague suggestion of a bony knee angling down toward the car's pedals, ticking slightly but making no move to alight from the vehicle. The engine idled while the driver remained behind the steering wheel.

I sighed and watched as the dashboard clock turned over to 3:00PM...3:03PM...3:05PM.

I returned by attention to the car still idling to my left. Was it up to *me* to make an approach? That didn't seem logical. Whoever had sent me the text obviously knew who I was. Why wouldn't they approach me? I unfastened my seat belt and hunkered down lower in my seat to see if I could make out any more of the driver and was startled when he leaned into view across the passenger seat, looking directly at me. His head was circled by dark, close-cropped hair that hugged the sides and back, the top of his pate smooth and shiny. He smirked at me beneath a bushy moustache, and abruptly, I pulled back, sitting bolt upright in my seat. I didn't recognize this man at all, but it sure seemed like he knew me.

I waited for another moment, focusing on my peripheral vision, but he made no move to emerge from his vehicle.

The clock read 3:07PM.

This was stupid. *Somebody* had to make the first move. I turned my engine off and looked across, just in time to see his hand through his passenger window, urging me forward. I was just about to open my door when he slid sideways into the passenger seat, and I suddenly realized he wasn't wearing any pants, and to say he was excited to see me was an understatement. I pulled my hand away from my door handle and gasped like a Puritan at a demon sacrifice.

This was followed by a tiny little bark of a scream courtesy of me when knuckles abruptly rapped sharply against my passenger window, scaring the living shit out of me. The door was already opening, and the person hopping up into my passenger seat was no more than a girl, tucking into my car with urgency and pulling the door shut behind her. Through the window, I spotted an aquamarine Toyota Prius parked in the next slot over, its stealthy hybrid engine masking my guest's arrival. She cowered in the seat, her green eyes massive behind thick glasses, and her close-cropped fiery red hair plastered to her head in soggy ringlets.

"Um, hi," she said, looking like she'd rather be anywhere than here. "I'm glad you came. I wasn't sure you would." Her eyes were everywhere at once, like she expected us to be interrupted at any moment.

"You were at the church this morning," I said as realization dawned. She had been one of the teens huddled together near the front of the cathedral.

She nodded, every movement an effort. A horn blared from my driver's side, startling us both, and I turned to see my would-be suitor backing out of his spot, flipping me off through his driver's window as he repositioned himself farther away in his continuing quest for fast relief.

"You've got me at a disadvantage," I said, keeping my voice even in the hopes it might help the girl stop vibrating like a chihuahua. "You already know who I am. Who are you?"

She hesitated long enough for me to wonder if I would be restricted to pronouns when she finally said, "Tammy. Tammy Tipton."

Another mental light bulb flickered on as I recalled the short list of Tina's friends that Anne Marie had provided. "Oh, okay. From the list."

Her eyes widened with fear, and an involuntarily strangled whimper gurgled from her mouth. She scrambled for the door handle.

"*Whoa! Whoa!* Wait a minute!" I said, placing a hand gently on her arm only to have her burst into tears. "Hey, hey—you called *me* here, remember? Don't get spooked now."

"But if I'm already on a-a-a-a *list*—"

"A list of Tina's *friends*," I clarified. "I asked her aunt who I might talk to who could maybe clue me in on her day-to-day life. I think she probably mentioned everyone you were with there at the church. What kind of list did you think I meant?"

Her tears slowed as her panic abated, but she still shivered like she was freezing to death. "A list of suspects."

"Is that how I should be looking at this list?"

She shook her head quickly. "N-n-n-o. But—"

"Why don't you just start at the beginning? I'm all ears."

I felt tension slowly ease as her breathing approximated something closer to normal, and I did my very best to bury my eagerness beneath a façade of calm, hoping it would be contagious. It seemed to be working.

"We *weren't* Tina's friends," she finally said. "In fact, I wish I never laid eyes on that girl."

She couldn't meet my eyes, her fidgety focus on everything else. All I could do was remain patient. I was afraid to spook her by saying the wrong thing.

"Do you remember high school?" she asked quite seriously, and I couldn't help but laugh.

"Well, sure," I said. "It wasn't *that* long ago."

The trace of an apologetic smile came and went. "Of course. Sorry. That didn't come out right. What I'm trying to ask is, what kind of kid were you?"

"I'm not sure I understand."

"Aw, you know—were you good at sports? Smart? *Popular?*"

I took a moment to consider her question. "Well, I *definitely* wasn't good at sports. Too many rules and too little interest—too little talent, too, if I'm completely honest. My grades were okay, nothing special. I had some buddies I hung out with, but I don't know if we would have qualified as popular. Why?"

"You know what I'm talking about, right? The cliques. You've got your jocks, cheerleaders, band kids, geeks, druggies—almost everyone falls into one or more of those groups, you know? Sometimes they overlap a little. Sure, there are a handful of rebels who don't really wanna be like anyone, and that's fine. They show up because they have to, but you'll never see them at any extracurricular activities. They're just killing time."

She squirmed in the passenger seat, her gaze a million miles away while I wondered where she was going with all this. It was difficult not to urge her along, but she still seemed skittish. My eyes drifted to the entrance of the rest area as a couple new arrivals eased into slots near the restrooms.

"Tina McAlister wasn't *anybody*," she finally said, and her hand immediately flew to her mouth, her cheeks flushing a deep shade of crimson. "Oh my God, I didn't mean that. Of *course*, she was somebody. *Everybody's* somebody. What I meant to say is that she didn't fit into any of those cliques. She was practically invisible. At least, until this year."

"What was so different about this year?"

She stared at fingernails that had been chewed to nubs and burst into tears again, her body shaking piteously as she hugged herself tight. Her deep, gulping sobs begged for reassurance and comfort that I was ill-equipped to provide. I felt sympathy rising as a lump in my own throat while I fumbled with words intended to soothe but that were ultimately inane and meaningless. It was nearly as awkward as funeral chit-chat. All I could do was wait for her to wind down again and continue. After a few minutes, her sobs turned to hiccups, and I handed her some napkins I had stashed in my center console.

"This was the year that Tina McAlister got tired of being invisible," she said, shrugging before offering a tremulous, tight-lipped smile.

"Her aunt said she became surprisingly popular this year," I said. "But she said it was because you and your friends sort of took her in."

That drew a surprised bark of laughter. "Oh, no. We didn't invite this upon ourselves, I promise you. It started with Chandler."

"The preacher's son."

She nodded. "Out of nowhere, he started bringing her around. It was awkward and weird. She was always saying the oddest things, and no one felt comfortable around her, but she was suddenly everywhere."

"Why did he bring her around?"

Her mouth opened and closed several times, but no words found their way past the gate. Finally, she said, "He didn't really have a choice."

I sighed, wishing she would stop being cryptic and get to the point. "This isn't making a whole lot of sense, Tammy. What kind of hold could Tina have possibly had over Chandler, and what was she expecting him to do for her?"

"She had something on *all* of us!" she blurted out. "I don't know how she got her information, but she had it, and she made sure we *knew* she had it."

"She was blackmailing everyone."

She nodded, and tears were spilling over again. "Why else would Jesse take her to Homecoming? Do you think he *wanted* to do that? No, it was all because of *her*."

"I don't get it," I said. "Tina's aunt said she was voted Homecoming Queen. At my school, that's an honor that is determined by a vote of the entire student body. Tina couldn't have possibly been blackmailing *everyone*."

"No, that one was on me," she said, dabbing at her eyes with the sodden napkin. I fished another one from the center console and handed it to her. "I work in the school office one period a day instead of having study hall. I help process mail by scanning it into the system, and I do some other data entry. Mrs. Bramblett, the office secretary keeps all her login information on a Post-it underneath her keyboard, so I can access pretty much anything."

"Including the voting tally," I surmised, groaning. "That's nuts, Tammy. Do you know the kind of trouble you could get into for tampering with the school's records?"

"Of course, I do," she almost snapped. "It would be instant expulsion. But I didn't have a choice."

"What could she have possibly had on you that would make you take such a risk?"

"My entire future is all!" she said, raking her fingers through her short curls. "Look, I'll tell you what she had on me, but *please* don't ask me about the others. It's not my place to tell their secrets."

"All right." At this point, I would take whatever I could get.

"My mother died when I was a baby, and I never knew my father. I was mostly raised by my grandma who was doing the best she could on a widow's pension and Social Security. That is, until she got too sick to take care of herself or me. She developed rapidly progressive dementia and was gone within a year after being diagnosed. All I've ever dreamed about was becoming a doctor. I want to revolutionize the field in Alzheimer's care, and I've had my eye on Johns Hopkins since the beginning. Do you have any idea how hard they are to get into?"

I could only shake my head. I had only barely dipped my toe into collegiate waters at my parents' urging, racking up enough student loan debt to decide it wasn't for me.

"Their acceptance rate is right around eight percent," she said. "And even with financial aid, they're expensive, although I'm committed to doing what I have to between grants and loans to see it through. What I didn't count on was tanking the SAT. I only managed a 1390."

"That's bad?"

"Well—no, not exactly," she said. "But it's not good enough for Johns Hopkins. They're looking for something closer to 1500. I'm just not good at standardized tests. I was throwing up the whole night before and felt awful while I was taking it. I knew it wouldn't be good."

"It's not the end of the world," I said. "So, you could always go to a different school—"

"*No,*" she said emphatically. "My whole life has been one disappointment after another, and I wasn't about to give up now."

"So, what did you do?"

She chewed on her bottom lip and went back to studying her decimated fingernails, clearly ashamed of whatever it was that she had done. "I had just enough time before applying to Johns Hopkins to take my SAT again. I scheduled it, but I couldn't afford to blow it. So, I started digging around on the internet. It took some time, but I found someone who would take it for me for $1,000. She would provide a fake ID to get herself in and guaranteed a 1500 or better."

"*Guaranteed?*" I marveled. "Like a money-back guarantee?"

She shrugged and nodded. "She had testimonials…"

"And you *believed* all that?" I don't know why, but I was incredulous. In my consulting business, I spend a good bit of my time educating folks about trusting strangers in a transactional capacity on the internet while always doing damage control after the fact. "That's a whole lot of money to chance on what amounts to little more than a pinky swear. Where did you even get your hands on money like that?"

"It's not like I *stole* it," she said, suddenly defensive. "I work part-time at the Dairy Queen. I've been saving as much as I can from every paycheck."

"Let me guess: The girl was secretly Tina. She took your money and screwed you over."

"Not even close," she said. "The girl was legit. She took the test and got me a 1520. I've completed the application to Johns Hopkins and sent it off along with a handful of recommendations from faculty. I really had a good feeling about all this. And then *she* came along."

241

"Tina."

She nodded. "She was complaining about a science project she couldn't get her head around, and Chandler pretty much volunteered my services. I didn't know then that she had already gotten to him—and a few of the others. I agreed to meet her after school at the library so she could show me where she was having trouble, but what she showed me didn't have anything to do with schoolwork at all. She handed me one of those thumb drives, *this* thumb drive." She extracted a cutesy little novelty device from her pocket that was shaped like a duck and pulled its head off to reveal a Type A USB male plug underneath. "When I plugged it into my laptop, I discovered she had a copy of the fake ID used by the girl who took the SATs for me. She had copies of the Paypal transaction showing the money going from my account to hers. She had a time-stamped video of me at work when I should have been taking the test. It didn't even occur to me that someone might notice."

"But how—?"

"I don't *know* how she got it," she said, sliding the yellow ducky back into her pocket. "I guess being invisible has its advantages. She told me what she expected me to do as far as fixing the vote and made sure I knew she wouldn't hesitate to share what she had with the admissions board at Johns Hopkins. She also made sure to let me know this wasn't her only copy. If anything happened to her computer, she had it all backed up on the cloud, and if anything happened to her, she left instructions somewhere that would make sure it would all come out."

My mind was struggling with the improbabilities of it all. This wasn't some well-trained government operative we were talking about. Tina McAlister was just a schoolgirl. How could she have marshalled the resources to secretly collect all that information and hold it hostage, and not just for Tammy, but for all of those other kids, as well?

"You don't believe me." She read my expression and was instantly sullen.

"I'm just trying to figure out how a girl her age—a girl of her *means*—could manage all of this without some sort of help."

"How should I know?" She was getting upset again. "Maybe she *did* have some sort of help. Does it really matter? But one thing's for sure. I don't believe for a second that Tina McAlister killed herself. I mean, why would she? She was getting everything she ever wanted."

"But now that she's dead, you're afraid that it's all going to hit the fan." She nodded. "That's why I went to her house yesterday."

It took me longer than it should have to realize my vague recollection of the silhouette on the other side of Tina's bedroom window was now sitting beside me in my car. "That was *you?*"

She nodded again, sniffling. "I had to go back. I've got her email address, but without access to her phone, I can't recover the password. I was hoping I might find somewhere she kept her passwords. If I could just get to her cloud account before anybody else, I could permanently delete all of the things she's been holding over our heads. It would free us all."

I mulled this over for a moment. "*If* Tina was blackmailing your friends—"

"She *was.*"

"—and *if* she didn't kill herself, doesn't it worry you that one of your friends might be responsible?"

She squirmed in the passenger seat. "It's crossed my mind, but I'd have a hard time believing any of them were capable. I don't think we're the only ones she's been blackmailing. She was getting money from somewhere, and it sure wasn't from any of us."

Her cell phone pinged in her hand, startling us both. She pressed her thumb to the screen, unlocking it as she pivoted in her seat, shielding its contents from me with no pretense of subtlety. Her eyes grew impossibly wide. "Oh, *no*—"

"What is it?"

She flicked the screen with her thumb, terror growing with each pass. After one last flick, she slammed her phone down into her lap, the blood draining from her face. "I have to go," she mumbled, reaching for the door release.

"What *is* it, Tammy?" I urged, reaching out to her. "You came to me for help—"

"*No*," she said, pulling away and practically falling out of my car. "This was a mistake."

She kept looking over her shoulder toward the bridge as she fumbled with her keys, scrambling to get behind the wheel of her car. My view of the bridge was obstructed from where I sat, so I opened my door and hopped down into the lot, moving around to the back of my SUV. Before I reached my hatch, Tammy was already speeding off, her little hybrid gliding silently around the bend toward the exit. I scanned the bridge and surrounding area for anything out of the ordinary but there was nothing to see.

CHAPTER NINETEEN

I let myself into Cheryl's kitchen through the screen door after knocking futilely. Every female in the family was crowded into the room and were talking over one another. Mackenzie and Amanda were arguing over something in high-pitched, whiny tones unique to girls their age while Maggie was practically reenacting the movie they had seen earlier for Cheryl, who was barely paying attention. She was up to her elbows in creating what looked like an enormous pot pie from the Thanksgiving leftovers.

Cheryl's van had returned in my absence, but it took me a moment to find Melanie as she paced back and forth from the living room to the kitchen, her phone pressed to her ear and a look of exasperation on her face. She spotted me on her next pass through and put her phone aside and gave me a quick peck on the cheek.

"Hey, you," she said, considerably less frosty than she was when last we spoke.

"Everything all right?"

"Yes," she said, but she was clearly frustrated. She scowled at her phone. "I'm swear I'm gonna strangle that child."

"Jasmine?"

"Who else? Pestered me forever to get her that damned cell phone, and when I finally did, my only condition was that she keep it charged and on her any time she's out. I don't think that's too much to ask."

"She's not here?" I was surprised. Everyone else certainly was.

"No, Katie offered to take her to get her nails done, which I think is a complete waste of money. Cheryl can do it for free, but Katie offered to pay, so whatever. I know Jasmine looks up to Katie and enjoys spending time with her when it's not with everyone else, too." Melanie lowered her voice and indicated the squabbling sisters whose row had only intensified since I last tuned in. "These two can shred your nerves after a while."

I immediately flashed on Katie smoking pot on the porch the night we arrived and again wondered about the wisdom of leaving Jasmine in her care, but I held my tongue, remembering how Craig had rankled when I suggested Katie might not be the best influence. Those who raise children rarely appreciate the criticism of those who have none.

I decided a change of subject was in order. "I heard you went to see Sarah," I said, testing the waters.

"I did." She crossed the room to where Cheryl was chopping vegetables. "You need any help, Sis?"

Cheryl blew her bangs up and out of her eyes. "Just get these demon children away from me," she pleaded, casting an exaggerated look at her bickering daughters. "I can handle the rest."

"All right," said Melanie, getting the girls' attention as she snagged Maggie through the elbow. "You heard the woman, and dinner depends on it. Mags, take these two over to your trailer, will ya? We'll shout when dinner's ready, but whatever you do, sort this nonsense out before you even think about coming back, do you hear me? We've got a tree to decorate this evening, and nothing kills the Christmas spirit faster than a couple of whiny sisters trying to claw each other's eyes out—believe me, I know."

Amanda stuck her tongue out while Mackenzie looked wounded, and I would've expected no less. Maggie tucked each one under an arm and guided them toward the door. "Come along, ladies," she said. "No need to hang with the kitchen staff."

It was Melanie's turn to stick out her tongue as she swatted her younger sister's bottom with a dish towel. The animated bickering resumed between Cheryl's girls, drifting out the back door like a storm cloud tethered to them, leaving behind a silence that was only broken by the sound of water boiling on the stove. I dropped into one of the chairs at the dinette table while Melanie inserted herself into Cheryl's process, grabbing a few potatoes from the stack on the counter and setting to work peeling them.

"So?" I asked as the silence extended.

"So, what?"

I sighed. *"Melanie!* Are you really gonna make me beg? How did it go with Sarah? Did you meet Jordan?"

"I did," she repeated, slicing away at the helpless potato.

"And?"

"And nothing," she said, studying that potato like it was the most fascinating root vegetable she'd ever seen. "It is what it is, and I'm gonna have to learn to deal with it."

I waited a beat before continuing. I didn't like the way she was wielding that paring knife. I could almost hear the potato screaming. "Will we be visiting Sarah as a family before we head back?"

"That's the plan," she said breezily, the light over the sink glinting off metal with each flick of the knife. "That's why I was trying to get hold of Jasmine. I wanted to make sure she comes back right after they're finished getting their nails done. I thought we might go after dinner, if that's alright with you."

"Um, sure," I said, surprised by her sudden about-face. Melanie handed what was left of the potato to Cheryl and grabbed her next victim. I waited

247

a moment longer before venturing, "So, how's this all going to work? I mean, Sarah still works full-time, and—"

She slammed the knife to the counter and sent the potato flying into the sink, and Cheryl practically jumped out of her skin. I could practically see the tension knotting up her neck and shoulders. She took a deep, steadying breath and said, "Why don't you tell me about *your* day?" She finally turned toward me, leveling me with a withering glare. "And let's not leave anything out this time. Do you think you can manage that?"

So much for being out of the doghouse.

I started with my ill-fated attempt at reconnaissance at New Life Apostolic, getting only partway through the story before Cheryl's howling laughter brought Craig in from the living room, his face lit with expectation.

"What am I missing?" he asked.

"Oh, darlin'," she said between guffaws. "Just have a seat. We need to have Dwayne over more often."

He nabbed the chair across from me like he was in the front row of a comedy club, and I could feel the back of my neck burning to the tips of my ears as he gave me his undivided attention. He was sorely disappointed when I shifted gears and told them about my much more disturbing encounter with Tammy Tipton at the Greenup Dam. I will confess I omitted the part where the dude tried to woo me with his junk, but I felt fairly certain this wasn't something that could come back to bite me in the ass later. By the time I finished, I had everyone's ear.

"Was Doug mad that you went without him?" asked Melanie.

"I'm sure he will be. I haven't been able to reach him, and believe me, I've been trying since I left the dam. It just goes straight to voicemail."

"Shouldn't you have tried *before* you went to the dam?" asked Melanie, wiping her hands on a dishtowel.

I shrugged the question off. "There really wasn't time."

"Have you tried calling his house? His cell phone's ancient. It barely holds a charge anymore."

I looked at her incredulously. "How do you know so much about Doug Boggs' personal communication devices?"

She swatted me with the towel. "I pay attention. It's something you might want to start doing if you're serious about all this detective bullshit. You should try and call him there before it gets any later. He's already pulled you off of the case. You don't want to give him any more reason to make your life hell."

"I left him a message to call me."

"Which won't be good enough, and you know that." She picked my phone up off the table and handed it to me. "Trust me. Call him."

I turned my phone over in my hands and fiddled with the screen, never quite managing to unlock it.

"What's wrong?" asked Melanie before a knowing smile crept across her face. "You're afraid Loretta will answer."

"*Well*—"

She laughed and snatched the phone from my hand. "Oh, for heaven's sake." She bypassed fingerprint verification by using my not-so-secret PIN number and was already making the call before I had a chance to react. "Allow me to run interference for you—oh, hi. Loretta? It's Melanie. Melanie. *Mel-a-nie!*"

She hooked a finger into her free ear and squinted, as if that might make it easier to hear whatever was going on through the phone.

"Can you turn your television down? I can barely hear you. Wow! Yeah, that's much better. I could almost hear Vanna White breathing." Her bogus laughter would have never passed a lie detector as she covered the mouthpiece of the phone and grinned at me. "Celebrity Wheel of Fortune. Looks like Mama Boggs is in the market for some hearing aids."

She returned her attention to the call.

"Listen, I'm going to put you on speakerphone. Dwayne needs to talk to Doug." She activated the speaker and set the phone on the table, as Loretta's booming voice filled the kitchen.

"—was only giving it 'til the end of my show before I called *him*. I think his phone is dead. Keeps going to voicemail. This here's a holiday weekend, you know, and since you came around with that new case, I've seen less of my boy than I do through the week," she said.

I sighed. "Hi, Loretta. Is he there? I really need to talk to him."

"Weren't you listening to a dang word I just said?"

Do I ever?

"Come on, Loretta. This might be urgent."

There was a moment of near silence save for the vague sound of applause in the background as another celebrity contestant successfully solved a puzzle. "I thought he was still out with you," she said. "I haven't seen him since he left this morning. Should I be worried?"

Melanie and I exchanged glances while Cheryl and Craig didn't even bother to pretend they weren't listening.

"I'm sure it's nothing, Loretta," I said. "He probably just had some errands to run on his way home. I was getting his voicemail, too, which is why I'm calling. Can you have him call me when he gets there?"

"Sure," she said, sounding quite the opposite. "And if you talk to him first, have him give me a call, okay?"

"Will do," I said, disconnecting the call and sitting back in my chair.

Cheryl cleared her throat. "Should she?" she asked. "Be worried, I mean."

I shook my head. "I honestly don't know."

"Dinner will be ready in about fifteen minutes," Melanie said, stepping out onto the back porch where I sat in the shadows, alone with my darkening thoughts. After the sun had settled beneath the western hills, a gentle rain moved in, providing a timpani rhythm on the tin roof overhead. It was both soothing and annoying as hell. The temperature had also begun to drop, and Cheryl lent us each a jacket from the back of their closet. Betsy slept at my feet, smelling like the wet dog she was. She was a little slow on the uptake when the rain had started to fall, and I wore traces of the excess moisture she had shaken off before settling in for her nap.

"Did you get hold of Jasmine?" I asked.

"Sort of," she said. "Katie texted Maggie that she and Jasmine were running a little late, and Maggie just forwarded the text to me. I asked her to let them know we still have a tree to decorate, and it's not fair to Cheryl's girls to make them wait on Katie and Jasmine. I also told her to tell Jasmine to plug her damn phone in." She leaned in and placed a cool hand against my cheek. "You're worried about Doug."

I shrugged, uncomfortable with the admission. "It's just not like him to wander off his mommy's radar, that's all."

"Maybe he went to see that old girlfriend of his," she said, perching on the edge of the chair beside me. "You know, try and rekindle that old flame."

"Lucy Graves?" I smiled at the thought. "I sincerely doubt it. I think she's married now. Her last name isn't what it was when Doug was in the police academy with her." My smile morphed into a wince.

"What is it?" asked Melanie, reading my expression.

"She was at the church this morning to witness that whole debacle."

"She *wasn't*."

"Oh, yeah," I said, rubbing my tired eyes. It felt so much later than it was. "It's a good thing for me the church is across state lines, because I'm pretty sure she would have really enjoyed arresting me. Doug's worried she

251

might still cause trouble for Boggs Investigations, and that's just one of the reasons he sidelined me on this case."

"Well, maybe you should just let it go," she said, taking my hand into her own.

"I'm trying," I insisted. "I wasn't looking for Tammy Tipton to reach out to me, although truthfully, I don't think she would have talked to Doug, even if he had been able to make it to Greenup in time. She was so jittery she was practically coming out of her skin."

"And you have no idea what spooked her at the dam?"

"She got a text, and she was done. She was out of my car so fast I barely had time to react. She was looking everywhere at once, like she expected to see whoever sent the text, but then she was gone. I was right behind her, but I didn't see anything or anyone out of the ordinary. No one followed her as she left the lot."

We sat in companionable silence as the gentle rainfall intensified, and I replayed the day's events over in my mind. Tammy's revelation that Tina had been blackmailing seemingly everyone certainly provided more motive for murder than suicide, but it also raised far more questions than it answered. What kind of secrets was she keeping that would be worth killing over? It was everything I could do to keep from reaching out to Reverend Keaton to see if he had any luck contacting the other teens, but Doug had expressly forbidden me to do so.

And then there was Doug.

Where *was* he? I didn't know why it was bothering me. If I could go whole weeks without crossing paths with the guy, I would normally consider it a gift from God. I knew there were times he sought to maintain his sanity by stepping away from his mother for a bit, but he always let her know where he was going, lest she blow up the phones of all their mutual contacts trying to locate him. In fact, just the other evening, he had gone out fishing, and lucky for me he did, or—

I sat up in my chair. "Mel? Where's Chip?"

"I don't know," she said, wrapping herself tighter in Cheryl's jacket. "He was gone when I got back. Why?"

"Do you think Cheryl or Craig might know where he is?" I started to get to my feet, but she placed a hand over my arm, holding me in place.

"What's the sudden interest in Chip's whereabouts? I got the distinct impression you guys weren't exactly fond of one another. Personally, I was considering it a small blessing not to have him underfoot tonight. I was sick of being a referee."

"Can you call him?" I asked, urgency creeping into my voice. I really didn't want to spell it out, but the perplexity on her face suggested that was the direction in which we were headed.

"Why would I do that?"

I sighed, massaging the bridge of my nose as I looked for words that wouldn't reopen a wound that had only just begun to heal. "That night, out on the bridge," I said. "Doug was the one who broke it all up. If it hadn't been for him, I'm not sure I wouldn't have gone over the side of that bridge."

"That's ridiculous," she said, leaning forward in her chair and pulling her hand away from me. "Chip would have never taken it that far."

"Chip wasn't the one who had hold of me," I said. "I'm not sure he had much say in what was happening. It was more of a mob mentality."

"So, where are you going with this?"

"Guys like that want the last word," I said. "What if they decided to teach Doug a lesson for interrupting their fun?"

"*Guys like that?*" she repeated. "You're talking about my brother like he's homicidal! Next, you'll be accusing him of killing the McAlister girl!"

It hadn't even crossed my mind until she said it, and the consideration that swept across my face brought her to her feet.

"You have *got* to be kidding me!" she said incredulously, her rising voice bringing Cheryl to the screen door.

"Y'all okay out here?" she asked tentatively.

"Just call him," I urged, ignoring Cheryl's question.

"Call who?" Cheryl asked, poking her head through the door.

Melanie rankled. "Apparently, Dwayne thinks our brother is some kind of crazed killer."

"Yeah? Who'd he kill?" Cheryl seemed more amused than upset.

"The McAlister girl and maybe his boss, too."

"I didn't *say* that, Mel," I protested, keeping the tone of my voice even in the hopes that it might keep this from escalating. I was beginning to feel like I'd done nothing but argue my way through this entire holiday.

"It's what you were thinking. Go ahead—convince me otherwise." She defiantly crossed her arms in front of her while Cheryl joined us on the porch.

"But that's impossible," said Cheryl. "Chip couldn't have had anything to do with Tina McAlister. He only got home from Fort Moore a few days ago. She was already missing."

"*See?*" Melanie gestured toward her sister.

"I never said he did!" My protests were getting louder, and despite my good intentions, I was beginning to lose my cool. "But after what your brother and his friends did to me the other night, it doesn't seem so farfetched they might have been looking for some payback for Doug. If you could just be a little more open-minded—"

"You did *not* just say that to me," Melanie said, leaning over me with her eyes blazing. "Your mind is already made up! As far as you're concerned, Chip has been tried and convicted, and you don't even know if there's anything *wrong* yet!"

Cheryl rent the air with an ear-splitting whistle that brought a startled yelp from Betsy. She held her phone to her ear while motioning for us to quiet down with her free hand. "Can you two just shut it for a minute? I can't hear a—oh, hey, Bub! Just wondering if you were planning on dropping by this evening. Dinner's almost ready, and we'll be putting up the Christmas tree after."

She nodded as his muffled words came across the phone.

"Really? I thought you two were done. Uh-huh. Can you repeat that?" She activated her speakerphone and held it out between me and Melanie.

"Ummm—okay," Chip said, uncertainty in his voice. "Jenny and I are spending the night out at her gram's, helping her get her Christmas decorations put up. She ain't got no business bein' up on a ladder at her age. Why are you acting so weird?"

Cheryl ignored the question. "Where does her grandmama live?"

"Otway. You know that. Why are you—"

"I suppose you just got there."

"Shit, no. Been here all day. Jen's been helping tidy up around the house while I went hunting for a tree with her brother. Now, what in the hell is going on?"

Cheryl cast a self-satisfied smirk in our direction. "Not a thing, Bubby. Just wanted to know if I needed to set an extra place at the table. Say, you haven't seen Dwayne's boss by any chance?"

"Dwayne's *what?* Sis, you're being extra weird, even for you."

"*Awww*...you say the sweetest things. By-*eee*." She disconnected the call and looked from Mel to me and back again. "There. Y'all can stop bickering now. Chip's been too busy helping a little old lady put up her Christmas decorations to continue his life of crime."

Melanie opened her mouth to respond, but Cheryl silenced her with a forefinger.

"Before you say *anything*, Melanie, Dwayne wasn't wrong to wonder. Whether Chip was the ringleader of what happened the other night or not, he was a willing participant, and those fellas he's running around with are nothing but a bunch of trouble. I know it's your first instinct to play mama bear and defend all of us. It has been ever since Mama died. But sometimes we don't deserve your righteous indignation, and in this particular instance, Chip most certainly does not."

I looked at Cheryl appreciatively while Melanie's mouth snapped shut. "Thank you," I said.

She smiled. "I've decided I like having your face around. You're okay to look at, and there's never a dull moment. I didn't want my big sister's obstinance to scare you away." She elbowed Melanie playfully and got a half-hearted swat in return.

Cheryl's phone screen brightened, and a generic version of "Macarena" began cycling. Even from where I sat, I recognized the helmet of chestnut brown hair that identified the caller as Molly. Cheryl connected the call, putting the phone to her ear as she hit the ground running.

"I'm not sure I even want to speak to you, sister dear. What was all that bullshit with bringing Daddy around here? You know—"

Molly's words were unintelligible, but her volume rose, cutting Cheryl off.

"Well—no," she said, her own righteous indignation evaporating in an instant. "Why do you ask? She and Katie are out getting their nails done. I—"

Molly's next words came in a hysterical avalanche, and as I watched Cheryl's expression shift to dread, I got to my feet, putting an arm protectively around Melanie, waiting to hear words no parent should ever hear.

CHAPTER TWENTY

"*Stop the car! Stop the car!*"

My eyes flickered sideways toward the passenger seat where I found Melanie doubled over in the eerie luminescence of my Hyundai's dashboard lights. She looked awful.

I cut to my right with little regard for the traffic around me. I was greeted by a chorus of angry horns as I awkwardly bumped my front passenger tire up onto the curb and slammed on my brakes. Rain fell in sheets across the pavement, illuminated by headlights as cars swept by on this dark, dismal evening I desperately wished belonged to anybody else.

"I'm going to be sick," she mumbled, covering her mouth with one hand while fighting the seatbelt with the other.

I unlatched my own and threw my door open into oncoming traffic. More angry honking, and as I stepped down to the glistening pavement, I alternated between flipping a pair of angry birds and apologetic, palms-forward hand waving. I scurried around the back of the car to where Melanie knelt by the curb, retching herself into dry heaves. I helped to steady her against the car as she gulped for air between expulsions.

I've never felt so helpless in all my life.

Cars continued to whiz by in both directions along the two-lane city street, and I hated everyone inside of them. They were bound for destinations made by choice, and absolutely no one would choose to go where Melanie and I were heading.

Woefully inept at saying the right things at times like these, I stuck with the simple and inane, soothingly repeating things like, "I'm right here, sweetheart," and "Just breathe…breathe…"

Eventually, her hiccupping breath slowed and settled into a pattern approximating normal. I held her steady with my right hand as I rubbed her back with the palm of my left. "Do you think you can stand?" I asked.

She nodded, wiping the corners of her mouth with the back of her hand. I helped her to her feet, and once she was upright, she leaned against the SUV, a fresh wave of anguish sweeping over her. "Oh, God—I don't think I can *do* this," she cried.

"*Shhh, shhh,*" I soothed, folding her into my arms and tucking her head beneath my chin. I could feel rather than hear the sobs that caused her body to quake against mine. I was afraid to say anything more as we clung to each other in the pouring rain.

For everything I *had* been through, I'd never attempted to identify the body of a loved one, much less someone so young.

It should have come as no surprise to learn that Molly frequently filled her evenings listening to a police scanner. Another young girl's body had been found near the riverbank. Carrying no identification, her description alone caught Molly's attention, but when she heard there was a coffin-shaped backpack found near the body, she had immediately thought of Jasmine. She had been actively trying to dissuade Jasmine's burgeoning interest in Demon Academy for months, as if there was such a thing as a gateway toy to set its owner on a direct path to surrendering her soul to Satan.

I eased Melanie back into the passenger seat before racing around to my side of the car, oblivious to the horns of oncoming traffic. I slid behind the wheel and fastened my seatbelt, prepared to work my way back into traffic when Cheryl nearly sent me into cardiac arrest from the backseat.

"It's just going straight to voicemail," she said, frustrated. "Slow down. You'll want to turn left here."

She had been doggedly persistent in trying to reach Katie's cell, and I had completely forgotten she was lurking in the shadows. More familiar with the layout of Ironton and the best ways down to the riverbank, she also acted as our guide. I waited for the light to change before turning left at the next intersection.

I tried to cling to the tiny sliver of hope that remained, but I couldn't bring myself to say it out loud. As much as I wanted to soothe Melanie's distress, I couldn't give voice to the possibility without certainty of the outcome. I'd never forgive myself for being wrong. There had been no official notification, but we couldn't just sit and wait for the Grim Reaper to arrive. Now, as we drew nearer the point of no return, I fought the overwhelming urge to turn around and drive away just as far and as fast as I could go.

I blew through a red light and nearly broadsided a minivan, swerving and sliding on the wet pavement as Melanie got an uncomfortably close glimpse into the other driver's terrified eyes.

"Sorry, sorry, sorry," I repeated to everyone and no one, checking all of my mirrors for the police lights I figured were inevitable—anything to prolong this torture.

None came.

Cheryl directed me toward the entrance to the floodgate, and it was impossible to miss the flashing light bars painting the night red and blue from patrol cars parked along both sides of the wall. One had been pulled across the entrance, effectively blocking it, while a square-jawed female officer stood guard in the driving rain, protected by a bright yellow rain slicker as she turned away gawking onlookers drawn to the scene by the activity. We were fifth in line, and I don't know why we should expect any different reception than those who came and went before us, but I was already rolling down Melanie's window as we approached the officer.

"Keep it moving, folks. Nothing to see here," she said, waving us left with a Maglite.

"Excuse me, officer," I called, stretching across Melanie as she shielded her tear-stained face from the bright glare. "Can we—"

"I need you to keep moving, sir," interrupted the officer in her even tone, her expression unchanged. She was completely oblivious to the distress right in front of her face.

"I don't think you understand—*officer*," I tried again, unable to keep a little attitude from creeping into my voice. "We—"

"I don't think *you* understand," said the officer, shining the light directly into my face and raising her voice slightly. "This is an active crime scene. No one without authorization will be permitted to enter. Now, I'm going to need you to move along."

"But—"

"Now!" she barked, thumping her palm repeatedly against the side of my car before stepping back and directing her attention to the car behind me.

As I slowly eased left, all I could see was Melanie sobbing helplessly out of the corner of my eye. I couldn't let her suffer this uncertainty any longer. I pulled ahead just enough to fake compliance before slamming the car into park and hustling out into the rain, racing directly back toward the startled officer. I was barely aware of her fumbling for something on her belt as I pushed past her and ran into the area behind the floodwall, breaching the secured perimeter. Just as it occurred to me that she might have been reaching for her gun, I heard her sounding the alarm on a handheld radio, alerting others to my impending arrival. I broke into an erratic, side-to-side advance, nonetheless. Getting shot in the back wasn't high on my list of priorities.

A large tent had been erected near the water's edge to shield the crime scene from the inclement weather. Bright interior lighting leaked out through its seams, pushing back the night just a little. Two or three silhouettes worked inside the tent while a handful of darkened figures huddled in small groups around its exterior. A pair of EMTs waited inside the relative comfort of a darkened ambulance for their eventual cue to collect the victim's body. One by one, flashlights turned my way as the radio alert began to register with the officers I raced toward.

Would I have plunged headlong into that tent, potentially compromising a crime scene before it was officially cleared? I'd have to guess I would have. My need to know was simply too great. But just as I neared the small group of uniformed officers and plainclothes detectives who were hurriedly scrambling to block my path, I was abruptly clotheslined from the shadows to my right. My feet flew into the air as my head snapped back and I was driven to the ground, landing painfully on my back on the wet, uneven soil. My breath whooshed out of me as my diaphragm contracted, and I didn't even register stars before I winked out.

••••••●◦◦●••••••

I woke to the taste of dirt in my mouth.

I was cold, wet and on my stomach, my face pressed into the dank earth. I felt a knee in the small of my back as my hands were pulled behind me and bound tightly with a plastic zip tie. I didn't think much time had passed. Straining, I was able to lift my head up off of the ground and see the brightly lit tent before me. The detectives had resumed their huddled discussions, no longer concerned with the threat I no longer was. A hand clamped down on my shoulder and roughly flipped me over onto my back. With my arms bound behind me, all I could do was squint up into the blinding flashlight that shone directly into my eyes.

261

"Son of a *bitch!*" muttered a somewhat familiar voice. "What in the Sam Hill are *you* doing here?"

"Do you have to shine that thing straight into my face?" I said, squirming helplessly on the ground.

The light fell away, and I found myself under the intense scrutiny of Officer Lucy Graves. She suddenly stood up, shining her flashlight every which way. *"Please* tell me that idiot boss of yours is somewhere out here, too." Her laugh was ugly.

"It's just me," I said, struggling to sit up and getting no assistance. "I have no idea where Doug is. Listen, I just—"

"Is *this* the kind of training that man offers?" she asked. "Do you even know the kind of trouble you're in?"

"Please," I implored, grinding my teeth as my patience continued to erode. "I just need to see who's underneath that tent."

She threw her head back and laughed. "Well, that ain't happening. What's your business in all this, anyway?"

"Please—" I tried again, but my voice caught in my throat as a year's worth of memories washed over me of the young girl I had grown to love every bit as much as if she were my own. "My girlfriend—*our* daughter. We can't find her, and then we heard about the backpack, and—oh, *God!"*

I was fighting a losing battle for control of my emotions, and it took a moment before my hitching breath allowed me to attempt speech again.

"We just have to know. *Please,"* I begged, staring unflinchingly at Officer Graves as the pouring rain helped obscure my free-flowing tears. Frankly, I was long past caring about appearances.

Uncertainty flickered across the officer's face as she returned my stare. I prayed it was an ounce of humanity. She finally looked away, scouring the nearby area before calling out, "Ray?"

One of the nearby officers jogged over, and I recognized him as her partner, Officer Palmer. "Hey, Luce. What's up?"

"I've got our interloper secured here on the ground, but I don't want him going anywhere. Can you babysit for a sec? I need to check something."

"Sure," he said, giving me the once-over. If my face sparked any recognition whatsoever, he gave no indication. Lucy jogged toward the tent, her yellow slicker flapping in the wind, and after conferring with someone just inside its entrance, she carefully stepped through the tent's opening.

It was the longest five minutes of my life.

My heart sank as Lucy emerged from the tent, returning much more slowly than she had gone. The rain was beginning to taper off, and I could see the distress on her face more clearly as she bridged the distance. I could barely breathe by the time she arrived.

"It's not your girl," she said, and I blinked, unable to comprehend what she was telling me.

"But—are you *sure?* You don't even know what Jasmine looks like. I'm sure I've got a picture on my phone if you could just—"

"It's not her," she repeated, her expression troubled but sure.

I couldn't make myself believe it was true. "But—how do you know?"

"Because I recognize her. It's another young lady from the youth group at my church. You might have met her when you were nosing around up there this morning."

She had my full attention.

"Tipton," she said, struggling to keep her own emotions in check. "Tammy Tipton."

It took everything I had not to react.

"Give me a hand, Ray," she said, grabbing one of my arms while nodding to my other. He took hold and together, they boosted me to my feet.

Apparently, it was time to be charged with whatever laws I had broken here tonight, and I hoped they were something my attorney, Sally Sheaffer, would be able to handle.

"I know it's probably too much to ask," I said. "But can we please stop by my car on the way out so I can tell Melanie the—" I could almost hear myself skid to a stop as I realized I was about to say, 'good news.' This wasn't good news. It was some other parents' nightmare, and only a small reprieve for us. We still had no idea where Jasmine was.

Officer Graves reached behind me and abruptly cut the zip tie, telling her partner he could rejoin the others.

"Why don't you go tell her yourself," she said. "We've got enough to deal with here tonight without having to arrest you, too."

I coaxed blood back into my hands as I stared at her, stunned. "I'm free to go?"

"You are," she said with a tight smile. "I've got a little girl, too, and in your place, I doubt I'd have done much different. Do we need to get an Amber alert out?"

The question caught me off guard. My first instinct was to say yes, but this entire episode had been triggered by Molly's hysterical interpretation of a transmission on the police scanner. Amber alerts were typically reserved for minors who had either been taken by estranged parents or someone else who was putting the child in immediate jeopardy. I don't know that Katie's impunctuality after an impromptu nail session qualified. In fact, it seemed ludicrous to suggest such a thing at this point. I ended up shaking my head.

"I don't think so," I said. "At least not yet. She's late getting home, but not all *that* late. We just panicked when we heard what was going on down here."

She stared at me about ten seconds past my comfort level. "Well—if you're sure."

"I am."

She directed a forefinger at my nose. "Two things: One, don't mention that girl's name to anyone, do you hear me?"

I quickly nodded. Anything to get away from here.

"I shouldn't have even told you that, and I'd hate for her poor parents to find out from the media or, God forbid, the rumor mill. And two—"

Her forefinger inched closer to my nose.

"Find someone other than Douglas Boggs to train with," she said. "He's not gonna do anything but hurt your reputation before you even have one. Believe me, I should know."

She headed back toward her colleagues, and I hauled ass in the opposite direction before she could change her mind.

······•••••●◌◦●•••••·····

I hurried past the officer who was still busily diverting cars away from the floodgate entrance, hoping I would escape her notice. I headed to where I had improperly parked my car, but it was no longer there. Mildly perplexed, I walked in a slow circle, looking everywhere for my vehicle and the two sisters I had left inside it. My gaze finally connected with that of the officer I had been trying to avoid. She had now halted all traffic and was staring at me impatiently, wandering out into the street like an idiot as I soaked up more of the nighttime drizzle. She pointed straight ahead and to the left, and following her indication, I spotted my Hyundai about three blocks down, parked along the curb facing the wrong way with its hazard lights winking. As I started across the street, Melanie jumped down from the driver's seat and ran toward me, her cell phone clutched in her hand. From that distance, it was hard to be certain, but it looked like she was— smiling?

I was practically breathless as we met midway, cars slowing to gawk as they inched past us. I took her face into my hands. "It wasn't her, Mel. It wasn't her."

"I know," she said, tears streaming down her face as her relief manifested itself in giggles. She indicated her cell phone. "Craig just called. She's home."

• • • • • • ● ◠◠ ● • • • • • • •

Melanie was out of the car before I could come to a complete stop, sprinting across the gravel expanse to disappear through the back door, Cheryl hot on her heels. I didn't fully realize how much anxiety I still carried until I walked into the kitchen and saw Jasmine for myself, wide-eyed and standing ramrod straight in the living room between two kneeling, hysterical women who alternated between blubbering nonsense and showering her with hugs and kisses. She shot me a look that was pure WTF, and my throat was thick when I laughed, my eyes threatening to spill over. I casually dabbed at the corners as Craig crossed into the kitchen from the living room.

He smiled and clapped an arm around my shoulders. "I didn't know how much you guys wanted me to tell her, so I went with nothing," he said quietly. "Other than the fact that she scared the living shit out of you both. I've only told Maggie as much as necessary to keep my girls over with her at the trailer until you all got back and had a chance to talk with Jasmine. I'm not in any hurry to let Kenzie know another body was found down by the river. She's gonna be sleeping between me and Cheryl for the next year."

"Thanks, man," I said, giving him an appreciative nod before joining the trio in the living room where they stood in a close circle. Melanie had shifted gears and was now mid-lecture.

"—once, I've told you a million times. You *have* to keep that phone charged. It's not optional—it's part of the deal. Do you realize how worried I've been since I couldn't reach you? I thought you were—" She couldn't bring herself to say it. "Let's just say my imagination went dark."

266

Jasmine looked from her mother to Cheryl then to me before her eyes finally came to rest on the floor. "It *is* charged," she finally said, holding her phone out for her mother to see.

"But—I don't understand." Melanie eyes shifted from the phone's brightly lit display to her daughter's suddenly guilty expression and back to the phone, settling on the hand that held it. She grabbed Jasmine's hand and turned it over. "You didn't get your nails done."

She slowly shook her head. "I talked Katie into taking me out to Gramma's house. You know how bad cell phone reception is out there."

Melanie's mouth fell open. "You *what?!?*"

"I was tired of waiting, and you were never going to take me!" protested Jasmine in an insolent tone she's perfected over the years that drives Melanie absolutely wild. "I don't care what you say, it wasn't right for you to keep me from my brother."

Melanie stared at her beyond the point of comfort, and I didn't dare intercede. It would be like stepping between two fighting Dobermans. When Melanie finally found her voice, it was surprisingly calm. "That was never my plan. In fact, we were going to go visit them tonight after dinner, but I'm guessing you already know that. Gramma sure must have been surprised when you showed up without us."

Jasmine shrugged, but her face softened as she sensed the foundation of her argument collapsing underneath her.

"Did you have a nice visit?" Melanie asked.

Jasmine shrugged again, unable to look her mother in the face but sensing the fury hiding just beneath her dulcet tone. "S'pose."

"Well, as long as you were able to satisfy your curiosity," said Melanie, cupping her hand under her daughter's chin and demanding her undivided attention. Her cheekbones were flushed but her voice remained deceptively mellifluous. "Do you want to know where me, Dwayne, and your Aunt Cheryl have been? Hmm?"

"Um, sure."

"We just got back from the river where another young lady's body washed up. Did I mention she fit your general description?" Melanie's volume continued to rise as her composure went right out the window. *"Oh! And all of this was while we couldn't get you to answer your goddamn phone!"*

Jasmine's face crumpled, and I couldn't see what good could come of this. Melanie's emotions were completely out of control. "Melanie—"

"Stay out of it!" she shrieked at me, so angry she was shaking.

Cheryl took Melanie by the shoulders, turning her away from Jasmine while Melanie fought her every step of the way. Finally, she burst into angry tears and collapsed against her sister's shoulder. Cheryl eased her towards the stairs and up to the bedroom she shared with her husband, guiding her inside, and closing the door behind them.

I knelt down to Jasmine as she stood there quietly weeping, and all I could think about was what a complete clusterfuck this weekend had become. I pinched the bridge of my nose, wishing like hell we had just stayed home.

"Are you g-g-gonna yell at me, too?" she hiccupped.

I gave her a reassuring smile. "Nope. I sure am glad to see you, though."

Despite my sad, soggy state, she threw her arms around my neck and let it all out, sobbing on my shoulder. Damnedest thing about tears—they're contagious. It took no time before a lump had worked its way into my throat and my own chin was quivering.

"Hey, hey, hey," I said, forcing that lump right back down. "It'll all be okay."

She pulled back to give me a doubtful look, and I chuckled, running a thumb underneath her leaky eyes.

"Eventually," I added, and we put our foreheads together while she got herself under control. "So, what did you think of your little brother?"

"He's loud, and he slobbers a lot," she said, allowing herself the trace of a grin before it dropped away. "He looks just like Daddy."

I nodded. "I think so, too. A little shorter, maybe…"

I winked at her and was rewarded with a giggle.

"I know this isn't the point," Jasmine said solemnly. "But why in the world would you all think something like that had happened to me? I wasn't even that late."

"Apparently, your Aunt Molly spends her evenings listening to the police band for entertainment. She heard that the body of another young girl had been found by the river, but what really caught her attention was the mention of what sounded like a Demon Academy backpack—"

Jasmine inhaled sharply.

"What?" I asked, as her eyes widened.

"I loaned my backpack to one of Katie's friends just before we headed out to Gramma's," she said. "Her name was Tammy something. Was it her?"

I didn't need to answer. It was written all over my face.

CHAPTER TWENTY-ONE

"Let me get this straight. Tammy was with you earlier this afternoon, and you didn't think this was worth mentioning when we were down at the floodwall?" Officer Lucy Graves asked me incredulously, pacing her way through Cheryl's living room as Melanie and I sat side-by-side on the couch with Jasmine between us. The disembodied artificial tree limbs that had been scattered about the floor were moved to line the wall beneath the stair railing. It was looking less and less likely the Christmas tree would be going up tonight. Craig and Cheryl had gone to the trailer to break the latest news to Maggie and their daughters before they caught wind of it on TV.

"I wasn't exactly thinking clearly," I said. "I was worried about Jasmine."

"And you're telling me the backpack we found at the scene belonged to your daughter."

"Yes, ma'am," said Jasmine, nodding. "Tammy asked if she could borrow it."

Melanie's eyebrows shot up. "You never loan your Demon Academy stuff out. You won't even bring the dolls into the house for fear Mandy and Kenzi will mess up their hair."

Jasmine shrugged, squirming between us. "I didn't really want to. But she was picking a bunch of stuff up from Katie, and it was too much for her to carry. She promised to give my bag to Katie just as soon as she was through, and Katie said it would be fine, and not to be a big—"

"A big what?" asked Melanie, shifting sideways to look into her daughter's downcast face.

"Nothing," she said sullenly, and suddenly, I liked Katie even less. Fear of manhandling wasn't the only reason Jasmine didn't share her Demon Academy obsession. Jasmine was at that precarious stage where other girls her age were as likely to ridicule her for playing with dolls as to appreciate them in any way. Older girls like Katie had no interest at all, and in my head, I could hear her calling Jasmine a big baby just as plainly as if she were standing in the room.

Lucy stopped pacing and looked at Jasmine. "Wait a minute. Katie? You mean Katie Hamilton?"

Jasmine shrugged but another light winked on in my head.

"I don't know her last name," she said. "She's best friends with my Aunt Maggie."

"Is Katie short for Kaitlyn?" I asked, remembering the list of church friends Anne Marie had sent me.

Lucy looked at me expectantly. "Don't tell me you know her, too."

"No, not really," I said, shaking my head dismissively. "Other than meeting her briefly when we first arrived Wednesday evening. It's just that hers was one of the names given to me by Tina McAlister's aunt—you know, when she hired us to check things out. Tammy's name was on the list, too."

"Didn't I just tell your boss to stay away from this case? Let me guess, he split the list with you and gave you the ones you hadn't already scared to death."

I didn't appreciate the dig, which made my next admission a little more humiliating. "*No.* As a matter of fact, he told me to back off. He's taking the lead."

Lucy threw her head back and laughed. "Oh, *man!* How embarrassing. Sidelined by Doug Boggs. Wow. Just *wow!* So, how did Tammy end up in your car?"

"She texted me," I said, unlocking my phone and finding the cryptic message. "I didn't know who it was. All I knew was that Doug didn't have time to make it all the way back to Greenup. I was also worried that whoever it was would bolt if Doug showed up with me or in my place. It said to come alone, so that's what I did."

"So, what was the big urgency?"

"She told me Tina was blackmailing them—*all* of them," I said. I had already decided against withholding anything, not that I knew all that much to begin with. This wasn't a competition. People were dying.

"*Blackmailing* them?" Lucy repeated incredulously. She checked the levels on the voice recorder on her phone to make sure she was still getting all of this down. "Seems awfully complicated for a bunch of teenagers. What could Tina have possibly had to hold over them? She was such a mousy little thing."

"Apparently not so much this past year. Tammy said she had an agenda, and one by one, Tina was pressing these kids into helping her achieve certain goals. She was relying on Tammy to rig the computer vote so she would win Homecoming Queen."

"And why would Tammy do that?" asked Lucy.

"Tina had video proof that Tammy hired another girl to take her SATs for her. It would've ruined Tammy's academic career if it had gotten out."

Lucy processed that for a moment before exhaling in a whistle. "And what about the others?"

"Tammy wouldn't talk about them. She said it wasn't her place to tell their secrets. But whatever Tina had over Jesse was enough to get him to ask her to go the Homecoming Dance. And Tina told Tammy that she and her friends had better hope that nothing happened to her. She somehow had it fixed to make these secrets public if something did."

Lucy resumed pacing the floor, chewing on her thumbnail as she deliberated. "Okay, let's back up a bit. Jasmine, did you see what Tammy was putting into your backpack?"

"I wasn't really paying attention. Some papers. Maybe a tablet—I'm not sure."

"Wasn't there anything in the backpack when you found her?" I asked.

Lucy scowled at me. "We are not engaged in an information exchange here," she said dryly, but I could read between the lines. She wouldn't have asked the question if she had already known the answer. "Is Katie still here?"

Jasmine shook her head. "No, she just dropped me off and left. She said she had some things to do, but I think she was afraid of running into Mom."

Lucy went on point. "Does she have reason to fear your mother?"

Melanie laughed awkwardly. "She drove the getaway car in an unauthorized expedition to Jasmine's grandmother's in Lymont. I'm sure she wouldn't have enjoyed what I would have had to say, but it's not like I was going to—"

She left the sentence hanging, but we all knew what her next two words would have been.

"Is there anything else you might want to share with me?" asked Lucy, treading back and forth while boring holes through us with her eyes. I was starting to think this was some form of hypnosis, and she was the pendulum. "Even if you think it's insignificant—why don't you tell me, and let me be the judge?"

I opened my mouth and closed it, but not quickly enough to escape notice.

"Yes, Mr. Morrow?" asked Lucy impatiently. From the corner of my eye, Melanie's face was riddled with concern, anticipating my revelation that

Chip and his buddies had assaulted me on the U.S. Grant Bridge, but the thought honestly hadn't even crossed my mind.

"I'm sure it's nothing," I said. "But I haven't been able to get hold of Doug since this afternoon."

"Did you try his mother's?" she asked, and I caught her slight eye roll. "Loretta usually keeps him on a very short leash."

"Well, yeah. It was the first place I tried," I said, noting Lucy's familiarity with Doug's living arrangements and wondering once again exactly how close they had once been. "She hasn't seen him since he left this morning to meet me in Flatwoods, and I haven't seen him since he—you know what? I'm sure it's nothing. His phone doesn't hold a charge for shit, and he's probably out fishing. Ran into him doing that just the other day, trying to catch a break from Loretta and his aunt who's visiting for the holiday."

"Was he planning on questioning anybody else today?" she asked, and despite her casual nonchalance, I was pretty sure I caught the faintest hint of concern. "I mean, is there any reason to think he could be in any immediate danger?"

"I don't think so," I said. "He was really pissed at me about what happened at the church, and he was worried that any more immediate missteps could cause trouble for Boggs Investigations. He was headed back to Lymont to cool off. It actually kinda makes sense that he wouldn't go straight home. His aunt brought her poodles, and they aren't very fond of him."

She chewed her bottom lip and slowly nodded. "All right, then. That's all I have for now, but I want you to remain available should I have any more questions. Here's one of my cards in case you think of anything else I should know."

Melanie leaned forward and took the card. "We were planning to head back to Grove City tomorrow. I hope that won't be a problem. I have to work on Monday, and I'm still fairly new—"

"That's fine. Just don't drop off the face of the earth," said Lucy, heading toward the kitchen but stopping under the arched entrance to aim a forefinger in my direction. "And you. I don't want you anywhere *near* this case or anyone involved with it. If I catch you nosing around, I will personally lock up you for obstruction of justice, do you understand me?"

I held her glare, but my grin was tight, and I was barely able to suppress a salute. "Yes, ma'am."

• • • • ● ● ⌒◌⌒ ● ● • • • • • •

Officer Graves had been gone no more than a few minutes before everyone from the trailer filed back into the house. Craig, Cheryl, and Maggie were a little more subtle with their questioning, but Kenzie and Mandy went after Jasmine with a vengeance, barraging her with queries she couldn't even begin to answer while simultaneously testing out theories of what might have happened to Tina and Tammy, including a particularly imaginative scenario involving the Mothman. After all, Point Pleasant wasn't so far away.

I don't think anyone was in the mood to put up the Christmas tree, but that's exactly what Melanie and Cheryl decided was the best distraction for the girls to occupy the rest of their evening. We were startled to learn it was barely eight o'clock—it felt so much later. Since Jasmine had already visited with her grandmother, Melanie gave Sarah a quick call to see if we could postpone our family visit until the following day, which was starting to get a little full. We were supposed to spend some time with my folks, too, and I made a mental note to call Mom to keep her in the loop. I'd never hear the end of it if we didn't spend some more time with them before we headed back home.

The local CBS affiliate was playing a bunch of animated Christmas specials, so we left the television on in the background while the girls went

275

to work. It was such an unusual juxtaposition to hear the Grinch's instantly recognizable theme song segue into Mandy's latest conjecture on what was *really* going on down by the river. After broaching human sacrifice, Cheryl put her foot down, declaring the subject off limits for the rest of the evening. Everyone except for her own two girls seemed relieved.

"I think I'll go out and see if I can get a fire started," suggested Craig, sliding on his coat. "What do you think, ladies? Smores by the fire after you get that sucker up?"

Squeals of delight followed, and Cheryl seized the opportunity to unfold her crisscrossed legs and, with a bit of a grunt, rose to her feet. She had been sitting in that position for long enough to lose all feeling as she untangled lights. She passed the remaining knot to Melanie and hobbled toward the kitchen. "I'll get the hot chocolate going."

It felt perverse to be doing anything that approximated normal, but keeping the girls preoccupied was the priority. Craig nudged me. "Give me a hand with the firewood?" he asked, nodding toward the back door.

"Sure," I said, grabbing my jacket and slipping it on. "Lead the way, sir."

We stepped out onto the porch where Craig paused long enough to dig a couple pair of filthy work gloves out of a milk crate. He tossed me one, and I slid my hands into their warm lining. The temperature had dipped low enough to make our exhalations visible against the moonlit night. Mercifully, the rain had stopped before it would have turned to snow, and I sincerely hoped it stayed that way. We each loaded up with an armful of wood from the cord stacked under a tarp at the far end of the porch, and I followed Craig around to the northwest corner of their front yard where he had arranged four outdoor benches in a loose circle around an oft-used section of scorched earth that currently held the incendiary evidence of bonfires recently past.

"Do you think the ground's too wet?" I asked, noting the standing water on the benches.

"Nah," said Craig as he unloaded his firewood directly into the blackened pit. He indicated an area between the benches for me to drop mine. "The wood's dry, and once I get it going, everything else will dry out pretty quickly. Might have to wipe down the benches, though. Why don't you go ask Cheryl for some towels, and I'll grab a canister of gasoline from the garage?"

"Roger that," I said, jogging toward the house with my breath pluming in front of me as Craig veered left, his movement activating the security light mounted near the entrance to his garage.

I was about halfway to the porch when my phone launched into the opening chords of "Running Down a Dream," indicating a call was incoming. A humorous, albeit less than flattering picture of my mother appeared onscreen, in which she was taking an enormous bite from a sandwich. It always made me grin. I took a beat to stop panting like a dog before connecting the call.

"Hey, Mom," I said. "What's up?"

"Just checking to see if you're still out there somewhere," she said, and I could tell from her tone she was less than pleased. Her cadence was clipped, her choice of words precise and maximized for effect. "After you bailed on us yesterday, I was sort of looking for you and the ladies to pop in all day. Your Aunt Jane has already headed back to Cincinnati. She's worried about snow."

I winced. "I'm sorry, Mom, but that case I told you about has taken some really odd turns. I've been a lot busier than I thought I would be."

"Nothing too dangerous, I should hope," she said irritably, and I wasn't about to get into the details. "I can't say I'm a big fan of this new career choice of yours. What was so bad about your consulting service? It seemed to be providing nicely for you."

"It was—it *is*," I said, correcting myself. "But it's also gotten very boring. It's the same thing day in and day out, week after week after week. I like most of what I'm doing with Boggs Investigations."

"Seems to me like you're just trying to impress your girlfriend."

"Where's this coming from?" I asked, surprised by the ugliness creeping into her voice. "Melanie isn't the reason I'm working with Doug. Why are you blaming her? I thought you liked her."

"I do," she said, shifting gears with a sigh. "It's just—I don't know. It just seems like I hardly get to see you anymore. If you're not spending time with her family, you're picking up some new case. You know, even God rested on the seventh day."

"It's not like I *planned* for this to happen," I said. "Frankly, I'm surprised Doug even took the case on at all."

"Are you planning on stopping by tomorrow? It would certainly be nice to have all of my children under the same roof at the same time, at least for a *few* minutes. I doubt Matt and Sheila will stay much past noon."

"Jeez, Mom, you make it sound like it's been forever. We were all just there for Thanksgiving dinner."

"And you were gone just as fast as you could break away," she accused, and she was getting upset again. "I don't *like* this new thing you're doing. It's dangerous, reckless, and thoughtless!"

I stood there, wisps of frosty exhalation escaping my open mouth. I didn't like the sounds coming from the other end of the connection. No one wants to see or hear their mother cry, although she was doing her damnedest to stave it off.

"Mom—" I began, wondering how in the hell I could reason with her in this state.

"No," she said, cutting me off abruptly. "Forget about it. If you can make time, you know where to find us. I'm making enough chili for everyone, but don't feel obligated. I'll freeze whatever's left and your dad can just have it for lunch."

"*Mom*—" I tried again.

"You know what really *pisses* me off?"

Oh, shit. She lowered her voice and hissed the pejorative. She never swore. This was trouble.

"It's almost unbearable to lose one of my children," she said, her words cutting me to the bone. "It's something I wouldn't wish on anyone. But somehow, lately it feels like I've lost two, and it's just not fair."

"Oh, *Mom*—"

But I was talking to empty air. She had hung up on me.

"What's wrong?" asked Melanie, reading my expression as soon as I walked into the kitchen.

"Nothing," I groused, not really up for the instant replay.

"Bull," she said, placing her fingers gently against my cheek which burned with shame.

Despite everything we had been through earlier that evening with Jasmine, I had no idea the kind of pain my mother was enduring. It had never once occurred to me that by avoiding my childhood home and protecting my own feelings, it might affect anyone other than myself. I felt incredibly selfish and stupid—*cowardly*.

"It's just my mom," I finally said. "We have to make it to lunch tomorrow. Whatever else we do, we need to be there."

"Of course," she said, continuing to stroke my cheek while she patiently waited to see if I was willing to share more. I wasn't. No matter how I told the story, I was the asshole in the end.

I clumsily dabbed at the corners of my eyes which were threatening to betray me and exactly how upset I was. "Craig sent me up to get some towels. The benches out there are still wet from the rain."

Her gaze lingered for a moment longer before she turned and headed down the hallway toward the bathroom. I took the opportunity to dampen a paper towel and run it across my face and then stared at the yellowing tile of the drop ceiling until I felt my eyes were no longer in danger of leaking. She came back holding three ratty towels.

"Will this be enough?"

"Should be plenty." I took the towels from her and peeked into the living room, where I saw that the tree was nearly finished. The girls took turns handing ornaments to Maggie and telling her where to put them, since she was the only one tall enough to reach the upper portion of the tree. "Looks like they're about finished in there."

"Yep," said Melanie, sliding an arm around my waist and giving me a gentle squeeze. I rested my chin on top of her head.

"I love you," I said quietly, still fighting the constriction in my throat.

"You better. You know I'm here for you."

I nodded and sighed. No use fretting about things I couldn't change tonight. I would fix things with Mom over lunch the following day, or at least as much as I could. It was beginning to feel like this evening was never going to end.

"Craig's probably got the fire started by now," I said, reluctantly extracting myself from her embrace. "I should probably—"

"Holy moly!" Cheryl exclaimed from the living room. "Guys! *Guys! Come here. You've got to see this. Hurry!*"

Melanie and I exchanged a puzzled glance as I set the towels aside on the dinette table, and we crossed to the living room where everybody was focused on the TV. I had a sinking feeling as I tried to absorb what was onscreen, prepared for breaking news about yet another teen body washing up along the banks of the Ohio.

It wasn't a breaking news alert. Whatever animated Christmas fare had been playing had gone to commercial, and I found myself staring at a rapid-fire sequence of images that preyed on consumer insecurities set to music designed to make the pulse race. A hammer smashing through a pane of glass on a residential door followed by a leather-gloved hand reaching through to release the lock. A grieving mother passing out missing persons photos of her young daughter as she silently begged passersby for information. An elderly woman checking her email on a computer model I hadn't seen in years, panicking as her screen starts populating with porn—pixelated, of course—this was a television ad, after all. And centered right there at the bottom of the screen and in bold letters:

BOGGS INVESTIGATIONS
(740) 555-HELP (4357)

"Isn't this where you work?" asked Cheryl excitedly.

"Uh-huh," I confirmed absently, transfixed by the ad. Doug's upper torso appeared in the lower left corner of the screen, stuffed uncomfortably into the same corduroy getup he had worn to church earlier that day.

I shushed the room and waved to Cheryl. "Can you turn it up?"

Cheryl obliged, and soon the room was filled with the stumbling cadence of Doug Boggs reading in a monotone from cue cards he visibly squinted to decipher.

"—anything from a cheating spouse to a missing pet, my team is the affordable solution for any budget. Cybercrimes? No problem. We've recently expanded our services and can help you out if you're the victim of ransomware. My team is equipped with the know-how to free your data without emptying your bank account."

A horrific black-and-white photo of me with my mouth hanging open appeared in the lower right corner of the screen, captioned, 'Dwayne Morrow, IT Expert,' and I gasped out loud as the younger girls looked from the screen to me and burst out laughing. I looked positively deranged, like a person you wouldn't trust to scoop your puppy's poop, much less restore valuable data from your computer equipment. That damn picture had been floating around in the media since I had solved my best friend's murder, and if I never saw it again, it would be too soon. I couldn't believe it was the best of Doug's options. I suspected Loretta was behind this, the cantankerous old troll. And what, exactly, was he suggesting I could do? I was no cybersecurity expert. He was making promises we would never be able to keep. I tuned back in just as he announced our satellite office on West Broad in Columbus, and I could only guess he was running the ad in that market, too.

"I didn't realize you were doing commercials," said Melanie.

Wide-eyed, I watched the commercial segue into an ad for Burger King, nearly speechless. "Neither did I."

CHAPTER TWENTY-TWO

"Wh-wh-*what?!?*"

I flinched and pulled the phone away from my ear. I stood on the ground at the corner of the back porch, enviously watching the folks at the far end of the yard where they huddled around the sizable fire Craig had managed to build. They were loading marshmallows onto thoroughly seared metal skewers while fragments of animated chatter and laughter drifted my way on dissipating wisps of frosty breath. Fun for everyone but me. The rain had moved out leaving the cloud cover behind, and the temperature continued to drop. My knuckles were beginning to ache.

"Nice way to *finally* answer the phone, Loretta," I said, thinking she sounded more than a little like Cartman's mother from *South Park*. Hmm— the comparison didn't exactly stop there.

There was a brief pause.

"Who is this?"

"Cut the shit, Loretta," I said. "It's me—Dwayne."

"Oh." She sounded less than pleased. "Well, what did you expect? It's a wonder I heard the phone at all over my CPAP."

"Well, is he home? Of course, he is. You'd have never gone to bed without seeing your little man safely in the door. Didn't you pass along my message? I really need to talk to him."

She yawned loudly. "Listen, Mr. Smart Guy, I'm not gonna be pulled out of a sound sleep just to listen to your filthy mouth. I've got church bright and early. What's this all about?"

"I just caught our new television advertisement," I said. "When did *that* happen?"

"Are you kidding me? This is on the agenda for Monday's staff meeting. Why are you bothering me with it now?"

"I'm not trying to bother you, I'm trying to bother Doug," I said. "But his phone still goes straight to voicemail. Can you get him for me, please? I need to talk to him about more than just false advertising. There have been some developments on this case he needs to know."

"What do you mean, 'false advertising?'" she challenged. "I was very hands-on with the production of that commercial."

"Well, you might have checked with me to see if the things you advertised were things I could actually *do*."

"You're kidding me, right? You said you could do anything."

"*Nobody* can do everything."

She harrumphed. "I have heard you say more than once that you were like a bulldog with computer problems. You dig in 'til you figure it out. Am I wrong?"

I laughed incredulously. "Loretta, there's a *huge* difference between being tenacious in resolving networking issues and cracking a system that's been locked down by ransomware. This isn't even apples and oranges. It's more like apples and chainsaws. You're promising a service we can't provide. These commercials have got to go."

"We paid a lot of money for those spots! I'm not pulling anything."

"We're going to get sued."

"Well, that's on *you*," she said hotly. "You misrepresented your capabilities."

My blood pressure was skyrocketing. "I don't know why I'm even talking to you. Will you put Doug on? *Please?*"

"No can do," she said. "He's not here."

I was perplexed by her sudden nonchalance. "Where is he?"

"He decided to grab a room at the Cop-a-Squat in Greenup. It's cheaper than running gas out to and from, especially since he wanted to talk to more of those Holy Rollers in the—wait a minute. I thought you were working this case together. Why do I know more than you?"

I wasn't about to tell her I had been sidelined after Saturday's service. I'd never hear the end of it. Diversion seemed the best approach.

"Did you even tell him I'd been trying to reach him?" I asked, and this was met with stone cold silence. "Do you even *remember* me calling earlier?"

"Of course, I do," she snapped. "But I didn't really have the chance."

"It was a simple message. How hard could it have been?"

"I didn't exactly speak to him," she said. "He sent a text."

I let that sink in for a second. Doug wasn't a fan of texting, or anything else that required spelling for that matter. "I don't understand. Why wouldn't he just call?"

"His phone is pretty much shot," she said. "He's gonna have to get it replaced. He dropped it in—some water."

Ah! The picture was clarifying. Doug kept his phone in a faux leather case that snapped onto his belt. Time had softened the clasp's hold, and a healthy appetite had stretched his belt to its outer limits. He had already dropped that sucker, case and all, not once, but twice into the toilet. I guess the third time was the fatal charm.

"It won't hold a charge at all and even plugged into the wall it dies within minutes of him trying to use it. He tried to call before he settled on texting. I couldn't understand a word he said. It was all jibber-jabber. When he finally got through with the text, your message just didn't seem all that important."

"Alright, it's 8:45, and I'm writing that down," I said, doing nothing of the sort although filing it away in my mental lockbox. "When Doug crawls my ass for not touching base, you're my get of out jail free card."

I disconnected without waiting for her undoubtedly sarcastic retort and slid my chilly hands deep into my pants pockets, stifling a shiver. A tiny voice in my head whispered that something was off, but for the life of me, I couldn't find a nit to pick. Resigned for the moment, I headed toward the fire pit where the girls were now singing Christmas classics to a decidedly hip-hop beat.

One of these days, I'm gonna learn to listen to that little voice.

·····•••◦◦•••·····

"You haven't heard a word I've said," said Melanie, jabbing me in ribs I had exposed as I absently draped my arm around her.

Cheryl was in the kitchen loading the dishwasher, and Craig had chased me off while he tamped out the last of the smoldering embers in the fire pit. I hadn't dressed for the sudden drop in temperature, and my teeth were practically chattering as the fireside festivities drew to a close. Melanie and I sat on the couch staring at the next spate of Christmas animation, instantly forgettable CGI that couldn't even hold the attention of the youngest of the girls. They had all gathered their things and crossed the gravel expanse for one last sleepover in Maggie's trailer before the holiday weekend ended. We had muted the sound, opting for classic Christmas fare, courtesy of SiriusXM and a decent Bluetooth speaker playing softly in the background. It should have been peaceful and relaxing, but after the emotional rollercoaster of our day, I couldn't seem to keep my thoughts from gathering like storm clouds.

"I'm sorry," I said, giving her a squeeze. "What were you saying?"

She shifted positions and studied my face, the twinkling lights from the Christmas tree reflected in her eyes. "Nothing important. What's going on in that head of yours? Jasmine's home and safe—"

"Thank *God*," I interjected.

"—so that's not it," she continued. "Was it your mom? I know her call upset you."

"No. I mean, *yes*, she was using guilt as only a mother knows how," I said with a humorless laugh. "But that's not it. I'm just—I'm feeling really helpless right at the moment."

"How so?"

"I can't get my mind off that girl," I said.

"Which girl?"

"Tammy. I mean, she was right there in my car, alive and well, not even *seven hours ago*. I knew she was scared, but I thought it was about being found out. Now, when I play it over in my mind—which I can't seem to *stop* doing—it seems obvious she knew she was in real danger. Whatever that last text was—" I shook my head. "But now she's gone. Just like that. If I could have just kept her in the car, I—"

"*Shhh*." Melanie gently placed her fingertips against my lips. "Don't do that to yourself. You were there trying to help her. You had no way of knowing what was going to happen, and short of restraining her, you couldn't have kept her in your car."

I chewed at my thumbnail, considering the day as a whole. "Anne Marie was convinced her niece wouldn't have killed herself, and knowing Tina was actively blackmailing an entire group of kids lends more than a little credence to that theory. The fact that Tammy Tipton has turned up in an almost identical manner can't be coincidence. I'm wondering what injuries they might have sustained, and if the cause of death was the same. If only Molly worked for the hospital up here, or I had some other connection—"

I sat up straight.

"What are you thinking?"

"I don't have any connections, but Doug does."

I was on my feet in an instant, patting my pockets to make sure I had my wallet and cell phone. Melanie followed as I crossed to the kitchen, where Cheryl was wiping down the counters.

"You headin' out again?" she asked, flicking me with her towel as Craig entered through the back door, bringing the scent of scorched firepit with him.

"Just for a bit."

I slid my lightweight jacket on, wishing once more I had the foresight to bring something heavier, and scooped my keys up from the dinette table.

"Hang on a second, mister." Melanie was dubious. "Doug doesn't have any connections. What's really going on?"

"I can't just sit around here doing nothing," I said. "Loretta told me where Doug was staying, and it feels like I ought to bring him up to speed before he attempts to interview anyone else tomorrow morning." Down by the fire, we had already laughed about the untimely demise of his phone by Ty-D-Bol, so I didn't need to explain why I had to do this in person. "And I know it sounds ridiculous, but Doug might actually have a connection, if he's willing to use it."

"Lucy," said Melanie, connecting my dots without need for further explanation. It was comforting and a little spooky. "But do you really think he can talk her into sharing information with him? From what you said, she's harboring one hell of a grudge."

"I'm hoping that I can make them both see that whatever it is isn't important in light of what's going on. It just feels like everything is escalating."

"Well, that makes a certain sort of sense," said Melanie. "If Tina has somehow scheduled a public information dump from her cloud account, time's running out."

"I need to talk to those other kids on the list and see if I can find out what Tina was holding over their heads."

Melanie shook her head. "I don't like it. It's dangerous. One of those kids might just be a murderer."

"And any of the others might be in danger of being the next victim."

"I'm coming with you," Melanie said, reaching up to adjust the way the jacket's hood fell against my shoulders. "This isn't something you should be doing alone."

I kissed her forehead. "I won't be. I'll make Doug go with me. We'll start with the preacher's son, Chandler, since I know where to find him. He should be able to help me find the others. If you really want to help, why don't you see if Maggie can locate Katie and invite her to spend the night again? I'd like to talk to her when I get back."

"Katie?" Craig interjected, surprised. "I was just thinking how nice it is not to worry about my girls catching her smoking weed or, God forbid, another Ouija board incident. Why do you need to talk to her?"

"She's on Anne Marie's list," I said with a shrug. "I need to know why."

I crossed the bridge into Kentucky from Ironton, picking up US 23 on the other side and turning right toward Greenup. The outside temperature on my dashboard was reading forty-three degrees, and traffic was light. It felt good to be doing something, but I couldn't shake the paranoid feeling that I was being followed, and I kept checking my rearview mirror, unwilling to be caught by surprise like I was Thanksgiving night down by the Grant Bridge.

The Cop-a-Squat was closer to Flatwoods than it was Greenup, a cinder-block rectangle of eight tiny rooms and an office, set back from the highway on a strip of asphalt that was in desperate need of repair. Unlikely to ever boast a recommendation from AAA, the motel was a favorite for truckers, teens, and anyone else who might be looking for a room that could be rented by the hour. Most of the neon in its sign had long-since expired, leaving behind "Squat" and "V cancy" to shimmer in cautious trepidation for the impending moment when it, too, would go dark. A single sodium vapor lamp mounted high on a utility pole near the office provided scant illumination for motel guests, and the place had seen more than its share of police activity over the years. An eighteen-wheeler was parked perpendicular to the motel's end, its front grille modified to show sharpened metal teeth of a snarling beast. Light flickered though the window of Room #8, suggesting its trucker occupant was watching television in the dark. I didn't care to know what. Pay-per-view porn was one of the motel's few amenities. There were only two other cars in the lot, and I was relieved to see that one of them was Doug's rusting Pontiac Aztek. It was parked in front of the darkened window of Room #2, while the other, a compact Toyota, occupied the spot in front of Room #5. I eased in beside Doug's SUV and killed my lights and engine, but not before catching a curious onlooker duck back behind the curtain of #5. I wondered fleetingly if they were expecting company before wondering if Doug even knew what kind of place this was. Somehow, I doubted it.

I considered visiting the office first to confirm which room Doug was in, but it was dimly lit and unoccupied as far as I could see through its own signage covered windows, one of which proclaimed, "Yes! We're OPEN!" I decided to go straight to the room and knock. Why would he park anywhere other than in front of his own door? It wasn't as if the lot was full.

I rapped my knuckles on the door and shivered, tucking my hands into the armpits of my hoodie. My frosty breath rose toward the unobstructed night sky as I waited. After a moment, I knocked again, putting a little more into it. While I didn't really want to attract any of the other patrons, Doug was known to sleep almost as soundly as his mother. When that brought no response, I tried again, thumping the door with the edge of my closed fist.

"C'mon, Boggs," I grumbled to myself. "Answer your damn door."

I leaned my ear against the door and heard nothing. I was beginning to get uneasy. I tried the doorknob and found it was locked. I stepped back to examine the other rooms just in time to see the curtain fall back into place in Room #5. Whoever was inside was awfully invested in my agenda. I briefly considered knocking on the door and asking if they had seen Doug, but right about then, the light in the office brightened, and a skeletal older man poked his head through the door, shielding his eyes as he located the source of his interrupted slumber.

"What the fuck you doin' down there?" he yelled. "You gonna wake all my customers."

I held my hands up in apology and headed his way, allowing my left hand to drop on the hood of Doug's Aztek as I passed. It was stone cold; it had been parked here for some time.

"Sorry about that," I said. "I was just trying to wake up one of your customers, and he's my boss, but maybe I've got the wrong room. Would you be able to verify that for me?"

I offered a hand to shake, but he was more concerned with keeping his terrycloth bathrobe cinched around his bony waist, and I was just fine with that. He scowled at me through narrowed eyes beneath bushy eyebrows. "I ain't gotta show you my guest register. At the Cop-a-Squat, we are known for our privacy and dee-scretion."

"That's fine," I said. "I don't need to see your register. I was just hoping if I gave you my boss's name, you might be able to tell me what room he's in. I wouldn't bother you if it wasn't important. The name's Boggs, Doug Boggs."

"Ain't nobody here by that name," he said immediately, taking a step back so he could close the door, and I barely managed to wedge my foot inside, blocking his retreat.

"Are you certain?" I asked. "I mean, maybe he arrived before you came on duty."

He sighed, staring daggers at my foot before shifting his attention to my face. "Son, I been on duty since 1999," he said. "I got a couple in Room #5, and a long hauler in Room #8 who's stayed here twice a month for years. And now you, but you don't seem to be int'rested in booking a room. Why don't you move along and let an old man get some shut eye?"

"But that's his car right there," I said, pointing to the lot.

"I s'pose I could have it towed. Only motel guests are allowed to park here. But it's a whole lot of trouble for me, and your 'boss' would get stuck with the towing fee, so he might not be real happy with you by the end of all this. Do we really need to go through all that? C'mon, man. It's fucking cold out here."

Something clearly wasn't right here. No one had laid eyes on Doug since we had angrily parted ways at lunchtime, the only communication coming in the form of a text message to his mother because his phone was down for the count. And while, sure enough, his car was where the text had indicated he'd be staying, he wasn't there. Alarms were going off inside my head.

"Why don't you grab your master key and meet me outside Room #2?" I suggested. "I'd like a little visual confirmation he isn't lying in there hurt or something. In fact, bring the whole set. I'd like to clear all of the rooms you believe to be unoccupied."

"The fuck you say!" he protested loudly. "Who the hell do you think you are? I ain't doin' all that."

"I'm investigating the deaths of a couple of locals, and I have reason to believe my boss might be in one of these rooms. You can either do as I ask, or I can call the police and ask for their assistance, but either way, I'm going to see inside, and you'd better hope to God he's not lying in there needing medical attention. That would be on *you*."

I fixed him with what I hoped was my most intimidating glare and held it until he finally cracked, muttering a string of obscenities before stepping back into his office and leaving the door ajar. "Hold yer fuckin' horses," he grumbled. "Let me grab some clothes here."

I stepped onto the ribbon of aging linoleum that passed as a lobby while he shut himself into a tiny room just behind the narrow counter. The guest register lay flat on the countertop, visible to one and all, so I took the opportunity to peek. Only two names were listed on the lined page, and neither signature looked anything like Doug's heavy-handed primary school script. Beside it, an ashtray overflowing with spent butts explained the dubious quality of the air and the hint of yellow that had attached to all visible surfaces.

The old man returned in jeans and a wearing a dark blue puffy synthetic coat that seemed to nearly swallow him whole. He was still dropping expletives as he picked a handful of keys from a pegboard on the wall behind his desk.

"I'm Dwayne Morrow, by the way. I work for Boggs Investigations," I said, knowing better than to attempt shaking hands again, but thinking a tardy introduction might help ease the chill from dude's frosty reception.

Yeah, right.

He looked at me like I had just dropped a turd in front of him. "I don't give a good goddamn who you are. I want you out of here just as quick as I can be done with you, you understand? Now, c'mon. Let's get this over with."

He elbowed past me and hobbled toward the first room, its key already extended in one hand. As I followed behind, I saw more movement at the curtain of Room #5. They were as committed to seeing this thing through as I was. "Can you at least tell me your name?" I asked. "I don't even know what to call you."

He paused after unlocking the door, and called tightly over his shoulder, "Sir will do just fine, you fucktard."

Well. Alrighty, then.

He threw the door open, bellowing, *"Housekeeping!"* He reached inside and flipped a switch. Low-wattage orange illumination bathed the room. The bathroom door stood open at the rear of the room, and it was plain to see both were unoccupied.

He moved to Room #2, and I found myself reflexively holding my breath. This was where Doug's car was parked. This was where I most anticipated a crime scene to appear once the lights were thrown, but after another bark of *"Housekeeping!"* from my less-than-congenial host, I exhaled pure relief. There was no sign that anyone had been in the room at all. Its bed was more or less neatly made, and the surfaces were free of the normal clutter that accompanies guests.

We continued down the line, skipping only Rooms #5 and #8, as the manager seemed familiar enough with the occupancy to think it was a waste of time. I only agreed with half of that assessment, as I continued to catch movement at the curtain to #5. Was it possible that Doug was being held against his will in that very room?

"There," the old man said, pocketing his keys. "Are you satisfied?" He didn't wait for an answer before shuffling across the lot back toward his office.

"Not entirely," I said, pausing in front of Room #5. "Who's in here?"

"Paying customers, that's who," he said. "They have a right to privacy, and I ain't waking 'em up, if that's what you're thinking."

I was already closing the distance to the door. "I'm not really worried about waking them up," I said. "They've been watching my progress from the window this whole time, and I'm wondering why it is that I'm so fascinating." I rapped my knuckles sharply against the wooden door and turned back towards the manager as I watched him reverse direction on a dime.

A string of inventive new invectives that referenced not only my mother but also the occasional farm animal spewed forth as he stomped his way towards me with his arms flailing, his dander fully flared. "Git yer ass away from that door! I'm not gonna have you bothering my guests with this foolishness, and if *I* have to call the police to be done with ya, I won't even—"

"It's alright, Clint," said a voice from behind me. "I'll talk to him. You can go on back to your office. Thanks."

I turned to find myself face-to-face with Chandler Keaton, blond hair tousled and looking completely busted.

CHAPTER TWENTY-THREE

"Might as well come in," said Chandler, stepping back and allowing me to enter the small room. He wore baggy gray sweats and a loose white t-shirt with the Rolling Stones' iconic red lips and tongue emblazoned on the back. The bed looked like a hurricane had struck, and the shower was running in the bathroom. He perched on the corner of the bed and nodded me toward a padded metal folding chair that served as the room's only other seating.

"Chandler Keaton, right?" I asked, and he nodded, brushing his wavy bangs out of his eyes. I extended a hand, and this time, it was taken, although cautiously. "I'm Dwayne Morrow. You might remember me from that embarrassing little go-round at the church this morning." I rolled my eyes and grinned sheepishly, hoping a little self-deprecation might lighten the mood.

"I heard you were a private eye," he said, struggling to meet my gaze.

"That's almost true," I said, nodding. "I'm still in training. I work as an apprentice at Boggs Investigations. That's why I'm here."

"Did my dad send you here?" This time, his eyes locked onto mine, gauging my reaction.

All I could return was a look of surprise. "Huh? No. *No.* Why would he do that?"

Chandler heaved a sigh of tremendous relief and flopped back onto the bed, staring at the ceiling. "I thought for sure he knew."

"Knew what?"

He sat back up and shook his head, once again taming his errant bangs. "Never mind. So, wait a minute. If you aren't here looking for me, then what are you doing here?"

"Actually, I was looking for my boss, Doug Boggs. He was with me at the church this morning."

"The short guy stuffed into the old man's suit?"

"That's him. And that's his ugly-ass SUV parked out there in front of Room #2, but I can't seem to find him." I nodded toward the bathroom, where the shower abruptly stopped. "I don't suppose he's in there?"

That pulled a genuine laugh from Chandler. "Umm, *no-o-o.*"

"Of course not," I said, laughing with him. "Had to ask, though. I can't figure for the life of me where he's gone off to without his car."

"I haven't seen him since we—" The hint of a smile crossed his face, and his eyes wandered to the bathroom door. "—since we got here, but the car's been here the whole time. I didn't know who it belonged to. Like you, I just figured it was someone else staying at the motel."

"It's actually pretty convenient running into you here," I said. "You would have been my next stop after picking Doug up."

"Yeah? How so?"

"We're investigating Tina McAllister's death," I said, and he instantly stiffened.

"Look, we barely *knew* the girl," he said, his words escalating in volume as they rushed out. "She just kept showing up wherever we went. We didn't *invite* her—"

"*Whoa, whoa, whoa,*" I said, holding up my hands. "You're not on trial here. But there have been some recent developments I'm not sure you're aware of."

"Developments? What kind of developments?" he asked nervously.

Dammit. This wasn't the kind of news I was good at breaking, but I had backed myself into a corner. I could only hope Chandler had already caught word, but I suspected he hadn't.

"Your friend, Tammy Tipton?" I began.

"Yeah?"

"I'm so sorry. Her body washed up on the riverbank in Ironton a few hours ago. I—"

A strangled scream stopped me in my tracks, and I realized the bathroom door had opened while I was talking. Wide-eyed and standing with a hand clamped over his gaping mouth was the dark-haired young man I had chased down the church corridor earlier that morning.

Chandler held the young man against his shoulder, gently rocking and shushing him while he sobbed convulsively. His narrow shoulders hitched beneath the plain white t-shirt he wore with a pair of navy basketball shorts.

I tried not to stare, but it was difficult as pieces began to drop into place. "Jesse Baker?" I asked quietly, and Chandler nodded, continuing to soothe his—friend? No. Their body language told me everything I needed to know.

It all felt voyeuristic, so I shifted uncomfortably on my padded folding chair, waiting for Jesse's grief to taper, but he was only gaining momentum, and as the awkwardness of the moment grew, I found myself offering up a loathsome platitude. "I'm sorry for your loss."

Chandler accepted my words with a nod, which unfortunately encouraged me to say more.

"You were close?"

Oh, for shit's sake, Dwayne! I groaned inwardly. *Find better words or keep your stupid mouth shut.*

Nevertheless, it did elicit a response from Chandler.

"Yeah, we were," he said, continuing to rock gently as Jesse's grief finally showed signs of quietening. "Jesse knew her way better than I did. Her family lived across the street from Jesse and his grandmother down on Dixon Hollow. They've been friends forever. In fact, I doubt Jesse would have given me the time of day if Tammy hadn't approved."

"She loved you from the minute she met you," said Jesse, easing away from Chandler's tear-dampened t-shirt and blotting at his eyes.

"So, she knew the two of you were—together?" I asked.

Chandler nodded, his chin quivering as he looked at me beseechingly. *"Please,"* he implored, his own eyes brimming with tears. "You can't say anything to my father."

I was already shaking my head. "Of course not. I'm not working for him. I've got no obligation to tell him anything."

"Do you *swear?*"

"Absolutely," I assured him. "But I think you've just confirmed what I came to ask. This is what Tina McAllister was holding over you both, isn't it?"

His panic returned nearly full force. "You already *knew?* How?"

"I *didn't* know. Tammy came to see me earlier today. She told me Tina was holding something over each of you to use against you, but she would only tell me what Tina had on her. She said it wasn't her place to share everyone else's secrets. She was a good friend."

Words I hoped might provide comfort only brought a fresh wave of anguish from Jesse, and Chandler resumed rocking him, kissing his forehead gently between soothing words too soft for me to understand. I got up from my chair and crossed to the window, peeking outside, and doing the best I could to give them a little privacy, but there was only so much I could do short of leaving the room, and I wasn't quite done yet.

After an uncomfortably lengthy stretch, Chandler returned his attention to me. "Were you able to help Tammy?"

I turned, letting the curtain fall back into place. "I don't even know what she wanted," I said apologetically. "She had heard that my partner and I were looking into what happened to Tina on behalf of her aunt, and she wanted to make sure I knew that Tina wasn't as innocent as people seem to believe. She was worried that all this information that was being held over you would go public now that Tina was dead. At least that's what Tina told her would happen. It seems like Tina recognized the precarious position she was putting herself in by threatening you all with your most guarded secrets."

"Yeah, she told us the same thing," said Chandler. "Can she really do that? I mean, releasing information from beyond the grave? It sounds like the plot of some bad spy movie."

"I wish I could ease your minds," I said, frowning. "But frankly, it wouldn't be that difficult to orchestrate. All she would have to do is draft an email with a link to the folder on her cloud account and schedule it to be sent out to whoever she wanted at a preselected time. As long as she was alive and well, she could always log back in and reset the schedule to keep it from being sent."

"So, what you're saying is we're fucked," said Chandler.

"I don't know what I'm saying," I said, pacing the room. "I wish I knew why Tammy came to see me. It feels like she thought I could help, but I have no idea how. She was only there a few minutes before she got a text that scared the shit out of her, and she was gone."

"And now she's dead," said Jesse. "Just like Tina. It just doesn't make any sense. Do we need to be worried about our safety?"

"I think it would be smart to remain alert," I said. "Stick together as much as possible. Safety in numbers isn't just some old saying, you know."

"Perfect," said Chandler, sarcastically. "Give my dad even more reason to suspect something's going on between us."

"I don't know what else to tell you. You might be facing discovery sooner rather than later anyway if Tina's files are released. Tammy said she thought Tina was also blackmailing folks outside your circle of friends. I don't suppose you have any idea who that might be?"

Chandler and Jesse exchanged a blank look.

"How about Kaitlyn—*Katie?*" I said, correcting myself. "Any idea what Tina had on her?"

"Not really, but if I had to guess, I'd say it was weed," said Jesse.

"Weed?"

"Yeah," said Chandler. "Katie doesn't really hang with us. She's older. But she's the one to see if you're looking for some dispensary-grade bud."

I would have gotten his message even if he hadn't emulated smoking a fat doobie and floating into outer space.

We sat in silence for a long moment before Chandler asked, "So, do you really think this is all going to come out?"

I sat across from the two and leaned in. "I wish I could tell you with any degree of confidence that it won't, but you're both smarter than that, and I'm not going to lie to you. You know, acceptance for alternative lifestyles has come a very long way in the past couple of decades. Your father seemed like a reasonable man when I met him earlier today. Is it possible you've convinced yourself of what his reaction will be because you're afraid to have the conversation? Maybe you're not giving him enough credit."

Chandler and Jesse exchanged a glance before slowly shaking their heads, almost in unison. "No disrespect intended, Mr. Morrow, but you don't know what in the hell you're talking about," said Chandler. "You spent what, a half-hour with my father? You saw exactly what he wanted you to see, and he's been perfecting that image for as long as I've known him. If my father knew about Jesse and me, I'd be sent away before the sun set, I promise you."

"Sent away?"

"You know," he said, bitterness creeping into his tone. "Pray the gay away—that sort of thing. I've heard about some of the methods they use. No, thanks." He shuddered.

"Conversion camps?" I shook my head in disbelief. "I didn't think those operations were legal anymore."

Chandler chuckled. "You make it sound like band camp. I'm sorry to say, but you are woefully undereducated on this subject. I think you're confusing conversion therapy with women's reproductive rights. Easy mistake when you don't have a horse in either race." My cheeks grew warm at being schooled by a boy nearly half my age, and he wasn't done yet. "Yeah, a handful of progressive states have passed legislature banning conversion therapy, but there are still quite a few with no laws on the books at all, and wouldn't you know, all three in our tri-state area are completely silent on the matter."

"Is this, like, an official church position?" I asked. I knew some denominations were more tolerant of homosexuality than others, but I honestly had no idea what the official position of the Apostolic church was— or if there even *was* such a thing. "Official positions" are all too often informed by the personal agendas of those in power, and they end up hurting whole swaths of folks; that's why I keep my spirituality to myself and organized religion at arm's length.

Chandler's smile was little more than a smirk. "I don't think you'll see any reference to conversion therapy on the campus brochures, no, but I'm sure more than a fair share of the congregation would support my father's position if it were."

"What about your mother?" Even sporting fresh teeth marks on my rear end from my earlier conversation with my mother, I couldn't imagine a world in which she wouldn't ultimately have my back.

Chandler exhaled in a long whoosh. "If it was just her, maybe. But she has followed my father's lead for so long, I don't think she even allows herself to have an opinion anymore. I mean, she certainly didn't stand up for Dustin."

"Who's Dustin?" The name was vaguely familiar, but it eluded me.

"My older brother," said Chandler, and I flashed back to the family portrait sitting on the edge of the reverend's desk.

"He was—" I started to whisper the word, 'gay,' felt foolish and rolled my eyes. "—too?"

Jesse startled me by laughing. "You *can* say the word. Gay. See? It isn't a slur."

The warmth in my cheeks spread to my ears. "Of course," I said, smiling apologetically. I'm at my offensive best when I least suspect it coming.

"But to answer your question," interjected Chandler. "No, he wasn't. I can't say I really know what happened to him. He just—went dark when no one was paying attention."

"What does that mean?"

Chandler just shook his head. "I wish I could tell you. We weren't close, even before he got so—so—empty, but something changed. He was almost fifteen, and he just stopped caring about everything. I don't know if he was bipolar or if it was some other chemical imbalance, but my father never believed in those things anyway. He thinks psychiatry preys on spiritual weakness, and the drugs prescribed only mask symptoms, not address the actual cause. That is what *he's* for, and it was up to him to help guide Dustin back to a virtuous path."

"But it didn't work."

"No," Chandler said grimly. "Dustin had escalating anger issues. You just never knew what would set him off. Most of these episodes happened at home, but at one point, he really lost it with some girl at school. I think he really hurt her."

I narrowed my eyes. "You *think?*"

"I was only eleven," said Chandler. "It wasn't like we discussed it around the dinner table, you know? All I can tell you is after that, Dustin was sent away. We went to see him a couple of times early on, but he refused to acknowledge we were even there. It was especially upsetting for my little sister, so we just stopped going. I haven't seen him in over five years."

"What about the girl?" I asked. "I mean, if he really hurt her, wouldn't the police have been involved?"

"You would think, wouldn't you?" Chandler grimaced. "They were members of the church. This happened on church property, back when the Christian academy was being run out of a handful of trailers lined up along the ridge beside the original church out on Sweeney Hollow. The attendance back then wasn't what it is now, and I guess there weren't any real witnesses, so it was basically Dustin's word against the girl's. Honestly, I've heard she didn't have the best reputation herself. My father and his lawyers circled the wagons. The girl and her family moved away shortly after that, and most folks believe they received a pretty good payout to keep everything under wraps. Keeping things quiet was always my father's priority, not the well-being of his son. He's got a real vision for expanding his ministry, and there's no room for any scandal, including what he would undoubtedly perceive as my own."

I considered his words silently while instantly experiencing a newfound appreciation for my own parents. They may not be perfect—who is?—but at least their fundamental priorities are in order. I had trouble reconciling everything Chandler told me with the man I had met earlier that day who still displayed the family portrait, including his eldest son, on the corner of his desk. I suspected Reverend Keaton was a lot more complicated than Chandler knew, but I recognized the futility of pressing the issue.

"We're just trying to make it through our senior years at school and past our eighteenth birthdays, and then we'll be free to live the lives we want without worrying," said Chandler.

"You should just go," Jesse said, pulling his hand free from Chandler's. For a second, I thought Jesse was talking to me, but then I realized I was no longer part of the conversation. "Get out while you can."

"*No*," said Chandler flatly. "I'm not leaving you behind."

"Every day it's getting harder," Jesse protested. "And if Tina's files are made public—"

"*No*." Chandler was firm, and Jesse cast his eyes downward, studying his own fingernails. Chandler's gaze flicked back to me. "Jesse's six months younger than I am. I turn eighteen in a couple of weeks. I could leave then, but I'd rather finish the school year here, and I'll be goddamned if I'm leaving Jesse behind. We'll just have to hope Tina was bluffing and be more careful in the future."

Jesse jumped to his feet, pacing a small semi-circle in the area between the bed and bathroom. "That's funny coming from you. You get off on the rush."

"Do we really have to go into this now? You're being hysterical."

Jesse looked as if he had been slapped. "Hysterical? Are you kidding me?" He leaned down, snagging a pair of jeans from the floor beside the bed and rifling through the pockets. He pulled out a ring of keys and held them up, my eyes landing on something that wasn't a key. "You take unnecessary risks all the time! You've been carrying around the very thing that Tina was blackmailing us with! Don't you think your mom or dad might notice? Maybe even *Tessa?* All it would take is a little bit of curiosity."

Jesse was showing a small plastic cow whose collar was tethered to the key ring by a thin chain of metal links.

"She gave Tammy a duck," I mumbled, remembering the innocuous novelty item that contained enough evidence to derail Tammy Tipton's entire academic future. I reached for the keychain but not before Chandler intercepted it. "It's a USB drive, isn't it?"

Chandler's face had flushed crimson, but he gave a curt nod as he tucked the keys into the pockets of his sweats. "Let's just say she caught us by surprise."

"More like she caught us with our pants down," said Jesse before turning to me. "Just like you almost did this morning."

For a brief moment, I didn't know what he was talking about, but then it all fell together. "You two were hooking up at church? During *services?*"

My expression must have been comical because Chandler suddenly laughed. "It's not like *anyone* could just walk in on us. All of the offices are secured by key cards. I happen to have access to one. I ain't gonna lie, it adds a little something extra. And don't let Jesse tell you otherwise. He's as into it as I am." The look he gave me was unexpectedly dismissive. "Look, I don't mean to embarrass you, but I'm guessing you and your old lady are strictly missionary and only with all the lights off?"

I stammered as another wave of heat rushed into my face. "We—I mean our—" I took a deep breath and shook my head. "We're not talking about my sex life. Tina was blackmailing you over yours. So, what is it? Pictures?"

Jesse turned away, embarrassed, but Chandler only smirked, and his self-confidence was both superior and ugly. "Hi-def video, and in my father's office, of all places. I can't imagine how she got the vantage point, but—" He whistled appreciatively. "Not gonna lie, I keep it because it's hot. We are never gonna look any better than we do on that video, and it's a memory we'll appreciate when we're your age. Surely, you can understand that."

I blinked and gave myself a quick once-over. "I'm only thirty-four."

Chandler merely shrugged. "You *do* realize that's almost twice our age, right?"

Ouch.

I was never particularly good at math in my head, but this was a simple computation that even I couldn't bungle. I could only gape at him.

Jesse nudged Chandler. "Stop it, babe," he said quietly. "You're being rude."

But Chandler was on a roll, his eyes twinkling. "Before you know it, you'll be as old as Clint." Jesse turned away, embarrassed, while I struggled to keep up. "Clint?"

"The old queen who runs this place," he said, hooking a thumb in the general direction of the office. "Don't get me wrong, we love her dearly. She knows about my family and has sort of become a surrogate mother to us both. She lets us have a room whenever we want, and it's not likely anyone is going to recognize us here. But when she's all dolled up and doing her act at The Stonehenge in Huntington, all I see are wrinkles, and frankly, it's embarrassing. Heaven help us, one of these days, that will be us. I always want to remember us like we are now."

"Chandler," scolded Jesse. "That's hurtful and awful. You don't have to be such a dick."

"I'm just being honest. You wanted to know why I held onto the drive."

"I don't think Mr. Morrow needed to hear all that."

"Mr. Morrow most certainly did *not* need to hear all that," I agreed, deciding that while I might sympathize with Chandler's plight, I really didn't care much for him one-to-one. He was far too self-assured and smug. "But it does raise a question. If all the offices were secured by key card, how did Tina get into your father's office to capture the video? I mean, I'm assuming she wasn't standing right there where you could see her. She must have hidden a camera or something. How did she get access to your father's office? How would she have even known you'd go in there?"

"She must have followed us," said Chandler, avoiding my gaze.

"Well, exactly how often did you go in there?" I asked incredulously. "I can understand a cheap thrill, but this is almost like you've been *trying* to get caught."

He looked at me sharply. "Look, the girl was a real creeper. She was catching us by surprise all the fucking time. For all I know, she had cameras that she could operate remotely in every office. And I imagine she got into the offices the same way I did. Her aunt works in my dad's office. She probably left her own key card laying around."

Okay, that was new information.

"Wait a minute," I said. "Back up. You're saying that Anne Marie Brown works for the church?"

"Sure. She has for years. I figured you knew."

CHAPTER TWENTY-FOUR

I sat in the parking lot with my teeth chattering as I waited for the heat in my SUV to engage. It was a little after ten—a little late to be socially acceptable, but I pressed the button on my steering wheel anyway, repeating the voice command for the third time.

"Call Anne Marie Brown."

The Hyundai's integrated concierge confirmed my request in a cool, feminine voice, and soon I was surrounded by the familiar trilling of a ringing line projected through all the speakers in my sound system, waiting to be answered. After five rounds, I was once again connected to Anne Marie's voicemail, and I jabbed the disconnect button. I'd already left one voicemail; there wasn't any point in leaving another. She was probably in bed for the night, and while I was curious if Doug had been in contact with her since he and I had earlier parted ways, I wasn't sure it warranted interrupting her sleep.

I glanced over at Doug's Aztek, mocking me from where it sat beside my car, moonlight reflecting dully from the fading white paint of its hood. I had given it a more thorough look before climbing into my own vehicle, testing its doors and windows, pressing my face against the glass, and shining the flashlight from my cellphone into floorboards that were littered with fast food wrappers and spent lottery tickets. This was all ordinary disarray. There were no telltale spatters of blood or anything else that might indicate Doug had done anything other than emerge from his car and lock it up tight before disappearing into the ether.

I didn't like it.

After adding both of their cell phone numbers into my phone, I had left a business card with Chandler and Jesse, making them promise they would watch each other's backs, at least until I found out what was going on with Doug. Jesse seemed to take me more seriously than Chandler, but that was no real surprise. Over the course of our short conversation, Chandler had shown signs of being a complete narcissist. I wasn't even sure he could picture a world without himself in it. Two girls were dead, yet he still made time to brag over his sexual exploits and make fun of what he assumed would constitute mine.

There was a sudden rapping at my driver's window, startling me out of my thoughts. I turned to find Clint staring at me, urging me impatiently to roll the window down. As I complied, I noticed he had slipped back into his terrycloth robe, holding it together with a hand sporting an expertly executed French manicure, and I wondered how the length of his nails had escaped my attention before. I was going to have to work on my observational skills.

"Look, Mr. whoever-the-fuck-you-are," he said. "You either need to rent a room or move it along. I don't need someone out in the parking lot steaming up his own windows, capiche?"

"Sorry, of course," I said, fumbling for my wallet so I could extract another business card. "If you should see anyone or anything, please give me a call."

I passed the card through the window, and just when I thought he wasn't going to take it, his fingers snaked out and snagged it, quickly tucking it away into the pocket of his robe.

"Fine, whatever," he said. "Just get outta here. I won't tolerate you hassling my friends."

I held my hands up in surrender and offered what I hoped was a reassuring smile. He glared for just a moment longer before shaking his head and pivoting on what a double take revealed to be six-inch hot pink feathered open-toed mules.

Was he wearing those before? It was entirely possible. I *really* needed to work on my observational skills.

I sighed, shifting into reverse, and pulled out of the lot.

I was out of ideas anyway.

"Hello? Are you still there?"

Melanie had asked me a question, but my focus was on the coffee machine.

I fumbled with the lid for my jumbo beverage, wondering to myself—and not for the first time—how I could reseat tiny microchips on circuit boards but almost always had to ask for help in making my scalding hot beverage safe for conveyance. As my phone slipped farther down my shoulder and away from my ear, I opted to save it and set the lid and coffee back on the counter.

"Yeah, I'm still here," I said, stepping aside and nodding apologetically to a tattooed behemoth who was growing tired of waiting for access to the coffee dispenser. Speedway was a circus tonight with representatives from almost every road-weary demographic stumbling their way through the crowded aisles, looking for some little pick-me-up to make the rest of their journey more palatable.

"So, are you going to call the police?" Melanie asked.

"And tell them what? My boss isn't where he told his mama he would be? I don't think he's been out of touch long enough for them to issue any kind of missing person's alert. And they would undoubtedly want to search the motel, which would only bring a heap of trouble down on Chandler and Jesse. I'm not sure exactly what to make of what Chandler told me about his father, but I'm not willing to break their confidence, especially considering I've already gotten the manager to show me the other rooms. Doug's car may be there, but he's not."

"I don't like it," said Melanie. "This just isn't like Doug. He's never seemed much like the type to put in overtime."

"You've got that right. He's much more of a delegator."

"Have you contacted Officer Graves yet?"

I started fiddling with the lid to my coffee again. "I was really hoping to have Doug with me when I made that call. She was pretty clear in telling me to stay out of things, but I don't guess I have a choice now. She doesn't have any jurisdiction here in Kentucky, but maybe she can help me figure out what to do next. That is, unless she keeps her promise and throws me in jail for obstruction. With my luck, you might want to brace yourself for that probability. Not sure what bail might be. How's your bank account?"

"Very funny." She wasn't even slightly amused.

"Did you have any luck getting hold of Katie?" I asked.

"It took a while for Maggie to track her down, but she finally got hold of her. She's on her way here now."

"Good," I said. "I'll be interested in—a-*ha!*"

"A-ha?"

"Sorry," I said, moving away from the coffee counter and into the general flow of munchies shoppers. "I finally got the lid to my coffee on."

She laughed, having saved me with some degree of frequency from this particular form of self-immolation. "Well, hooray for you! This day's been enough of a shit-sucker without you dumping piping hot coffee in your lap."

"Amen," I agreed, my eyes traversing the rows of brightly wrapped confectionary goodness. I plucked up a Payday until I remembered how winded I was after my little riverfront sprint earlier. Frowning, I put it back down. "What were we talking about?"

"Katie," Melanie reminded me. "You'll be interested in seeing what her part in all this is. Am I close?"

"You are. Of course, I don't know if she'll be willing to share whatever Tina's been holding over her, but at least we'll know she's safe." In the parking lot, a car alarm started whooping obnoxiously as another thought popped into my head. "How well do you know Katie?"

"Katie?" repeated Melanie. "She and Mags have been friends forever, but—what *is* that ruckus in the background?"

I sighed. "Some idiot's car alarm is going off in the parking lot."

I interrupted my perusal of the healthy, protein-infused nut bars to scowl through the plate glass frontage of the convenience store and discovered that idiot was *me*. All of my Hyundai's exterior illumination pulsed in time with a ululating screech that drew disgusted glares from customers both inside and outside of the store.

"Shit," I muttered, weaving my way through the folks who stood between me and the door. "I'm gonna have to call you right back." I disconnected the call and slid the phone into my pocket.

"Hey!" yelled the startled cashier as I elbowed my way through the door, my unpaid coffee still clutched in my hand. She started waving her bony arms and pointing in my direction. *"Smile*, you asshole! You're on candid camera, and we persecute shoplifters, you stupid son of a bitch!"

"I'll be right back!" I yelled over my shoulder, not bothering to quibble over what they actually might do to shoplifters. For all I knew, she might be correct. As I neared my pulsating vehicle, I couldn't help but notice how everyone's attention was on me and not the vehicle that was screaming for assistance. Apparently, people have become so accustomed to cars that cry wolf they no longer feel the need to check and see if help is actually needed.

I used my key fob to silence the alarm, and the resulting silence made it impossible to miss the sounds of tennis shoes slapping against the pavement. I hurried around the front of my car to find the passenger-side window bashed in and the door hanging open. A diminutive figure in a dark hoodie was hauling ass just beyond the perimeter of light thrown by the fluorescents mounted underneath the canopy shielding the twin bank of pumps from the elements. A vehicle waited in the shadows at the far end of the lot with only its running lights on.

"Somebody stop him!" I yelled, dropping my coffee, and gesticulating wildly in the general direction of the vandal, but all eyes remained focused on me, as if my accidental pilferage of a stupid cup of coffee was far more egregious than this forced entry into my locked vehicle.

I groaned in frustration and took off after him, nearly getting nailed by a car entering the parking lot way too fast. The driver's eyes were wide as saucers as he stopped to mime his apologies, but all he was doing was effectively blocking my pursuit.

"STOP HIM!" I shrieked, literally hopping mad, flailing my arms like a lunatic.

By then, the vandal was already ducking into the passenger side of the waiting car which didn't even wait for the door to close before squealing its tires and rocketing out onto the highway, the roar of its throaty engine receding quickly as it sped away.

Sirens were coming from the opposite direction, and as I fumbled for my phone, I wondered who they were after, me for stealing the coffee or the asshole who had vandalized my car. Either way, I wasn't getting out of there anytime soon. I hurriedly called Melanie back.

"What happened?" she answered, alarm in her voice.

"Later," I said as the first Flatwoods police SUV bumped into the lot, its lightbar painting the entire parking lot as a crime scene. "I need you to locate Chip."

She was confused. "Chip? I told you earlier, he's out at Jenny's grandmother's—"

"That was hours ago," I interrupted. "I need to know where he is now."

A second SUV joined the first, and they blocked the lot by parking across each exit, effectively sealing everyone in place.

"I don't understand," said Melanie. "Is that police sirens I hear?"

"I'll explain just as soon as I can," I said, watching as the cashier met one of the officers just outside the door. Her lips were moving a mile a minute, but every gesture pointed to me. Customers were collecting in small groups, transfixed by the scene unfolding before them, and yet I could almost guarantee that not one of them had gotten a good look at the person who did this to my car. "*Listen.* You need to find out where your brother is *right now.* It's important."

I disconnected the call and started to slide my phone back into my pocket but decided it might be best to keep my hands visible. The officer, who was now approaching me, had his hand hovering just beside his holstered weapon, a scowl etched across his face. It wasn't hard to imagine getting myself shot at this point.

I didn't have time to explain much of anything to Melanie, and I could only hope she would do as I asked. I thought the getaway car was vaguely familiar, but just as soon as it sped away, I knew where I had last seen it, although I hadn't recognized it even then. It was Thanksgiving night, and I was dangling over the side of the U.S. Grant Bridge.

"You have *got* to be kidding me." I stared at the splintered, low-resolution video displayed on a tiny 10" monitor. "What's wrong with the picture?"

The grumpy cashier who I now knew as Gerd—yes, as in gastroesophageal reflux disease—had accompanied grim-faced Officer Huntley and me into the closet serving as a manager's office to review security footage, and she was impatiently leaning against the wall, toking on a vape and filling the room with the sickly-sweet scent of cotton candy. Apparently, it wasn't store policy for anyone to be left in the manager's office unchaperoned, even if one of those people was an officer of the law.

"Camera lens is broke," she grumbled, shifting on her feet. "We've been complaining to corporate for weeks. Is this gonna take much longer? Colby's getting slammed out there, and this is only her third day. I'm afraid she's gonna bolt."

"Are there any other angles we can see?" asked Officer Huntley, leaning in and squinting, as if that might clarify the kaleidoscope in front of us. His slow, easy drawl suggested he was a local boy.

Gerd sighed. "You've seen everything we have."

"Mr. Marlow," he said, turning to me.

"Morrow," I corrected, but he looked inconvenienced rather than enlightened.

"You said you recognized the car," he said.

I hedged. "I said I recognized the *type* of car. Sort of." I glanced at my cell phone for probably the twentieth time since we had entered this claustrophobic little hole, hoping for a text from Melanie confirming her brother's whereabouts, but there was still nothing.

Officer Huntley sighed. "How do you 'sort of' recognize it? Either you do or you don't."

"It was either a Mustang or a Challenger," I said. "It had a real throaty engine, you know?"

"So, it was a muscle car."

"Yes." I nodded, adding tentatively, "I think it might have been orange."

After experiencing nuclear sibling blowback from questioning Chip's involvement earlier, I was reluctant to say too much, at least until I heard back from Melanie. It wasn't like the car belonged to Chip, so it didn't feel like a betrayal to offer that much.

"And you saw the perp fleeing the scene, but it wasn't anyone you recognized?"

"That's correct," I said, and technically I wasn't lying. The vandal was too short to be Chip, although he could very well have been waiting inside the idling car. I thought back to my assault on the Grant Bridge, and it seemed possible that one or more of his buddies might fit the physical description, but as it was, I couldn't remember any of their names.

"Well, alright, then," said Officer Huntley, rising to his feet and prompting me to do the same. "I'll put out a BOLO for a vehicle matching your description, but I wouldn't hold my breath. Even if one turns up, you can't identify any of the occupants. If it turns out to be kids, which I think is likely, sometimes just the sight of a police officer is enough of a bluff to make them crack. Did you notice if anything was missing from your car?"

"I don't keep anything in there worth stealing."

He nodded. "If you discover something after you've had more time to look, we can always amend the report, but in the meanwhile, contact your insurance company. They can assist with getting your window replaced. I'll forward you a copy of the police report once it's finalized. They'll need that."

"Okay, thank you, Officer," I said, extending a hand, and I was almost surprised when he shook it. I guess he had decided my dine and dash with the coffee wasn't worth pursuing.

Gerd looked less satisfied.

"I don't suppose you might have something I could put over the hole where my passenger window used to be?" I asked her, earning another eyeroll to the heavens.

She snagged a roll of cellophane tape from the desktop and tossed it to me, ushering us out of the office and locking it behind her. "If I give you some bags from the checkout, will you just go away?"

•••••••◦◯◦••••••••

The makeshift "window" I had clumsily taped together from the thin convenience store plastic bags lasted a little more than a mile before getting sucked out and spiraling away into the Kentucky night. The resultant sonic ripple it created threatened the integrity of my eardrums, but only reducing my speed slowed its assault, and I was very aware of the lateness of the hour. I had wasted over an hour giving questions non-answers and reviewing security footage that was indecipherable. My eyes kept wandering to the passenger seat, where tiny shards of tempered glass glittered like diamonds. In the middle of the wreckage, the darkened screen of a Samsung smartphone stared back at me with its single, dead eye.

It wasn't my phone. Mine was connected to the car's USB port, providing navigation services to the address I hoped belonged to Officer Lucy Graves. It was an unusual last name, and I had been able to locate a public record on Google matching one 'L. Graves' who was the correct approximate age. I had tried to call the number on her card several times, but her phone went to voicemail, instructing callers to dial 9-1-1 if they needed immediate assistance. 9-1-1 didn't feel like the appropriate choice, so I had opted to seek Lucy out on my own. I was operating under the assumption that her shift had ended, and she would be going home afterward. I doubted she would be happy to see me, but now more than ever, I felt I had no choice.

As I had stood outside the Speedway, constructing a flimsy barrier for my window while onlookers continued to gawk, I had caught the corner of something peeking out from the underside of my passenger seat. I'll be the first to admit I'm not the best housekeeper, but I'm surprisingly fastidious with the cleanliness of my vehicle. I am constantly reminding both Melanie and Jasmine that "what goes in comes back out." I'd said it to the point of eye-rolling irritation if I'm completely honest. Whatever this was, it hadn't been there for long. I carefully reached beneath the seat, trying to avoid cutting my fingers on the shattered glass, and fished the phone out and looked it over. It was powered off and wouldn't power back on, the red outline of a battery flashing "0%" when I tried.

It wasn't Melanie's phone.

I had placed a quick call to her just as soon as I was out of earshot from Officer Huntley to let her know what happened and why I needed her to locate her brother as soon as possible. While I felt certain it was the same car, I knew it didn't belong to Chip, so I was hoping beyond hope he'd be where he said he was so I could eliminate his involvement without having to suggest its possibility. I really didn't want to face the united sibling wall of defense treatment I had received when I suggested his involvement before.

Unfortunately, she had been unable to confirm anything.

"There isn't cell service out where Jen's grandma lives," she had told me. "Chip's phone is going straight to voicemail."

"Or he isn't answering," I had muttered. "Doesn't the grandmother have a phone?"

"She has a landline, but the number is unlisted. I already checked with Cheryl and Mags, but neither of them has it. I'm sorry."

"*Shit.*"

Melanie had sighed. "I really don't think Chip's capable of being involved in this, but I appreciate you handling this discreetly. You owe

Craig a great big favor. He's not totally thrilled about it, but he's on his way right now to Otway to see if Chip is where he says he is."

I was relieved. At least it was *something*. "Thanks, babe. For what it's worth, I really hope he finds him right where he's supposed to be. It would be helpful to know who owns that orange Challenger, though. Oh, and the names of those other guys he runs around with."

"I'll try and catch Craig before he's out of coverage. Are you still planning on contacting Lucy Graves?"

"Yep," I had replied, dreading the very thought. "Keep that bail money handy."

"Not funny. Dwayne?"

"Yes, dear?"

"Be careful. I love you."

"Love you, too," I had responded, smiling as I disconnected the call. It was comforting to know there was someone who worried about my well-being and waited for me to come home safely. It wasn't so long ago that role was filled exclusively by my feline companion, Dexter, and frankly, I suspected his concern was more for his continued sustenance than my own personal safety. Cats make no bones about who's Number One in their books; it's *always* them.

I crossed the Oakley C. Collins Memorial Bridge into Ironton as directed by the soothing voice of Google Maps, my eyes coming to rest again on the cell phone lying in my passenger seat. Ambient light from passing traffic skimmed across its darkened screen, and I tried to remember what Tammy's phone had looked like as she answered the text that had sent her fleeing my car and racing toward her own death. I supposed it *could* be hers, but I hadn't been expecting a pop quiz, so I couldn't be certain. But only three people had ridden in my passenger seat in the past few days: Melanie, Tammy, and Doug, and it certainly wasn't Doug's. *His* flip phone I would have recognized.

320

GPS advised me to turn onto Spruce Street with my destination just around the corner on South 8th. I eased in behind a police SUV that was parked along the curb in front of the house bearing the street number I was searching for and killed my lights and engine. I scooped the phone into my hand and forced myself out of the car before I could change my mind. This wasn't going to be fun, but I couldn't think of anything else to do.

I pressed the unlit doorbell and heard nothing in response. I rapped a knuckle against the door, triggering the baying of what sounded like a dog of mythological proportions. I heard the beast scratching at the door as the porch light suddenly flared, blinding me. I shielded my eyes and squinted at the trio of narrow, staggered windows mounted high in the door, eliminating the need for a peephole.

"*Quiet*, Beowulf!" I heard Lucy bark from the other side of the door. "Ma? Can you take Wulfie into your room with you? Someone's at the door who should realize it's too late to come calling."

I winced as I heard another voice faintly beckon to the dog, and his rumbunctious barking faded as he was dragged away. A moment later, the door opened, and Lucy, clad in quilted pajamas, stared at me, her hand on her hip.

"What in the *world* are you doing here?" she asked.

"I'm really sorry, Officer Graves," I said. "But I need to talk to you. There've been some new developments, and—"

"Didn't I tell you to stay out of this?" she interrupted, rubbing her eyes. I wondered if I had woken her up.

"Well—yes, but—"

"Mama? Who is it?" The child's voice came from behind Lucy, bleary and wrapped around a yawn.

"It's nothing, Brianna. Go on back to bed. I'll tuck you back in just as soon as I can."

321

But children are nothing if not curious, and before Lucy could stop her, Brianna poked her head around her mother, looking at me inquisitively.

All my words escaped me as my mouth dropped open.

The little girl was undeniably beautiful, her long, raven hair framing her delicate face. Yet somehow, in a twist that seemed completely unfathomable, she was the spitting image of Doug Boggs.

CHAPTER TWENTY-FIVE

'*B*rianna!*" Lucy said sharply. "Get back to your room!"

The girl gave me one last look before scurrying away. Lucy leaned against the door, rubbing the ridge between her eyebrows while I struggled to regain my composure.

"Is that—?"

"My daughter, Brianna," Lucy answered flatly.

"Does he—?"

"Stop," she said, shaking her head. "We're not going to do this. You didn't come here to ask me about my daughter. I just got off a fourteen-hour shift, and I just want to go to bed. Why are you here?"

"Can I come in?" I asked. "It's kinda chilly out here."

She stepped back, granting me conditional entrance accompanied by a look of warning. I stepped into a tidy little living room with various toys and dolls scattered around its beige carpeting. A modest sofa and matching chair were aimed towards a smallish flatscreen television that was currently switched off. Department store artwork occupied some of the wall space not already covered by pictures of a smiling Brianna at various stages of her life. In one, she was a tiny infant swaddled in a pink blanket, Lucy beaming down at her while a man who most definitely was not Doug looked proudly over Lucy's shoulder.

"It's actually Doug who I'm here about," I said, perching on the edge of the sofa. "He's sort of gone missing."

She snorted. "Did you check with his mother?"

I nodded earnestly. "Of course. That was my first call."

She laughed and rolled her eyes. "Well, if that woman doesn't know where he is, I don't know who else would. Why would you think I could help?"

"It's gotten a little—weird," I said, and began filling her in on Doug's mysterious disappearance, including the loss of his cell phone and the text he had sent Loretta informing her of his whereabouts. I told her that I had found Doug's SUV abandoned in the parking lot of the Cop-a-Squat but stopped short of telling her about Chandler and Jesse. I didn't think it was relevant to whatever was going on with Doug, and I wasn't comfortable sharing the boys' secret when it might just make its way straight back to Chandler's father. I remembered Melanie's sister, Molly, had been maid of honor at Lucy's wedding and was also little Brianna's godmother. I had no way of knowing if Lucy enjoyed gossiping as much as Molly did. I followed that up with the vandalism of my own vehicle in the Speedway parking lot.

"So, you think somebody's following you?" she asked, taking a seat in the chair catercorner from me. I had her attention, and it gave me a twinkle of hope that my visit wouldn't end in arrest.

I blinked. I was so occupied with everyone else's whereabouts that I hadn't really given it much thought. "I guess so," I said.

"Why?"

I pulled my find from out of my pocket and handed it to her. "Maybe they were looking for this? I found it under my passenger seat after they got away. I think it might be Tammy's."

Lucy turned it over in her hand, handling it by the edges. I don't know if she was trying to keep from adding to the multitude of fingerprints already covering the screen, but I hadn't been nearly so thoughtful. She attempted to turn it on and received the same flashing red battery outline in response.

"It's not Tammy's," she said, more to herself than to anyone else.

"You're sure?"

Lucy nodded. "Tammy's phone was in her pocket when we recovered the body. This couldn't possibly be…" Her voice trailed away as she turned her thoughts inward.

I had a moment of sudden revelation. "You think it's Tina's, don't you?"

"I didn't say that," she said, but her face told me otherwise.

"Anne Marie mentioned that her phone hadn't been recovered."

"And we don't know for sure that it has been yet," she cautioned. "I'll want this kept under wraps for the time being. Are you even capable of discretion, Mr. Morrow?"

I fumbled through a maneuver that began as cross my heart and ended in a weird sort of pinky swear, and she looked at me like I was contagious. I dropped my pinky and cleared my throat. "Yeah. I can be discreet."

Her eyes briefly skimmed the pictures on the wall, and I realized she wasn't just talking about the case.

"What about Doug?" I asked, and her eyes narrowed.

"What do you mean?"

"Do you have any connections in Flatwoods who might be able to help find him?"

She looked relieved. "Oh, that. Yeah. Let me put a little thought into it, but I'm sure I can get some assistance. Was there anything else?"

"*Well—*" My eyes were drawn back to the framed pictures, and she sighed. "Does he even know?"

"Yes," she snapped, her cheeks flushing angrily. "No. *Dammit.* I can't make him believe what he doesn't want to believe."

"It's fairly obvious to the naked eye," I countered.

"Not if that eye is blind."

325

"A paternity test, then," I suggested, and she was on her feet in an instant.

"*Stop it!* You sound just like that horrible mother of his. She never believed this was his baby for an instant, and I'll be damned if I'm going to force someone to be a father based on the outcome of some stupid test. I don't need his support. I don't *want* it."

Her heightened state registered with Beowulf, and he started howling in the other room, followed immediately by a concerned elderly voice. "Lucy? Is everything all right out there?"

"It's fine, Mother," she called, working at the lines in her forehead again. "Mr. Morrow is about to leave."

I stood and made my way to the door. "Will you let me know if you are able to locate Doug?"

"I will if I can."

I paused in the open doorway, turning to face her. "Look, I know it's none of my business," I said. "I know the kind of iron grip Loretta has over her son. We've known each other for a lot of years, and believe me, she's no fan of mine, either. When we were in school, she was one of those moms who all the other kids were scared of. I can see her convincing Doug that this wasn't his responsibility. What I *can't* see is him walking away if he knew otherwise. I really don't think he has a clue."

"I, for one, would like to keep it that way," she said, crossing her arms in front of herself.

"*Lucy*—"

"Would you *stop* that? I don't recall how we suddenly got on a first name basis. I didn't ask for your opinion, and I would thank you kindly to just stay out of my business. Didn't I tell you I would have your ass hauled to jail if you didn't stay put?"

I raised my hands in surrender, stepping out onto the tiny square concrete porch. "I'm done. I'm headed back to Melanie's sister's house where I plan to go straight to bed."

"That's the best idea you've had all night," she said, stepping back and closing the door in my face. The porch light winked out before I had even taken the single step down into the yard.

······●●●◉◎●●●······

I was deep enough into my own thoughts as I traveled along State Route 93 that I barely noticed a light snow had begun to fall, that is, until enough had collected along my windshield wipers to warrant a swipe. My wipers screeched in horror as I triggered them, and I made a mental note to replace the blades before we headed home the following day. They were the automotive equivalent to fingernails on a chalkboard.

The more I thought about it, the more certain I was that the phone I had found was Tina's. While Tammy hadn't stuck around long enough to tell me why she was seeking my help, I was starting to piece it together on my own, and it felt plausible. Jasmine had told us that Tammy wanted to borrow her Demon Academy backpack so that she could carry a tablet and some other things in it. I believed what Tammy actually had was the laptop missing from Tina's desk when Doug and I had investigated her room. After confessing to being the masked bandit I had encountered during that investigation, Tammy had made the comment that she had to 'go back' in search of Tina's passwords. She wouldn't have phrased it that way if she hadn't already been there before. I was guessing she had both Tina's phone and laptop but was unable to access either without biometrics or a password, and once she encountered me and Doug in Tina's room, her plan to toss the place in the hopes of finding a password list was officially thwarted. She was resigned to asking for my help in accessing one or the other through more conventional means, and she was hoping that as an IT specialist, I would be up for the challenge.

Sadly, I probably wouldn't have been.

There was a time in the early days of computing when accessing material on the hard drive of a password protected computer was as easy as removing the hard drive and installing it into an external hard drive enclosure, which could then be plugged into another computer via USB port, making its contents fully accessible. While that's still a pretty tall order for the average computer user, Google has pretty thoroughly documented the hack over the years, and YouTube even offers step-by-step guides on how to accomplish it. By necessity, Microsoft and Apple have stepped up their approaches to security, and many of those older hacks no longer work on newer machines. Hacking was never my specialty, anyway. I was more of a Mr. Fix-It.

I was worried about Doug a whole lot more than I wanted to admit.

It felt nothing short of sinister to see the profile of his aesthetically appalling Aztek abandoned in the parking lot of the Cop-a-Squat where his trail went ice cold. Someone had to have taken him somewhere. I had subconsciously elected to leave the radio off as I drove, fearful of another news bulletin announcing the latest body pulled from the Ohio River. While I prayed that wouldn't be the outcome, I refused to let the news be delivered in such a manner. It was a form of denial, sure, but I just couldn't deal with any more bad news that evening.

I couldn't help thinking about the little girl he knew nothing about, and my opinion of Loretta somehow managed to dip even lower. It was easy enough to picture her intervening in any of Doug's potential romantic entanglements, but this? She was not only robbing her son of the opportunity to experience fatherhood, but herself of the opportunity to be a grandmother, and to what end? Guaranteeing herself a live-in caretaker for as long as she haunted this earthly plane? I couldn't even imagine our next meeting. How could I ever keep my mouth shut? I wasn't particularly good at that anyway, and lately I felt like I was drowning under the weight of secrets. I wasn't sure I could contain even one more. And none of this even mattered if Doug was…

I couldn't bring myself to even *think* the word.

A light dusting of snow covered the gravel in the Mullins' driveway. Craig's truck was still gone, but an older silver Honda was parked beside Cheryl's minivan, and I recognized it as Katie's from my first night here.

Good. One less person to worry about.

I parked near the back porch of the house, yawning as I checked the time on my phone. It was 11:05, and I was exhausted.

I let myself in through the back door, stomping my feet on the mat just inside the kitchen to rid myself of the thin layer of snow that had collected on my shoes. Looking through the kitchen to the living room, I could see half of the Christmas tree from where I stood. The twinkling, multicolored lights bathed the room in holiday magic, and Christmas music played softly in the background. It smelled like Cheryl had unleashed something tinged with evergreen and cinnamon into the air.

"Hello?" I called out, crossing the hallway to find the living room empty. I didn't even have time to wonder where everyone was before my phone rang in my pocket. It was Melanie.

"Hey, guy," she said. "I'm glad to see I didn't have to bail you out."

I laughed. "Not this time, although it was a little touch-and-go at times. I see that Katie made it."

"Yeah, she's less than happy to be here. I pulled her aside and asked if there was something Tina might have been holding over her, but she laughed it off. Said she barely knew the girl. It feels like she's holding back. Were you able to locate Doug?"

"No," I said. "Although I did manage to track down Lucy Graves, and she said she'd put some feelers out with some of her police buddies in Flatwoods. You won't believe what I *did* find."

"Yeah?"

I whistled. *"Complete* mindblower, but it can wait until I see you. Where are you?"

"Cheryl and I decided to join the sleepover in the trailer," she said. She lowered her voice. "With everything that's been going on, it was a little creepy staying in the house after Craig left. But hey, you'll be happy to know that Chip's whereabouts have been confirmed. Craig called about ten minutes ago. Chip and Jen are watching *The Nightmare Before Christmas* in their PJs while Jen's gram saws logs in her La-Z-Boy. They didn't go anywhere all evening. Had dinner delivered from Giovanni's."

She was justifiably smug, and I was okay with that. I really didn't want to lock horns with her over her brother again. "Was Craig able to find out any information about those other guys Chip's been running around with?"

"Yes, sir," she said. "He texted me names and numbers. Why don't you join us over here, and we can put our information together."

I grinned. "I love it when you want to collate facts with me. Total turn on. But you know what? If you don't mind, I think I'd like to run through the shower before I head over. Between the rain, the sweat, and all of that smoke from the campfire, I feel gross, and my clothes haven't completely dried out since we were at the riverfront. I hate to admit it, but I might just be a little whiffy. A nice, hot shower without the risk of Molly walking in on me sounds extremely appealing."

She sighed. "Fine but hurry up. You can't tease a woman with a complete mindblower and then just walk away."

"Ten—fifteen minutes, tops," I promised.

"I'm timing you, mister."

She made a smoochy sound and disconnected.

••••••••◦◦••••••••

I showered under water as warm as I could possibly endure, and the pressure was glorious. My ten or fifteen minutes turned into twenty before I knew it, but it was worth every second. I felt rejuvenated and comfortable for the first time in hours—hell, *days*.

I chased the moisture from my dark brown hair with a compact blow dryer Melanie had packed, noting it was getting just long enough to curl at the ends. That was new. My hair had always been straight as a board.

I pulled a clean pair of jeans from my duffel bag and stepped into them and donned a Pink Floyd tee that wasn't remotely warm enough, but it was all I had left. I wished I had the foresight to throw my lightweight jacket in the dryer while I was showering, but it was a little late for that now. It was just a short jaunt across the way to the trailer; I would survive.

The snow had tapered off, but the wind had picked up, and I was hit with a frosty gust just as soon as I stepped out onto the porch. It felt like the temperature had dropped another ten degrees. I hugged myself, shivering convulsively as I started across the expanse. I can't even say what made me look as I crossed in front of Katie's Honda, but as my eyes skimmed across the snow collecting on her windshield, the moonlight glinted against something hanging from her rearview mirror. I moved closer, leaning in to get a better look.

Suspended by a keyring attached to an OSU lanyard was a small plastic shark.

I glanced at the trailer to make sure no one had noticed my approach before crouching down by the driver's door and reaching for its handle. The car was old enough I wasn't particularly concerned about a car alarm.

If it was Katie's habit to lock her vehicle, my quest was over. I didn't have a Slim Jim and her locks weren't the type to be defeated by a coat hanger. My raging curiosity wouldn't justify putting an elbow through her window.

The door popped open, and the dome light flared.

I hesitated only a second as I was suddenly framed in the light. I reached in and snagged the lanyard, pulling it off of the mirror before quickly easing the door shut, bumping it with my backside to latch the door and kill the telltale light. I turned around and scurried back to the house, hoping my luck would hold for just a moment longer.

Once inside the kitchen, I pulled my phone out of my pocket and called Melanie.

"Longest fifteen minutes *ever*," she answered.

"Listen," I whispered, caught up in the moment. It wasn't as if there was anyone in the house other than me. "I think I've found the USB drive Tina was blackmailing Katie with."

"Okay," she said cautiously.

"Can you make sure everyone stays put over there?" I asked. "I'm going to take a peek and put it back."

"That shouldn't be a problem," she said. "How long do you need?"

"Ten—fifteen minutes, tops."

"Dwayne."

"Fine. Twenty-five." I disconnected the call and slid my phone back into my pocket.

It took me a moment to find my laptop bag. I had left it leaning against the dining room table, but Melanie must have carried it back to our room. I sat on the edge of the twin bed and pulled my MacBook out of the bag, firing it up. After it loaded, I pulled the gray and white plastic head off of the shark, exposing its USB connector.

I turned my laptop from one side to the other before checking its backside in desperation. I only had two ports on my MacBook, and they were both for the newer, smaller USB-C standard. I required either a port for USB-A or an adapter.

Shit.

I could pocket the drive and hope that Katie wouldn't notice it was missing before I had a chance to examine it, but I figured the odds were next to nil. She kept it hanging around her rearview mirror, right out in the open where its absence would be immediately apparent. I was almost resigned to returning it unviewed when another thought occurred to me. I pocketed the drive and headed for the back porch once more.

It had started snowing again. Big, fat flakes collected with considerable haste on the windshields and hoods of the vehicles in the drive. Ambient light from whatever movie the girls were watching flickered through the curtains covering the rectangular window of the trailer, but there were no curious onlookers monitoring my activity.

I skirted the outer edge of the drive closest to the house and headed towards Craig's garage. My heart jumped into my throat as the motion-detected security light burst to life, illuminating me as plainly as if I were on a Broadway stage. I looked behind me, but no one had rushed to the door of the trailer to see what prompted the light. I hurried to the door on the far-left side and grabbed the cold metal knob, twisting it.

It was locked.

Shi-i-i-it!

I knelt down to examine the knob and saw that it really wasn't anything particularly fancy. There was no deadbolt. No sticker warning me of a security company who would be dispatched via silent alarm. I fumbled in my pocket for my wallet and fished out a credit card. I'd seen this maneuver on TV plenty, but could it actually work? I was about to find out.

I slid my card between the metal frame and the door, just above the latch. I cringed as I felt the card buckle and warp, and I knew I'd be calling for a replacement on Monday morning. The first pass did nothing but destroy the integrity of the card. With my second attempt, I did less sliding and applied more pressure, and I almost laughed out loud when the door popped open.

I hurried inside and closed the door behind me, standing stock-still until the exterior light flickered out. I pulled my cell phone from my pocket and activated the flashlight, shining it back towards Craig's desk where his computer sat on his desk.

I pulled the task chair out and sat behind the keyboard, moving the mouse, and bringing the monitor to life. The screensaver cleared, bringing up a login prompt that was thankfully no challenge at all. I typed '1234' into the password prompt and was rewarded with the Windows' 'Welcome' chime.

The computer was a little slow to load, but I used the time to find the desktop's USB-A ports, and it had plenty. Two in the front and six in the back. I pulled the head back off of the shark and inserted the drive into one of the front-facing slots. A dialog box popped up in the lower right corner asking what I wanted do, and I selected the option to view files. There was only one, and it was a video.

I double-clicked the filename and sat back in the chair as Windows Media Player came to life.

At first, I wasn't sure what I was watching. The point of view changed as the camera was carried around, but after a second, I recognized the inside of Maggie's trailer from the brief glimpse I had gotten of it my first night here. It appeared to be some sort of party. Laughter and voices comingled with country karaoke which was being executed with a surprising level of skill just offscreen. As the camera panned left, Cheryl and Maggie were revealed as the harmonious duo, with Cheryl singing as much into her glass of amber liquid as she was the microphone. Couples I didn't recognize passed through, and one girl nodded toward the camera with a distinct lack of recognition. As the camera continued left, Tina's reflection was momentarily captured as she exited the trailer through the storm door and stepped down into the yard. Cars were piled into the drive, and I had no sooner wondered if this was the big Fourth of July party that had been previously mentioned when multicolored fireworks blossomed in the distance, visible over the roof of the house.

Noises from the party faded as Tina continued toward the house, where only a light in the kitchen shone through a window, but rather than head in that direction, she cut right, skirting the western end of the house, and crossing into the front yard. When she turned back to the house, only a boxwood shrub and ten feet separated her from the window that belonged to Maggie's old room—the room Melanie and I currently occupied.

The curtains were wide open, and Katie's nubile shape came into view. She was lost in the moment, straddling her partner, and grinding away, her head thrown back as her breasts rose and fell. For longer than I was comfortable watching, I could only see Katie and the suggestion of the man underneath her, his thick hand clasping her milky white hip to hold her in place. A wedding ring reflected moonlight from his fourth finger.

As their rhythm intensified, approaching climax, he abruptly sat upright, pulling Katie into the thatch of fur on his chest as he nuzzled her shoulder. My heart sank as I recognized the face of Cheryl's husband, Craig, and suddenly the fluorescent overhead lights sprang to life. I turned to see the man himself, filling the doorframe with his considerable bulk and staring at me in disbelief.

"I really wish you hadn't seen that," he said.

In his hand, he held a gun, and it was pointed directly at me.

CHAPTER TWENTY-SIX

This was becoming an all-too-common occurrence for me, but the novelty of terror hadn't even begun to wear off. My eyes were everywhere at once, looking for something—*anything*—I might use to defend myself. All of the good wrenches were across the room, and I sincerely doubted I could pierce his eye with the barely sharpened pencil at my fingertips before he could end my life with the simple squeeze of a trigger. Still, I scooped it into my palm and slid it into my pocket. Anything was better than nothing.

I stood, looking for something to hide behind, but I had effectively cornered myself behind the counter. The only exit was a straight shot in his direction, no pun intended. The recorded sounds of a cascading orgasm continued to spill through the shitty computer speakers, elevating the awkwardness of the scene to new heights.

"Turn that off, please," Craig said.

I complied, closing the video program before snatching the plastic shark by its tail, plucking it out of the USB port. I held it up in front of me as words started spilling out of my mouth in a torrent. "Hey, listen, Craig. There's no need to make this any worse than it already is. You can just take this. It's yours." I almost tossed it to him but had second thoughts as I pictured the gun firing in response, my story ending far more abruptly than intended. "You know, if you pull that trigger, everyone's gonna come running. You'll never get away with it."

He looked down at the gun, genuinely surprised, as if he had forgotten it was even there. He lowered it to his side. "I'm not going to shoot you," he said, and his startled tone gave me the faintest glimmer of hope. "When I pulled into the drive, I saw your flashlight moving around in the garage. I thought you were a burglar. I *wish* you were a burglar."

We regarded each other in silence, avoiding eye contact.

"So-o-o," I ventured before holding up the USB drive. "Is this still a thing?"

"*No!*" he said angrily, flailing his arms a bit in frustration. "There never *was* a thing. Just one stupid, drunken slip that I would give anything to take back."

My eyes followed his gesticulations carefully. "You know, I'd feel a whole lot better about this conversation if you would just put the gun down."

He looked, surprised again to find it in his hand. He made a point of engaging the safety before slowly lowering it to the concrete floor. "I'm not going to shoot you," he repeated, nudging it out of reach with his foot.

I felt like I could suddenly breathe again. "I'm a big fan of that," I said with a shaky smile. "I don't get it. You and Cheryl seem so—together."

"We *are*," he insisted, finally meeting my eyes. "She is the best thing that's ever happened to me! I wouldn't trade my life—our *girls*—"

He clamped a hand over his mouth just as his voice broke, and his red-rimmed eyes found the fluorescents. I waited for him to pull himself together and continue.

"Katie had been flirting with me for years. I didn't take it seriously at first. She was Maggie's best friend, and I've known her since she was just a kid. Even Cheryl thought it was innocent, and that woman gets jealous if someone stares at me the wrong way at the Kroger. I never meant for this to happen."

"Then how could you let it?" I sincerely wanted to know. I didn't have a lengthy history of relationships to draw upon, and the one I was in with Melanie felt like a gift I didn't deserve. I couldn't imagine jeopardizing it by sleeping around. The guilt would live on my face for the whole world to see.

He just shook his head, staring at the fluorescent fixtures above.

"Well, come *on*," I challenged. "You know the old saying. It takes two—"

"Three, if you count Jim Beam," he said. "It was that stupid Fourth of July party Cheryl throws every goddamn year. It's the one big blowout she insists on."

"Thanksgiving wasn't exactly small," I said.

"Not at all the same," he said. "Thanksgiving is mostly family, and even when it's folks you don't particularly want to see, you've got a good idea of when it's gonna start, and when it's gonna end. These Fourth of July parties are a free-for-all. Cheryl invites all her co-workers from the salon, and they bring whoever they want to bring, and Maggie and Chip do the same. My guys from the shop bring their wives and girlfriends, and I don't even know half of the people who are here."

"Sounds like loads of fun for Kenzie and Mandy," I said.

"Oh, fuck *you*," he said, pointing an angry forefinger in my direction. "Just because we have kids doesn't mean we're done living. You sound just like Molly, which is kinda funny, because that's exactly who Kenzie and Mandy spent the night with. This is an adults-only party. Children are not welcome, and I can't believe you would think that they were."

"I'm having a little trouble knowing *what* to believe here."

"Fuck *you!* I'm trying to tell you what happened, but what's the point if you've already made up your mind?"

338

Frankly, I wasn't sure what the point was, either. I was no priest, and this was not a confessional, but I had seen something I couldn't unsee, and even though I was beginning to believe Craig had nothing to do with deaths of the two girls, I suspected I knew where we were heading. It was one more secret I was going to be expected to keep from Melanie, and I wasn't sure I wanted to. I wasn't sure I *could.*

"I had way too much to drink," he continued, not waiting for an invitation. "When Cheryl gets lit, her go-to is karaoke. She and her sisters can sing just as sweet as angels, and she and Maggie usually put on a little show. I'm more for darts or poker, but that night, we were throwing horseshoes down by the firepit, waiting for Chip and his buddies to get back with some fireworks they promised to bring. Chip had some Army connection where he could get the good stuff real cheap. I started feeling real sick to my stomach, you know? Everything was spinning, and my throws were getting wilder and wilder. I decided I'd better put my head down for a bit, so I headed up to the house. I must've got turned around because I ended up in Maggie's old bedroom, but by that point, a bed was a bed. I laid down and fell asleep almost immediately. Next thing I know, someone is helping me off with my pants. I thought it was Cheryl. I didn't even open my eyes."

I couldn't help but snort. "You're kidding me, right? *'I didn't even open my eyes.'* What a load of horseshit. Your eyes were open in that video."

"Would you let me finish?" he implored. *"At first,* I thought it was Cheryl. But she was doing things to me that Cheryl's never done. I was just so wasted. I thought maybe it was just a dream—"

I laughed out loud. "A *dream?* Is that the best you've got?"

"Like you would have done anything different if you'd been in my place," he said earnestly, closing the distance between us. "You might *think* you would, but you can't know for sure. I don't know what more to tell you. I never claimed to be perfect. It only happened that one time, and I would give anything to be able to take it back—that's the God's truth. I don't know why you're getting so bent out of shape anyway."

I looked at him incredulously. "Because I *liked* you, you idiot! You and Cheryl both. You've made me feel welcome in your home, and I want Melanie's family to like me. I've already got two strikes against me with Molly and Chip, but having you, Cheryl, and Maggie on my side would have made up for that. But now there's this *thing* hanging between us, and the next thing you're going to do is ask me to keep quiet about what I've seen, right? Just keep it between us two bros—"

"I don't want to lose my family," he said plaintively, his eyes practically pleading.

"And I don't want to lose mine, either!" I snapped, louder than intended. I cleared my throat and adjusted my volume. "Do you know the kind of trouble I'd be in with Melanie if this all came out, and she found out I *knew?*"

"So, just don't *say* anything," he urged.

"Wow. You just don't get it," I said, beginning to pace in a tight circle. "Exactly what do you know about this video?"

He shook his head. "What do you mean?"

"I mean, how long have you known about it? Was Tina blackmailing you, too? Do you have your own copy?"

"No," he said. "I'd never met Tina. She came as Katie's guest, and while I might have said hello or something, I didn't notice her again for the rest of the evening. She was a real wallflower. Katie showed me the video about a month or so ago and told me Tina was blackmailing her, but she acted like it was no big deal. She said Tina wanted her help getting a makeover before the school year started. Tina never approached me directly."

"A month ago? That would've been before Tina disappeared."

Craig nodded. "So?"

"Why would Katie suddenly decide to show you the video?"

340

Craig was sheepish as he reached out and took the plastic USB drive from my hand. "I think she was hoping that seeing us in action would make me want to do it again. I told her it was a mistake, a one-time thing, but she's relentless. I honestly don't think she cares if the video comes out. While she hasn't come right out and said it, I think she's been working herself up to a little blackmail of her own with this." He let the plastic shark drop to the concrete floor and crushed it beneath the heel of his work boot. "At least this solves one problem. No more instant replay. Look, I don't like the thought, but if it's down to a matter of he-said, she-said, I will lie through my teeth to protect what I've got. It would sure help if I knew I didn't have to worry about you taking Katie's side."

I groaned, shaking my head. I knew it was coming, but now that he had actually spoken his request aloud, I was going to have to take a position, and I wasn't comfortable with either of my choices. I just wanted to punch him in his stupid face.

"You know that's not the end of it, right?" I said, shifting gears and pointing to the shattered USB drive. "Tina supposedly had cloud backups of all this shit. Several of the kids I've spoken to said she had arranged to have the files made public if anything were to happen to her. It was her own safety net, to keep anyone from deciding that maybe getting rid of her was the easiest way to free themselves from her."

Craig's face clouded as my words sunk in. "So, this is all still going to come out."

"What's all going to come out?"

Cheryl stood just inside the doorway with Melanie right behind her. She could only see her husband's back since he was facing me, and that's a good thing, because Craig couldn't have looked more guilty if he tried. While his complexion roamed the warmer hues of the color palette, I leaned into the visible jumpstarts she'd given us both.

"Jeez, Cheryl, you're peeling the years off me two at a time," I said, clutching at my chest.

"I saw Craig's truck in the drive and noticed the lights were on out here in the garage," said Cheryl. "So, what's going to come out?"

As I watched Craig's lips work soundlessly, I was suddenly afraid of what might emerge from them. I recognized that I was a famously bad liar, but I had no idea of this guy's potential. If the tale he told stretched the boundaries of truth too far past the breaking point, there would be no turning back.

"Your Christmas present," I blurted out, bustling past Craig while he looked at me incredulously. I only hoped I could keep Cheryl's attention from her husband's absolutely vacant expression. "Turn around! *Hurry!* You're going to ruin *everything!*"

Cheryl's eyebrows knit together, but her face lit up. "Babe? I thought we were focusing on the girls this year—?"

"I—um, uh—we—" Craig was a useless, stammering fool.

By then, my arms were practically pinwheeling, urging Cheryl and Melanie back through the door. I avoided Melanie's eyes at all costs, certain she would see right through me. This was everything I never wanted, playing out as high-speed farce. "Go! Go! Go!"

As I ushered them back into the snowy night, I risked a last-minute glance at Craig, pointing first to the gun on the floor and then to the fragments of gray shark and its shattered circuit board entrails surrounding his boots.

"Hurry and put that away before she sees it!" I urged, relieved to finally see a light come on behind Craig's eyes. As he reached for a push broom, I pulled the door shut behind me, guiding the ladies back toward the trailer.

"I still don't understand," said Cheryl, but whatever her reservations, they couldn't erase the smile from her face. "I mean, we said we were going to focus our budget on the girls this year. If he got me some secret surprise—well, of *course* it would come out on Christmas, right?"

"He's talking about how much it cost," I said. In for a penny, might as well be in for the whole goddamn pound. I still had approximately four weeks to bring Craig up to speed on what these new expectations would be, and it served the idiot right. "But please don't tell him I said that."

Cheryl's eyes glistened as visions of sugar plums—or their equivalent—took hold of her imagination, putting a little extra spring in her step. My eyes skirted Melanie's, and she was a whole lot less enthusiastic. In fact, her expression indicated a private consultation was imminent.

Somehow, I didn't think Craig was going to come riding to my rescue. *Shit.*

* * *

"Will you stay still for just one second?" Melanie whispered, as she cornered me in the tiny nook that served as Maggie's kitchen.

Only a half-wall separated us from everyone else, all of whom were fully invested in *The Polar Express*. Well, all but Katie, who had curled into a ball in the recliner and was currently rumbling like an asthmatic kitten. Maggie had already begged off because she had to work in the morning. Jasmine, Kenzie, and Mandy shared a blanket, propped on elbows with hot chocolate at the ready. Craig sat at the far end of Maggie's threadbare sofa, his arm draped around Cheryl's shoulders, looking like he belonged on death row. His mind was on anything but the movie, but then again, so was Cheryl's. She was tucked into her husband's side, and unabashedly blissful contemplation made her look like a girl dreaming of Santa Claus. Lord only knew the disappointment I had primed for her on Christmas morning. It may have served Craig right, but it was unnecessarily cruel to Cheryl, and I already felt bad for being vindictive instead of inventive.

"What's up?" I asked in an octave foreign to my own ear. I busied myself with fixing another bag of microwave popcorn, trying my best to avoid Melanie's probing gaze.

"Did you get a chance to look at it?" she whispered.

"Look at what?"

"Katie's USB drive," she said, impatience throttling her volume. She cast a furtive glance over her shoulder to confirm Katie was still sawing logs. "What did you find out?"

"Nothing," I said as the microwave sounded. I retrieved the bag by a corner and held it upside down over the sink, shaking it to encourage the last of the kernels to pop.

"Nothing?"

"My MacBook doesn't have the right kind of port to plug it in."

"Well, where is it? My laptop is older than yours. It might have the type of port you're looking for."

She stared at me expectantly while I paid far too much attention to distributing the popcorn evenly between three plastic bowls. "Huh. I didn't think of that. Well, it's too late now."

She blinked, her frustration mounting. "What do you mean?"

"I put it back in her car," I said, venturing out into the minefield of improvisation. I wish I'd never mentioned that damned flash drive to Melanie, but how could I have possibly known what was on it?

"Why would you do that?" Her volume was rising again, and I shushed her, snagging the bowls of popcorn.

"Craig pulled in and wanted to show me Cheryl's present in the garage," I lied. "I told him I'd left my phone in the house, and I'd meet him there. Once he went inside, I hurried and put it back. I barely had time to think."

I didn't give her a chance to respond before carrying the popcorn out into the living room.

"Last call for popcorn," I said. "Any takers?"

Jasmine reached for a bowl to share with her cousins, and I offered one to Cheryl, but she waved it away, still daydreaming about Christmas morning. I handed one to Melanie and kept the other for myself, perching on the open end of the couch and leaning forward to signify my focus was on the runaway train skittering across a lake of ice onscreen. I patted the cushion beside me, but she just rolled her eyes and went back into the kitchen. I leaned back, hoping I had bought myself a little time while trying to commit the bullshit I had already spoken to memory.

This wasn't going to go away.

At some point, Mandy extricated herself from underneath the blanket and joined her parents on the couch beside me. She had tucked herself under Cheryl's arm, her mouth ringed with chocolate, and both were sawing logs as the movie entered its final stretch. I couldn't tell if Craig was asleep or praying for a quick death. His head rested against the back of the sofa, and his eyes were closed. Jasmine and Kenzie, both fighting yawns, were determined to see this movie through to the very end.

After tidying up the kitchen, Melanie pulled one of the rickety chairs in from the dinette and sat down, but her leg ticked with nervous energy, and I sensed her watching me out of the corner of my eye. I tried my best to remain focused on the movie, but when she loudly cleared her throat, I had no choice but to look over.

"You alright, babe?" I asked.

She nodded toward the door and winked. "I don't suppose you'd be a dear and go get my laptop for me?" she asked sweetly.

"Now?"

"I just got an idea for my book, and I don't want to lose it," she said. "I'd go myself, but I'm already dressed for bed. Please? I'll make it up to you later."

"*Mo-o-m*," said Jasmine without missing a beat. "Gross."

"We're at the very end of the movie, Mel," I hedged, the words lame in my own ears.

"In the end, Christmas is saved, and the kids make it home safely," she said, with a saccharine smile. "Now, hurry back."

I got to my feet, wondering how in the world I was going to get out of this now. Would it be too excessive to set Katie's car on fire?

"And don't forget my storage drive," she added, emphasizing the last two words. Katie snorted in her sleep and turned over, mumbling something incoherent.

I grabbed my jacket and slipped it on, surprised by the arctic blast that hit me in the face when I opened the door. At least two inches of fat, fluffy snow had fallen and was still falling, covering the cars, and erasing the boundaries between the gravel expanse and lawn. I stepped down carefully onto the cinderblock stoop and pulled the door closed behind me, my mind racing from one implausible excuse to another.

I could tell Melanie that Katie's car had been broken into, and the drive was stolen, but Katie's vehicle was the least likely to attract burglars. My eyes were drawn to my own Hyundai and the hole where its passenger window used to be. Snow had blown in to fill the seat and drift across the armrest into the driver's side. Wonderful.

I was contemplating the practicality of faking a fall while carrying Melanie's laptop back to the trailer, smashing it into as many pieces as possible when I heard a text notification land on the phone in my pocket. I fished it out and unlocked my screen.

It was another from the ubiquitous 'CALLER UNKNOWN.'

Running out of time. 3688 Sweeney Hollow. Flatwoods.

Another text landed as I read the first. It was a picture, and the lighting was bad. I squinted, trying to determine what I was looking at, but only after examining it at arm's length could I recognize it as an extreme close-up of the lower side of a man's bloodied face. His eye was swollen shut, and his bottom lip was split in multiple places, a thick rope of bloody saliva trailing down his stubbled chin. If it hadn't been for the corduroy collar that was barely visible in the corner of the picture, I would have never even recognized Doug.

Another text landed.

Come alone.

This wasn't the solution I had hoped for, but what choice did I really have?

I glanced back at the trailer to confirm the coast was clear before changing direction and making a beeline to my SUV. I used the sleeves of my jacket to quickly clear the windshield before easing behind the wheel. Once I started my engine, stealth would not be an option, and I couldn't afford to get stuck in the driveway.

I put my foot on the brake and counted to three before pressing the ignition button, immediately shifting into drive to begin what may have been the sloppiest three-point turn in the history of maneuverability. With each sweep, my tires struggled for purchase, and I nearly hit all three of the other parked cars before finally righting myself, aimed towards the road. One last glance through my driver's side window, and I saw Melanie framed in the open door of the trailer, her hands on her hips as she watched me execute this lunacy.

I gave it too much gas and fishtailed out onto the icy pavement of State Route 93, fueled only by adrenaline and without a single clue of what I was headed into.

CHAPTER TWENTY-SEVEN

Melanie called me repeatedly, and I shuttled each call off to voicemail. I'd beg her forgiveness later, but I couldn't debate it now. Twelve calls in, she gave up, and I would be hearing about this for a while. It couldn't be helped.

Traffic was nearly non-existent as I crossed back into Kentucky. I passed the first salt trucks as I neared Flatwoods, but they were headed in the opposite direction, so I had only my SUV's four-wheel drive to rely on to keep me on course along the untreated highway.

Something about the address was familiar, but it wasn't until I neared the snow-covered lot of New Life Apostolic on Kentucky Route 207 that it registered. The original church site was on Sweeney Hollow. Why did everything seem connected to the good Reverend Keaton and his church? It felt like we were well past the point of coincidence. And now that I thought about it, what better place to hold a hostage than its abandoned campus? I had my choice of spots in the massive but empty lot, not that I could tell where any of them were underneath the glistening blanket of white, but I pulled in and parked, consulting Google Maps on my phone to try and find alternative entry points to my final destination. I was discouraged to learn there was only one way in and one way out of the hollow itself. I wouldn't be catching anyone by surprise tonight.

I'd like to say I was anything other than scared to death, but I'd only be lying, and by now, you should know I don't do that very well. I kept telling myself that whoever was behind all this wanted something out of me, and I wasn't in any *real* danger until I knew what that thing was. What they might do *after*—well, that was another matter, but I refused to think that far ahead. I wasn't *that* brave. I needed to stay focused and alert. Doug's life most likely depended on it.

Mine, too.

I pulled back out onto the highway, traveling south for a few more miles before being directed onto Route 503, also known as Naples Road. I crawled along for miles until the GPS warned me of an impending turn to my left, but for the life of me, I couldn't see where the road was. There was no streetlight courteously mounted near the unmarked entrance, and guard rails had been hit or miss for miles. The likelihood of dropping the front end of my car into a culvert was high. With no traffic in either direction, I slowed to a stop, examining my surroundings. The outermost edge of my headlights illuminated what remained of an ancient, hand-painted sign for New Life Apostolic with an arrow pointing back into the snow-capped treetops. It had since been spray-painted and vandalized but seemed very sure of itself as it bobbed and teetered in the wind, and upon closer examination, there was just enough room for a narrow lane directly in front of it. I started to ease my SUV left, then reconsidered. I couldn't see two feet in front of me with my headlights off, but with them on, I would be announcing my arrival to anyone paying attention. Another idea occurred to me, and while I wasn't completely in love with it, it seemed smarter than approaching in a hail of a white-hot halogen. I straightened my wheel and continued along Route 503, squinting into the distance, and looking for a place to pull off.

I found what I was looking for less than a half-mile ahead, a wide shoulder with six mailboxes nailed to a plywood frame. The far end of the shoulder dipped down into a lot where six trailers squatted around a utility pole, drawing power while sending fossil fuel exhaust into the air through matching metal chimneys. I tucked in behind the mailboxes and killed my engine, stepping out into the frigid night. I hurried to the rear of my SUV, using my key fob to trigger the automated hatch. I slid the weatherproof cabin liner aside, revealing a storage area where I fully expected to find all the tools needed to change a flat. While I may not have my gun with me, a tire iron might help offset my jangling nerves. Imagine my surprise to discover only a basic inflation kit, designed to help me limp to safety where my tire could be repaired or replaced by a Hyundai-certified professional.

Shit.

A quick pass through the car's interior revealed nothing more fearsome than a long-handled snow scraper, which I promptly tucked underneath my arm before signaling the hatch to close. It was better than nothing.

My breath plumed out before me as I retraced my path along the disappearing roadway, quickening my pace upon the realization that I had underestimated how fucking cold it would be. My jeans were adequate, but my Skechers were not, and soon enough, my feet were cold, damp, and complaining. I hurried along, wanting to be done with this.

The night was preternaturally quiet, its nocturnal creatures shocked into a collective silence borne of a surprise snowfall the weathermen hadn't seen coming. I stopped short when I reached Sweeney Hollow. A fresh set of tire tracks cut across the snowy highway, dropping down onto the rutted dirt and gravel path leading back into the woods. They weren't there just moments before. I honestly couldn't tell if it was my imagination, but I thought I heard an engine receding in the distance, although no lights betrayed its presence.

I followed along.

I had ventured far enough to lose sight of the highway behind me, but I hadn't encountered any other signs of life. The trail meandered underneath a tangle of interlocking limbs from ancient oaks and pines, their branches weighed down by heavy snow that continued to fall. My heart hammered double-time whenever a heavy clump performed a kamikaze maneuver, breaking the fragile silence.

My eyes had acclimated to the darkness, aided by moonlight peeking through pregnant clouds and reflecting off fallen snow, and the world had taken on an ethereal quality. The silence was deeper, and my vision was sharper. I kept to the rightmost tire track, thinking I could plunge into the brush if necessary but doubting my ability to pull the maneuver off without face planting. Who was I fooling? I rubbed my hands together and shoved them into my pockets, keeping the snow scraper tucked firmly under my arm and focusing on the tire tracks ahead.

A cascade of breaking foliage culminating in a metallic sequence of thunks sounded just ahead and to my left, and there was no mistaking it now. I heard the sound of an ignition being attempted again and again. I cut across the road, clinging to shadows as I moved forward, rounding the bend slowly.

Just ahead, a small silver sedan had slid off the path, its passenger front tire dropping into a culvert. After one more elongated attempt to re-engage the engine, the driver gave up, flinging open the door and getting out of the car. The silhouette was short, dark, and angry as it unleashed a torrent of obscenities into the air and planted a few futile kicks into the rear door panel before stepping away, hands on hips and staring into the night sky. From this distance, I couldn't tell if it was a man or a woman, only that they were highly agitated, but infinitely better prepared for the inclement weather than me. Its dark, insulated jacket with a fuzzy hood was stark against the snowy backdrop, and there was no exposed flesh where its hands would be. After a moment, the figure began a slow, circular examination of its surroundings, and I did my best impression of a Virginia Pine rooted in the brush, still thirty feet away and obscured by shadows.

Well, all except for my breath, which rose above me in voluminous plumes.

"Who's there?!?"

The voice was high-pitched, female, and frantic. It was also vaguely familiar. I suddenly realized she had extended her right arm and appeared to be pointing something in my direction.

"If you don't come out *right now*, I'm going to shoot, so help me God!" she warned, her voice trembling.

I didn't move a single muscle, yet thunder cracked, and the muzzle flared orange, and I hit the ground, momentarily unsure if it was reflex or if I'd been hit. Nothing hurt any worse than usual, so I was going with reflex. I stole a glance at my assailant and realized I wasn't the only one taken by surprise. The figure dropped the gun as soon as it jumped in her hand, and she was rooting around in the snow trying to recover it, a running monologue of self-deprecation carrying across the way.

"Anne Marie?" I called out, recognition dawning.

She froze, looking over her shoulder in my general direction. "O-o-oh, who *is* it?" she pleaded. "What do you *want* from me?"

I crawled out from my cover of shadows before she could locate the firearm. "It's Dwayne," I called, trying to keep my voice at least somewhat subdued. I had no idea who else might be listening. "Dwayne Morrow."

"Oh, Mr. Morrow!" she squealed, not a second thought given to volume. She bridged the distance as I got to my feet, brushing snow off my jeans. "I didn't shoot you, did I? Oh, please God, tell me I didn't shoot you."

"No," I said, and she was close enough that I could finally see her face underneath the furry hood. "But please—*shhh*. We've got to keep our voices down."

She clamped a hand to her mouth and nodded, her eyes wide.

"What are you doing here?" I asked, guiding her back toward where she had dropped the gun.

"I got this text," she said, fumbling through her puffy pockets before realizing she had left her phone in her car. She hurried over to retrieve it while I nudged around in the snow with my foot, locating the gun a couple of feet away from where she had originally stood. I plucked it from the snow, my knuckles screaming in protest the whole way.

"Found your gun," I said as she came back, peeling off a glove and unlocking her phone.

"Keep it," she said. *"Please.* I hate that thing, but I thought it was stupid to come unarmed."

I looked at the snow scraper I had tossed aside and kept my mouth shut. Probably not the best move to let the client know she came better prepared than me. I engaged the safety and slipped the gun into my pocket.

"It's Marlene," Anne Marie said, turning her phone so I could see the screen. She had received a matching set of texts to my own, also from 'CALLER UNKNOWN.' The only difference was the picture in the second one. A closeup of Anne Marie's sister filled the picture, her eyes wide, and her mouth opened in surprise. Thankfully, other than looking surprised, she didn't show any signs of physical abuse.

"I thought your sister was in the hospital," I said.

"They released her this afternoon into my care. I took her to my apartment rather than back to that big ole empty house where she'd have nothing to occupy her mind but memories of poor Tina. I can't see her stayin' there anymore, and she's welcome to stay with me just as long as she wants, but there was some things I needed to get from her house—clothes, medicine—you know. I waited until she took her meds and went to bed before I headed over to her house to collect her things, never once thinking it wasn't safe to leave her locked in my own apartment, but once I was over there, I got this, and I—" Her face crumpled, tears glistening in the corners of her eyes. "I just can't lose anyone else."

I nodded solemnly. "Well, let's see what we can do to prevent that, okay? Why would someone want to lure you out here?"

"I got no idea! Me and Marlene didn't do nothin' to no one!" She was getting agitated again, her voice on the rise. I shushed her, motioning for her to take it down a notch.

"I guess we'll find out soon enough, but we don't want to broadcast our approach. We've got to keep our voices down. Can you do that?"

She nodded, blotting her eyes with the backs of her gloves.

"Do you know how much farther it is to the old church site?"

"It's just a little ways round the bend," she said, gesturing toward the path her car had been following until she lost control. We began walking in that direction. "Why are *you* out here?"

"I got a text, just like you," I said.

"About Marlene?"

"No. It was Doug—Mr. Boggs. Everything else was the same, though." I didn't offer to show her my own phone. I imagined her reaction to the damage done to Doug's face would only lead her back to hysteria, and nothing good would come of that.

"Oh, my heavens, no!" she said, clamping a hand to her mouth. "That poor man. He was trying so hard to be helpful, I'll never forgive myself if something happens to him. It must be a real pleasure to work with someone so patient and kind."

I chewed on my bottom lip to keep from laughing. Under the circumstances, it would've been the height of bad taste, but I couldn't help wondering if we were even talking about the same person.

"We've known each other a while," I said. "Went to school together, in fact. This 'working relationship' is still pretty new."

"Yes, that's what he told me," she said. "He said that business at your high school reunion last fall gave him the spark of an idea of what y'all

355

might be able to do if you put your skills together, so he brought you into his company."

Now *that* sounded like the Doug I knew, taking all the credit for the creation of our partnership, when, in fact, it had taken me solving two cases on my own to convince him to even give my apprenticeship a chance. We'd been on shaky ground ever since.

"Hmmm. When did he find time to share all this with you?" I asked.

"This afternoon—you know." She looked at me sheepishly as we continued to plod along.

I slowly shook my head. "Know *what?*"

She shuffled her feet in the snow, suddenly unable to look my way. "After all that business with you in the church this morning. He came by to—well—this is just so awkward."

"It's okay, Anne Marie, just say it."

"He came by to apologize for your behavior, not that I thought you had anything to apologize for. He wanted me to know that he would be handling the case personally and wanted to make sure I was comfortable with that, and I'm not gonna lie, I was surprised he seemed so put out—"

"Wait a minute," I interrupted, stopping to process. "You spoke with Doug *after* you saw us in the church?"

She nodded her head. "He caught me at my apartment, just as I was leaving to pick up Marlene from the hospital. Said he wanted to make sure he had the same facts I'd already sent to you because he'd be taking the lead, and he was afraid you mighta held something out of spite."

Out of spite. It most *definitely* sounded like the Doug I knew, but with conscious effort, I forced myself to focus on what was important, not petty. This was the only definitive sighting of Doug to be reported after he and I parted ways at the McDonald's in Flatwoods.

"Did he give you any indication of what his plans were for the rest of the day?" I asked.

"Not exactly, but I was in a hurry to get Marlene. I know he was gonna try and talk to some of the kids whose names I texted you, but I couldn't say when. Honestly, I think he was there to make sure I was okay with him staying on the case after you—" She shrugged apologetically.

We walked in silence for a few moments while my thoughts churned inside my head, looking for nits to pick. For all of the moving pieces in this particular puzzle, the common thread was New Life Apostolic, and I found myself replaying my conversation with Reverend Keaton from earlier in the day. His entire demeanor was so self-assured and calm in the face of my own aggressive breach of his inner sanctum. I don't think I would have maintained my cool were the roles reversed. It was difficult to imagine him being the same angry and judgmental father figure Chandler spoke of earlier. Maybe years of keeping secrets had made him an expert at it.

Or maybe he was just a sociopath.

"I didn't realize you worked at New Life," I said.

"Really? I thought I mentioned Molly Ridenour recommended you to me. She didn't mention it?"

"I actually don't know Molly all that well. I'm dating her sister, Melanie, but I've only spoken to Molly a handful of times."

She looked at me questioningly. "Does it matter?"

"No. It just occurs to me that everything that has happened so far seems to lead one way or another back to the church. How long have you been part of the flock?"

"All my life. Reverend Keaton—Donald's daddy, Lawrence, that is, took my family as a sort of personal project back when my daddy was killed. Daddy was police in Greenup County and got himself shot trying to talk some drunk fool out of killing his wife and kids."

"Oh my God, that's awful! I'm so sorry!"

She shrugged. "I really don't even remember him. I was just a baby. But he was a real hero that day. Daddy's partner was able to take the man out before he hurt anyone else. But poor Mama was just lost. She had never worked a day in her life, and now it was up to her to raise her two little girls on her own. Reverend Keaton took mercy on us and offered her a job as the church secretary, even though she didn't have no training. He had the patience of a saint. Others from the congregation stepped up, too. Old Mr. Endicott had one of those pull-along camper trailers that he and his wife used to explore the country in 'til she got too sick with the cancer to travel. It was just rusting in his backyard, so he signed it over to Mama, and the Reverend let us park it on the church lot where we could plug right into the utilities there. He never charged her for rent or utilities. It wasn't much, but it was plenty for me, Marlene, and Mama."

I thought of the stern-faced man I had seen on the church's official website and would have never guessed that man had the capacity for this amount of selfless generosity. That whole idiom about not judging a book by its fearsome cover was proving itself true yet again, and I was embarrassed that I had been so quick to assume he would be as harsh and judgmental as—well, Melanie's father, Charles. I realized Anne Marie was still talking, and I had missed the last of what she said.

"I'm sorry, what was that?" I asked.

"Hmm? Oh, I was just saying that I reckon the trailer is still up there, along with the others that were brought to run the school from. I've got a lot of memories from those days."

"You attended the church school?"

"Sure did," she said. "Me and Marlene and really just a handful of other kids. It was just getting started back then."

I grabbed her arm, stopping us in our tracks. "So, wait a minute. You grew up out here?"

She turned toward me, puzzled. "Well—yeah. That's what I've been telling you."

"So, you should know this area like the back of your hand, right?"

"Sure. We was all over these woods when we was kids. Why?"

I felt the weight of the gun in my pocket and couldn't help but smile. What felt like a glimmer of hope was finally taking shape. "I want you to think hard, Anne Marie. Coming straight in like we are, we're probably walking right into a trap. Surely there are some paths through the woods we could use to come in from behind the church."

She nodded slowly before looking me over dubiously. "I'm not sure you're wearing the right kind of shoes for this."

My grin widened. "You let me worry about that. If you'll just lead the way, I'll follow in your footsteps. If we can gain the element of surprise, I think I might be able to get us out of here before anyone else gets hurt."

She looked relieved. "I just knew you could help me. All right, then. Let's go."

We backtracked just a little before Anne Marie carefully picked her way through some tangled branches on our right, careful to make as little noise as possible while keeping them from smacking into me as I fumbled through. Once on the other side, a narrow trail was visible, leading up the ridge before bending left. I would have never seen it, but Anne Marie remained surefooted, and all I had to do was stay close. While my Skechers weren't particularly warm, they provided a surprising amount of traction. Once we reached the crest, Anne Marie stopped.

"There it is," she whispered.

I peered over her shoulder to see the remains of the old church site below us. A row of three trailers were lined end-to-end fairly close to us while the camper trailer Anne Marie had described as her home was set off on its own to the extreme left. All were darkened husks, vandalized over the years, with broken windows and spray-painted graffiti evident from where we stood at the edge of the woods. Beer cans and other garbage littered the grounds, and we picked our way through the debris to get a closer look. It didn't take long to conclude they were currently unoccupied.

359

That only left the church itself, narrow and long, nestled into the tall grass below. Its siding was warped and peeling, missing in places and entire sections of the roof were missing, granting unfettered access to the elements. Only the trace of a semicircular expanse that had served as a hard-packed dirt parking area remained at the front of the building, partially reclaimed by Mother Nature and covered by an unbroken blanket of snow. At the top of a steep and crumbling set of stairs, one of the cathedral doors hung askew on its hinges, while the other was propped open by a cinder block, an open invitation to anyone foolish enough to take it. We proceeded through the tall grass down into the valley, approaching the church from the side to keep ourselves invisible to anyone who might be watching from inside.

"Do you see that?" Anne Marie whispered, stopping to point toward the entrance.

My eyes followed, but it took a long moment before I noticed a mild flickering luminescence emanating from deep inside the building. Someone was inside. I nodded, pulling the gun from my pocket, and motioning for Anne Marie to stay behind me as we resumed our approach from the side. Once we reached the foot of the stairs, I pulled Anne Marie aside.

"It's going to get a little hairy from here," I whispered. "We can't both go up those stairs without being seen by whoever's inside, so I'm going to go first to get an idea of what we're getting ourselves into. You wait here until I call for you, okay?"

She clutched my arm. "I'm scared."

I showed her the gun. "I've got this, remember? Just stay put."

Staying low to the ground, I began climbing the crumbling concrete of the stairs, keeping to the side where the broken cathedral door obscured part of the entrance. Halfway there, I hesitated, detecting a low, throaty grumble, and it was getting closer. I looked over my shoulder to discover headlights sweeping through the trees at a distance.

"Oh, *shit*, Anne Marie," I yelled. "We've got company. Come on!"

She squealed before hustling up the stairs to join me, and we hesitated only a second before plunging into the shadowy interior. The headlights were almost upon us, sweeping the snow-covered expanse that used to serve as parishioner parking. There was no time to clear every nook and cranny of the abandoned space. Between the twin rows of pews straddling the center aisle and the chancel surrounding the altar, there were far too many places to hide. I could only hope the fact we hadn't been attacked yet was a good sign.

It was a straight shot down the long aisle to the altar, which had been surrounded by trays of flickering votive candles. Sprawled in a heap at the foot of the altar, Doug Boggs was motionless, his arms bound behind him, and a rag secured in his mouth by what looked like duct tape. His eyes were closed, and it was impossible to see if there was any rise or fall to his chest. I dropped to my knees and placed my hand underneath his nostrils, and just as relief washed over me when I felt his hot breath against my skin, I realized that I recognized the sound of that engine. I had heard it twice before, once on a bridge and once in a Speedway parking lot.

Headlights shone brightly through the open cathedral doors, and the engine abruptly shut off.

"Just stay behind me," I directed Anne Marie, as I checked the gun, making sure I had released the safety. Her response was a stifled mewling, but she did as I said.

Time went into a long, slow crawl as perspiration trickled down the inside of my armpits, and the sound of my own breathing seemed unusually loud. Anne Marie continued to fret as we waited for something, *anything* to happen.

Finally, there was motion, as a tall, broad figure crested the stairs, backlit from the headlights, practically filling the entrance. I recognized the dark jeans and hoodie, the gloved hands and knit mask. More importantly, I recognized the stature. This was the same monster who had attempted to send my ass over the U.S. Grant Bridge on Thanksgiving night. He paused, just inside the entrance, flexing his hands at his sides.

"Stay right where you are, asshole," I said, rising to my feet and pointing the gun in his direction.

He cocked his head to the side as if evaluating my command and took a step forward.

"*I mean it!*" I barked, lifting the gun above my head, and pulling the trigger.

It only clicked.

I looked at it stupidly then back toward Anne Marie, who had gotten to her feet as I did.

"Sur-*pri*-se!" she said in a sing-song voice, just before I was hit with what felt like a bolt of lightning.

My head snapped back, and my eyes bugged like they were going to burst from my head.

Everything went dark.

CHAPTER TWENTY-EIGHT

Low and muffled grumbling penetrated the layers of invisible cotton that seemed to fill my ear canals.

"—I did *not*. Look, his eyelids are fluttering."

The voices seemed to be coming from the far end of a long tunnel, and my eyelids were just too heavy to lift. My body felt like I'd been hit by a truck. Every single muscle complained.

I flinched as a hand persistently smacked my cheek.

"Wakey, wakey!" It was Anne Marie's voice. "Time to rise and shine, big fella. You've got work to do."

One eye slowly opened, followed by the other. Anne Marie's face was inches from mine, but it wasn't exactly concern I saw in her expression. It was more like rabid impatience. The behemoth from the muscle car hovered just over her shoulder. He had removed his knit mask and studied me with clinical detachment with his icy blue eyes. His sweat-soaked hair was dirty blond, short and tousled, and although his features were familiar, I couldn't quite place him.

"Anne Marie?" I croaked, trying to sit up only to find my wrists and ankles had been bound with twine. "Wha—what's all this?"

She set what looked like a walkie-talkie at the foot of the altar and grabbed my elbow, tugging me into a seated position. I looked around to get my bearings. I sat on the floor to the left of the altar with Doug's prostrate form to my right. Upon closer examination, I could see the device Anne Marie had laid down was not a walkie-talkie but a two-prong, handheld stun gun. Her eyes followed mine, and she picked it up, slipping it into the pocket of her coat.

The room's luminescence had changed. Bright, halogen headlights no longer spilled through the cathedral doors, and several of the votive candles had winked out, the stench of burnt wicks hanging in the frosty air. Moonlight spilled through tiny breeches in the roof, and every hair follicle on my body felt like it was standing on end, electrified.

"You *stunned* me," I said, startled by the realization. Processing thoughts was like slogging through quicksand. "Why would you do that? I don't understand."

She was rummaging through a duffel that sat at the blond man's feet.

"I wish we had more time to chat," she said, extracting a laptop and placing it on my legs as it booted. "But I'm kinda playin' beat the clock here. Battery is all charged up. I'm gonna need you to do what you do best."

When the lock screen finally appeared, the username was prepopulated with "Tina," and a selfie of Ms. McAlister vamping with duck lips served as her profile pic.

"But—you said that Tina's laptop disappeared when she did," I said.

"I said a lot of things," said Anne Marie. "I'm afraid I haven't been completely straight with you, Mr. Morrow, but I really need you to focus and get me into that laptop."

I looked at her blankly. "What makes you think I can do that?"

She scowled at me. "You damn well better be able to do it," she said. "Ain't that what your TV commercials say? No password too tough, no encryption too rough?"

I groaned inwardly. Loretta Boggs and her goddamn television commercials were literally going to be the death of me. It didn't seem prudent to mention how greatly those commercials had overstated my abilities. It was the only value I brought to the table. All I could do was stall and pray for another opportunity to present itself.

"I'm going to free your hands, but don't get any bright ideas. Dustin's got his eyes locked on you. One wrong move, and he'll put a bullet through your kneecap, won't you, Baby?"

The behemoth grunted, and he grinned, his eyes twinkling with menace, but what caught my attention was the gun nearly swallowed up by his hand, pointed in my general direction. Again, Anne Marie's gaze followed mine, and she sneered. "Same gun, but it's loaded now. Did you really think I'd hand you a loaded gun?"

Dustin.

As in Reverend Keaton's oldest son, Dustin. If I squinted, I could almost recognize features from the expressionless boy whose picture still occupied the corner of his father's desk. The rest of him was undoubtedly the byproduct of hours spent in the gym. And probably steroids.

Anne Marie cut the twine that bound my wrists with a pocketknife, and I flexed my fingers, coaxing the feeling back into my frosty phalanges. I pressed a sequence of keys to reboot the laptop and tapped the appropriate function key to cause it to boot into Windows Safe Mode with a Command Prompt. It was all just really for show but typing commands into a black window with a prompt at least gave the illusion I was doing something productive while I looked for a way out of this mess. She and Dustin stood over me, watching my fingers fly across the keyboard.

"So, you're buddies with Reverend Keaton's son," I said.

Her smile widened. "We're much more than buddies. We pretty much go all the way back. We were in that very first class together, right here on this site. This is sort of like our own homecoming, ain't it, Baby? There isn't a thing I wouldn't do for him."

The look she gave him was pure adulation, and it creeped the living shit out of me.

"What's your stake in all this?" I asked, indicating the computer. "I mean, Tammy Tipton told me how your niece was blackmailing a bunch of her friends into doing whatever she wanted. She told me what Tina was holding over her head, but she wouldn't share her friends' secrets. I figured out what Tina had on Chandler—"

Anne Marie threw her head back and laughed. "That mincing little pantywaist? *Everybody* knows what's going on with him and his little cuddle buddy except maybe the good Reverend, but I think it's more a matter of clinging to false hope, don't you agree, Baby? He doesn't want to be disappointed in *all* his children."

Dustin's canine teeth were unnaturally sharp in the low, flickering light.

"Okay, so you already know what's on here. Why do you care?"

Anne Marie pursed her lips and turned to Dustin. "Do you think I should tell him?"

His smirk was ugly. "Why not? He ain't gonna be around long enough to repeat it."

My throat ran dry.

"I really haven't lied to you *all* that much, Mr. Morrow," said Anne Marie. "Tina and I was always very close. I was more of a mom to her than Marlene ever was. My sister was too busy playing a victim of her own life, and Tina spent most of her school years getting laughed at by these idiots who thought they was better than her. I'm ashamed to say I didn't see how it bothered her until last year, when Nathan Engles invited her to junior prom and then stood her up. It was a nasty thing to do, and from that point, I was determined to help Tina turn things around. It was my idea for her to start collecting things she could use against those little monsters, and it was really working. I even helped her get some of the videos. I was the one who showed her how she could schedule Outlook to send a shared link to her files. They're set to go out to everyone on New Life's mailing list at eight o'clock sharp each Monday morning—unless, of course, she logs in and snoozes the schedule. I worried one of those kids might decide that hurting my niece would be the end of all their troubles, so it would be good to put the fear of God into 'em, and I really think it did.

"Tina got a whole new wardrobe out of Kaitlyn, not that I really care for that whole slutty schoolgirl look myself, but whatever. For the first time in her whole life, she felt pretty, and you could see it in the way her face would light up when she saw her own reflection. She went to Homecoming with the boy she's had a crush on since I don't know when—"

"Jesse Baker," I interrupted, continuing to enter meaningless command after command into the laptop. "She had the videos of him and Chandler. She had to have known he was gay."

"Oh, she knew, she just didn't care. She thought she could change him if she had the chance."

"That's ridiculous."

"Well, of *course* it is!" she said, kicking my foot and nearly knocking the computer off my lap. "But there was some things I couldn't just *tell* her, and heartbreak was somethin' she was going to have to figure out for herself. But it was a lovely evening. She was just so beautiful."

Her face clouded, and she turned away. Dustin kept the gun on me, but his eyes followed Anne Marie, and it felt like the temperature in the room had dropped.

"I loved that girl with my whole heart, and there wasn't nothin' I wouldn't do to help her dreams come true. I always figured she felt the same about me. I never expected—"

"You never expected what?"

Her laugh was mirthless as she dabbed at her nose with the back of her gloves. "I never expected her to give me my own flash drive," she said, and she was mad all over again reliving the moment. "Can you believe that? After everything I did for her. I would have given her anything she asked for, but no. She decided to just help herself. She used every single thing I taught her against me."

"What happened?" I asked.

Dustin rewarded my curiosity by kicking my foot harder. He pointed to the laptop with the muzzle of his gun, silently urging me to continue as Anne Marie turned to face me once more, tears on her cheek.

"She was just so damn smug, showing me the Quicken files she had managed to copy from my work computer while I was busy doing other things. It wasn't nothing for her to hang out with me after school until I finished up for the day, and then I'd give her a ride home. She was on my computer all the damn time, I just never expected her to do something so low. See, I don't just work for Reverend Keaton, I'm his bookkeeper."

My brain was finally catching up. "You've been skimming money."

"Just a little here and there," she said defensively. "The church has just got so *much*, it would never be missed, with just a little creative accounting and a second set of books. Ain't gonna lie, I held my breath all through our first audit. But when no flags were raised, I maybe stepped it up a little bit. Dustin and I will be long gone before the next one."

She kicked my foot again, and I yelped.

"For heaven's sake, ain't you made no progress yet?" she demanded.

"I'm working on it!" I insisted, typing another command at the prompt, this one bringing up the computer's current IP configuration. It was entirely irrelevant but populated the screen with a bunch of gibberish that looked a whole lot more impressive than Windows' standard retort, '*Such-and-such* is not recognized as an internal or external command.' "If this were easy, anyone could do it."

I was beginning to get the hint of an idea, but it was a dangerous one and it almost felt like giving up. If Anne Marie caught on to what I was doing, she wouldn't hesitate to order my execution—Doug's too, but I knew a way to render the laptop useless without ever having to log in. Using

Windows Recovery Console, I could reset the PC and format the hard drive, effectively wiping any saved credentials Tina had stored on the machine. It would prevent Anne Marie from accessing both Tina's email and her cloud account and would ensure delivery of the incriminating evidence against Anne Marie and Dustin the following Monday morning. Unfortunately, it would also assure the airing of everyone else's dirty laundry, but uneasy at the prospect of becoming the subject of a future episode of *Unsolved Mysteries*, I decided it was the best way to make sure the guilty parties would eventually be discovered. I needed to keep Anne Marie's attention away from the screen as I processed the keystrokes necessary to boot into the Recovery Console and based on her visceral reaction to her niece's betrayal, it felt like a good straw to grasp.

"I don't understand," I began, using the trackpad and keyboard to further my progress. "Tina's been missing for over a week. Shouldn't those emails have already gone out to the New Life congregation?"

"I may have glossed over the facts of her disappearance just a little," Anne Marie said, almost apologetically. "All that horseshit about her being kidnapped was exactly that. I had given Tina a ride home that Friday afternoon—the Friday she went missing. Marlene was still at work, and when Tina took me up to her room, all excited about something she just *had* to show me, I thought it was bound to be some other sleazy outfit she squeezed out of Kaitlyn or something dumb like that. When she showed me my flash drive, I thought it was some sort of joke. When she showed me what was on it, that shit-eatin' grin just *plastered* across her face—well, I may have lost my mind a little."

She began pacing in front of me, reliving the memory.

"I've never laid a hand on that girl, never once in her entire life, but Lord help me, I damn near made up for it in that moment. The only thing that kept me from throwing her out that window was the damn sash wouldn't give way, and it's a wonder she didn't get cut to pieces when I tried to push

369

her through. Instead, the little bitch bit me, and I lost my grip. She came at me just like a hellcat on crack, punching and swinging until she finally got her hands around my neck, and I ain't gonna lie, I thought I was in real trouble for a minute. I musta blacked out for just a second, but by the time I caught my senses, she was gone, and so was her laptop and phone. I didn't even have time to clean up the mess before Marlene was home, and by then Tina had already texted her."

I paused, looking up. "She told Marlene that you attacked her?"

"No. You saw the text she sent."

Aw, fuck—a pop quiz. Something or the other about not being able to do it anymore—no, can't *be* here anymore. That was it. "So, she really *did* run away."

She couldn't help but laugh at the irony. "Before I knew it, Marlene had called the police, and it was all anyone was talking about down at the church. Oh, I pointed out the broken window and the mess in the room, trying to get the cops to believe Tina was in immediate danger, but there wasn't any bloodshed to see. Tina hadn't been getting along with her mama because Marlene wanted to know where all of these new clothes were coming from. Marlene's ex had a bad habit of raising enough hell to get the cops called out to the house on more than one occasion before he finally left 'em both, and that dipshit Officer Graves couldn't stop bringing it up. She was sure it was some mother-daughter spat. I couldn't see Tina goin' far, but I was stumped. She didn't have any friends to speak of. She was smart enough to turn her cell phone off so's the police couldn't track her that way."

She paused to smile at me, making my skin crawl. I casually shifted the computer in my lap to obscure more of its screen from her view. The formatting progress bar had begun its slow upward climb, but it was nowhere near far enough at this point.

"And that's where you came in," she said. "At church on Sunday, you was all Molly Ridenour could talk about. Her sister's big shot detective beau, coming to visit for the Thanksgiving holiday and meet the family. She couldn't have spoken any higher of you. There wasn't a thing in this world you couldn't figure out, and she was just sure you could find Tina in no time. Well, that put a bug in my ear, but I wasn't about to bring an actual detective in for fear of what else you might find out.

"It was just dumb luck that Dustin happened on to where Tina was staying, and I have to say, I was really disappointed in myself for not coming up with it sooner. No, she didn't have any friends, but here she had all these kids she was blackmailing. Most of 'em was still school age and living at home, but not Katie Hamilton. She had her own little apartment right above the laundromat over on Long Street. Dustin was out running around with his buddies on Monday when one of 'em asked if Dustin could drop his lady friend over to her apartment so's she could get ready for work. I believe you know the fella. His name is Charles, but he goes by Chip, and wouldn't you know it? He's brother to Molly and your sweet Melanie, and the girl he had tucked underneath his arm was none other than little Katie. Sometimes, I am *amazed* at how truly small this world is! When they stopped to drop Katie off, Dustin saw Tina doing her laundry through the big glass window on the first floor. He called me just as soon as he could get free, and I left work early that day with a migraine. I had surprise on my side, and I wasn't about to let her get away from me again."

She slowly rolled her neck on her shoulders, and I could hear vertebrae popping in response.

"I didn't mean to kill her," she finally said, staring at the ceiling while lost in the memory playing out behind her eyes. "I only wanted to talk some sense into her, get my goddamn *files* from her. She was family, after all, and we could work this thing out. But as soon as she opened the apartment door, she started screaming. I had to make her stop. Someone in the

371

laundromat was bound to hear her. I shoved her inside, and she got tangled up in her own feet and went down. The sound her head made when it hit the coffee table—"

Her voice faltered as she grimaced and cursed underneath her breath. Her gloved hands were knotted at her sides, and her small frame was practically shaking. Dustin put an arm around her and pulled her closer, resting his square chin on the top of her fur-lined hat. After a moment, her trembling eased.

"We knew Katie was working 'til close, so there was plenty of time for Dustin to come back after the sun went down. While I waited, I searched that entire goddamn apartment, but I couldn't find Tina's laptop or phone. I knew she wouldn't have gotten rid of them, but they sure as hell weren't there. Once it was good and dark, we managed to smuggle Tina's body out using one of the laundromat's own carts, and no one saw a thing. In fact, we brought her out here until we could figure out what to do. I can almost still see her sitting right there in the front row, like she's asking the good Lord to forgive her for what she done. But by Wednesday, she was startin' to stink up the place, so droppin' her in the river seemed like a good idea."

I shuddered, halfway expecting to see a moldering corpse staring up at me. My hands were growing numb, and I rubbed them together while I kept an eye on the laptop's progress bar, which had only just reached thirty percent.

"But see, now I *really* had a problem," Anne Marie continued. "I didn't have a way to stop that email from going out. And just like a message from God himself, your commercial came on while I was watching *Big Brother*, and I saw my way clear. All I had to do was convince you to at least take a look. Molly said you were a softie with a big ole heart, but I gotta admit, I thought I'd have to beg a whole lot harder than I did."

She had me there. I had swallowed her story without reservation, and I suspected my vulnerability stemmed from my own family's grief over Gina.

What I couldn't figure out was why Doug had been so amenable to everything. He was usually the one to put on the brakes, but once he had learned of Lucy Graves' involvement, he was bound and determined to stay on the case. He groaned, stirring slightly where he lay, and I again was left to wonder the extent of his injuries.

"But first, I needed to find that laptop," she said, once again pacing the floor in front of me. "With Tina stayin' at Katie's, I was pretty sure Katie knew where it was hid, and after Tina disappeared, it was like a hot potato no one wanted to get caught holding. All them kids was shakin' in their shoes, waiting for something else to happen but not knowin' when it would. Dustin kept a pretty easy eye on Katie 'cause she spent all her free time hangin' onto Chip, but he didn't see no sign of the laptop until the day after Thanksgiving, when Katie had all the girls over to her place for a sleepover. I'm thinkin' they must've caught one of your commercials while watching whatever it is girls watch at a sleepover. I'm guessin' it gave her the same idea as me. Beg your help in cracking the password and then everybody would be free. She had Tammy swing by the laundromat the next day to pick up Tina's laptop and the phone. She had 'em both stashed under her spare tire in her car. After that, Tammy reached out to you."

I flashed back to the nervous young woman who hopped into my car at the rest area by the Greenup Dam, and it all seemed to gel. She had borrowed Jasmine's Demon Academy bag to transport the laptop, but she must have left it in her car until she was sure she had me on board. The phone must have been in her coat pocket and fallen beneath my seat in her hurry to get away.

"So, what was in the text that sent Tammy running?" I asked.

Anne Marie's smirk was ugly. "Just a little picture Dustin snapped from the side of the road up on the bridge. It's really amazing how good these cell phone cameras are these days, don't you think? He was able to zoom right in on Tammy sitting in your passenger seat. She couldn't see him, but she sure as shootin' knew he was watching her. The poor thing went to pieces, and all Dustin had to do was follow her. Her family is a ways down Schoonover Run, and there ain't no shortage of places to run a car off the road through there. That girl didn't have to die, and that one's on Katie."

It was a rationalization she could someday try on God, but I suspected it wouldn't hold any more water with the Big Guy than it did with me. I glanced at the progress bar on the laptop. Formatting was forty-eight percent complete.

"How about Doug?" I asked. "He was only trying to help you, and you didn't need him for this part of your scheme. Why is he here? Are you gonna try and blame that on Katie, too?"

Anne Marie laughed. "Oh, no. That one's all on you. Mr. Boggs spent a goodly part of the day tryin' to interview the kids on my list. He had the bright idea to check in with me before he headed home for the night, and if he had the good sense just to call, he wouldn't be in this mess right now. But no. He decided to just drop by my apartment while he was in the area. He remembered Dustin's car from the night those boys dangled you off a bridge, and while he sure ain't the sharpest crayon in the box, he was beginning to put things together. He's damn lucky the thought occurred to me of using him to lure you out here, otherwise he mighta joined Tammy in the river."

Doug shifted and groaned, and I seriously doubted he felt very lucky. My eyes drifted toward the twine binding his arms and legs, and it looked no less sufficient than the coils binding my own ankles.

"What in the hell is *that?*" asked Anne Marie sharply, and I suddenly realized she had closed in when I wasn't paying attention, a gloved forefinger jabbing at the computer screen. "Formatting? *NO!* What the hell do you think you're *doing?* Stop it. *STOP IT!*"

"Baby?" Dustin hurried over, unsure of what was happening.

She snatched the laptop from my outstretched legs, frantically pushing buttons as her panic escalated. The only key to elicit a response was the Escape key, which warned her that canceling the formatting operation would likely render the device unusable. A strangled cry erupted from her throat as she flung the laptop to the ground, its case cracking as the screen dissolved behind a spiderweb of static before winking out entirely.

The look she gave me was pure hatred.

"Shoot them," she said through gritted teeth, nudging Dustin. "Shoot them *now!*"

"I wouldn't do that if I were you."

The voice, surprisingly close, startled us all. I nearly giggled when I saw Lucy Graves, already halfway down the cathedral's center aisle, holding her gun steady with both hands in front of her. She continued to inch forward, a look of steely determination on her face.

"I want everyone to stay just where they are, no sudden moves," Lucy said, and for a fraction of a second, everyone complied.

And then all hell broke loose around me.

Anne Marie ducked behind Dustin as he brought his arm around and fired at Lucy just as she managed to squeeze off one round that went wide before she dropped like a stone.

"Lucy!" Even from behind the rag duct taped into his mouth, Doug's anguished cry was intelligible, surprising us all because we hadn't realized he had regained consciousness. With a low growl, he used his bound legs to sweep Dustin's feet out from under him, sending him crashing into Anne Marie as the gun went flying from his hand.

Anne Marie landed directly on top of me, hammering my face with a steady series of blows before settling her hands around my neck, putting all of her weight into choking me. I couldn't bring my arms up to protect myself because she had them pinned under her knees where they flapped helplessly against the bulk of her coat.

As my vision began to blur, my fingertips brushed against something blunt and square. I focused every bit of my remaining effort on taking hold of that object and pushing it against Anne Marie's body, locating its trigger by feel and squeezing like my life depended on it—which I guess it did. The stun gun crackled, but the look of surprise on her face wasn't exactly what I'd hoped for. She merely looked annoyed and reached down to try and wrest the device away from me, and it turned out to be exactly the break I needed. Her insulated coat was shielding her from the full effect of the stun gun, and I pulled with renewed determination, ripping her pocket to free the device. I pulled my arm out from beneath her knee, and this time, I aimed for her neck. Her body pulsed and jerked before falling to the side, leaving me defenseless to face the full fury of Dustin, who now hovered over me, arms flexed and ready to inflict grievous bodily harm.

I suddenly realized the lighting in the room had once again brightened, and a sea of red and blue pulsing lights shone through the cathedral door against the backdrop of ululating sirens. I heard the distinct click of a handgun being cocked.

"Let's try this again, asshole." It was Lucy, her gun pointed at Dustin's head.

I was completely confused, and if I wasn't mistaken, Doug was actually crying. "Lucy?" I sputtered. "I thought he—"

"Flak jacket," she said with a shrug and a quick thump of her chest, as a stream of officers stormed the premises with their weapons drawn.

EPILOGUE

Monday came and went without incident. No automated emails were sent to the New Life congregation, and with the passing of each subsequent Monday, it appeared that Tina may have been bluffing, after all. All of Tina's victims began to breathe a little easier—well, except for Anne Marie Brown. A subsequent audit triggered by the events of that night uncovered her creative accounting, and the full extent of her and Dustin's crime spree continues to unfold.

We would later learn that the incident Chandler had described to me when Dustin was first sent away involved another student, Jenny Burchett, who was considered by others to be a bit of a wild child. She had been beaten, raped, and threatened with a knife, and while Dustin had been implicated, Anne Marie provided the alibi that kept him out of any real trouble. Crumbling under intense scrutiny, Jenny had killed herself, and all of the ugliness was covered up in its entirety. Jenny's parents had received a sealed settlement from the church, and while it was rumored to be substantial, it was definitely enough for them to pull up stakes and move far, far away. Recent events would cause Jenny's case to be reopened, and it seemed likely that Jenny had received some unwanted assistance in her suicide from none other than Anne Marie, who couldn't have been more than fifteen at the time.

Anne Marie Brown and Dustin Keaton were a hometown Leopold and Loeb, dabbling in thrill kills since adolescence. Excavation of the old church site would begin in December, and by mid-January, the skeletal remains of three young women would be discovered buried on the grounds. Three billboards along US 52 would come down, as families finally learned the grisly fates of their missing daughters. A handful of billboards remained, but the investigation is ongoing and not everything ties up in a neat little package like it does on TV. Anne Marie and Dustin certainly aren't talking. They're being held separately in maximum security prison facilities, awaiting trial for a multitude of crimes ranging from kidnapping and theft to murder.

Reverend Donald Keaton held a tearful press conference surrounded by his wife and children—Chandler included—to apologize for both his and his late father's shortcomings in leadership, both as parents and pastors, temporarily stepping away from his position with New Life and begging for privacy while he focused on fixing his broken family. Surprisingly, the congregation was largely supportive, circling the wagons around their fallen leader and refusing to share speculative gossip with the throngs of media that descended in the aftermath. I honestly believed the good reverend was taken by surprise by virtually everything, guilty only of making the same mistakes any parent might make, locked in denial about the depths of depravity plumbed by his own flesh and blood. Given time, I expected he would return as the face of the church.

I suppose I should get back to what happened that night—I guess it was Sunday morning by then. It's not my favorite part of the story.

Who needed sleep anyway?

By the time Anne Marie and Dustin had been shackled and loaded into separate squad cars, an ambulance had arrived to transport Doug and Lucy

378

to the hospital for evaluation. I was thoroughly debriefed by both Flatwoods and Kentucky State Police before finally being returned to my own car. The sun was nibbling at the horizon, and the snow had finally stopped, but even the heater on high couldn't chase the chill from my bones.

It wasn't completely attributable to the missing glass of my passenger window.

I had called Melanie before my interrogation began to let her know I was safe, and after asking tersely if Doug was alright, she told me that she was going to bed. She was too exhausted to hear details. It didn't entirely escape my notice that she didn't ask how I was doing.

It was after six by the time my tires crunched across the snowy expanse between Craig and Cheryl's house and the trailer. The windows at both places were dark, and no one waited to greet me at the doors of either, so I opted left toward the house, figuring it offered the best choice for a comfortable nap. I had to try and squeeze a few hours in.

I quietly let myself into the kitchen and crept down the hall toward the bedroom Melanie and I had been sharing. The bed was unmade and empty, and I could only assume the slumber party had continued in Maggie's trailer. I stripped down to my boxers and crawled underneath the frilly pink comforter on the twin mattress, asleep practically before my head hit the pillow.

I awoke with a jolt as Melanie nudged me.

"We're going to be late for your parents," she said. "You need to get up. Jaz and I are already packed and ready to go, and I've loaded the car. Craig put a painter's tarp over your passenger window until you can get it replaced."

"You didn't have to do that all by yourself," I groused. "Why didn't you wake me?"

But she had already left the room.

We piled into the car after hugs and goodbyes with Melanie's family. Craig held onto my hand just a little longer than necessary, nodding with an unspoken appreciation for me holding my tongue, and it just made me mad all over again. Why did *I* have to be the storage vault for everyone's secrets? I never asked for the position, and I was increasingly resentful.

The car ride from Ironton to Lymont was interminable, and any small talk I attempted was met with monosyllabic responses or silence. Jasmine looked absolutely miserable in the backseat, tethered to her phone by her earbuds, and if she could hear me, she gave no indication. I finally asked Melanie if everything was alright, and she didn't even look up.

"Sure," she said, and I sighed, letting it go for the moment.

We arrived at Mom and Dad's a little past noon, just as Mom was preparing to serve dinner. The house was filled with the mouth-watering aroma of her secret recipe chili, and Abbie was asleep in her Pack 'n Play, having already had her lunch. Mom greeted each of us with a reminder to keep our volume down so as not to wake the baby before leading us back to the family room where Dad, Matt, and Sheila were watching yet another football game. I found it interesting that the only thing capable of moderating my brother's one-sided screeching at televised sporting events was the tiny sleeping princess tucked beneath her Little Mermaid blanket.

Hugs made the rounds, and I couldn't help but steal glances at Melanie, but she was all smiles as she and Sheila chatted about how much Christmas shopping each had left to complete, and I allowed myself to relax a little. I knew we had yet to discuss the previous evening, but this felt normal. Matt distracted me with yet another round of bluster about finally edging Dad out in bowling, and for his part, Dad seemed to take it in stride, challenging him to a rematch any day of the week. That was the Dad I knew, and whatever expression I thought had been captured in the pic Matt sent me must have been tainted by my concern.

A fresh round of shushing from Mom served to remind us we were getting too loud as we went through the motions of catching up on the events of the past few days, but nothing of any real substance. I certainly didn't feel the need to invoke the ire of Mom's earlier phone call by divulging the events of the previous evening; it would only add fuel to her fire. I was already dreading a conversation that, as it turns out, we would never have.

As we seated ourselves at the table, her eyes found mine for just a second, long enough so she could nod almost imperceptibly, and I did the same. I don't know how it is in your family, but with mine, even the ugliest of disagreements can be wiped away with a simple gesture, and we go on as if nothing ever happened. It can't be healthy. Anger and hurt aren't meant to live in a vacuum, hanging unresolved in perpetuity, but it's such an easy out, and we're so goddamn good at it, it's become our go-to move.

Around three, all parties agreed we should hit the road and try to get the biggest part of our travel behind us while there was still daylight. I reminded Melanie we were supposed to check in with Sarah before we left, but she shook her head and told me she had postponed until the following weekend. I wanted to argue the point, but her expression was set, and I didn't want to force her into spending more time with Jordan than she was ready to.

Matt and Dad fussed over Jasmine while I held my beautiful niece, Abbie, in the crook of my arm, captivated by her tiny perfection. I only needed a couple of nervous reminders from Sheila to support her little head before I started to get the hang of it, the fear that I might drop her at any moment beginning to fade.

Mom thanked Melanie for the desserts she brought to Thanksgiving dinner, returning the sparkling clean baking dishes. They hugged, and Mom kissed her on the cheek. "I look forward to seeing you all again at

Christmas," she said, smiling. "Hopefully, we'll get to spend a little more time together than we've been able to this go 'round."

Ah, Mom. Master of that last minute passive-aggressive dig. At least her tone wasn't bitchy, and Melanie took it in stride.

The drive north was no less frosty than the drive from Ironton had been. Jasmine immediately popped her earbuds in, and Melanie pretended to doze before we even hit Lucasville. By the time we reached South Bloomfield, I couldn't take it anymore.

"You know I'm sorry about the way I left last night, don't you?" I asked.

"Are you?"

"If there had been time to explain, I would have, but I could see from the text I got that Doug was in real trouble. Here, let me show you." I started to fumble with my phone, but she put her hand over mine, guiding it back to its resting place in the center console.

"I don't need to see that."

I was perplexed. "Don't you even want to know what happened?"

She sighed, rubbing her temples. "Fine."

Melanie stared straight ahead, expressionless as I took her through my evening, telling her everything I knew, with the exception of what was on Katie's flash drive. It wasn't paramount to the gist of the story.

I pulled into my driveway as my story was winding down. "One thing I haven't been able to figure out is how Lucy Graves found us all the way out there in the middle of nowhere," I said.

Melanie had unfastened her seatbelt and was rummaging through her purse. "That was me," she said, retrieving her keys and handing them to Jasmine in the backseat. Jasmine plucked the buds from her ears and took them, scowling at her mother.

I unbuckled my own seatbelt and turned towards Melanie. "What do you mean?"

"I installed Mother Knows Best on your phone after we got back from Marble Toe Island. I've known where you were the whole time. I pulled Officer Graves out of bed and practically begged her to follow up on you."

My mouth snapped shut. Mother Knows Best was a popular tracking app used by many to keep tabs on friends and family. I could understand its value to a parent but hadn't given it much thought in this context. The fact it had been installed on my phone without my consent rankled me.

"You *what?*"

Melanie turned to her daughter. "Would you give us a few minutes, sweetheart? Go inside and do as we discussed."

Jasmine rolled her eyes and sighed, getting out of the car before practically stomping toward my porch. She used her mother's key to let herself inside and slammed the door, knocking the harvest wreath Melanie had hung out onto the porch. All the tiny hairs on the back of my neck rose as one, warning me to choose my next words carefully, but my mouth was already running.

"Don't you think you might have asked me before doing that, Mel? It's more than a little Big Brother. Don't you trust me?"

She howled with laughter, and when she looked at me, her eyes were ablaze. "Are you fucking *kidding* me? You've made a science out of keeping me in the dark! You've got me on a goddamn need-to-know basis, and I'm telling you right now, I'm gonna need a whole lot more than what you've been giving me. I spent years with Ryan doing the same thing only to find out he was practically living a double life. *Everyone* knew but me, and I felt stupid and foolish, and I will *not* go down that same path again!"

"Mel—you know I'm not like that."

Hot tears streamed down her cheeks, but as I reached to dry them, she flinched and pulled away. "Do not *touch* me! I don't know *anything* anymore! It's been months since whatever happened to you in West Virginia, and you *still* haven't decided to take me into your confidence. I've been there for you *every fucking step of the way*. Lord knows, you've challenged my patience more than once, but at some point, I've gotta ask myself, are you ever going to trust me with *anything?* Because I can't do this—this—*whatever* this is any longer."

I didn't know what was happening, but it was happening fast, and I felt panic clawing at my throat. I needed to do something to slam the brakes on. "Alright, you want to know what happened in West Virginia? I'll tell you. I've wanted to tell you from the very beginning, but I was sworn to secrecy, and I've struggled with making the right choice. Do I keep my promise, or do I shut you out?"

"Who?" she demanded. *"Who* made you promise?"

"Gina!" I practically screamed. "She's *alive*—or at least I think she still is."

She looked at me, stunned, her mouth hanging open. I gave her the quick version of Gina's appearance in the ambulance as I was transported to the hospital after surviving that last night in Briarstaff. I explained the deep political connections Gina had uncovered, and the threat made against my entire family that required Gina to fake her own death. Only then would everyone be safe, so I had no choice but to carry the impossible burden of her secret. I had sworn to investigate no further, all the while watching my parents struggle beneath the crushing weight of their grief.

Once I'd finished speaking, the silence was nearly deafening. Melanie's tears had dried, and she stared through the windshield, chewing her thumbnail.

"Aren't you going to say anything?" I finally ventured.

She shook her head slowly. "I don't really know what to say. I mean, *wow*. How very *capable* you must feel."

I didn't care for the way she was looking at me. Her hand was on the door latch, and when I looked toward my house, Jasmine stood just inside the storm door, cradling Dexter in her arms, nuzzling his neck. There was a bag at her feet.

"I don't understand. You said if I told you—"

She held up a finger, stopping me cold. "We've been moving too fast, and I'm going to need some time by myself to think. I suppose it's turned out to be a lucky thing that no one snapped up the remainder of my lease on Wilson Road."

My stomach was filling with acid. "But Melanie! *Mel.* You don't need to do this. We can work through this together."

"We may be able to work through this, but not together. I have to figure out exactly what I'm willing to put up with, and you need to understand what it's like to really share your life with someone. I need somebody whose first instinct is to want to trust me, not to offer trust as a last resort, only to get out of trouble, like it's some sort of fucking currency. I might've been able to make these last few months a little easier for you if you had just let me in, but I guess we'll never know, will we?"

"Melanie, I—"

"I'll give you your keys back after I come back for the rest of our things. Surely, you can trust me with them for that long."

She got out of the car and slammed the door, nodding to Jasmine before going to the back of my SUV to activate the automated hatch. I was momentarily paralyzed, and my head was reeling. Jasmine gave Dexter a kiss on the top of his head and another protracted squeeze before putting him down and picking up her bag, scurrying out the door and down to her mother's waiting silver Mazda, never once looking my way. I scrambled out of my car just as Melanie triggered the hatch to close, hers and Jasmine's luggage in hand. I couldn't believe this was happening.

"Melanie!" I called, panic overriding common sense. She paused, turning towards me expectantly. *"Please*—you can't tell anyone what I've told you— you know. About Gina."

She shook her head and laughed. "You really are *unbelievable*, do you know that? Of all the things you could have said, I can't believe you went with something so completely insulting."

She tossed her bags into the back of her car, and got behind the wheel, her Mazda's cold engine protesting as she over-cranked the ignition. I watched helplessly as she awkwardly maneuvered around my Hyundai and exited the drive, her tires kicking up loose dirt as she accelerated east on Orin Way. I ran after her, standing in the middle of the narrow country lane, watching her taillights recede until they disappeared completely.

Had I just destroyed the best thing I ever had going for me?

THE END...?

NEXT UP…

DECEPTION
Dwayne Morrow Mystery #7

ACKNOWLEDGEMENTS

They say it takes a village…

I am so grateful for Teri Lott, Lynne Hobstetter, and Traci Steele, who were once again willing to work me into their busy schedules and provide essential feedback on this latest Dwayne Morrow outing. They catch things my tired eyes can no longer see, alert me when my continuity has gone out the window and let me know if my characters are doing things that are—well, out of character. Every single one of these books has been better for these ladies' invaluable input, and any mistakes that remain are mine, mine, all mine.

Special thanks to V.R. Tapscott for emailing me after *Isolation* was released to tell me my covers were shit. Okay, *fine*, with a lot more tact than that, but the conversation opened my eyes to elements of cover design I hadn't fully considered, and that is why the entire series got a facelift shortly after *Isolation* was released. Not only are the new covers more vivid, but the titling no longer competes with the background image for legibility. It was a good call. Sales have increased, and people have stopped calling me Darin Mitter—if you've seen the original cover for *Retribution*, you know what I mean. If you're looking for some humorous sci-fi, you should check out Tapscott's own Jane Bond series. I think she and Dwayne would be terrific friends.

Marketing and promotion are hard. I'm still just mostly making it up as I go along, and tooting my own horn is never gonna come naturally. As such, I have been astounded by the groundswell of support that I have received from my FB friends and followers, some of whom are fellow authors and some of whom are voracious readers. I would like to especially thank Charly Cox, Katie Mettner, and Lizzie Qnert for all the words of encouragement. You have an uncanny knack of saying just the right things when I need to hear them most. You make this dream seem possible.

But most of all, I want to thank each and every one of you who has given Dwayne Morrow a chance. Stay tuned! We've got a lot more road to cover...

Until next time,
Darin Miller
Grove City, Ohio – January 2024

ALSO AVAILABLE

REUNION
Dwayne Morrow Mystery #1

CIRCUMVENTION
Dwayne Morrow Mystery #2

RETRIBUTION
Dwayne Morrow Mystery #3

DIVERSION
Dwayne Morrow Mystery #4

ISOLATION
Dwayne Morrow Mystery #5

DECEPTION
Dwayne Morrow Mystery #7

DELUSION
Dwayne Morrow Mystery #8

OVER CONSUMPTION
*A Dwayne Morrow and Jane Bond
Novella
(Co-written with V.R. Tapscott)*

OTHER WORK

BROKEN BITS AND BOBS
*A Collection of What Ifs, What Was,
and What Never Should Be*

HOUSE OF SECRETS
*Every Room Holds a Story
(Contributor, "Redemption")*

EQUILIBRIUM

THE LIBRARY
CENTENNIAL
ANTHOLOGY
*Celebrating the Lives and People of the
SPL Community
(Contributor, "Meredith's Bad Day")*

DID YOU LIKE ME?

☐ Yes! ☐ No ☐ Maybe?

May I ask a favor?

If you enjoyed reading this book as much as I enjoyed writing it, won't you please consider leaving a rating and/or review on Amazon, Goodreads, Barnes & Noble, BookBub, or anywhere else you might see fit? It only takes a moment to leave a rating and a maybe a couple more for a short review— even a simple 'I would recommend this book!' will do nicely.

Word of mouth is the single most powerful tool in an Indie author's toolkit, and ratings and reviews help more than you may realize in growing our audience. Think of it as a gratuity you might leave a server after an evening of fine dining, but this gratuity doesn't cost a thing—only a few moments of your time.

Thank you for your kind consideration.

Darin

Amazon

Goodreads

Barnes & Noble

BookBub

ABOUT THE AUTHOR

Darin Miller was born in Portsmouth but currently resides in Grove City, both of which are located in Ohio. While he has worked in Information Technology for three decades, he has *not* solved a single, solitary crime to date. He is the BookFest award-winning author of the Ohio-based *Dwayne Morrow Mystery* series, as well as an unrelated short story collection, *Broken Bits and Bobs,* and a standalone psychological horror thriller, *Equilibrium.* With equal parts action, humor, suspense and mystery, the *Dwayne Morrow* series features characters you're sure to love—and in some cases, loathe.

Stay current with updates, short stories, and other special promotions at www.darin-miller.com.